# SOLDIER ON

## ERICA NYDEN

First Edition

Printed in the United States of America.

Library of Congress Control Number: 2020903213

ISBN 978-1-7333450-0-2

Published by Creative Raven Press
P.O. Box 6114
Bend, OR 97708
Cover Design by Annemieke Beemster Leverenz

*For Scott*

# SOLDIER ON

By
Erica Nyden

# CHAPTER 1

ONLY TWO OTHER passengers disembarked from the train in Par along with Olivia. The telegram she clutched told her the tall man in a black topcoat and driver's cap who was waiting on the platform must be James. It hadn't warned her of the downturned mouth or abject silence she would be subjected to once he'd confirmed she was indeed Nurse Olivia Talbot from London. That was all right, though; she wasn't in the mood for talking either.

Inside the roomy motorcar, she pulled her coat closed and adjusted the strap of her gas mask that had fallen from her shoulder. The required apparatus seemed unnecessary here in the country. The window, inches from her face, emitted a chill that clung to her cheeks like London fog, only cleaner. Olivia suppressed a smile at James's ostrich-shaped head bouncing up and down as they jostled along the narrowing road. He drove boldly down its center until the corners grew tight and the descent increased. His speed slowed, and the dense hedges on either side fell away, replaced by tall oaks crowned with masses of yellowing leaves that twisted and skipped in front of the motorcar.

She'd been told her new job would be at a country estate, but it was hard knowing what that meant these days. Estates had lost the grandeur of the past. Updating old houses to twentieth-century standards was expensive, and many had been left to crumble—that or the government had requisitioned them for war use, converting them into dormitories for rowdy soldiers.

As the motorcar crawled down the graveled drive, her new home emerged through the streaked windscreen. A stone railing smothered in wandering vines separated the drive from the house, a honey-hued fortress in the sunlight. Thick walls supported a shingled slate roof heightened by a multitude of chimneys. But even in the bright afternoon, the place looked sad —eerie, even. Most windowpanes were black as ink, and the ones that weren't stared vacantly, as if in shock. The landscape wore a similar expression. Random branches protruded from hunched shrubbery, causing once-regal plants to look defeated. The grass grew so long in some areas that the blades lay over themselves like the hairs of a Scottish terrier.

War had visited here, too. The sloping grounds and wooded glens didn't swarm with sirens, yet despair pervaded this place the same way cancer grows, quiet and lethal.

"Storm's coming," James said, bringing the motorcar to a stop.

Surprise at hearing his voice kept her quiet.

"The sun may shine, but it's the wind, miss. In these parts, wind always brings a storm."

He hefted her bags, and the two made their way up the granite steps. A gray-haired woman opened the massive black door, hands resting on her wide aproned hips and confusion flooding her face.

Praying there hadn't been some mistake, Olivia mustered a smile she didn't feel. "How do you do? My name is Olivia Talbot. I'm the nurse?"

"Oh my, but you're just a child, aren't you? James, take Nurse Talbot's things on up to her room. Come in, nurse.

Welcome to Keldor." The *r* at the end of Keldor hung in the air between them. Like James, her words were peppered with the West Country accent; unlike James, she was much more talkative. "I apologize. I thought Dr. Butler was sending someone more—"

"Experienced?"

"Oh no, my dear. I'm sure you've plenty experience, coming from London, what with all the wounded returning home from Dunkirk, like." She shook her head. Gray wisps danced around her kind careworn face. "I suppose I pictured someone more my age. But I'm sure you're quite capable, and we're glad to have you. My name is Mrs. Pollard. Come. Let's get you to your room. Are you hungry, miss?"

"No, thank you. I'm a little nauseated from the train, actually." Olivia smiled genuinely this time.

At the top of the stairs, a dark passage lined with rows of closed doors stretched to the left and right. Portraits of important-looking people hung in gold-leaf frames. These were likely the Morgans, the family who owned the estate.

"This way," Mrs. Pollard said, turning left. "The major's room be here." She lowered her voice as she swept her hand toward a door on the right. "And I've got you in the room across the way from him."

They entered a bedroom the size of her parents' entire house. The white cushioned headboard of the bed matched the vanity and wardrobe. The bedspread, the color of a robin's egg, complemented pale drapes of the same hue that bordered a wall of windows blotted by blackout curtains. A narrow doorway led to a small lavatory on the right.

"This is lovely," she said.

"Wonderful." Mrs. Pollard gave a soft handclap. "I hope you'll be comfortable. You settle in, and then we'll have tea. The room's been shut up, so take the blackout down if you like. The sun won't set for a couple of hours yet. Your patient be napping, but

3

I'll let him know you've arrived as soon as he wakes. He'll be eager to—"

A horrible moan like something from *The Son of Frankenstein* issued from the hall. Olivia's eyes met Mrs. Pollard's. Before either of them could speak, the bellow came again, long and guttural.

Mrs. Pollard's face fell.

"What was that?" Olivia asked, fearing the rebuke of a resident ghost.

"That'd be Mr. William." The housekeeper's eyes darted to the door, then back to Olivia. She raised an eyebrow. "Your patient."

Olivia darted past the housekeeper and across the hall. In the center of a four-poster bed, a man lay curled on his side. His hands covering his face, he rolled onto his back, kicking a heap of bedclothes to the floor that barely missed a large black dog and unveiled his skeletal form. Her patient indeed: Major William Morgan, thirty-two years old, officer in the British Army who'd spent the last two months as a prisoner of war in North Africa. The experience had left him blind and riddled by shell shock, which likely provoked the horrible sound that sliced the uncomfortable silence.

She stepped over the hound and blankets, climbed onto the bed, and gripped the man's damp arms to turn him slightly, exposing his stricken face. "Major Morgan, my name is Olivia Talbot. I'm your nurse. It's time you woke up, sir."

Left and right he lurched, struggling for release. He sat up and pushed her. "Not again—I won't allow it!"

She caught herself and pushed back, but lost hold on his shoulders. Up and down she bobbed, dodging his haphazard blows, until his arms went limp at his sides.

"Please," he whispered, opening his eyes. His face twitched fearfully, as if he awaited a pounding.

She sat primly at his side, smoothing a hand up and down his shoulder. "You're all right, Major."

He pulled away, locking his arms around his bony knees. Though his arms held fast, his white-knuckled hands trembled. "Who are you? What do you want?"

"My name is Olivia Talbot. I'm your nurse. Dr. Butler sent me."

"Mr. William?" Mrs. Pollard stood at the door twisting her pinafore, her face swollen with apology.

"I'm all right, Mrs. Pollard, I'm fine," he said.

He was far from fine. "Mrs. Pollard, would you mind putting the kettle on? I need a pot of plain hot water. And before you leave, would you fetch me one damp flannel and one dry?" She turned her attention back to the shivering man, his shoulders hunched up to his ears. "We've got to get you out of your night-clothes, sir. They're soaked through."

She patted his knees, prompting him to stretch out. With the expertise brought by wartime nursing, she nimbly unfastened the buttons of his nightshirt. She'd dressed and undressed many patients, some unconscious, others with severed limbs, many wailing and writhing in pain. By comparison, the major appeared an easy subject. She peeled the clinging fabric from his skin like a coat of old paint until his body jerked and he snorted.

"Are you all right, sir?"

He didn't respond, so she continued drawing the nightshirt away but found she couldn't. Pull as she might, the garment held fast. He grunted, this time with snarling lips.

She stood and peered over his shoulder. Worn bandages flapped across the top of his back over encrusted and bleeding lacerations of every shape and size. In some areas, silk sutures secured the inflamed flesh, dark as barbed wire and just as ugly. In others, the bloated bandages had lost their tackiness and revealed avulsions, places where chunks of skin had been carved from his back as though it were sandstone. Shallower cuts possessed no bandage at all. Blood and pus had seeped into his nightshirt and cemented the material to his skin, and Olivia's tugging had reopened several wounds. Blood, brilliant and alive, coursed the length of his back and pooled in the folds of his nightshirt.

"Oh, dear," she whispered, whilst in her head she shouted the few profanities she knew. "Mrs. Pollard?"

Somewhere in the house, a faucet turned off before a shuffle brought Mrs. Pollard back to the bedroom, bearing flannels.

Olivia dabbed the raw flesh before continuing to work on Major Morgan's nightshirt. She saturated the fabric with the wet washcloth until, bit by bit, she could bring the shirt away. His sharp intakes of breath disguised the screams he deserved to release. He listed to the left, and she righted him by his shoulders, massaging his taut unmarked skin, hoping to rub away several layers of tension before carrying on.

"Mrs. Pollard, before bringing that pot of water, would you mind fetching my medical bag from my room? It's the smaller of the two."

"Right away." The woman bowed her head and left.

She bent back to her task. "I'm sorry we had to meet this way, Major Morgan. Again, I'm Olivia Talbot. Dr. Butler sent me to stay with you for as long as you need. I am at your disposal."

Under her ministrations, the bent figure responded with small heaves and shivers—out of pain or mere contact, she wasn't sure.

Mrs. Pollard returned, trading Olivia's medical bag and more clean cloths for the soiled nightshirt and bloodied flannels. After drying the major's lesions and stanching most of the blood flow, Olivia found the ointment she needed. The salve's greasy sheen only amplified the gore before her. The network of bright red horizontals, verticals, circles, and diagonals left her confounded.

"When was the doctor here last, Major?"

"Two, three days ago." He answered as if each word tapped his last stores of energy.

"I see. Your bandages were quite worn. I'm glad I arrived when I did."

She was putting the final dressings on when a girl not much younger than herself entered the room. Eyes averted, she placed a tray holding a teapot and two teacups on the small table beside the bed. Olivia nodded a quick thank-you before the girl scurried away in silence.

From her medicine bag, Olivia pulled a satchel of dried herbs. She approximated two tablespoons and sprinkled them into the pot.

She kept her voice soft and gentle. "What you've experienced is a night terror, Major. I gather you've had them before? Do they come often?"

Mrs. Pollard nodded as she reentered. "They've come every night since he's been home, and during the day, too. Mr. William doesn't sleep much, I'm afraid."

"And what has Dr. Butler prescribed for your sleep, sir?"

Mrs. Pollard opened the bedside table drawer and handed her a bottle. "These. He's to take two an hour before bed."

Barbiturates. "Are you taking these as directed, Major Morgan?"

"Yes." He closed his eyes.

Night terrors were common amongst those with war trauma, and their effects were terrifying to witness. This wasn't the first time Olivia had wrestled a grown man as he shook and cried, only to awaken him to his new reality—not of falling bombs and piercing shrapnel but of missing limbs, lost friends, and a future of replaying the past every time he closed his eyes. Night terrors were often stronger than the treatment prescribed, and yet doctors still promoted these useless remedies.

Despite having her own ideas about what the boys should or shouldn't be taking, at St. Mary Abbot's Hospital, she'd never administered anything outside of doctors' orders. But tonight, not one hour at her new job, she would try something different.

And why not? Clearly her new post came with an opportunity to make her own decisions as a professional.

"Let's see if this helps you sleep any better." She peeked into the teapot.

"What is it you've got there?" Mrs. Pollard rose on her tiptoes for a better look.

"An herbal tea my grandmother makes."

"For sleep?"

"Yes, and to reduce anxiety. Harvested directly from her garden and dried in her kitchen." Olivia gave a knowing smile to Mrs. Pollard, hoping she shared an affinity for homegrown remedies. There was none, only a creased forehead and skeptical eyes.

"Sounds like a witch's brew," came the unexpected muttering of Major Morgan. "I suppose you read the leaves, too?"

Not the friendliest tone, but at least he could speak for himself. "Not at all, Major. But I believe this tea may work better than what you've been taking."

She picked up the cup next to the pot and poured the light green, steaming tea into it, leaves and all. She guided one of his hands to cup. "Here you are. It's hot, sir. Please be careful."

"I'm quite used to hot tea, Nurse Talbot, even if it smells as dreadful as this."

He couldn't see her embarrassment, but Mrs. Pollard could. The woman gave a sympathetic smile and handed Olivia a clean nightshirt.

"Thank you, Mrs. Pollard. I'll let you know if we need anything further."

"Of course. Come along, Jasper."

"Leave Jasper—please, Polly," the major said, his voice faint.

"Very well, Mr. William."

Olivia scratched the dog's head. Her father had their spaniel destroyed once the war started. It was the humane thing to do, he'd claimed, for an anxious dog that would be exposed to the chaos of war and who knew what else. Veterinarians in London had been up to their necks in animal carcasses, her Laddy one of them.

She turned back toward the major. "Are you hungry, sir? Would you like something to eat?"

"No. I'm just bloody tired."

"I'm sure you are. Tomorrow, before breakfast, we'll be sure you"—she struggled to word her intent without making the man sound a child—"get your bath in."

The major finished his tea and held the cup out, lips pursed. He said nothing.

"Here we are," Olivia took the cup and held his right hand aloft. "Let's get you dressed and back to bed, Major."

Though it was still early, the skies had grown dark, proving James's forecast correct. Coastal rain fell in sheets outside the tall windows, echoing in the vast kitchen where Olivia and Mrs. Pollard were taking tea. The flicker of pillar candles cast warmth on their modest supper of boiled pork, potatoes, and carrots. The older woman likely took her meals here alone, for James and Annie, the young girl she'd seen upstairs, were nowhere about.

"Tell me, Mrs. Pollard, how long has the major been home?"

"One week exactly. Haven't seen Dr. Butler for days. Seems he had to travel to London, so it's good you're here." She leant across the table and patted Olivia's hand.

"Have you worked for the family long?"

"I came to Keldor as a young woman, nineteen years old and already a widow. The sea took my husband a month after we wed, and I needed work. Mistress Charlotte knew of my plight and asked if I'd serve as nursemaid to her child once he or she arrived. Mr. William was born, and I took care of that little man like he was mine." Her eyes brightened, and the shallow creases around them deepened when she smiled. "Years passed and he went away to school—he didn't need me anymore, not in the same way, like. So when Mrs. Carne retired, I took her job as head housekeeper. A fine family to work for. Even after all these years, I can't imagine myself anywhere else." Long wrinkles shortened, and the sober face from upstairs returned. "But through the years, this house has endured one tragedy after another. Sweet, selfless Charlotte died of Spanish flu when Mr. William was still a boy, after his father, Colonel Morgan, returned home from war. The doctor told you about the colonel?"

Olivia shook her head. "I'm afraid I know nothing about the family."

"Mr. William had been missing for months, like. And the colonel, I found him dead"—she thumped the table between them —"just weeks before they found Mr. William."

The poor man upstairs had no one, then. "Dear God."

Mrs. Pollard nodded and wiped her eyes with her cloth napkin. "Such a shock, too. It'd been James and me working for the late colonel. When he died, and with poor Mr. William missing so long, Mr. Bather, the family's solicitor, told us the house would sit empty. Requisitioned, more like. We'd had our bags packed. But the day before we was to leave, James to his brother's and me to my sister's, a telegram came. Mr. William was coming home. I can't recall having been so happy. He's like a son, you know."

Immersed in the darkness of her new bedroom, Olivia struggled to sleep. The storm clouds outside had waned, and the night's stillness ushered in a blanket of maddening doubts over her new assignment.

Her first few weeks at St. Mary Abbot's had been miserable

too. Back then she'd been reprimanded for minor yet frequent mistakes. Meaningful friendships were scarce, and homesickness constant. She'd begun questioning her career choice until, in late May, Dunkirk happened. On temporary assignment at an emergency hospital in Sutton, she witnessed horrors they never told her about in nursing school: bleeding stumps, faces blown away, men begging for death.

But amidst the stress of tending to the endless stream of critically injured soldiers, she thrived. She assisted the doctors in surgery, managed her own caseload, and picked up the slack of her more delicate colleagues. Her tender hand brought smiles to all men, even those who no longer could physically show it. She learned the names of each patient she met, and because of her efficacy, the doctors and head nurses learned hers. After the crisis, they praised her attention to detail. Knowing she'd helped so many boys—boys who fell over themselves with gratitude—had given her a sense of satisfaction she had yet to feel here.

She likely never would.

Before taking herself to bed earlier this evening, she stopped by the major's room. He woke as soon as the door creaked open and sat up with a grimace. Mrs. Pollard scampered in behind her, announcing their presence and placing his meal tray by the bed before coaxing Jasper to join her for a quick trip outside. Obviously unhappy with the intrusion, the major climbed out of bed and plodded to the toilet, finding his way there and back quicker than Olivia expected.

Mrs. Pollard had prepared something he could consume independently, a broth-based soup easily sipped from the bowl and a hunk of crusty bread. But despite Olivia's urging that he eat, the major only grumbled.

"You need to eat, sir," she said. "You'll not get better otherwise."

"And why should I want to do that, Nurse Talbot?"

11

She wouldn't be baited by his rancor. "How did you sleep this afternoon?"

Rather than answer, he reached for his meal. She handed him a piece of bread and he stuffed it into his mouth. He chewed slowly.

"I'll ask again, sir: How did you sleep?"

He held his hand out for whatever else she had to offer and took a swallow of broth. "Fine."

"Brilliant. I'd like you to drink more of the tea I gave you earlier. Mrs. Pollard will bring a pot up with Jasper. And I'll not be giving you your prescription tonight."

"You're in charge."

Yes, she was. Once they'd settled the major in for the night, Olivia strode alone to her new bedroom, flush with promise.

But her optimism was dwindling. The unhappy man across the corridor clearly resented her presence here. He had no wish of getting better, and it was impossible to change the mind of someone who had no desire to change. A lifetime of refusal from her mother to her most benign requests had taught her this much.

Olivia hugged her pillow and snuggled the blankets around her shoulders. A soft rhythmic sound from the open door across the hall broke the silence. She lifted her head. The major was in deep slumber. Reduced to skin and bones on the outside, he was filled with misery on the inside, where her greatest challenge would lie. She couldn't fix his despair, but once he regained his health and she taught him to become self-reliant, perhaps that would wane.

She lay back down, somewhat encouraged. He was her patient, not her mother. Despite the major's contempt, she had a job to do, and as she'd done in Sutton, she would succeed.

# CHAPTER 2

THE BEDSIDE CLOCK read 7:02 a.m. Olivia stretched, ready to get a head start on the morning. Hopes that the major had managed the night soundly buoyed her through the open door across the hall.

Beside the bed of his sleeping master, the Labrador sat up at her approach. Olivia tapped her leg and the dog followed her out, tail wagging. She closed the door behind them and exhaled between her growing smile.

Mrs. Pollard was already busying herself in the kitchen. "Is the major still asleep?"

She nodded. "And when he wakes, I'd like to give him his bath. Then we'll have breakfast. Where would you like us? In a room with many windows, perhaps?"

"You mean to get him out of his room?"

"Oh, yes. You said yourself he never leaves it, so why not? I know he can't see the sun, but being someplace its presence can be felt will do him a world of good."

Mrs. Pollard's brows knit. "Whatever I told you about the major hasn't touched who the man really is—or was. He's never been like this. Backalong, the man I knew was full of life. He

13

played at pranks, making us laugh, even if his antics were some-times wicked. But to get him to leave his room? I can't even get him to the cellar during an air raid. Don't you think you're being a bit ambitious, like? He's some stubborn. Nothing's changed there."

She had to start somewhere. "I think it's worth a try."

"Well then, I wish you luck."

Olivia reentered the major's bedroom, her earnestness impossible to puncture. He lay on his back, blinking sleepily. She strode straight to the windows and stripped the blackout drapes. The view was spectacular. The green meadow below stretched until the land descended into woods and bramble. Beyond that, the flat top of the noiseless ocean extended forever. Last night's storm had left a handful of puffy clouds dotting the horizon.

On tiptoes, she removed the curtains from the en suite bath-room windows, which showed the same view. From the shelf next to the washbasin, she pulled a clean towel and placed it on the floor beside the porcelain tub. Steam and the sweet smell of lilac bath salts enveloped her face as warm water spewed from the spigot. The vessel would take time to fill, so she returned to the major's bedroom.

Last night, the wainscoting had looked as dark as black coffee. This morning, ribbons of blond and amber meandered throughout the mahogany paneling like caramel at the center of a chocolate bar. Within the room's patterned wallpaper, crimson flowers with black and gold stems twisted across the upper half of each wall, accentuating the blood-red bedspread.

Under that bedspread, the major struggled to sit up. His tired eyes squinted in the bright morning light.

Olivia glanced at the window and back at him. "Can you see that?"

"See what?" He pinched the bridge of his nose. "I can't see anything."

"The light. I've had blind patients in the past who could detect brightness and sometimes shapes."

"Well, I cannot."

"Yes, well, let's get your day started. We'll begin with your bath."

His wasted body hunched forward. His beard, several shades lighter than the dark hair on his head, had grown in unevenly without proper upkeep, and whoever last cut his hair had butchered it. Although it was short at his neck and around his ears, long hunks fell over his forehead.

She took his hand. "Would you stand please, Major?"

He flinched. "I don't need your help."

"Of course."

She let go, and he stood. "Are you really going to bathe me?"

His smirk, or maybe it was a smile, did not intimidate her. He wasn't the first man she'd seen undressed.

"Not entirely. You've enough water for a sponge bath, and I'll see that you don't fall or bump yourself. You can manage most of your own washing, but I'll check your bandages and change them if need be. Will that do?"

He mumbled consent and shuffled toward the bathroom.

"Ouch!"

"Forgive me, Major." Olivia dabbed another rivulet of blood from his chin. "All faces are different. I've shaved many, and it takes two or three times before I'm used to the particular curves and contours."

She sat back and admired her handiwork. Not as stick-straight as before, his newly trimmed hair swept across the top of his head in dapper waves. His eyes, though vacant, shone like the English Channel, slate-blue and cold. He might even be attractive if it weren't for his permanent scowl.

15

"I thought we'd go downstairs for breakfast." She'd learned early in her career that stating one's intent (rather than asking) was the best way to make it happen—usually.

His eyes darted and settled on her face as though he could see her. "Nurse Talbot."

She stalled with a fake cough, bracing for what was clearly coming next.

His eyelids fluttered with renewed impatience. "Nurse Talbot, if Mrs. Pollard hasn't told you, I prefer to have meals in my room. Alone."

"But Major—"

"No."

"You must leave this room someday—"

"And it won't be today."

"All right, then. We'll have breakfast up here. Together." She rose briskly. "I'll tell Annie."

In less than an hour, Mrs. Pollard had transformed the stuffy bedroom into a clean and cozy haven. A floral cloth draped the round table by the bedroom hearth, where a hearty fire glowed. Comfortable in a sturdy chair that had no business accompanying such a small table, Olivia rubbed her ankles together, basking in glorious heat. Keldor, though majestic and grand, was also drafty and cold. Her eyes drifted to the window. France wasn't far away, and the Channel Islands were even closer. War and occupation raged not much farther than the horizon, yet here on this estate, all seemed calm and peaceful.

"Is there tea?"

"What? Oh, yes." She reprimanded herself for letting her mind stray. That was twice today. She handed him a cup from among the plates of eggs, toast, and jam made from Keldor's own strawberries. "Tell me, Major, how have you been managing to eat?"

"Excuse me?" He lowered his teacup.

Her hand shot out, halting the cup's unintended track to his plate and placing it on the table herself.

"How are you eating? Have you been finding food with utensils yourself, or has someone been feeding you?"

"Mrs. Pollard helps me eat sometimes. I find it extremely unpleasant."

His honesty surprised her.

"I ask her to leave a plate in my room so I can fend for myself," he finished. "I've managed."

She smiled and hoped he heard it in her voice. "So that explains the bits of food and crumbs in your bed, then."

He folded his arms.

"It's humiliating to have someone feed you as though you were a child, which you are not," she said, "and it's rotten feeling helpless. Whilst I'm here, I'll do my best to teach you how to care for yourself. I hope you'll be cooperative in the process, sir."

"I'll try," he said, as though it was the last thing he'd do.

"Excellent. Let's begin with this morning's breakfast."

She stood and took his fork. With it, she scooped a pile of scrambled egg. As soon as she transferred the load to his hand, the food tumbled to his plate.

"Right, then," she muttered. She traded the fork for a teaspoon, which proved a more reliable vessel. A bigger one would be even better. She made a mental note: next time.

Once the spoon was in his grasp, the major found his mouth easily, if without much enthusiasm. After several bites like this, he asked, "When will you eat, Nurse Talbot?"

On the other side of the table sat her steaming eggs and toast. The glistening dollop of jam made her mouth water.

"I'll eat now," she said brightly.

With little fanfare, she dragged her bulky chair beside his so they touched. The heat from the fire felt miles away, but far worse was the view. A closed door and a blank wall weren't

nearly as captivating as the swaying treetops and endless sea. In
the future, she'd face them both toward the window. Heaven
knew she'd take cheer anywhere she could find it.

∼

Not surprisingly, Major Morgan found little interest in anything,
not just his breakfast. Olivia's attempts at conversation were met
with monosyllabic grunts. When she asked about his childhood
and the experience of growing up in such a fine home, he said
he'd been away at school for much of his upbringing. Questions
about his schooling went unanswered. He scorned the idea of
being read to, and since he refused to leave his room, Olivia
abandoned the idea of a walk.

The wireless might've been something they could both enjoy,
until he dashed her desire to hear music by insisting upon
listening to the news. Activity in North Africa topped the
bulletin, whilst Hitler's meeting with Spain's leader, Franco, filled
the rest. The raging Nazi, expertly translated by the British
reporter, choked the room like a poisonous gas.

The major's brows rose and fell as he slumped in his leather
chair by the window. When the reports intensified, so too did his
response. His arms and shoulders quivered. Olivia called his
name softly, but he didn't respond. His eyes squinted and his
mouth twisted as though he were experiencing dreadful pain.

She moved to touch him and then stopped, unsure. As a girl,
she'd befriended sparrows, squirrels, and bunnies, devising fantastic
schemes for mending a broken wing or torn ear. She'd even considered becoming a veterinarian until the time a neighbor's cantan-
kerous cat got its claw stuck in her palm. The gash was deep and the
pain severe. The incident had put her off animal care, especially after
her father had informed her that humans were much more civil—a
statement she'd begun to question over the last twenty-four hours.

The news report ended. Olivia retracted her hand, thankful for the harmonious sounds of the Andrews Sisters that dispersed the room's toxicity.

Next to her, the major straightened as his antipathy returned. As though nothing had been amiss, he coolly asked, "How old are you, Nurse Talbot?"

"Twenty-one, sir," she said, perhaps too eagerly.

"Hmm, I'm curious. I assumed young people were keen on doing their bit for the war. Isn't that why you became a nurse? If so, then why are you here in the country and not in the thick of the action in London? Or on the Continent, even?" He sat back, resting his elbows on the arms of his chair with his index fingers together, poking the flesh under his chin. "You find war a bit too frightening, do you?"

Perhaps she misheard him. Not likely.

She leant forward, her hands balling into fists. "Sorry?"

"I simply cannot find another explanation as to why a young woman like yourself would take a job like this, isolated in the far corner of southwest England to help an ungrateful, privileged chap like myself. Pray tell me, Nurse Talbot." He too bent forward, his striking features sullied by his arrogance. "Why … are … you … here?"

This was the longest conversation they'd had yet. She drew a deep breath to keep her temper in check. "I've been a nurse for two years. I chose this career because it's something I've always wanted to do. My father is a doctor and my mother a midwife. Healing and care run in our family."

"Ah! So you *are* experienced. A relief, surely, but it doesn't explain why you're here. I assume my theory is correct: You've had your share of the action, then? Did the bombings come too close one day? You've relocated to the country looking for peace, have you? Safety? Migrating like the rest of England's city children? Not that anywhere in England, Cornwall included, is safe from Jerry. Look at Falmouth, bloody hell. You hear the rumbles every night, same as I do, no doubt."

The fact that his accusations hit close to home drove her mad, but she'd no intention of telling him that.

"If you should know, Major," she said, hoping he couldn't hear her struggle for civility, "I'm here because of my parents. If it were my choice, I would still be in London, where I worked at St. Mary Abbot's Hospital. I left an important position, not to mention a sense of daily fulfillment."

"Something you'll not find here, I gather. But why for your parents? You're not a child any longer. You must've wanted to come."

That was the thing, wasn't it? She hadn't. She wasn't even sure she'd wanted to stay at St. Mary Abbot's. Weeks ago, many girls she knew from nursing school had signed up with Air Raid Precautions, not as wardens or messengers but as ambulance drivers. They'd set out at the first siren, determined to save what lives they could whilst dodging bombs from above. Hospital work was important, but Olivia didn't feel she was helping win the war unless she was risking her life to do so. It was for this reason alone that Mother said the ARP job was too dangerous and therefore forbade it, even part time. And so here Olivia was, hardly doing her bit, cooped up in a fancy house with a disagreeable patient.

"That's right, sir, I'm no longer a child. But sometimes one must make sacrifices for those they love, especially during wartime. My father, a friend of Dr. Butler's, heard he needed someone able to drop everything to come here to help you. I'm unmarried with no other commitments—save my job, which they filled easily because like you said, sir, so many young people want to do their bit."

Her father had asked that she stay in Cornwall for at least six months. But whether the major needed her or not, come March, she'd be off, away to work at a children's hospital. Or if the war was still on, perhaps she'd cast her lot with the army instead. Her parents wouldn't like her working in a field hospital, but she wouldn't be disabled by their fears forever.

"So here I am, Major," she said, standing. "I'm sorry I'm not the matron you were hoping for."

With that, she stamped from the room, her steps infuriatingly muted by her rubber-soled oxfords.

# CHAPTER 3

According to Mrs. Pollard, the sun was shining. But for William, all was dark and had been for close to a month. If not for the familiar sounds of home—Polly's household routines and Jasper's disappointed sighs—William could be anywhere—like in his North African cell. But even Nurse Talbot's tireless footfalls, a noise he'd already grown accustomed to, weren't clipped like those of his jailors.

Nurse Talbot.

Dr. Butler should've known better. He didn't need a bloody nurse, and he certainly didn't need the whippersnapper downstairs ordering him about for an entire week now as though she were his governess. If only he could suffer alone. He was a soldier, after all; suffering was a part of his job.

His father would've understood, had he lived. The colonel had kept his personal torments buried. William hadn't understood the triggers until he'd become a man himself: innocent questions regarding family history, or issues surrounding the estate his father had never been meant to inherit. Talk of William's mother could send his father into withdrawal for days, after which he smoldered like a battlefield hours after the enemy had annihilated it. The topic of war, however, bolstered him. Colonel Morgan recounted stories of valiant leadership, which prompted his son to follow his career path. William served and fought as his father had, and now he suffered like him too, allowing the most banal things to stir his anger like a nest of provoked wasps.

At least the worst was over. He was home. He was home—and again, he didn't need a bloody nurse. He had his dog. He had Polly. She could take care of him; she always had. Throughout his early life she'd played an authoritative role, similar to the one Nurse Talbot was attempting to usurp, demanding he wash behind his ears and speak without the whine he so preferred when young. But when his mother died, she softened. Polly cushioned his sadness and buffered the grief William couldn't commiserate with his father, earning her an honorable place in his heart beside his mother.

Outside the partially open bedroom door, the footsteps of his diligent nurse approached. It creaked open, allowing her voice to fill the space between them.

"The sun is shining, Major. We should be out in it."

"Help yourself, Nurse Talbot. I'm not stopping you."

"But I'm afraid you are, as I'd fancy a tour of your gardens. Mrs. Pollard is busy, Annie claims she doesn't know the place at all, and James has gone to the village. Would you be a gentleman and show me around your home?"

Was she truly this insufferable?

Silence ruled the span of time he hoped to her felt like an eternity before he relented.

"Fine."

"All right, sir," Olivia said, squaring her shoulders against the chill, "about three feet away, we've more stairs to descend. This time, you're to use your white cane and slowly tap it back and forth. If any tap sounds differently from the others, you'll know you've hit either an object or a change in elevation."

The major revealed his usual scowl. He'd managed the inside staircase rather slowly. Surely the shallow stone steps would prove less trying.

"Go ahead, sir. Tap away and let's see if you can recognize the stairs. And please, do so slowly, or you'll hit poor Jasper."

With the timid shuffle of an elderly person, Major Morgan slid his feet forward. Inches from Jasper's oscillating tail, the stick's tip bounced madly until the major took command. At the first sound of a different *tap*, his lips bowed slightly. He lifted his feet with confidence and trundled forward.

Still at his side, Olivia matched his pace. She held her tongue —and her breath. If he fell, well, she wouldn't think about that.

"There's a handrail here, I remember." His hand on the stone, he tapped the thin cane every which way and tore down the steps.

Jasper stayed a few feet in front of him, scarcely missing the random thwacking.

"Major Morgan, please wait—"

He plowed forward without her. A curse only she could hear flew from her lips as she went after him. She recaptured his left arm, but that hardly slowed him; still tapping, he took her with him.

Then he stopped. The sound had changed, and he'd recognized it.

"Well done, sir! You're getting the hang of it."

"I want to go this way," he said, pointing the stick to the right. Its shiny red tip, dusty from gravel, bobbed toward the overgrown landscape Olivia was eager to explore. "My favorite garden is over here. I'd like you to see it."

They stopped a short distance away where two heavily berried rowan trees marked the garden's entry. At the base of each, stone pots overflowed with the crunchy brown remnants of flowering plants; waxy ivy trailed down their sides and snaked across the path.

The major discovered one planter with his stick, then tapped the grassy carpet adjacent to the gravel.

"This is it," he murmured. The wrinkles between his eyes disappeared. He inhaled deeply and almost smiled.

With softer footfalls, they entered a garden obscured by tall, unruly hedges. At its center, heirloom rosebushes surrounded a towering wych elm in perfect symmetry. Leaves twirled lazily to the ground from its looming height, cloaking the ground in yellow. Jasper trotted away, sniffing his way round the familiar territory.

"How beautiful," she whispered.

The major held his white cane in front of him like a knight with his sword. "This garden was my refuge as a child. The elm's at least two hundred years old, majestic, beautiful, but frightening on stormy nights. From my nursery window, its grotesque shadows produced a monster able to reach our house in a handful of steps."

Olivia smiled. As predicted, the outdoors had cast a spell of calm upon her patient. But the magic didn't last long. Clouds began to obscure the sun she'd been so happy to see·that morning. A light mist followed. Led by the confident major and his white cane, the pair strolled the garden's circumference in silence until the wind stirred uproariously. She shivered and suggested they return indoors.

Back at the front steps, she placed the major's left hand on the balustrade. "You were brilliant coming down, Major Morgan. Let's see how you manage going up. Here's the handrail. The first step is before you. Use your stick, and remember to listen for changes."

His right foot went up, followed by his left on the step above it. He proceeded this way, one foot per step, increasing his speed and Olivia's anxiety.

"Major Mor—"

His right foot hit the edge of the next step, forcing him down. The cane went flying, and he crumpled with his face just short of the sharp step.

"Damn!"

"Oh, no." She knelt and tried lifting him.

"Back away!"

Stunned, she did as she was told. "Yes, of course. Forgive me." The major heaved himself up.

"Your hands certainly look better than I thought they would," she offered.

"It's not my hands, Nurse Talbot. It's my bloody knee."

"Please, let me help get you inside." She took his right arm and surprisingly, he let her. Together they hobbled up the stairs, whilst Olivia chided herself for apologizing. It wasn't her fault he'd bolted up the steps.

His thin frame shuddered as he clenched the railing, slowing their ascent.

In the small reception room off the foyer, she tended to his knee. Mrs. Pollard proposed tea, but he refused. Reading Olivia's mind, he said he'd rather lie down for a while.

"Can I help you change into something more comfortable, Major?" she asked when they entered his room.

"I'd like to be left alone," he said, still holding his white cane, although he hadn't used it since they reentered the house. His free hand squeezed the bridge of his nose, as if the simple act of speaking gave him a headache. "Leave something out for me to change into, if you must. I'll manage. Please."

"Of course, Major. I'll collect you for supper in the dining room, then, at half seven, sharp."

His jaw tightened. "Very well."

William inhaled deeply and let it out with a dejected sigh. The dining room smelled of neglect. Never again would it serve as the hub of the Morgan family, and using the space now seemed wasteful. This room had defined Keldor's majesty through the ages. Local pastoral scenes and portraits of ancestors crowded the walls, including a life-size representation of his father dressed in battlefield finery. Ornate sconces, a detail his mother had added after the passing of his grandmother, dotted the areas in between. Behind him, and undoubtedly covered with blackout, the windows stretched from floor to ceiling. At the room's center stood a long table capable of seating sixteen.

Tonight, it sat two.

He sat quietly while Nurse Talbot placed his napkin over his lap and reviewed the placement of his utensils. She announced the entrance of Annie, the young girl who never spoke (surely the reason Polly had hired her), delivering the meal of roast chicken and potatoes. Mrs. Pollard followed with a carafe of wine she'd retrieved from the cellar, unearthed, she said, in honor of his return home and Nurse Talbot's arrival.

William found neither event worth celebrating, yet he gladly accepted the glass thrust into his hand.

"Why are we eating in here, Mrs. Pollard?" he asked once the liquid had finished warming his throat.

"Wouldn't you want to be eating in here, sir? This is the dining hall, and pardon my saying so, but it's about time you stopped eating meals in your bedchamber."

"Aside from where I've been eating my meals, Mrs. Pollard, it hardly seems appropriate that we use this room. There are two of us, an invalid in his pajamas and his nurse. Please, take no offense, Nurse Talbot, but even though I can't see it, I know what this room is like, and eating here seems extravagant under the circumstances. Am I wrong to think so?"

He turned his head back and forth toward their voices, awaiting a response.

"I understand your concern, Major," Nurse Talbot said. "But this room in its current state isn't extravagant at all." She paused as if scanning their surroundings. "The chandeliers are unlit. The only light comes from a lamp on the sideboard and two candles on the table. The rest is quite dark."

"That's right," Mrs. Pollard said with a breathy huff, "and really, Mr. William, meals are to be eaten properly, even if we haven't much." Her tone sharpened, making way for her inescapable scolding. "The only way we're going to make it through this bloody war is by keeping our civilities. Three-quarters of this house is shut up, like. Can't we at least use a portion of this grand room as a reminder of who we are?"

The table shook. A chair moved, and Nurse Talbot's unsure voice followed. "Here, Mrs. Pollard. Would you like to sit down? May I pour you a glass of wine?"

"Thank you, Nurse Talbot." She fell into a chair with a thud. Liquid poured, and the room fell quiet save her unmistakable murmur. "Honestly."

"Why, Polly," he said, amused by her agitation, "I haven't witnessed you this upset since I had you convinced my great-grandmother's kitchen maid haunted the pantry."

And then, imagining the shock that undoubtedly decorated both women's faces, he laughed.

His mirth met a wall of silence. He drained his wine glass before covering his face with his hand, erasing his humor. "I'm sorry, Polly. I appreciate what you're doing for this house and my family, though I'm the only one left in it."

Mrs. Pollard seized his shoulders, and a kiss was planted atop his head. "Not a worry, my handsome. Please, get better now, will you?"

After their first meal in the dining room, the major stated he'd been downstairs long enough and wished to return to his room. Olivia invited herself to join him despite his ongoing request to be left alone. She was glad she did. The humor he enjoyed earlier influenced his mood the rest of the evening. The nine o'clock bulletin passed painlessly, followed by music. Conversation remained limited, of course, but the major's face softened during more than one song. His fingers twiddled to mellow rhythms and once, she spied a foot tapping to the beat. A hint of his earlier smile reappeared. Like a good nurse, she pretended not to notice.

Before bed, she checked his bandages, gave him his tea, and offered to help him into his nightclothes. As always, he claimed he didn't need her help. Why couldn't she leave him be? But although his words commanded she go, his face begged her to stay. Empty eyes widened in fear, erasing irritable lines. His hands, large and bony, fidgeted with his shirt like those of a child awaiting punishment.

Every night had been like that, and every night, Olivia had respected his wishes. She left him alone with the promise to leave both of their doors open. If he required anything at all, he needed only to call.

And call he did.

Beginning her third night at Keldor, she'd been awakened by shouting: "Not again! Not again!" She'd run to his room, where he stirred wildly in the center of his bed. When his racket didn't cease, she pressed her hands upon him, begging him to wake. He opened his eyes and pulled away, rubbing his shoulders as if erasing the imprint of her touch. He shouted, but consciously this time. Wasn't she aware he needed to suffer through these episodes? How else would he get any rest? Every time she interrupted his nightmare, he had a hell of a time getting back to sleep because his brain did nothing but dwell on it. No matter what she heard, she was to ignore it.

And still, the calls came.

This night, after their nearly companionable day, his cries, pitiful and incessant, nudged her from sleep.

"Help me," he whimpered. "Someone, please. Please help me."

She crept in and knelt beside him, his laments tearing at her heart. Powerless and conflicted, her hands hovered above his damp, wrinkled forehead. It took all her will not to flatten her palms against it, to wake him and remind him that everything was all right.

But for him, she suspected, nothing would ever be all right.

# CHAPTER 4

OLIVIA'S REQUEST TO start eating breakfast in the sitting room was met with surprisingly little opposition. Mrs. Pollard said the room had once been a favorite of the major's mother, Mistress Charlotte. Tea-rose walls and creamy white coving enclosed a comfortable space with cushioned chairs and a large sofa. Above an inviting hearth, Mistress Charlotte herself smiled down at the room's knickknacks, lamps, and drapes trimmed in gold, all of which recalled a home of affluence and took some getting used to.

For two weeks Olivia and the major had breakfasted facing the idyllic courtyard aptly called Charlotte's Garden. At its center, fronds of a tall palm tree dipped under a light rain shower. The view was perfect despite the rain, chock-full of early autumn foliage. Hopefully the major still remembered it.

This morning, before allowing him to attack his breakfast, she gave him the layout of his plate: eggs at 12:00, herring at 3:00, toast at 6:00, and the season's last fresh tomatoes fried and placed at 9:00. Since she'd implemented this system, the major had become a master at navigating his meals. Wielding a large spoon, he scooped with adept efficiency and rarely lost a crumb. His eating habits weren't perfect, though. He still used his fingers often, asking something at the same time in hopes, she imagined, of distracting her from his misconduct, forgetting that she could answer his question and watch him finger his food at the same time. Her biggest concern was hiding the smile in her response.

"Mr. William," Mrs. Pollard called before she entered the room. "Mr. William, I'm sorry to interrupt your breakfast, but there's someone here for you."

"Tell them I'm not taking visitors, would you, Mrs. Pollard?"

"Yes sir, but aren't you curious who it is?"

"No."

"But Mr. William, it's Miss Jenna. She's just heard you was found and—"

"I said no visitors. Please respect my wishes."

"But she's very upset, sir, and tomorrow she's off. She's signed on with the Auxiliary Territorial Service and she—"

Olivia put down her fork. "What if I talk to her, Major, as your nurse? I can calm her fears about your condition and tell her it's best you don't have callers right now. Would that be acceptable?"

"Very well."

In the foyer, an attractive woman with flushed cheeks paced the tiled floor. Her slender frame halted at Olivia's approach. Dark and shiny, her hair gleamed like a freshly picked blackberry. Silver barrettes glittering with tiny gemstones held the silky strands back from her ears. Under charcoal brows, sapphire-blue orbs sparkled as if backlit. They flitted to Mrs. Pollard, then back to Olivia.

"Hello, I'm Olivia Talbot, Major Morgan's nurse." She offered her hand.

The woman took it. "I'm Jenna Werren. I need to see William." She twisted the life out of her black leather gloves before shoving them into the pockets of her dripping mackintosh. "Is he awake? Will you take me to him?"

"I'm terribly sorry to disappoint you, Miss Werren, but he cannot have callers at this—"

"Can't you make an exception? I discovered only this morning he was alive. I haven't heard a word in months! I thought he was dead; we all did. Even the colonel—"

Olivia stepped forward. "Mrs. Pollard, I'd like to sit with Miss Werren for a moment. Would you mind bringing us a pot of tea?"

"Not at all, Nurse Talbot."

Miss Werren's black heels clicked behind Olivia's muffled tread on the way to the receiving room. "Where has he been? What's happened to him?"

Even distraught with worry, the demure woman radiated a charm that made it hard to look elsewhere. They settled onto a small sofa.

"I understand he's blind," Miss Werren said. "What else?"

"He was found in North Africa. He's blind, yes, and flesh wounds cover his legs and back. He has trouble sleeping and therefore needs much rest." She didn't want to intrude, but learning more about the major's life could better help him back to it. "I assume the two of you were close?"

Miss Werren's voice dropped. "Yes, we were close—we *are* close. He was to announce our engagement when he returned from North Africa. His last letter stated he'd be home in June. I didn't hear from him again." Quiet tears cut lines down her red cheeks. "I'm leaving for Bristol tomorrow. I don't know for how long." She pulled a powder-blue kerchief from her tiny leather purse. Embroidered with a red *J*, it draped her varnished red fingernails as she dabbed her eyes. "I need to see him."

Mrs. Pollard returned and placed a tray on the table between them.

"Mrs. Pollard," Miss Werren pleaded, reaching for her hand, "are you sure William understands it's *me* who's here?"

"He does, my bird, but you must understand he's not the same. He rarely speaks and when he does, he's some fair teasy like, cross all the time. I've never known him to be so irritable. Seems he's lost his spirit and love for life, poor man."

"Perhaps Miss Werren could leave the major a note," Olivia said. "Miss Werren, have you an address where he could send you a letter? As part of the major's rehabilitation, I think it best he ease back into his former life."

Miss Werren took the pen and paper from Mrs. Pollard. "Will he recover, do you think, or will he forever remain this different person?"

"It's too soon to tell. We'll see what time brings us, and hope for small miracles every day. Mrs. Pollard tells me he was once enjoyable to be around."

The young woman's face was unreadable. "He was." Head bent, she penned letters and numbers into a sophisticated work of art.

Olivia excused herself and strode back to the sitting room where the major sat comfortably in his chair facing the garden, appearing incredibly at ease. If Miss Werren saw him, she'd think both nurse and housekeeper were frauds.

"What is it, Nurse Talbot?" he asked.

Startled, she rocked forward. "You knew I was here?"

"Of course." He raised his eyebrows, seemingly impressed with himself.

Surely Miss Werren could find someone more suited to her than this unromantic bore. She stormed toward him. "Why won't you welcome this woman? She tells me you were to be engaged upon your return home. You're being extremely unkind. Please, let her see that you are in fact alive after everyone thought you weren't. If this woman was to be your wife, you at least owe her that."

The major turned his head toward her, his eyes staring past her right side. "This is none of your business, Nurse Talbot."

"But sir, you said you had no one left in the world who cared about you except Mrs. Pollard, and here is this woman—your fiancée!"

"She's not my fiancée."

"Well close to it, then." She was seething. Why did she even care?

The major's face darkened. "I won't have Jenna seeing me like this. She's young and has yet to experience the real world. She deserves a better life than the one I can give her. I've made my decision." He faced the window.

"But tomorrow she's off to Bristol and—"

"And what, Nurse Talbot?"

This was going nowhere. She dropped her head. "Nothing. Never mind."

Back in the foyer, Olivia collected Miss Werren's letter, squeezed her hand, and offered her sincerest hopes that once the war ended, relationships amongst those still standing would be restored. But Miss Werren barely met her eyes, leaving Olivia unsure of whom she felt more sorry: her patient or the stunning woman longing to be Mrs. Morgan.

Down the corridor, Olivia's heart dragged a burden she hadn't signed up for. Aware that her voice would give away her frustration, she took a deep breath and forced a smile before reentering the sitting room. But from the petering fire to the gray windows, the empty settee, and the chairs in between, the major was nowhere about. Thumbnail trapped between her top and bottom teeth, she racked her brain. Since she'd arrived three weeks ago, he hadn't wandered anywhere by himself, yet even his cane was missing. At least he'd come round to using it without her nagging.

She scurried back down the passage, charging doors left and right. Those that opened gave onto rooms housing furniture and artwork sheathed in white. In the deserted foyer, remnants of their departed visitor glistened in pools on the colorful mosaic tiles. Olivia avoided the wet spots and stopped at a pair of closed doors beyond the staircase.

An easy twist opened the left side, releasing the stale scent of smoke and leather. Blackout drapes covered the windows and white sheets clothed the furniture, almost glowing in the darkness. Instantly absorbed by the room's ambiance, she crossed her arms to fight the chill and searched for a light. On the corner of what she guessed was a desk sat a dusty, uncovered lamp. Switched on, it illuminated walls and walls of books. Even the wall encasing the hearth housed books.

As tall as a man, the sooty fireplace stood vacant and cold. A roaring fire and stripped furniture would have changed the room completely, symbolizing everything an ancient house like this should: tradition, majesty, and history. She'd spend every day in here if she could. Gravitating toward the shelves to her left, she traced a row of gold-embossed book spines. She must ask the major if he'd let her borrow one.

Damn. The major.

A white streak emerged from the dark like a blemish amidst the rich reds and browns of the Persian rug. Drawing closer, she peered over the sheathed sofa. There lay the major, a dark tuft of hair resting at one end whilst his feet, shoes on and ankles crossed, rested at the other. On the floor, Jasper thumped his tail happily.

Olivia knelt down and patted the dog's head.

"Hello, Nurse Talbot."

"Hello." Her voice remained calm, though her heart hammered. "I didn't know where you'd gone. Now that I do, I will leave you with your thoughts."

"You don't have to go."

"All right, then." She sat in a covered armchair beside the fireplace. "I left the foyer with Miss Werren moments ago. How did you manage to arrive here unseen—and with Jasper, no less?"

He sat up. "This house is full of secrets, Nurse Talbot. There are ways to stay hidden when one wants to, even when one is blind. Though I may have taken out a small table and vase on my way. Please tell Mrs. Pollard it was an accident."

"You can tell her yourself," she said, scanning the room. "I love libraries, especially private ones like this. It's a shame Mrs. Pollard had it closed."

"This was my favorite room as a child, a place to lay plans and tell secrets. The mustiness alone alluded to a history I wanted to be a part of. Though my father died in here, I still find the room comforting."

"Oh, forgive me. I didn't know."

Had he been ill, or was the death sudden? She would never ask. Still, her eyes roamed. Despite the tragedy, the room was as the major said: grand yet intimate, even comforting.

"A busy man, my father. I wanted to be just like him growing up. He would lock himself in here for hours. Sometimes I'd spy on him, watching his serious expression as he read over papers and wrote letters. Sometimes I'd catch him laughing."

"This fireplace must've kept the room toasty."

"Indeed. He received visitors here. From local estate matters to national security, whiskies were poured, cigars lit, and the world's problems were solved right here next to this hearth."

"Do you think we could convince Mrs. Pollard to reopen it?"

"I couldn't say. The place bothers her now. She hasn't said this, of course, but it's a feeling I get." He rested his elbows on his knees and yawned into both hands. "I gather Miss Werren has departed?"

"Yes, and she left you a note. I'll leave it. I'm sure Mrs. Pollard would be more than happy to—"

"Not at all, Nurse Talbot. Please, you may read me the note."

She wasn't keen to intrude on the Miss Werren's heartache,

but then again, women weren't so different from one another. She already knew what the letter would say.

"Very well. 'My Dearest William, I'm overjoyed to hear you are alive and home, yet saddened I could not visit you today. Despite your injuries and troubled mind, I still love you. I wish I had known sooner of your survival. I wouldn't have signed on with the ATS, a commitment I cannot forsake, and instead would have devoted my time to your recovery. Please tell me nothing's changed between us. And I must know: Did you think of me at all whilst you were away? Your Jenna.' "

Her breath caught as she read the last sentence.

"Does the letter upset you, Nurse Talbot?"

She wiped her cheek with the back of her hand. "Does it not tear at your emotions in the slightest? She was to be your wife."

"I learned to shut off my emotions long ago."

"Well, decide what you'd like to say in response, and I'll gather your writing utensils. In the meantime"—she stood and tugged on her skirt, straightening it—"I'll leave you to your afternoon. Do you wish to stay here longer, or would you like me to take you to your room?"

"I'll remain here with Jasper, thank you."

Sad to leave, Olivia gave the room one last glance from the double doors. A tapping sound caused her to linger long enough to see Jasper rise and ease his head onto his master's lap.

"Good boy," the major said, leaning down to nuzzle the dog's head with his own. Laughter surged out of him as the black dog licked his face. The crinkles around his eyes and the natural curve of his dimpled smile struck Olivia with another wave of sadness.

Poor Miss Werren.

William had lost the energy it took to argue with his nurse, so when she requested weeks ago that they spend their mornings in the sitting room, he'd yielded, reasoning it would make Mrs. Pollard happy. And too, the room reminded him of his mother. He missed seeing her portrait above the mantel, though. Memory depicted her in a satin gown as shimmering as the turquoise sea in which she loved to swim. They'd spent hours together in this room. Cozied beside him on the settee, she'd tell him troublesome tales of her childhood, expecting him to take them to heart and appreciate all he'd been born to. And he had.

Until lately.

Mrs. Pollard broke his thoughts. "Mr. William, I'm sorry to bother you, but Mr. Peder's here, and he insists—"

"I say, old boy, you look better than I'd feared."

"Now, Mr. Peder, I asked that—"

"Now, Polly," Peder said, fawning over the flustered woman. "I daresay your flushed cheeks brighten your eyes."

William smirked at the charm Peder effortlessly emitted around Mrs. Pollard.

"Major," Nurse Talbot whispered in his ear. Like a good girl, she didn't touch him. "Would you like me to ask your guest to leave? Though I'm not sure he will acqui—"

"William!"

He tried not to cower as two hands clasped his shoulders with the strength of Atlas. Peder enveloped him in a robust embrace that he struggled to receive with civility. He leant into the back of his chair, trapped.

"You're alive, my friend, you're alive!" Peder turned William's head left and right. "What the bloody hell happened to you down there?"

"Excuse me," Nurse Talbot said. "Mr. Peder, is it? How do you do? I'm Nurse Talbot, and I'm afraid the major—"

"It's fine, Nurse Talbot," William said, even as he recovered from Peder's assault. He cleared his throat and gripped his chair's armrests. "Peder is Miss Werren's brother. We've known one another for some time."

"'Some time?' Nurse Talbot, the major and I have a long history. Our families have been acquainted for decades."

A hand returned to William's shoulder. Surely Peder could feel the tremor beneath it.

"I'm sorry, mate, about your father."

"Thank you. Sit. Nurse Talbot, you may leave us."

"Yes, sir."

"Nurse Talbot, eh? My, my." The settee squeaked as her footsteps retreated. "Quite the looker, you know. Leave it to you to end up with a stunner of a nurse. And to think you get her all to yourself, lucky bugger."

"Why are you here, Peder? If this is regarding Jenna, you're wasting your time."

"I'm not here because of Jenna," Peder said, clasping his arm and making William start. "I'm here for you. Tell me what happened in North Africa. We all thought you'd died."

"I was captured. I escaped. The end."

"But your eyesight. What the hell did they do to you? Nazis, were they? How did you get out?"

If he sat silent long enough, Peder would end the interrogation. Perseverance wasn't his friend's strong suit.

"I joined, you know, the army," Peder said. "After you left. I've always admired your career choice, especially now that I've seen a bit of hell myself."

"Extraordinary. Where is it they've sent you?" He strived to picture his friend in uniform. Girls would love the look, but that wasn't the real Peder. Unlike his sister—tall, dark, and demanding—Peder's goofy smile and ginger locks the exact shade of his father's only accentuated his passivity. He could hardly command his own dogs. William questioned Peder's ability to withstand army life, especially during wartime. Still,

Peder was brainy, a trait he needed only capitalize on. Perhaps he'd found his chance.

"I'm a sapper, stationed along the southeast coast, shoring it up against invasion."

"You've joined the Royal Engineers, then? Suits you." William chuckled. "But what exactly is this 'bit of hell' you're referring to? No cream teas at camp?"

"Mm. I do believe North Africa has made your sharp tongue that much sharper. I'll not always exist in your shadow, my friend. I too, can do something heroic."

Maybe, if he wasn't so bloody sensitive.

"Upon my arrival in Dorset, the unit I'd been assigned were returning from Dunkirk in droves. The hell I'm referring to is the condition of these men. But I don't have to tell you. You've been trained to see it, to deal with it. I knew witnessing death would be grim, but to see it up close. To see so many suffer. It can change a man, if not ruin him."

William pitied his friend's diminishing morale so early in a war that was expected to last years. The conflict touched everyone now. Money and privilege, two things Peder Werren would never live without, could no longer shield him from war's unsavory truths.

William could write a manual on the topic.

"It's good you've still got Keldor, William. My parents haven't been so lucky. Our estate has been requisitioned, and they've moved to the dower house. It's not too tight a fit with Jenna gone, but I daresay the change has taken a toll on my father's health. And my mother's worried sick, with her husband ill and her two children in the thick of it."

The settee squeaked, and William readied himself for another collision.

"I'm here for a few days, staying in the flat above the stables. If you've a desire to get out, ring me."

There came the pat on his waiting shoulder.

41

"I'll leave you, but before I do, I must offer a word on your decision to cut ties with Jenna. Though I can't say I ever liked the idea you two together, I do believe you've broken the heart of the one person whose heart we thought unbreakable."

"Peder—"

"I know you well enough that when you make up your mind, there's nothing in the world to change it. But she's overlooked your past, William. Not many women would be willing to disregard the slew you've left behind."

"Peder—"

"And as your closest friend, I say, if ever you've needed someone permanent in your life—"

"I said enough!"

Nurse Talbot's feet scurried across the room. "Excuse me, Mr. Werren, but the major should rest."

At least she was good for something.

"Mm. Yes, of course." Peder's footsteps moved toward the door. "Best of luck to you, mate."

# CHAPTER 5

NOVEMBER BROUGHT the changeable days of October to an end. The sky no longer toggled between gray and blue, for the rain had come to stay. With it, unvarying cloud coverage kept even midday dark. Olivia and her patient spent many of these dim days in her new favorite room, the library. As soon as Mrs. Pollard knew the major wished the room reopened, she whisked away tarps, dusted shelves, and unearthed precious family heirlooms. A tapestry hung beside the marble bust of some unrecognizable figure. Daguerreotypes in gilt frames joined tomes of Cornish history bound in leather on the surrounding shelves.

Beside a radiant fire, Olivia practiced patience whilst knitting socks for soldiers. Annie had been kind enough to teach her how and even loaned her a few supplies, although her first pair proved a huge disappointment and would go nowhere but her drawer.

Just as industriously and with somewhat more success, the major responded to letters from well-wishers with a contraption designed to aid the blind in writing. Thick paper lay under a series of horizontal cords that guided the writer's pen in a straight line.

His first letter was to Miss Werren. He had granted Olivia

permission to read it; she insisted she need not but was glad when she did. The bit about wishing he hadn't survived North Africa was positively alarming.

4 November, 1940
    Miss Jenna Werren
    Auxiliary Territorial Service
    Bristol Branch
    Dear Jenna,

I'm sorry for the distress you suffered during your recent visit to Keldor. I know you're worried about me, but please, Jenna, don't be. My physical strength is returning and my outward wounds are healing. However, I'm no longer the man you fell in love with. I've witnessed and lived through events I shouldn't have. Oftentimes, I wish I hadn't survived them at all. Despite our former relationship and care for one another, I don't wish for you to spend the rest of your life managing my hardships. These experiences will haunt me the rest of my days and affect anyone who dares enter my life henceforth. I wish to suffer alone as only I can. You are free to pursue someone who completes your life and makes you truly happy.

I'm proud of you for joining the ATS. You're doing the right thing for your country. Your family must be proud. My best wishes to you, Jenna.

    Sincerely,
    William

"Excuse me, Mr. William, Nurse Talbot," Annie said at the library doors. "Dr. Butler has come for you both. Nurse Talbot, he'd like a word with you first."

Olivia glanced at the major. He possessed his father's desk as if it'd always been his. With clearly no need to address the visitor, he continued writing.

"Thank you, Annie," she said. "Major, I'll return shortly."

She swept yarn remnants off her blue pinafore and gave a silent thanks to God for giving her the sense to wear her uniform today. Nothing surpassed the comfort of casual dresses and here at Keldor, wearing the scratchy get-up hardly seemed necessary. Her patient couldn't tell if she wore her uniform or not, and Mrs. Pollard didn't seem to have an opinion one way or another. But instead of doing away with the outfit altogether, she'd chosen to wear it intermittently. She left the library with a smile. So far, this meeting was off to a good start.

"Ah, Nurse Talbot, splendid nice to see you," said the aged physician, drying his glasses with a handkerchief.

"Hello, Dr. Butler. We can sit in here."

She led him to the empty receiving room, where a budding fire endeavored to vanquish the damp day. They took seats across from one another and huddled close to tiny blaze.

"Someone will bring tea shortly," she said.

"No matter, my dear." He paused to look around. "Are you finding yourself at home?"

"Mrs. Pollard has been so welcoming."

"She's quite a brick. Your parents send their best." He reached into the breast pocket of his tweed jacket. "Here is a letter from your father. He's eager for a full report on your well-being. You aren't missing much, by the way. You may feel somewhat isolated here in the country after living in the city your entire life, but I tell you, London is no place to be. The situation is absolutely dreadful." He separated each syllable the way Mrs. Pollard chopped carrots. "Air raids, sirens, warplanes, the stench of fear and uncertainty looming round every corner ... I assume things are more peaceful here?"

It depended on how one defined the word *peaceful*. Yes, there were far fewer air raids here than in London, but they still happened, as did the major's maddening response to them. Arms crossed, he claimed the Nazis were seeking airfields and docks, and since Keldor was located far from both, they should all carry on without worry. It took Mrs. Pollard's commanding tone to force him down the narrow stairs to the wine cellar, a process as peaceful as immersing a cat in water. The steep steps confounded him. The ceiling was quite low as well, and every time he grazed his head, he spewed obscenities she'd never heard before, not even out of her older brother and his friends.

She smiled at the doctor.

"Well then," he continued, "tell me about our patient. How is the major doing?"

"He's shown some improvement since my arrival. The minor wounds on his back have healed. I've removed those sutures, but the deeper gashes are taking more time. The few marks on his legs have healed completely. He's gaining weight, and he's learning, ever so slowly, how to use his white cane."

"And what about nightmares? How's he sleeping? The pills I left, do you find they're effective?"

Her gut dropped. The major hadn't taken a single pill since she arrived; he'd had only her grandmother's tea. "He's been sleeping well, Doctor, though not perfectly. But he's no longer taking the medication you left him."

"And why is that, Nurse Talbot?" His frown reminded her of her father's the first (and last) time she'd bunked off school.

Still firm in her resolve to give the major a better remedy than the conventional prescription, she sat straighter and recounted her first hour at Keldor and the nightly administration of her grandmother's tea.

Dr. Butler chuckled at her confession, pulled a black notebook and pen from his leather medical bag, and began to jot some notes. "Oh, and how you remind me of your grandmother. He'd only been taking the medication two, maybe three days.

Results may not appear for an entire week. You hardly gave it a chance."

Heat crept up her neck to the tops of her ears. The flame burning her cheeks infuriated her. "I suppose you're right."

"I suppose I am."

"But the tea is working. I've been documenting every time he wakes with night terrors. Since that first day, there have only been a handful. He often moans in his sleep and sometimes he shouts or cries, but nothing like the day I arrived."

"No matter. I have something new for the major to try." He pulled a brown bottle from his bag. "Still in the experimental stage, but just in time to help these mutilated souls coming home from the war. The good news is that the major's system needed be clear of the other medication well before taking these. You say he's been off them for a month; therefore, he can begin the new medicine straightaway."

She took the bottle. The white pills shifted as she turned it over in her hand. Silently, she read the label, hoping her scrutiny hid her skepticism. "What are these for, Doctor? I don't mean to overstep my bounds, but I'm not sure the major needs a new sleep aid."

"These aren't only for sleep. They're for depression, anxiety, stress, even"—he paused, cocking an eyebrow—"suicidal inclinations. You haven't noticed these signs in the major, have you? Last I examined him I thought it likely, especially after he learned about his father."

The major's letter to Miss Werren had exposed this disturbing truth. "He broke off his engagement to his fiancée, claiming she shouldn't be exposed to his troubles—troubles he wished he hadn't lived through."

"That settles it, then. Before I leave today, I'll fix you with dosage information. I'm telling you, Nurse Talbot, physicians in London are witnessing remarkable results with soldiers who've come home with appendages intact but minds broken. These men have hope again. In a matter of days, you'll be amazed at what these pills will do for your patient."

∼

"William! How are you getting on, my boy?"

William stood at the doctor's entrance into the library, aware of his contrary demeanor. "I'm well, Dr. Butler." He shuffled around the massive desk and put forward his right hand.

"Very good."

The doctor's hand was familiar, like Mrs. Pollard's. Having known the man his entire life, William took comfort from it.

"I see you've put on weight—Mrs. Pollard's marvelous cooking, no doubt. Even with the latest round of rations, I'd wager she's a genius in the kitchen. And how is our Nurse Talbot treating you? I hope you're finding her services satisfactory?"

"She's been helpful, albeit dictatorial at times." The bite in his voice couldn't be helped. He wasn't brave enough to tell the doctor his true feelings about having a nurse, so perhaps the intimation would be enough.

"Precisely what I would expect from a proficient caregiver. I hope you haven't been too beastly."

"Nothing she can't handle, I'm sure."

Dr. Butler checked his vital signs. "I've known Nurse Talbot's family for many decades, almost as long as I've known yours. She's a lovely girl, very sweet and more than competent. You'll not have her forever, though; her time here is up come March. However, if you choose to dismiss her before then, do contact me well in advance of letting her go. I promised her father I'd keep her out of harm's way as long as I could."

So she'd come here for safety, and it was William's responsibility to see she remained. How brilliant that his dire situation had created a haven for this coddled city girl. Unwilling to discuss the matter further, William remained silent as the doctor took his time checking his eyes, turning his head this way and that.

"William, I still see nothing physically wrong with your eyes. These rudimentary instruments should detect *something* that shows your eyes aren't in proper working order. Can you tell me, now that some time has passed, were you exposed to anything that could've rendered you blind? Too close to an explosion, maybe?"

"No."

"That's good—and it would make sense, as I see no damage of that sort." The rustle of instruments ceased, and the doctor's bag clicked. "I believe you suffer from a condition called conversion disorder, once called hysterical blindness. Similar cases arose during the Great War, but rarely. The disorder is a psychological one, caused by a traumatic experience. I suspected as much during my last visit, but since you were unwilling to discuss North Africa, I couldn't be sure. Based on what you're saying today, I'm certain this is what you're dealing with."

*A traumatic experience.* The words knocked around the inside of William's head until memories of the villain's face dampened the back of his neck. The insults would come next, disguised as compliments, each word meant to wound, break, and eventually destroy.

A door slammed shut in his mind. *Help me, please. Is there anyone who can help me?*

"William? Are you all right, my boy? Why, you're shaking like the dickens." Dr. Butler placed a hand on his shoulder.

William recoiled. "I …" He had nothing to say: no explanation, no apology.

"Here, take this." The doctor pried William's hand from its tight grasp on his elbow and dropped a tablet into it. "I've given Nurse Talbot a new medication for you to try. It's working wonders for our wounded boys returned from battle, boys with a touch of shell shock. In a matter of days, you'll sleep better and your mood will improve, to boot."

The small pill scraped the back of William's dry throat.

"Some in the field of psychoneuroses believe that the more a patient reveals about their trauma, the quicker the disorder will disappear—but not forever, necessarily. We aren't completely certain how the brain works in such matters, you see." A friendly pat landed on his back. "If you're ready, let's get that shirt off. I'd like to check your back."

William fumbled over his buttons until the doctor swooped in to assist. Stripped bare to the waist, he allowed the doctor's silent scrutiny to torment him: the questions, the judgments, the bafflement. It was the same whenever Nurse Talbot examined him.

"I know that whatever you've gone through came close to killing you, and you're not willing to talk about these raw memories," Dr. Butler said. "A wise decision. I want you to put all that bad business out of your mind and enjoy the peaceful landscape here at Keldor. Understand?"

"Yes, Doctor."

Dr. Butler guided his arms through the sleeves of his shirt. The calm was immediate.

"Your back looks shipshape, William. Nurse Talbot is doing a fine job indeed."

"If you don't need me for anything else, Doctor, I'd like to lie down."

"Of course. I'll have Nurse Talbot take you to your room. I'm off to London tomorrow and not sure when I'll be back to Cornwall. I'm committed there until Hitler eases up on our cities, and I'm afraid that won't happen any time soon." He took William's hand and shook it. "Look after yourself, young man, and try thinking of happier times. It's what your father would've wanted."

~

The first changes in the major's behavior happened two days later, during his morning shave. Olivia had become an expert on his facial reliefs: his wide jawbone, chiseled chin, and narrow upper lip. His shave was usually a quiet time, save for the gentle scraping that echoed through the tiled room.

But not today.

"Nurse Talbot," he said as she rinsed his razor, "you've barely told me about yourself since you've been here, and I must know. Why aren't you married?"

Her wet hand paused, dripping, over the basin. "Well, I—I haven't met the right person, I suppose." She plunged the razor back into the water and splashed it around needlessly. "Nor have I had time to do so."

God help her to not sound so defensive.

"I see. You've been too busy. Nursing school, then the war. Does that sum up your last few years?" The more he prodded, the more playful his voice became.

She relaxed a little. "Yes, that's it exactly."

"But what about your soldiers in London? Your patients? You must've fancied a few of them. I'm sure they fancied you. Or"—he paused before erupting like a detective close to cracking a case —"perhaps there's a special sweetheart off fighting somewhere, and as soon as he returns, you're to be married and have loads of his children. Am I right?"

She laughed. "What does it matter to you?"

He shrugged. "Can't a man be curious about the woman charged with his care?"

She was patting his smooth face with a dry flannel when his hand found her wrist. He brought her forearm to his nose and sniffed. "Do you wear perfume here?"

"It's not perfume, it's oil," she said quietly, pulling from his grasp. A ring of warmth encircled her forearm for moments afterward.

"It reminds me of lavender, but not sweet like a perfume," he said. "It's fresh, like the plant that blooms in my mother's garden every June."

"It's also what I use on your back from time to time—that and jasmine oil. Both are good for anxiety. Lavender is especially good for burns."

"But why do you wear it? I'm not that much of a brute, am I?"

She wasn't about to answer the latter. "My grandmother, the one who makes your tea, created a mixture of geranium and lavender oil for me to wear a few years ago when I'd been quarreling with my mother an awful lot and struggling in school. It helped at the time. I've never stopped."

"Hmm, a lovely fragrance for a lovely woman. Dr. Butler was right, I'm sure." He turned on his broad smile and aimed his eyes toward her voice.

"Dr. Butler?"

"Dr. Butler told me you were a lovely young woman, and I daresay I believe him. Do you think you're pretty?"

What a morning this was turning out to be. "I'm sure the doctor was being kind. He's a friend of my father's."

"You haven't answered the question."

"Because it's not a fair one. If I think I'm pretty, then I'm conceited. If I state the opposite, I haven't an ounce of self-worth." She scraped her chair back across the floor tiles and rose. "I will not answer it."

He reclaimed her arm. "Please. Sit. I'd like to finish our conversation. You're right, the question isn't fair. But tell me, what do you look like? What color are your eyes?"

"Brown."

"And your hair? Is it wavy? Stick-straight? Dark as a raven?"

Miss Werren's sable tresses came to mind. "My hair is brown as well, and rather straight."

The major sighed. "I may be blind, but I'm not ignorant of the fact that there are many shades of brown, especially in the areas of eye and hair color. That being said, please take pity on a blind man and give me examples of your brown. What would you compare your shade to?"

She leaned forward, entranced by his captivating banter. "All right, then. My eyes are rather dark, like the brown of your father's desk in the library."

The major nodded as though he'd guessed the same.

"And have you ever seen a meadow after an unusually dry summer? My hair is the same shade as that lifeless brown straw, I'm afraid."

The major chuckled. "Dead grass? You *do* lack self-esteem. And I'm afraid the color you're describing is more golden than brown."

"I've plenty of self-esteem, and my hair is far from golden. My older brother called attention to this fact one year on a family trip to Scotland. He claimed the parched moors resembled my hair exactly. The comment upset me at the time, and of course my parents said nothing to counter his remark. Because really, he was right."

The major's eyes creased, a cool blue enhanced by his warm smile. She smiled back, wishing he could see it or at least get some sense of the strange pleasantness he shared with her this morning.

"I'm glad I asked," he said. "I have a better picture of you now, not just of the outside but the inside too."

# CHAPTER 6

"She wrote you back! Already!" Olivia was almost singing as she entered the sitting room clutching a small white envelope.

In his usual seat by the wireless, the major sat listening raptly. Olivia lowered the volume, souring the atmosphere at once.

"I was listening to that," he said.

"And you can in a moment. I want you to listen to Miss Werren's letter." Riding the wave of his recent good humor, she placed the envelope in his hands and sat beside him. "Will you open it or shall I open it for you? You want to hear it, don't you?"

"Not particularly."

"Why ever not?" Was she a fool for hoping she'd never again experience his disagreeable side?

"After hearing I've ended our relationship, I'm certain Miss Werren has replied with enough curses to last a lifetime. I'm in no mood for a lashing today."

"Then Major, you don't know women. I saw the look in her eyes. She still loves you, and this letter will prove it. Please, let's open it."

Elbow bent, he rested his forehead in his hand and sighed—a sure sign of consent. She snatched the envelope back and read.

"'My dear William, Thank you for your letter. I've read it at least ten times and find much of it hard to believe. You say you're a different person, but that cannot be. Your stubbornness shines through your written words, as does your blatant unselfishness. I've known you your entire life, sweetheart, and you will always be my William.'"

Olivia glanced at William, whose expression remained stoic, so she continued.

"'I'm committed to my responsibilities in Bristol currently, but say the word and I will apply for leave so I can come back to Cornwall and care for you. Through the good and the bad, my wish is to be by your side. Won't you have me? We don't have to marry right away. Just let me be with you. Your Jenna'"

Triumph curled Olivia's lips as she waited for the major to respond. When he didn't, she added, "Well?"

"Well, what?"

"I was right. She loves you and wants to be with you. I understand you don't want her to see you like this, but what you don't realize is that you need her. And if you don't mind my saying so, I believe you've forgotten how much you still love her."

Maybe not. His face had developed anger lines she'd not seen before. She refolded the letter and placed it on the table.

"You know nothing more of Jenna than what you witnessed the day you met her. Furthermore, you know nothing of me except for the scars on my back. And coming from someone so young and utterly ignorant of the world's cruelty, save your handful of patients, I find it infuriating that you think you know what I need."

He banged his fist on the chair's wooden armrest and crossed his arms.

Her composure scarcely eased her own rising anger. "You're right. I don't know Miss Werren, or you. But as far as experiencing pain and loss, you know nothing of me either."

"Do enlighten me."

She approached the window, praying she'd keep her temper. "My older brother, John, joined the RAF weeks before the war started. He'd wanted to fly since he was a boy. He was killed last summer in a dogfight against the Luftwaffe. He'd just turned twenty-five."

His birthday party a few weeks earlier had been sunny and warm. The scent of freshly cut grass and her mother's petunias had filled the air. John's fiancée was there. They'd been engaged for two months, and though Olivia didn't know her well, she liked the idea of having another woman in the family.

It was the last time they'd all been together.

She opened her palm on the cool glass windowpane. "They told my father first. He had the unlucky job of telling my mother, whose life also ended that day." Mother refused to mourn with the family. Johnny had been her first born, and without him in her life, no one else existed, not even Daddy. "She forced herself to go, to identify the body alongside my father. To see my brother one last time before they laid him to rest."

"I'm terribly sorry." The major's hushed voice startled her. "I had no idea."

"In September, when the Nazis started blowing London to hell, an incendiary bomb buried my younger brother, Henry, and three of his mates. He was fifteen."

She focused on the magnified raindrops trickling on the other side of the pane. Though she thought of her brothers daily, she'd stopped crying for them weeks ago. She'd even stopped crying for her parents: her father, whose lost sons would never carry on his name, and her mother, who clearly preferred her boys but was left with an exasperating daughter.

Outside, a great gust of wind hurled water at the window. She drew back as a fumbling hand touched her shoulder.

"Nurse Talbot—"

But her self-control had run its course. She nodded tersely and found satisfaction in pretending he could see it. "I believe you're the most insensitive, unappreciative, and selfish man I've ever met. For as much time and effort that Mrs. Pollard and I put into your well-being, we are relentlessly slapped in the face with your disregard, and I for one need a respite."

She wheeled about and came nose to nose with a puzzled Mrs. Pollard.

"Terribly sorry to interrupt, but there's a telephone call for you, Nurse Talbot."

"Thank you, Mrs. Pollard. I'll take it in the library." She looked over her shoulder on the way out of the room. "Enjoy the rest of your day, Major."

"Oh, Katie, you couldn't have rung at a better time."

Despite the welcome, chipper voice of her cousin and dearest friend, Olivia's childish tantrum in the sitting room had begun to solidify, making her queasy.

"You sound wretched. This isn't about your patient, is it? I thought the major would have developed into the dashing Maxim de Winter by now. What's happened?"

"An argument. A rather explosive one too, I'm afraid, especially on my part." She'd failed miserably and hadn't the pluck to share details, not even to Katie. She'd been a fool to push the matter of Miss Werren. The major was right: She knew neither of them. Their relationship was none of her business.

"Whatever's happened, it can't be that bad."

"It's bad enough that I'll be surprised if I'm not sacked as a result."

Allowing her emotions to take over and arguing with the major as if he was her mother had been incredibly unprofessional. Her father would be devastated—and the thought of the fury that only her mother could unleash turned Olivia's stomach. After losing two of their three children, her parents had been adamant that she leave London before she suffered the same fate. Many had left—children, mainly, boarding with strangers in the country indefinitely. Lucky for Olivia, her opportunity to leave came with a paying job in her profession, one that could propel her career if all went well.

And she'd botched the whole thing.

"You're panicking," Katie said. "I thought the doctor needed you so desperately that he promised a glowing recommendation in exchange for your services?"

"Only if things went well here. I doubt even Head Nurse Smythe would have me back after this."

Katie's pep vanished. "Livvy, Nurse Smythe was killed. The Nazis bombed St. Mary Abbot's two nights ago, completely destroying Block C. Four people are dead, all staff. Your mum hadn't the fortitude to ring and tell you, so I said I would. I'm sorry."

Olivia opened her mouth to reply, but nothing came out.

Katie waited a moment before softly saying, "Stop worrying about your quarrel. Your main concern is the major's well-being. All you need to do is remind him of that."

If she hadn't been so distraught, she'd have laughed.

"And don't forget," Katie continued, "Maxim De Winter was a moody sort as well. Give it more time. Perhaps the two of you shall become friends after all."

Katie laughed with her typical optimism, coaxing a chuckle out of Olivia who shook her head at her cousin's ridiculous comparison: William Morgan couldn't hold a candle to the charming Maxim de Winter, and he never would.

Olivia faced three frazzled reflections in her vanity mirror. Her nurse's cap sat utterly askew. To hell with it—she threw it on the bed. Static electricity set disorderly strands of gold and light brown standing on end. The guise fit her; she looked as crazy as she felt. The sight made her want to laugh. Knowing full well she shouldn't, she did anyway. But the madness didn't last long. Each snicker nudged her closer to a reality that made her palms sweat. From the top right drawer, she grabbed her hairbrush and began pulling it through her tangled mass of hair, wincing when it caught in knots. The pain was punishment for her bad behavior.

She didn't want to leave Keldor. This she readily confessed to Katie before ringing off. Though it was lonely here, her parents needed her safe, and she bore endless gratitude to the doctor who'd procured the assignment.

More importantly, her charge as a nurse kept her bound to the man she was sworn to care for. Before today, she'd assumed Dr. Butler's pills were working and the major had turned a corner. As his bitterness waned, he appeared on track to emerge as the wonderful man Mrs. Pollard bragged about. He smiled much more these days, making her heart skip. Yes, he could play the tyrant, but a good man resided there too. She just needed to alter her strategies if she ever wanted to see him again.

If she still had a job.

Sitting here, bullied by fear and duty wouldn't do. She needed a walk. The weather was foul, so she shed her uniform for clothing that could withstand the rain. In her navy mackintosh and a pair of Wellies found outside the scullery, she ventured out the back door and into the wet, driving wind.

"This war is far worse than the one your father and I fought when you were a lad. It seems bombing our cities isn't enough for Hitler. Three days ago he raided Penzance. Sixty bombs! Falmouth before that, of course. And whilst Jerry thinks he can distract us from the sky, he'll swarm our coastline, mark my words."

William slouched in his chair. Captain Dinham, who'd served with his father over twenty years ago, had arrived shortly after Nurse Talbot's unpleasant departure. If he hadn't been so rude to her, perhaps she would've warded off a visit from this (and his father would agree) most tiresome fellow.

And still the captain yammered on.

"Your portion of coastline is small and therefore dangerous. Air patrols on our end aren't enough. Secret streams and overgrown bramble could provide the perfect place for a group of unscrupulous Nazis to hide along our shores. You know we've fortified Steren Cove?"

"So I've been told," he said, increasing the exhaustion in his voice and sinking another inch in his chair.

"We've installed barbed wire across the two rivers that cut into your beach. We've yet to add beach scaffolding—depends on how HQ prioritizes. No room for mines, I'm afraid."

"I would love to help, Captain." William stifled a yawn. "You're right, this war is different from the one you fought with my father. I've seen hard evidence of that, and I'm most anxious for it to end. However, I've been discharged from His Majesty's Armed Forces and am unlikely to return. I haven't the stamina to do much more than thank you for your diligence."

"Haven't the stamina? You're an officer, Morgan. How can—"

"Excuse me." It was Nurse Talbot. Thank heavens.

"Please don't get up," she said.

But he stood immediately. "Nurse Talbot! Captain Dinham, this is my nurse, Olivia Talbot. This is Captain Dinham. He—he was a friend of my father's and is currently leading the local, er"—he turned to the captain—"the Local Defence Volunteers, is that right?"

"Home Guard now, Morgan. And it's serious business. We're not just enforcing blackout regulations." The captain's volume changed. William pictured him standing to his unimpressive height of five feet. "How do you do, Nurse Talbot?"

"Very well, thank you. Forgive me for disturbing your tea, but—"

"Not at all," William hurriedly added. "Please join us. Captain Dinham was saying how they've adorned our cove with barbed wire and mines, is it?"

"No mines, Morgan. Your beach is too rocky. However, it's secluded enough for Jerry to hide unsuspected. We're at risk living so close to the ocean, and we want to be ready and well defended in the unlikely event something should happen."

"I see." Nurse Talbot's voice moved closer. Her hand wrapped around his arm, setting him surprisingly at ease. "I'm sorry to interrupt, Captain Dinham, but I'm afraid the major needs rest."

"Yes, of course. Despite your lack of sight, Morgan, you look better than I'd feared. I hope you'll continue down the path of good health and follow the course of country first. It would make your father proud. I'll show myself out."

Once William was confident they were alone he said, "Thank you. I don't think I could've handled much more of him. I'm afraid the captain can be rather overbearing. He's also never wrong and knows everything about everything. Drove my father mad."

"You looked rather uncomfortable."

"I'm better now, thank you," he said. And he meant it.

This afternoon's quarrel had been entirely his fault. But like an angel, she'd returned and dismissed the captain as well. Her compassion hardly seemed warranted. If he'd been in her shoes, he'd have asked the captain to stay for supper as payback for his mistreatment of her.

Her grip loosened. Afraid she'd walk away, he groped for her shoulder. Instead, he caught the side of what he determined was her face. It was cool, as if she'd been outdoors. He rubbed his thumb across what felt like her chin and aimed his eyes, he hoped, toward hers.

"I apologize for my behavior earlier. It was deplorable."

"Maj—"

"I'm terribly sorry about your brothers. How awful for your parents—and for you. Now I understand why you're really in Cornwall, helping me, a miserable bloke who doesn't deserve your kindness."

"But sir, I'm the one who should apologize. I shouldn't have spoken to you the way I did. I'm not here to carry on about my problems. I'm here for you."

She could carry on as much as she liked—anything to detract from his own torments. "Will you sit?"

The sofa squeaked, and he sat beside her.

"Just because I'm unhappy doesn't mean you should be. You aren't unhappy here, are you?"

"No, not entirely," she said, her tone teasing.

"Good."

"And what about Miss Werren?" she asked.

"You're rather persistent, aren't you?"

"Always."

"Someday I will explain further the situation regarding Jenna and myself. But I don't need her. However, I do need you to pour me a cup of tea. And tell me more about your family. Please?"

He waited whilst china clinked and tea splashed. She said earlier that she needed a respite from him. He hoped their hour or so apart had been enough, for strangely, this London nurse was not so disagreeable a companion after all.

# CHAPTER 7

"How's the weather looking this morning, Polly?" William asked.

Full from breakfast, he turned to the sitting room window as if he could see out of it.

"It's raining and blowing. Has been since I woke this morning. Not as hard now, I reckon, but wet just the same."

"Excellent. I'd like a walk. Nurse Talbot, you'll accompany me?"

"Of course." Her voice lacked the zest he was used to. "Unless you'd like the rain to let up before venturing out? I'm happy to wait."

"Not long ago, I would've given anything for a walk on our rain-soaked property. Come, we'll have an adventure. Jasper will love it."

A short descent down the kitchen steps landed the pair in the southeast garden. Over the clamor of the rain, Keldor's chickens clucked about their coop. William recalled the vegetable plots dotting the grassy meadow and the surrounding stonewalls and wooden gates. At one time, this area was the picture of perfection —a painter's paradise, and a gardener's as well. It had certainly given his mother joy. Though many had cared for it after her death, her presence here still reigned.

"This reminds me of my grandmother's garden," Nurse Talbot said. "But hers isn't this big."

"My mother had full charge of her garden. She planted, harvested, and kept up the maintenance in between, even pulling weeds. My father told me she found gardening relaxing."

He kept one hand swinging his cane and one wrapped around Nurse Talbot's arm. Thanks to his practice and her patience, walking together had developed into a sort of dance where each partner instinctively knew when it was their turn to step.

"I'm glad my father kept things running after she died," he continued, "with hired help, of course."

Keldor had been known for its gardens. His grandmother's roses had been famous all over the county. But that wasn't why his father had kept them going. It was for William's mother. Keldor's gardens were forever enshrined in her loving memory.

The restless air sent a chill across his shoulders. Harder rain followed. He shouted over the kerfuffle of tree branches and dead leaves. "Take us to the glasshouse!"

He lifted his white cane and moved his hand down Nurse Talbot's arm until it locked onto hers. Trusting her lead, he kept pace as they rounded raised beds and garden sculptures. He caught fragments of her laughter as the rain blew at them head-on.

"We made it!" she announced, slowing her steps and then stopping altogether.

William's shoulder slammed hers, and they crashed into the wooden door. He was about to apologize but she was still laughing.

He chuckled as well, wiping his matted hair back from his forehead. "An adventure, see?"

The doorknob squeaked, but neither she nor the door moved. Olivia grumbled.

"Hang on." He lifted his left arm and thrust the door open.

Inside, the rain echoed as it pounded the glass panes above their heads. The wind whined through tiny chinks like curlews during breeding season. The damp, earthy smell again conjured his mother.

He waved left. "She started herbs on this side." Though the space felt cavernous, it was easy to picture the fragrant greens that had once crowded it from floor to ceiling. He gestured right, where at one time succulents, orchids, and a variety of palms had held sway. "Her tropical plants grew up front, here."

Nurse Talbot was quiet. Perhaps she had no interest in plants. Or perhaps the place was so gloomy she was having a hard time picturing what he described. Best to change the subject.

"One year ago today, Nurse Talbot, what were you doing?"

"From today? I have no idea."

"Okay, then close to a year ago. Where were you? What was your life like during the war's infancy?"

"Let me think." Despite the rain's hammering, her voice rang clear, as though she stood close. "I had been at St. Mary Abbot's for two months. I lived onsite, and my hours were long. My biggest worry was whether I'd see my family at Christmas."

"And did you? See your family at Christmas?"

"I got away for two days. We were all together, except for John. He was unable to get leave. I don't suppose Christmas will ever again be like it was before the war."

He agreed, though he didn't say so. He liked hearing her talk about her family and hoped she didn't find the subject too painful.

"What were you doing a year ago?" she asked.

"Me? I was conducting combat training north of here." He lowered his head. "Sometimes I feel this war has already lasted a decade. To think it's just been over a year."

"When did you get to North Africa?"

This was unexpected. "Not until May. I was in Norway before that."

"What was your assignment there?"

The patter of rain muted his courageous inhalation. "In North Africa? To gather information. Years before the war, I'd trained the Egyptians on how to strengthen their army whilst keeping watch over the Suez. When the war started, Egypt remained neutral. We still had plenty of people there, but rumors of Italy joining the Nazis began to surface. A friend of mine in Cairo, a man I'd met in thirty-seven, knew people, so because of our friendship and his connections, I went back—not as an officer, mind you, but a sort of spy, I suppose." He scratched his upper lip, ready to talk about something else. "You know, I wish I had a cigarette. You don't have one, do you?"

"Sorry, I don't smoke. My father's convinced they're deadly."

"Hmm." He frowned. "Do you see drawers over that way?" He pointed down what he remembered to be the narrow walkway.

"I do."

"Would you look through them for me? Perhaps the bottom one? There may still be a pack shoved in the back somewhere."

Several bumps and knocks said she was struggling with the drawer as she had the glasshouse door. Before he had a chance to assist, he heard it slide open.

"You hid smoking from your father?" she asked.

"When I was fifteen, yes. Did you find them?"

"You really want one of these?"

"Why not? And you'll join me?"

"I might, if they weren't twenty years old."

"There's no harm in old tobacco."

He accepted the cigarette she placed between his fingers. He put it in his mouth and waited. A scratch followed by a weak sputter. She said the second fizzled almost as quickly as the first.

"I think you're out of luck. These matches are too damp."

Finally, the tang of sulfur reached his nostrils.

"Got it, sir. Here's your light."

He took a drag. He couldn't remember the last time he'd had a cigarette. His father preferred a pipe, but William enjoyed cigarettes, mainly in social settings like parties or in pubs. The girls he knew liked to smoke. Was the last time he'd smoked in London, then? With Clementine, the night before he left for North Africa?

He held the smoke in his lungs. Visions of a pretty face dissolved into darkness. All he smelled was burning tobacco. All he felt was pain.

He exhaled and dropped the cigarette. "You were right, these aren't very good. In fact, that was positively dreadful." He opened his mouth and stuck out his tongue, as if the air would strip away the foul taste.

"I have chewing gum. Care for a piece?" Her voice dropped. "It's pretty old—well, not nearly as old as your cigarettes. It's from my stocking last Christmas. I had a feeling gum would be rationed first. Like chocolate."

"I couldn't take your last piece," he said, though at this moment, he would've killed for it.

"It's not my last piece. I've a few more."

He thanked her and popped the minty strip into his mouth.

"What's Egypt like?"

He was finished thinking about Egypt. He was finished talking about Egypt. But he wouldn't be rude to her, not again. "Dry and hot. I missed this cool, wet place, but I got used to the climate. There were more important things to focus—oh!"

Sharp pain assaulted his head as though someone was stabbing his temples with an awl, over and over. He bent forward.

"What is it?"

"A pain above my eyes. My temples, too." He pressed his palms to his head. He'd had headaches lately, usually in the middle of the night, but none this brutal.

"You should sit. Let me help you." She placed an arm around

him and squeezed gently, the way his mother would when he needed her most.

The pain vanished.

Still standing, he sniffed and tilted his head left then right. He almost laughed. "The headache—it's gone. I can't believe it."

"Brilliant! But let's go back so you can lie down, should it return."

It was as though the pain had never come. Had she healed him? It was a ridiculous thought, surely.

"Sir?"

"I—er, yes, let's go." He offered his left arm. "Lead the way, Nurse Talbot."

Color was returning to the major's face. That was good because the rain had yet to cease. The wind remained as well, and he'd need all his energy to make the trek back.

The water dripping down the back of her neck chilled her, yet Olivia was glad they'd ventured out. She'd never seen the major more at ease than he had been today. He'd answered questions about North Africa, too, a milestone that even his fleeting headache couldn't diminish. If he hadn't puffed that dreadful cigarette, he likely wouldn't have experienced it in the first place. Headache aside, she hadn't missed the other effect smoking had on him: the trembling hands, his face a white sheet.

With the major at her side, she tugged the glasshouse door open. The house felt miles away beneath the downpour. She led the major around the beds and through a stretch of long wet grass. Jasper trotted in their wake, undeterred by the wind that pummeled them head-on. The major's white cane bobbed with every step, and in his haste to keep up, he lost his hold on it. Down went the cane, and Major Morgan followed, his arms instinctively extended to break his fall.

Attached as they were by the arms, Olivia fell with him.

"Sir!" she shouted from the ground, the piercing rain stinging her face.

The major's right arm was draped across her hip, and he was laughing. Uproariously. "I don't know what happened!" His face bore the biggest, most striking grin she'd seen on him yet. He shifted his weight, unwittingly pulling her toward him.

His nearness sent her head spinning. She tilted her face back and caught a whiff of his warm, minty breath. Did he know they were this close?

"Nurse Talbot?" he asked softly, his nose a whisper from hers. Concern swept his handsome face. "Are you all right?"

"I am. Are you?"

"Yes."

In a Hollywood picture, this would have made quite a scene: two lonely souls thrown together by tragedy, impervious to the pouring rain above and the river of wet grass below, making passionate love …

Until a wet dog interjected his nose between the unsuspecting pair.

Laughing hard, the major rolled onto his back to allow Jasper to lick his face properly. His hand came free from Olivia's hip, breaking the spell. She sat up as well, no longer cold but more than a little muddled.

The mirth continued as she retrieved the major's cane. Arms crossed, she loomed above the two cutups still lolling in the grass.

As lightheartedly as she could, she asked, "Are you quite finished? I'm soaked through and dying for a cup of tea."

# CHAPTER 8

"Shall I tell you about Jenna, Nurse Talbot?" William asked as they finished their supper in the dining room.

Two weeks had passed since he'd scolded her for meddling in his affairs regarding Peder's sister. She hadn't brought the subject up again, but guilt over his mistreatment of both women had nagged him ever since.

"Sir, that's entirely up to you."

"I wish you wouldn't call me 'sir.' " She was his companion, for heaven's sake, not his servant. "If I tell you about Jenna, it may ease my conscience a bit, and perhaps you'll no longer think of me as a heartless bastard."

"But, s—I don't think of you as a heartless bastard, Major."

"You're incredibly kind."

But first, he needed a drink. He found the wine carafe easily. Glass clinked glass, and once his wineglass felt full enough, he took a mouthful.

"I've known Jenna her entire life. Peder and I were at Blundell's School together, and once upon a time, our families were rather close. But Jenna, you understand, was always younger and therefore a pest. Whilst Peder and I plotted to conquer the world, she would spy on us, then unleash taunts and run away, hoping we'd follow. For close to ten years, whenever I visited their family home, she proved to be a large thorn in our sides. But then, after years of not seeing her, all of that changed. She grew up. The quintessential squirmy caterpillar had transformed into the most beautiful butterfly."

He almost hadn't recognized her that day he called at Tredon and she answered the door. Having returned from holiday in Ibiza with her eccentric yet wealthy aunt, Jenna's sun-kissed skin and curvaceous figure stirred desires he'd never before associated with Peder's sister.

She was exquisite. Whereas Peder had to remind himself to be charming (William had caught him speaking to himself in the mirror once before walking out with a girl), Jenna's allure was inherent, like the sapphire-blue eyes that glimmered no matter what her emotion.

He drank. "Meanwhile, I'd worked a lot and perhaps played just as much. My father was miserable during his years alone, and I refused to go down that same path. So upon seeing this beautiful, striking woman whom I'd always known, the answer became obvious. Why shouldn't I spend the rest of my days with her?"

He recalled it as though it'd happened yesterday. "Remembering how she'd followed me like a puppy dog when we were young, I pursued her confidently. I imagined her face lighting up as I went down on one knee." His voice caught; he wanted to tell the story, not relive the pain. "I'll never forget the look on her face. She acted as though I was out of my mind, my proposal ridiculous. Seems she'd learned of my less-than-prudent behavior as a younger man and concluded I wasn't tame enough to be her husband." His forced smile did little to hide his bitterness. "Of course I wouldn't take no for an answer and spent weeks groveling for her affections. It took me a while, a long while, before I finally got the message."

He chuckled, remembering his audience. "But that's men for

you. I'm not sure if you're aware, Nurse Talbot, but we aren't very clever when it comes to love."

"Not at all, Major. What happened after that?"

"I left her alone, threw myself back into work. When the war started, I went north for a few months. Surprisingly, the day after I'd returned, she arrived at Keldor." He emptied his glass. "She told me she changed her mind—she did in fact want to marry me. Much to my father's disappointment and hers, I didn't jump at the offer. I was leaving for Egypt soon, and the trip would give me time to determine if marrying her was something I still wanted. That's why I chose to wait to announce our engagement."

His glass was empty. He tipped the carafe—empty as well. Bloody hell.

And then Nurse Talbot was securing his fingers round a glass sloshing with wine. He nodded his gratitude and drained it.

"Do you understand why I've so easily let her go?"

"I think so. You're convinced that because she initially turned you down, she didn't really love you, even though later she claimed to have a change of heart."

"Correct. She didn't love me then. And she doesn't love me now." Of this he was certain. He'd seen love in the way his mother gazed at his father. He'd seen it in the eyes of the few girls whose hearts he'd broken over the years. But he'd never seen it from Jenna—curiosity, maybe, but not love. And if he'd seen her face weeks ago, the look would've been pity.

No matter. He hadn't loved her, either.

"But—"

"Humor me for a moment. If you were Jenna and you'd been informed that the man you were meant to spend the rest of your life with had been found, that he wasn't dead like everyone believed, what would you have done the day you came to Keldor?"

"I would have come to you. Nothing could have kept me from it."

He'd been right—it wasn't ridiculous to expect more from true love. He slapped his hand on the table. "Exactly! And that is why I will not write her and why I will not ask her to return. I won't allow anyone to have me out of pity or guilt, most of all my wife."

Habit brought the empty glass back to his lips. He returned it to the table and covered his face. Nurse Talbot must think him a fool. Perhaps he was.

Perhaps he was destined to be alone.

"Polly, what did Father do with my gramophone? I'd like to dance," the major said, breezing into the library.

Over supper he divulged his relationship with Miss Werren, and now he wanted to dance? Olivia halted at the double doors.

Standing beside a newly lit fire, Mrs. Pollard looked from him to Olivia. "Dance, sir? And who is it you'd be dancing with?"

"Well if you won't dance with me, Polly, then maybe Nurse Talbot?"

He was serious. She stepped into the room.

"I enjoy the idea of dancing, but I'm not good at it, I'm afraid." As soon as Olivia uttered the words, she wished she hadn't. Any time the major expressed a desire to do something other than sit and listen to the damned wireless was a time to be taken advantage of. "But I suppose I could give it a go."

"Your gramophone is here, Mr. William, where you left it, with all your music."

"Perfect." Hands out like feelers, he found his way to Mrs. Pollard's voice, bumping a chair here and a table there. "This is ridiculous. There's no room in here! Polly, find James, would you? See if he'll move this furniture. We need an open space."

73

Mrs. Pollard grumbled through her radiant smile and went to fetch James. In no time, they moved the sofa closer to the hearth, freeing a portion of the room's center.

"I'll leave you young people," the housekeeper said once the major approved the new arrangement. "And good luck, Nurse Talbot."

With a wink, she closed the double doors behind her.

"Good luck?" the major called through the closed door. "And what would she need good luck for?"

"Good luck, indeed," Olivia murmured. She shuffled through a plethora of vinyl records individually wrapped in thin paper. The collection surprised her. She'd never have guessed that the man she'd met weeks ago would be interested in anything as diverting as modern music. "What would you like to hear, Major?"

He settled on Billie Holiday's "Fine and Mellow." Soft, rhythmic crackling filled their ears until the first notes hit the speaker.

The major held out his open palm. "Nurse Talbot?"

Not sure what she was getting herself into, she took it.

The major turned her body into his with remarkable confidence, holding one of her hands aloft whilst wrapping the other in the tidy bow of her dress at the base of her spine. He nudged her closer. Hoping to avoid his feet, she yielded. His jawline, so close, hosted a small cluster of stubble she'd missed that morning. Wafts of his aftershave filled her nose. Though she'd smelled it dozens of times before, this was the first time its piney undertones caught her attention.

Then he took his first step. She hadn't been lying when she said she wasn't much of a dancer. Every time she'd danced with her father, she'd failed to step properly and eventually tripped on his feet. He often teased her until her brothers joined in and they all had a good laugh at her expense. She stiffened.

"Major, I'm really not a dancer."

"There's nothing to it. Leave everything to me." The hand on her back pulled her nearer. "Allow me to guide, for once. Relax."

He carried her into measured currents, up and around and side to side, as light as a feather. Even without sight, his steps glided them smoothly where he intended. Reassured, she released all restraint and focused on the music. The tune was slow and sultry. Heavy with saxophone, the melody enveloped them in a sweet embrace as Ms. Holiday's hypnotic voice carried Olivia away from war, depression, and the fear of not being a good dancer.

"Do you know this song?" he asked, his lips brushing her ear.

"I don't."

"What do you think of it?" His whispered breath was warm, and the stale smell of alcohol threatened to overpower his aftershave.

"I like it. You dance very well, Major."

"Thank you. Despite other disabilities, I hope I will always be able to dance."

As the tempo intensified, his hand moved to her hip and set them both swaying. Their feet lifted in a sort of dance she'd never have practiced with her father. Occasionally the major stretched out his arms, causing her to do the same, before twirling her back to him, his hand securing her at the small of her back.

After two more cozy bends, he stopped and pulled his face far enough away that if he'd had his sight, he could've looked at her squarely. "Would you call me William?"

"William. Yes." She'd call him whatever he liked. "I—"

"And may I call you Olivia?"

Her name on his lips sounded as smooth as sweet cream, a treat denied since the war started but one she swore she tasted now. She bent her head with a girlish grin she was glad he couldn't see.

"Of course."

The irritable dictator she'd met weeks ago faded from memory whilst the music and his arms continued to carry her.

"Lavender oil," he murmured. "Do you wear it on your neck too?"

Her accomplished dance partner left her too entranced to respond. Rocking gently, she repositioned her left hand more snugly to his shoulder and laid her head on him, the fabric of his shirt a soft pillow for her cheek.

# CHAPTER 9

Dᴀɴᴄɪɴɢ with Nurse Talbot had rekindled feelings William had gone too long without—and in recent months, feelings he thought he'd never have again. It'd been a week since his hand smoothed the slight curve of her hip, pulling her toward him as he had so many other women so long ago. Dancing had been the talent that landed him in the beds of the women whose bodies he held on the dance floor. When the lights were out, restraint was never a concern; he wanted them, and they wanted him.

But with Nurse Talbot, restraint was a must. He couldn't crush her to him, though twice he'd come close. Three times he'd brushed her backside with his hand, hoping she'd think his blindness caused the fumble. There was no fumble. Every move had been intentional, and if Peder had been in the room, he'd have recognized William's misbehavior.

Olivia's velvety skin reminded him of Paula, a woman he'd met at a cocktail party in London back in '35. Cynthia had soft skin too, especially her neck and face, where her dimples deepened alongside her dazzling smile. Did Olivia have dimples? Or Marie, who had dimples and the fullest lips; even when she grinned, they pouted, luscious and heavenly to kiss. What were Olivia's lips like? Would he ever know?

Olivia's scent drifted into his memory as strongly as if she stood beside him. The slightest whiff of lavender made him think of her, and thinking of her brought sanity to his perpetual madness. If it weren't for the pall still corrupting his mind, he'd tell her so. Instead, he remained a negative, depressed, and most unworthy companion, as he'd proven again this evening.

At suppertime, Olivia had been ruminating on the upcoming Christmas holiday and hoping that at least part of her family would be together despite the war.

"The holiday can go hang for all I care." He'd reeled with regret as soon as his words took flight.

"Sorry?" she asked, surely outraged, though her voice remained tempered. He couldn't understand how she stayed so even-keeled whilst dodging his mood swings.

"Terrible time of year, truly. Never could abide it."

"Even when you were a boy? I don't believe you."

He considered taking her hands in hopes that her touch would somehow remove the pain from his forthcoming words, but he didn't dare. "The war ended when I was ten. I was in my fourth year at Blundell's, and my father was to be home in time for Christmas. It had been close to a year since the three of us had been together. I especially couldn't wait see my mother. Even at age ten, young boys miss their mums when away at boarding school."

"Of course they do."

"When I arrived home, as soon as James brought me through the front door, my father told me Mother had died a day earlier. But I'd no idea she was even ill."

His voice cracked, and he wished he hadn't broached the subject, until Olivia took his hands. Little by little, her gentle pressure coaxed open his clenched fists, allowing his fingers to link with hers.

"I'm terribly sorry, William."

"I remember nothing else about that time save the disbelief and the hollowness. I can't even recall crying for her." He tilted his head back. "Strange how the brain blocks events from our lives we'd rather forget. I have several recent events I wish it would bloody well block. Someday, perhaps."

"What do you remember about your mother besides her love of gardening?"

"Her beauty and compassion. My mother's upbringing differed greatly from my father's, and the struggles she endured as a child left an indelible mark. She was charitable. The village folk adored her. Everyone did." His voice had finally returned to some version of normal. "My father, a cold person by nature, was as malleable as clay where my mother was concerned. No one else held such esteem in his eyes, not even his son. Not even close. He doted upon her, and she in turn doted upon me."

Abruptly he took his hands from the comfort of Olivia's and rubbed his eyes. His lack of embarrassment at this emotional disclosure astounded him. Was it because he couldn't see her criticism? Or was she truly an angel come to rescue him?

"How hard it must have been to lose the person closest to you when so young. You're incredibly brave for telling me. Her portrait in the sitting room is stunning. You look like her, you know. I'm sure you've heard that before."

The smile in her voice made him smile, too.

She'd stood then. The dishes had clanked together; utensils tinkled. "I'd love to hear more about her some time, William, if you'd be willing to share. More wine?"

Like that, Olivia had taken a painful moment and turned it into something sweet: stories for another day, ones he longed to tell. She'd brightened a dark memory.

Thinking on that—and her—made the loneliness of his bedroom at this hour a little less gloomy.

∼

Since the death of his mother, the major and his father had preferred to be alone at Christmastime. As a result, the staff at Keldor was used to considering the Christmas holidays as time off. William said those who still had families should spend time with them. He encouraged Olivia to take days off opposite Mrs. Pollard, but she refused and so did her parents. Once she told him she could cook and even enjoyed it, it was settled: James, Annie, and Mrs. Pollard would take the entire week, all the way to New Year's Day, as a proper holiday.

Olivia was excited at the prospect of carrying the reins for Mrs. Pollard in her absence. She welcomed the new responsibilities, and since she had only to cook and clean for two, the assignment would be easy.

"I've changed the linens and dusted the open rooms. And remember to hang the blackout before sunset," Mrs. Pollard told her, gripping an extensive list. "I know times have changed, but I'm not sure how I feel about you cooking and keeping house, like."

"Do you think me incapable?" Olivia asked teasingly.

Mrs. Pollard patted Olivia's cheek. "Oh no, my bird, I know you're more than capable. But you already have your hands full with Mr. William. I don't feel comfortable adding to your workload."

"Not to worry. The major's overall health has improved immensely these past two months. We'll be fine."

Mrs. Pollard called attention to William's favorite recipes, which she left on the counter. In the larder, she identified specific food supplies and where to find them. For dinner, she'd prepared a hearty lamb stew; any leftovers would make for perfect luncheons over the next several days. She'd gathered enough ingredients to whip up a small Christmas pudding, to be accompanied by her special brandy sauce.

"Now don't tell Mr. William I've made a Christmas pudding. Let it be a surprise. If he knows, he'll sneak in here and search it out. His eyes may not work, but he has a wicked sense of smell. Not only will he find the pudding and the coin hidden inside, but the brandy sauce will disappear as well."

After finally dropping Annie and Mrs. Pollard at the train station, Olivia drove James to his brother's small cottage outside Charlestown. From there she headed to Fore Street in the village, armed with Mrs. Pollard's list of victuals and ration cards.

At the family-run grocer's, evergreen boughs swathed the handwritten adverts and timeworn baubles twirled idly above the heads of the bustling shoppers. In between animated voices and the din of bells from the main entrance, Bing Crosby crooned "Silent Night." The scents of cinnamon and cedar filled the air. For a few blissful moments, it was easy to pretend there wasn't a war on.

The fantasy didn't last long. After gathering extra goodies like Christmas surprises for William bought with her own money, Olivia longed to visit the shop next door to buy a new scarf or brooch. Reason chased away the notion as quickly as Mrs. Pollard after a housefly. The world was a different place now. She should be happy she had enough money to purchase some over-priced dried fruit and nuts. They weren't always available, and few could afford them—a cruel reminder, like National Margarine and the absence of bacon at the butcher's, that this Christmas would be unlike any other.

Olivia untangled herself from her negative thoughts. She needed to quit thinking of herself. William detested this time of year, and somehow she'd have to make it better for them both. She'd knitted him a scarf and found treats to share, and Mrs. Pollard had made a Christmas pudding, for heaven's sake. Perhaps he'd be willing to play his gramophone. Maybe they'd dance.

The idea of his arms around her propelled a familiar tingle

through her lower abdomen. Since their first dance, quelling these feelings had proven impossible. Sometimes when he listened to the wireless and most likely forgot she was in the room, she'd stare at his broad shoulders and the minor creases in his face. His eyes were her favorite—his eyes and his mouth, for when he smiled, they twinkled like stars at twilight. In deep thought, his pensive face reminded her not so much of Daphne du Maurier's Maxim de Winter but certainly of Jane Austen's Mr. Darcy: handsome, discerning, mysterious. When he laughed, delight shook his entire body the same way Jasper's tail wagged his.

Amidst the holiday decor and faint Christmas carols, a seed of optimism grew inside her. War or no war, she and her employer, having become fast friends, would generate their own peace in this turbulent world. They'd celebrate it.

Eager to get back to Keldor, she rose on her tiptoes to see ahead in the long queue. Movement beyond the scrim-covered shop windows caught her eye, and her heart leapt.

It was snowing.

On Christmas Eve, William waited as Olivia's feet scurried from dining room to kitchen to library and back again.

"Why didn't I dismiss the staff one at a time?"

"It's not so bad," she said, her voice breathless. She finally settled somewhere across from him. "I enjoy doing something different, preparing meals and such."

He sounded like a child, and he didn't care. "But you're always cooking or cleaning up or preparing a fire, for God's sake, and I'm left to sit here alone and wait. At least before, we were waiting together and I had someone to talk to."

"You're right. A horrible thing to sit and wait for someone else to serve you."

The smile in her voice gratified him, as usual. But still, he sulked.

She splashed wine into his glass. "Happy Christmas, William. Cheers."

He lifted it, drank, and promptly began to eat.

"Shouldn't we pray first?" she asked. "It's Christmas Eve."

"Pray? Pray to whom?" He bounced his fork above his waiting meal. He hadn't prayed in over a decade.

"Tomorrow is the birthday of Jesus. To whom do you think we should pray?"

How young she was, and so terribly naïve. "So we should pray, then, thanking him for the limited food on our table and for the family members we no longer have with us? Perhaps we should give thanks for our peaceful world as well? Do as you like. I'll respect it, but I'll take no part."

He found a morsel he could stab and popped it into his mouth.

"I never thought about it like that before. But God must have a purpose somewhere in his grand scheme of things."

"Well, I'm not interested in the plan. I confess I'm a tad bitter and have been since my mother died. Do you know she went to church every Sunday? She helped people. They often didn't have the chance to ask because she already knew of their plight. And she didn't give people what they required. She opened up opportunities for them, finding work or creating exchanges between neighbors for goods or services. Simply put, my mother was a selfless angel."

He took another bite and chewed a moment. Fairly certain he was ruining her meal, he went on anyway. "My father continued attending church after Mum's death, doing his best to accept her passing as a part of God's plan. He said God needed her in heaven more than we needed her here. What's that scripture, something about ours being a jealous God? So he took my mother; he'd shared her long enough. And now my father." Emotion he'd rather not reveal filled his eyes. "I'm sorry, Olivia."

"You needn't apologize."

"No, no, I'm ruining your holiday with this ridiculous talk. That wasn't my intent." He thumped the table, his heart as cold as her meal was becoming. "Pray if you like. Your food's getting cold."

# CHAPTER 10

FIXED on getting the dining room tidied as quickly as possible, Olivia extinguished the pillar candles on the buffet before clearing the plates from the table.

"Cleanup can wait, can't it?" William asked, standing. "Let's go into the library."

With arms waving like Frankenstein, he searched until she caught his left hand. Once in her grasp, though, he resisted her pull.

She turned, confused. "What's the matter?"

His pursed lips twitched somewhere between a frown and a smile. He plunged his right hand into his trousers pocket and retrieved a small black box.

"I know it's not Christmas yet, but I couldn't wait to give this to you."

Dried fruit and a lopsided scarf would barely compare to whatever was in that black box. She cleared her throat and hopefully, the dismay from her voice. "A Christmas gift? William, you didn't—"

"You're a light in my darkness, Olivia. I appreciate your being here and tolerating my insolence these past months. Happy Christmas."

Hesitantly, she took the box. It was heavier than she expected, and covered in velvet. In one hand she secured its bottom whilst the other slowly creaked open the lid. Inside, cradled in black satin, lay an oval moonstone set in a simple pendant of scored white gold. She plucked it from its hold, freeing the thick chain behind it.

"It's beautiful."

His eyes fluttered for a moment, like he didn't know what to say. But then he lifted his chin and spoke. "It was my mother's, a gift from my father on their first wedding anniversary. I remember her wearing it when I was young. Mrs. Pollard helped me find it before she left. Will you wear it?"

"Of course I will! It's lovely. I've never owned anything so elegant. Are you sure?"

He scoffed. "Don't insult me. I've never been more certain of anything in my life. Can I help you put it on?"

She placed the necklace into his waiting hands, hook and eye first. He linked the heavy chain easily under her lifted hair, as though familiar with the task. Her neck sizzled where his fingers had touched her.

She faced him. "Thank you. It goes perfectly with what I'm wearing tonight, exactly the pick-me-up this tired old dress needed. I love it."

Quickly, she took him by the shoulders and swept her lips across his cheek. She dared not look at his face. Rather, she gripped his hand and gave a small tug.

"Shall we?"

At the entrance to the library, she left him at the door and scuttled to her poor excuse of a fire.

"Damn," she whispered, "I forgot all about it."

"Thank heavens, or I would've eaten alone." William made

himself comfortable on the settee, which had been repositioned close to the hearth both to keep its occupants comfortable during the winter months and to allow for more dancing. If he didn't suggest it tonight, she would. It was Christmas Eve, after all.

"Would you like a brandy?" she asked, adding more kindling to her dying fire.

"Of course, thank you."

The fire sputtered back to life. She crossed to the sideboard under the cloth-covered windows, where Mrs. Pollard's festive pine cones and sprays of various evergreens lay amidst crystal glasses and a large, twinkling decanter. Olivia poured two snifters half-full, then lit a few candles. The small spruce tree James had found on the property came just to her shoulders. Bright red holly berries tucked amongst the boughs reflected the fire's glow. Underneath lay William's meagerly wrapped gifts.

"Sit by me, will you?" he asked, taking his drink. "I prefer you much more as my companion than my servant."

"I know. How about music first? What would you like to hear?" She flitted across the room, her free hand clasping the pendent at her neck. Her insides were melting. What else would the night bring?

"I presume holiday music would be appropriate. See what you can find over there." He stood, brandy in hand. "In fact, I shall come help you."

Perplexed at how he would help, she met him with an outstretched arm. "What would you recommend? Shall I read the titles?"

"There's a Guy Lombardo record in there somewhere with a festive song or two."

She found the disc and placed it on the gramophone.

He chuckled. "Would you look at that?"

"Look? What are you talking about? Look at what?" After so much wine, perhaps the brandy had been a bad idea.

His index finger pointed heavenward. "Mistletoe. And we're both under it."

Indeed, mistletoe hung above them, but nowhere near where he pointed. A foot away, suspended from the overhead lamp in the room's center, the tiny berries gleamed like pearls amongst dusty green leaves.

"How in the world?"

"After my brilliant idea of giving you the necklace, I supposed it fitting to keep a few other Christmas traditions alive this year, too—the pagan ones, anyway. Mrs. Pollard helped, of course."

"I see." Her mouth was as dry as a burnt mince pie.

"It'd be a shame to pretend it wasn't there." Candlelight danced in his mischievous eyes. "So may I kiss you, Olivia?"

She wanted to kiss him again, but not like she had in the dining room. Not like a girl, too self-conscious to give a real kiss. But that's what she did. Rising onto her tiptoes, she started out strong, one hand on the side of his face, but her lips barely brushed his. Too bashful for another go, she dropped back, flat on her feet.

She caught the disappointment in his weak smile. "The perfect gift, then: a kiss from a beautiful woman. That's two in one night."

She tried to sound unaffected, but her voice squeaked out unnaturally high. "Beautiful? My dear William, I'm afraid when your sight returns, you'll be sorely disappointed."

What a child she was—a fool who couldn't keep quiet and let the night's events unfold as they would.

"We've been over this before. You must think more highly of yourself. But in all fairness, perhaps I should learn for myself. Would I be out of order if I—" He raised his hands. "May I?"

"Be my guest."

He found her eyebrows first, smoothing each before tracing the rings of bone around her partially closed eyes. Fingertips soft as rain tapped along both cheekbones until his left hand slipped behind her neck. With one rotation, he amassed her hair in a loose coil before tilting her head. Feather-light caresses along her exposed jawline shuttered her eyes and unfurled her lips. As if sensing the shift within her, his fingers skimmed first her top lip, then the bottom before supplanting them with his open mouth.

Unhurried and indulgent, his lips brought all her romantic fancies to life. This was how she imagined herself with him, caught in an embrace so passionate it eliminated everything wrong with the world. Fireworks exploded instead of bombs. Peace and happiness reigned, and no one cried over loss or pain.

William withdrew his lips and rested his nose against her forehead. She sighed, savoring their closeness.

"Dance with me, Olivia."

On their makeshift dance floor, he guided her with awareness and agility. Twirled, dipped, and swayed, her new love of dancing had everything to do with her partner. Though the upbeat tunes were fun, she preferred the slower songs like "Auld Lang Syne" and "Shadow Waltz." She could stay forever locked in the sanctuary of William's arms, where his whispers caressed her ear and his breath massaged her neck.

"How are you?" he asked, attending to the slow sway of her hips with a steady hand.

"Happy."

He kissed the top of her head, showering her in disbelief. "You fit nicely in my arms, Nurse Talbot, have you noticed?"

Olivia relished his possessive hold and the electricity that sparked wherever he touched her. "Actually, sir, I noticed the first time I danced with you."

"Really? And you've been too shy to share this observation with me?"

"I—I can't say. Perhaps."

Eager to swim in his ocean-blue eyes, even if they reprimanded her for her reticence, she raised her head. But his blind eyes were squinting, and he inhaled shallowly as if in pain.

She froze. "What is it?"

"It's nothing." But he threw his head left to right like an angry toddler.

"I don't believe you. Come, sit down." She tried to lead him to the sofa, but with another great breath he doubled over and crumpled to the floor. "Is it your head?"

He grunted and circled his fingers over the small space of his temples.

Her fingers joined his, and she pushed as hard as she could. "Is that better?"

He nodded and made a soft moan.

"Has your head been bothering you all night?" she asked, her voice spiked with irritation.

"A dull headache, really."

This was more than a headache, and if she hadn't been caught up in unrealistic fancies, she would've noticed his discomfort sooner. "Why didn't you tell me?"

"I wanted to have a nice evening. More importantly, I wanted you to have a nice time. I didn't want to burden you with this."

She took a deep breath and digested his sentiment. Stray currents of desire wound themselves around her hips, shoulders, and neck. But this wasn't about her; this was about him and his health.

"All right, let's get you to bed. Can you stand?"

She left him upstairs on his bed whilst she retrieved a bottle of aspirin. By the time she returned, he was flat on his back, both hands squeezing the front of his skull as if juicing a grapefruit.

"I'm calling Dr. Butler," she announced.

"It's Christmas Eve. Don't call him tonight." His eyes were nailed shut, his face scrunched. "What are you going to tell him? That I have a headache?"

"Headaches, plural. You've had them in one form or another

ever since you started that new medication. Here, sit up." She thrust a glass into one hand and deposited two aspirin tablets into the other. "What else have you noticed since then?"

He swallowed the pills. "That I feel better."

"Better? How do you feel better? Please be specific, because if the medication is triggering your headaches yet helping you in other ways, you've got a tough decision ahead of you."

"It's hard to explain, but it's like I have hope in my life again. But that's not because of the medicine." Through his agony, he offered a wan smile. "It's because of you."

"William—"

"When you first arrived, I was alive in the sense that I could eat and drink and my heart still pumped blood through my veins. But inside, I was dead. I didn't know who I was or why I was even here. And Olivia, I didn't want to be here." He whispered the last part, his free hand searching for her. She took it. "I couldn't recall what it meant to be happy. But you've helped me remember."

Yes, she'd been there for him, but their friendship had taken time. For weeks he hardly spoke to her. She'd been uncertain of his recovery before Dr. Butler's visit, after which everything had changed. The attention, the flirting, his mother's necklace, and the incredible kiss—they were all because of the blasted medicine. How could she have been so stupid?

She took his glass and rubbed his forehead; the other hand pinched the bottom of his skull. His eyes rolled upward, then closed.

"I'm flattered you want to credit me with your change in disposition," she said, "but it wasn't me. It was your medicine. And now it's likely giving you severe headaches. If that's the case, I think you ought to stop taking it."

"Fine. Take me off it. Don't you see?" His smile became dopey, like a drunken fool's. "I don't need—oh, that feels good."

Why was he talking in riddles? She took a deep breath. "What do you mean? What don't you need?"

He cocked his head and grinned as though he'd never been in pain. "I no longer need the medicine because I have you, Olivia. Knowing you'll be here every morning when I wake gives me something to look forward to. And I haven't looked forward to anything for so long."

# CHAPTER 11

CONFIDENT THAT WILLIAM would soon drift to sleep, Olivia returned to the library. Numerous candles still flickered in what had become a romantic setting. The fire was petering out, yet a handful of coals still glowed against the soot-stained brick. From behind the late colonel's desk, she watched flames flare up then die as quickly. In her ear, Dr. Butler's house telephone rang and rang. It was only ten o'clock—not too late, considering it was Christmas Eve, though she couldn't be positive he'd be home.

"I'm sorry, no. My father is still in London." The girl on the line offered her father's London contact information, a phone number she already had and that rang with no answer. She'd try again in the morning.

In the meantime, she rang her father. She hadn't planned to speak to her parents until Christmas Day, but surely they wouldn't mind hearing from her a day early.

"Sweetheart!" her mother exclaimed once they were connected.

"Happy Christmas, Mother."

"Livvy, what is it?" She knew her daughter well.

"Is Daddy available? It's about Wi—the major. I can't reach Dr.

Butler."

"What's the problem? Is he all right?"

Speaking to her mother could be like traversing a country road with hairpin turns and endless bridges to cross. "I'm worried about the pills Dr. Butler prescribed. They're giving him terrible headaches. At first they came and went, but tonight he's got the most severe one yet. He can't even stand. I'm thinking of taking him off them."

"What are they for?"

"Depression. Anxiety. Sleep."

"And are they helping him?"

Olivia took a deep breath. "Well, yes, remarkably well. Is Dad at home?"

"No, dear, he's not."

She should've guessed.

"He's taken a double shift tonight. In fact, I've just returned home myself. Since the holiday is so different this year"—her voice caught—"with the war intensifying and without …"

Unable to bear the sorrow in her mother's voice, Olivia said, "So you both decided to work for Christmas."

Mother sniffed. "We miss you, Livvy."

"And I miss you both. Listen, you go to bed, and I'll phone tomorrow to wish you both a happy Christmas." She rested her forehead in her palm. "By the time I talk to you again, I'll have been in touch with Dr. Butler."

"All right, then. Your letters seem to find you in good spirits. Does Cornwall truly suit you?"

She glanced up at the mistletoe. The ghost of William's lips on hers nudged her toward disclosure. "It does. There's no other place I'd rather be."

The remnants of the evening's revelry had been cleared, and

Olivia lay wakeful in bed like so many of England's children, hopeful for what the next day would bring. Some lay in bomb shelters with their toys and perhaps a sweet treat and a stuffed companion. Others like her lay in beds that weren't their own, living with people they hadn't known a year ago, and missing their families. Olivia hoped they still found magic in the holiday, that they could set aside their fears for at least one glowing evening. The world wasn't always a scary place.

Light from the small lamp in the corridor caught her eye. Sure she'd be up and down throughout the evening, she'd left it on. But William's faint breathing from across the hall relaxed her, and she smoothed the stone at her throat. That he wanted her to have his mother's necklace was proof he shared her growing affection.

But even as bliss sought to elevate her, the weight of dread dragged her down. William's affections as of late were a result of his medication. As soon as the effects wore off, he'd undoubtedly reject her—a blow her heart could never withstand. The last year had brought enough pain as it was.

From now on, she'd ignore her silly flutters. Memories of his kiss must be stowed away, as well as the way his arms held her as though she belonged there. She tucked the moonstone beneath the neckline of her nightgown and rolled onto her side, brushing at her cheek, and dutifully steered her mind to the reason she was there to begin with: The major was ill. It was her job to see he recovered, whether he cared for her or not.

On Christmas morning, Olivia took a tray of tea, toast, and two boiled eggs to the major's room. There hadn't been a peep from him all night, which was a good sign.

"Happy Christmas, William," she said, surveying his every movement from the blink of his eyes to the rate of his breath.

"Hmm." Hand already at his forehead, he breathed in sharply. "Happy Christmas to you."

He was no better after all, and until she spoke with Dr. Butler, she was at a loss of what to do. Some nurse she was. "You're still hurting."

He coughed, squinting in discomfort. "Mm-hm."

She poured his tea and helped him eat his breakfast in bed. She dispensed more aspirin. "I'm not sure if these are even helping you, but they can't hurt. I couldn't reach Dr. Butler or my father last night, but I'll try again soon. I will not, however, give you another anti-anxiety pill this morning."

"You're the nurse."

Her second call to Dr. Butler was equally fruitless. She explained her situation and left a message and phone number, stressing that this was indeed an emergency. Next, she phoned her father. She was glad for his sympathetic voice, but he was no help.

"I'm afraid I haven't heard of it, Livvy. It must be new, and sadly, communication in the medical world is mostly through word of mouth these days. Do away with the pills if they're causing such adverse side effects. I say the major is lucky to have you there as his nurse."

She closed her eyes. She neither wanted nor needed to hear this.

"Dr. Butler says you're doing an excellent job, and your mother says you're happy. That's more than I ever wished for." His voice dropped. "I'm proud of you, Livvy."

She wasn't sure if she could handle a second conversation like this in less than twenty-four hours. Nevertheless, she thanked him and told him how much she loved and missed him.

Just as William considered her his savior, her parents' pride was undeserved. The guilt was numbing. This time when she hung up the phone, her tears were a mere trickle—nothing like the deluge the night before.

# CHAPTER 12

AFTER TWO DAYS without his prescription, William's pain came in pounding waves threatening to pull him under. Olivia was still trying to contact Dr. Butler, but he hadn't returned her telephone calls, and she remained steadfast in her decision to keep William off his medication.

Still, like faithful Jasper, she stayed close. When he was awake, she rubbed his head where the pain was most severe. Her diligence in keeping him comfortable these past few days was irreplaceable, though his anguish kept him from thanking her with the sincerity he would've liked. He felt useless, like a sailboat with a broken mast. Did she think him, too, dead in the water?

It took three full days before he could make it downstairs to eat at the table. At Olivia's suggestion, they went outdoors for a dose of fresh air. Snow had made another unusual appearance in Cornwall last night, but the sparkling white blanket she described was melting rapidly. Water dripped from Keldor's rooftops, splashing in a percussive patter.

He clung to Olivia on their way down the slippery stone staircase. She reminded him to take it slowly, but she needn't have worried. After days in bed, he moved at a snail's pace no matter where he was. Arm in arm, she led them down a narrow path south of the house. If they followed the entire quarter mile, they would arrive at Steren Cove, a favorite childhood landmark—nowhere he wished to visit today.

"The path is steep and hazardous enough without the addition of this snow," he groused. "Besides, Captain Dinham said the cove is marred with barbed wire fencing and who knows what." The thought of his beloved cove in such a state angered him to the point that his eyes filled. He lowered his head, hoping to hide his bitterness. It wasn't Olivia's fault he'd no interest in going there.

He raised his head for a deep breath when the darkness blazed white.

"What the devil?" he shouted, his body frozen. "Did you see that?"

"See?" Her voice twisted with emotion. "What did you see?"

"A flash. There." He pointed to what he knew was the ocean beyond. "You didn't see it?"

"Like a reflection?" Her skepticism made the question come out sounding playful.

"No, no, much more powerful than a reflection." She stood right beside him. How could she have missed it? "It was like lightning, or an explosion."

"An explo—"

"There it is again!" He squeezed her arm and squinted at the brightness. The enemy was here. In Cornwall, and coming for him. "Olivia, we must return to the house."

"Whatever for?"

"I have a bad feeling." The tremor in his chest traveled quickly to his perspiring limbs. "Something's going on down there, and the sooner we're away from it, the better."

"Down there? Down where?"

"Steren Cove." He took firm hold of her face once he found it.

"We need to get back inside, and I need to ring Captain Dinham. Now."

"Y-yes. Of course."

Confident with his cane, William strode toward the house. It was the fastest he'd moved in days.

"Wait, William!" Olivia scurried behind him to keep up. Her tugs on his arm did little to slow his momentum. "What do you think is happening? Perhaps your vision *is* returning and there wasn't a flash at all—it's your eyes beginning to work again."

"I know what I saw." Did she really doubt him?

"But William, I thought you couldn't see anything!"

"Olivia!" He wheeled around. "This has nothing to do with my vision. I know something's amiss because I can feel it! Please, help me up the steps. I need to make a telephone call."

William careened toward the library. Olivia followed silently as he scrabbled toward the desk, then patted every item until he found the telephone.

"Captain Dinham, please. Yes, Captain, this is Major William Morgan. I believe we may have intruders at Steren Cove ... Yes, I saw a flash—two of them ... No, not even halfway there. We came back straightaway to ring you." Shoulders squared, he appeared ready to fight, yet his jittery hands and colorless face said otherwise. "How long have they been there? And you're in current contact with them? If the flash didn't come from the cove, based on where we were standing, I'm sure it came from the south ... Well, no"—he chuckled uneasily—"my sight hasn't returned, but I know something sinister is going on here. It wouldn't surprise me in the least if Nazis were behind it."

Nazis?

"We're between major holidays, and those bastards are taking advantage of the peace we're struggling to enjoy, no matter how temporary ... Yes, I understand. Very well."

He clumsily dropped the phone into its cradle.

"Well?" she asked.

His chiseled jaw jutted forward and his eyes fluttered in time with his rapid words. "I realize we aren't anywhere near sunset, but I need you to cover the windows, upstairs and down, and secure all doors to the outside. If there are intruders, I don't want them knowing we're here."

"Intruders. You mean Nazis?"

"Yes."

Captain Dinham's warning from weeks ago grew legs. Remarks like "if the unlikely should happen" scrambled her thoughts. If bombing big cities wasn't giving the Nazis the results they were looking for, why wouldn't they invade Cornwall the same as they'd invaded Jersey and Guernsey, a mere hundred miles away?

She dashed to the window. "We don't want them to think the place is abandoned, do we? And—and what about our footsteps in the snow?"

He pinched his nose. "I forgot about the snow. Damn. Well, whether they think we're here or not, we need to hide completely out of sight. We'll go to the wine cellar."

Olivia approached the desk, hands on her hips. "William, what exactly did Captain Dinham say? Are there signs we're being invaded?"

"No evidence whatsoever. His men were at Steren Cove earlier this morning. They've seen nothing."

Thank heavens. If there'd been a flash big enough for a blind man to see—an explosion, as he put it—she would've seen it too. And wouldn't they have heard something as well?

William's pallid face had become speckled with drops of moisture below his hairline and along his upper lip. She'd seen

this look before. "I've a strong premonition we may be in danger
—and I'm a bit uneasy, to be honest."

He looked more than a bit uneasy.

She moved with calm authority toward the windows. "I'll
cover all the windows, but we'll stay in the library. From here, we
can survey the outside and listen for anything untoward. If we
need to relocate in a hurry, we'll have plenty of time."

He jerked his head up and down, swallowing in between.

"Can you manage here on your own whilst I go? I'm sure
you'll want to stay close to the telephone. I'll be quite quick."

"Thank you, Olivia."

She charged through the mansion draping the windows with
black, condensing a thirty-minute task into fifteen. At each
window, she scanned outside. Clouds were moving in, and the air
was warming. The crystalline carpet of snow was losing ground.
In its place were a growing collection of roundish yellow patches
—and absolutely no sign of Nazis.

As her eyes adjusted to the light in the library, a movement on
the floor between the sofa and hearth caught her eye.

"William?"

Drawing closer, she recognized the sheen of his black shoes.
Above them, he hugged his knees tightly to his chest. Most of his
face lay buried, and only his forehead and crop of dark hair were
visible. He rocked back and forth, making no acknowledgment of
her presence.

"William." She knelt beside him, placing her hand on his
shoulder. He stilled. "The house is secure and I've locked all the
doors. The windows are covered, and I've had a look at the
nearby grounds. We're alone. No visitors, no intruders."

He lifted his head. Across his knees, his hands locked as if to
keep the other from shaking.

It wasn't working.

"If I had my sight, Olivia, I could fight them. I'd kill them.
With my bare hands, I could do it."

"William—"

His arm flew at her. "These are dangerous men. I should never have taken Dr. Butler's advice in hiring a private nurse. And now you're involved, when all along I knew they'd be coming for me."

"When you knew who would be coming for you?"

"Wirth's men." His voice was so low she hardly heard it.

"Who's Wirth?"

"Wirth?" His voice softened, and he smiled as though he had fond memories of the man. "Wirth was my captor, Olivia."

"In North Africa?"

In fidgety jerks, he scratched his bent head, scattering his hair in all directions. "The medication! It fooled me into thinking we were safe. It put me off my guard."

"But surely these men wouldn't come all the way here after you?"

Hate soiled his face. "Yes, they would, because I did something awful." He held up his hands. "With these."

"What? What did you do?"

"I killed him. With joy. With his own knife. I cradled his head in my arms, and I slit his throat."

She couldn't picture it. All she could do was stare, captivated by William's culpable smile.

The telephone's peal broke the spell.

She sat in the desk's creaky wooden chair. "Keldor."

"Nurse Talbot, this is Dr. Butler."

Finally! She pressed the handset into her face. "Yes, yes, Dr. Butler, hello!"

"I've just received your message. Please tell me you've only phoned today?"

Her heart sank. "No, the first time I phoned was Christmas Eve."

"Nurse Talbot, you haven't stopped the medication, have you?"

She bit the tip of her thumbnail, her jaw clenched. "Oh, dear."

"How long has it been?"

"Since Christmas Eve. Dr. Butler, his headaches were unbearable—today's the first day he's got out of bed."

"I understand that." She could picture his thinning gray head shaking in disappointment. "Tell me what else you've noticed, aside from his headaches."

"Actually, Doctor, the major is here with me." William's hair, a black crown of chaos, hovered above the shaking hands that hid his face. "May I ring you right back?"

"I'll await your call."

She settled William on the sofa and made him promise to stay put while she was gone.

He nodded, face void of its former arrogance. "Do you think badly of me? This wasn't a detail of my life I had planned on sharing with you."

If she hadn't been in such a hurry to speak with the doctor— or so afraid of her own feelings—she would've wrapped her arms around him. "Not at all. We'll talk more when I return. But don't leave this room."

"Nurse Talbot," Dr. Butler began without preamble when she rang back. "The medication the major's been taking is not the kind you can abruptly stop. We're learning—the hard way, I might add—that patients need to be weaned off this medicine slowly. We've had boys become extremely paranoid. Have you noticed this with the major? You're not leaving him alone, are you? Under no circumstances should he be left alone."

"He's not far from me, no, but he's out of earshot. If I'd known about this, Dr. Butler, I never would've taken him off the pills. But I didn't know what else to do, and—" She gripped the telephone with both hands and lowered her voice. "He thinks Nazis have landed in Cornwall and are coming for him, though Captain Dinham said there's no evidence of it. What should I do?"

"If he hasn't taken them for three days, then it's been too long to start the pills up again and wean him off gradually. Since he's out of bed today, I assume his headaches have become less severe?"

"Yes," she whispered.

"Well, that's something. Just a matter of time, before it's completely out of his system." He stifled a yawn—exhausted, hopefully, from working long hours and not from placating his muck-up of a nurse. "But please, make sure you, Mrs. Pollard, or any of the staff stay with him at all times. We've had men jumping from windows around here."

"It's only me right now. The major gave the staff the week off."

"Well then, you've got your hands full unless you can convince Mrs. Pollard to come home early."

"Yes, Doctor. I'll see what I can do."

"I'm sure you'll manage. I'll call you tomorrow to check in. And I'm terribly sorry I didn't get your message any sooner. I hate to use the war as a crutch for the lack of communication around here."

"I understand, Dr. Butler. Thank you for your call."

# CHAPTER 13

OLIVIA RANG DR. BUTLER DAILY. He was eager to know the major's every move, so even when the doctor wasn't available, she left detailed updates. For days, the reports were the same. The major's outlook remained tainted with terror. No matter what room they were in, William's spine remained straight, his ears attentive, his shoulders thrown back, and his eyes, though out of order, appeared alert. He had no desire to listen to the wireless—apparently, news updates from the Continent meant nothing when someone was hunting you on your own property —so the house remained quiet. Sometimes after long periods of silence, Olivia would speak and he'd start as if he'd forgotten he wasn't alone. Once, she dropped a metal spoon on the tiled kitchen floor, causing him to leap to his feet with a yelp. Too often, she looked up from her reading or cooking to see him quaking so badly that the grip on his chair was the only thing keeping him upright. If a storm blew in, his panic attacks could eat up entire hours. When he fixated on a sound like the scraping of a branch against a window, his pleas sometimes had her believing him. Maybe someone *was* lurking outside.

But as long as she supported him, he did whatever she asked, so calling the staff home early was unnecessary. He didn't dare leave her side. He stayed with her in the kitchen whilst she prepared their meals, and he followed her outside to the garden behind the kitchen when she took Jasper out. The poor dog, used to more exercise, whined over the lack of it. He would rest his head on William's lap, hoping to penetrate the heart of his master with his wistful gaze.

William couldn't see him, but he sensed his presence. "Sorry, old boy," he would mutter whilst petting him mechanically, "we've all got sacrifices to make, haven't we?"

Olivia's sacrifice was living without natural light, and it irked her in unexpected ways. After two days of near darkness (for it was wasteful to use too many electric lights), she found herself not so much irritable as depressed. As an experiment, she removed a blackout panel in the library. William noticed it right away. Evidently, his eyes actually could sense brightness. Rather than argue, she replaced it and apologized for not attending to the fallen curtain quickly enough. Thank heavens the air raids had dwindled since November. Daytime blackout was bad enough, but spending more hours than necessary in the dank wine cellar (for certainly the all clear wouldn't satisfy William that it was safe enough to emerge) was unthinkable.

Imagined scenes of William throwing himself down the stairs forced her to get creative with sleeping arrangements. After her first conversation with Dr. Butler, she made a bed for herself on the chaise longue in his bedroom. With her own linens piled on top, she dragged it toward the bedroom door.

"What the devil is that noise?" he'd asked, emerging from his bathroom. In striped pajamas, with a freshly washed face and a line of white toothpaste outlining his bottom lip, he didn't appear fearful for once, just annoyed.

Slightly out of breath, she knelt on her new bed and appreciated the view. He'd slicked his hair back with water, which still dripped from his left ear. Even with a frown, he looked quite captivating. Despite all that had happened since Christmas Eve, she still had a hard time forgetting the feel of his lips on hers.

"I'm sleeping in here with you, on the chaise. I've pulled the linens off my bed and will stay here by the door. I thought this would be the safest place for us during the night."

He raised his eyebrows. A ghost of a smile appeared on his lips, as though something crossed his mind he'd rather not say. "Good idea."

It had been a very good idea. His night terrors were more severe than ever. When his screams woke her that first night, she abandoned her promise to leave him be. It took an eternity for him to wake, and once he did, he crumbled all over again. She was out of her grandmother's tea and at this point it likely wouldn't help.

Her hands held his in his lap as they sat on his bed.

"Damn this blindness! I can do nothing to protect either of us when they come. You should go. It's me they want, anyway, not you."

"I'm not going anywhere, and you're not to worry. I can protect us both." Surprised at her own composure, Olivia hoped to heaven he drew comfort from it.

"I don't understand why God let me live. There's no purpose for me on this earth anymore."

Unable to hold back any longer, she gave in and let the week's trauma rush down her cheeks. As much as she wanted to yell and criticize him for his cowardice and selfishness, she also wanted to take him in her arms.

"William," she said, trying to mask the stuffiness in her nose, "there's a reason you're here. It hasn't been shown to you yet." She smiled in the darkness. "And if I remember correctly, I thought you'd stopped believing in God."

~

On New Year's Day, Keldor's small staff of three returned. Olivia had arranged for James's brother to bring him back, and he in turn took the Morgan motorcar to retrieve Mrs. Pollard and Annie at the station later that afternoon.

"This is highly unusual, isn't it?" Mrs. Pollard said, making herself at home again in her kitchen. "And you're positive Nazis haven't landed nearby? My sister said—"

"Don't you start in on this, too. No matter what you've heard, they're rumors and not to be spread. We don't want to heighten the major's fears; we want to soothe them. Also, we can't leave him alone for reasons I've already explained. How nice to have more working eyes around here. I may actually get a bath in."

Mrs. Pollard looked her up and down. "You haven't been bathing?"

"Certainly not the way I'd like. How else could I keep an eye on the major? His moods change in a flash, from anxious and fearful to hopeless and possibly suicidal. Nights have been the worst. I've partially moved into his bedroom—"

"You've what?"

"You'll see what I've fixed when you go upstairs. At least by being in the same room, I can gauge if he tries to leave in the middle of the night."

"And has he?"

"No. No, he hasn't."

In another week, William finally began to sit more comfortably and stopped jumping like a skittish pussycat at every noise. His nightmares, though still horrendous, occurred less frequently. He even asked to listen to the wireless again.

It was time to contact their local home front security expert.

"Dinham here."

As soon as Olivia spoke, the man gushed as if he'd been

awaiting her call. She evaded small talk by diving headfirst into recent developments at Keldor: Due to severe side effects from his medication, Major Morgan still believed Nazis tiptoed on Cornwall's doorstep. If apprised of recent enemy whereabouts and the local military's defense plan, perhaps the major would feel less alone in his fears. What were the captain's thoughts? Would he be willing to help?

Authoritative as usual, Dinham praised Olivia for phoning; she'd done the right thing. He'd heard about the adverse effects different medications could have on certain soldiers—pity the major was one of them—and he'd be happy to give an official update on the local threat of intrusions and air strikes, and the Home Guard's plan to keep the area safe. Staging his visit as a drop-in house call was a brilliant idea, as he had an important document to deliver to the major anyway.

The man's self-importance was nauseating. "Any reassurance from a top local official would be much appreciated, sir."

That same afternoon, the windblown captain brought salutations to his hosts as he handed Mrs. Pollard his dripping greatcoat. Olivia led him and the major to the dark library, which was still shrouded in blackout yet warmed by a steady fire. Annie rushed in with tea, and once the men were settled, the women left together. Olivia lingered outside, hoping to catch any snippet of conversation. This proved a useless endeavor, as the thick doors muted even the captain's blaring voice.

After twenty minutes, the two military men emerged. Olivia's eyes flew to William, who stood calmly. This, of course, told her nothing.

"Nice to see you, Nurse Talbot," Captain Dinham said. "And my apologies for dropping in on you like this today." He winked.

Grateful for his visit even if it hadn't worked, she smiled back, acknowledging their little secret.

He huffed and puffed his way back into his damp greatcoat.

"Don't hesitate to call me, either one of you, if you're in need of anything."

Once the front door had closed behind him, William turned to Olivia with a dour expression. "I suppose we can remove the blackout. At least until sunset."

Mrs. Pollard scampered down the corridor toward them. "Oh, Mr. William, that sounds like wonderful news, it does!"

The smile in Olivia's voice was as big as the one on her face. "We can? Why? What did the captain say?"

"The coast is clear. Funny, I suspected as much these past few days. Glad Dinham could confirm it." But unease produced rows of thick lines across his forehead. He pressed on the skin between his eyes. "Olivia, would you mind terribly if I spent the afternoon alone? I've much to sort out."

Alone? As in without her?

"I realize my being unaccompanied could prove dangerous," he added, a dash of sarcasm peppering his tone. "However, you've nothing to worry about."

"Dangerous?" She forced a giggle. "What are you talking about?"

He laughed outright at her awkward attempt at innocence. It was a delightful sound she hadn't heard in weeks. "Have you forgotten that when one of the senses goes, the others are amplified? In all this blindness, my hearing has become quite sharp. I've overheard at least two of your conversations with Mrs. Pollard about how I may off myself if left alone."

Olivia looked away to hide her smile, though she needn't. At least he didn't seem cross.

He searched until he found her shoulders and pulled her forward. "Trust me, Olivia, my nurse and wartime companion, just because I spend the afternoon alone doesn't mean I won't be joining you for dinner tonight. I will, and I look forward to it." His thumb found her forehead and smoothed her eyebrows, sending tingles up her spine. "I appreciate what you're doing for me—and your patience. But I'd like to retire awhile by myself, if you'll allow it."

How close his eyes were to meeting hers. "Yes, William, of course."

"Brilliant. Come fetch me when it's time for tea."

# CHAPTER 14

"It'll be much easier to shave you this morning," Olivia said.

A light breeze told William she'd whisked down the bathroom blackout.

"I'll actually see what I'm doing," she continued, "and maybe you won't walk out of here bleeding today."

She had lost her touch lately, but such a triviality hardly bothered him. He had graver matters to settle with her—and she sensed it.

"William? What is it?"

He wasn't sure where to begin. "I'm sorry."

"You're not going to tell me to replace the blackout, are you?" She sounded sulky.

For once he was happy not to see her eyes. "No, no … I'm sorry for frightening you. I feel like a tremendous buffoon for keeping the house shut up all day, forcing you and everyone else to be as blind to the outside as I am."

Before he could say more, she was spreading the cool shaving cream onto his face. He continued despite the risk of getting a mouthful of foam. "And I regret telling you the Nazis were coming for me. And why. I'm certain my former captors won't come after me—at least, I don't think they will. The idea seems preposterous now. They have plenty of other things to do than avenge the murder of someone who wasn't very nice to them either." It was impossible to sound rational. The thought of North Africa infuriated him. "I hope to God we kill every last one of them."

Her wet hands closed over his.

"I've shared things with you that have brought back terrible memories, memories I don't want anymore. Things I've fought bloody hard to forget." Could she understand enough to forgive him? "Damn it, I hope you don't think poorly of me. I'm a good person."

"I know you are. And it was good you told me. You should've told me long ago."

What was she saying? "No, you don't—"

Her finger grazed his dripping chin. "What you've shared with me only nicked the surface of your time as prisoner. It's no wonder other recollections are filling your mind. But burying them won't get rid of them completely. That's why they keep returning. Instead, you've got to get them out—not one or two memories, but *all* of them."

She made it sound easy. "And how, Nurse Talbot, would you propose I do that?"

"Talk about them—not to me, necessarily. Or don't talk; write them down. Keep a journal. Any way to purge them. Your memories are like poison. Think of a blister filled with fluid or pus. It festers and grows until it's lanced and the poison is released. By releasing your memories, you'll heal." The brush tickled his nose. "And in the process, it wouldn't surprise me if your eyesight returned."

Decidedly the last thing he wanted as of late. "If I can see, then there's nothing wrong with me—nothing to prevent me from returning to war. They'll send me back. To kill or be killed."

"Nothing wrong with you?" Her volume rose, her voice close.

"If your vision returned, that would be a wondrous miracle—but you're nowhere near healed, William, not on the inside. After what you've already lived through, to do it all again would kill you quicker than any bomb or bullet."

She was right, but to agree would be a crime. "Men without the stomach to fight were executed during the Great War, killed for treason by their own government—and rightly so, according to my father."

"Then we wait," she said, her lilt returning. She whipped the shave cream. "You don't have your vision yet anyway. Whatever you decide, we'll take each day as they come. And in the meantime, let's finish your shave. And give your hair a trim as well."

She lathered his neck, her touch gentle yet diligent, like her care for him. In all of this—his paranoia, his fear, and his guilt—at least he had her.

Once William was presentable, Olivia settled him in the sitting room beside the wireless whilst she went in search of her latest knitting project. She scoured every room she'd frequented over the last few days and still couldn't find it. Mrs. Pollard hadn't seen it either. Finally, on her third pass through the library, she spotted something in the corner William had huddled in weeks ago. Subtly out of place, the sofa jutted forward; her knitting basket sat tilted behind it.

As she righted the furniture, she spied a flat brown triangle under the fringe of the rug. Basket in one hand, she grabbed what turned out to be an envelope with the other. It was addressed to Major William Morgan, and it had already been opened.

She did only what Dr. Butler would do in her position and tugged the contents from its envelope. William's business was her business—she was his caregiver, after all.

At once the letter, typed on Royal British Army letterhead, unfolded before her.

21 December, 1940

Attention: Major William Morgan

We hope this letter finds you well and in good health. We thank you for your loyal service to your country and king these past twelve years.

The initial report given us from Dr. Blair on the *HMHS Comfort* indicates that you suffered lacerations to your legs, neck, and back whilst held in captivity by the enemy in North Africa. You also suffered blindness. Dr. Butler, your current physician as of your return home, stated your injuries as "healing accordingly" and your blindness as temporary. We are happy to hear this news for your sake and for the sake of your country.

As soon as you recover, we look forward to hearing from you. As a highly qualified asset to our military, it's crucial you return to our ranks as soon as possible. Our aim is to capitalize upon your strengths and talents and therefore will consider your twelve years of military history and place you appropriately. We will disclose your new position in due time.

In the interim, please have Dr. Butler inform us of your current condition as soon as possible.

Regards,

Colonel Adams

151st Infantry Brigade

Sixth Battalion, DLI

She slid the letter back into the envelope, tucked it inside her knitting basket, and hurried from the library.

Back in the sitting room, William sat by the window. The

look on his face was tranquil, an expression she hadn't seen in some time. She hated to ruin it.

"William."

His head shot up.

She deposited the basket into a nearby chair and shook the envelope in front of him. "I found this."

His brow creased as if he realized exactly what she was speaking of, but she clarified anyway. "This letter from Colonel Adams. Did the captain bring you this?"

He nodded.

"The conversation we had this morning makes more sense now, but I don't understand why you wouldn't tell me about it."

"I—"

"And your hiding place for it? You did a better job hiding my knitting basket."

"I'm blind, Olivia, and I was in a hurry."

"Listen." She checked the door to confirm they were alone and went back to kneel in front of him. "If your vision returns, we won't tell anyone. Not a soul. Not Mrs. Pollard, not Dr. Butler, no one. Do you think you could do it? Fake it, I mean?"

"What, pretend I'm blind?"

"Yes."

"I think so, but—"

"This letter shouldn't deter you from wanting your sight back. You'll get it back, and I'll help you if you'll let me. But you are not going back to war." Without realizing it, she had gripped the tops of his knees. "Do you hear me?"

His face softened, his voice quiet. "I do."

"Forgive me." She smoothed the trousers over his knees, certain she'd left imprints on his skin. "I feel strongly about this. Do you think I'm being silly?"

"I like that you're looking out for me. I'm touched, really. But—"

"I'll ring Dr. Butler this afternoon to update him on your

condition. He can write Colonel Adams and give an update of his own. That should appease your superiors for a time. Then when your sight returns"—she refused to say *if*—"I'll help you practice your acting around here with the staff, and then with the captain, should he come by, so that you'll eventually be ready to meet with Dr. Butler. What do you say, Major?"

He raised a hand and finding the curve of her cheek, pulled her closer. "I say that I'm glad you're here. Thank you, Olivia."

Olivia's knitting needles clicked a steady rhythm that was occasionally overcome by the music from the radio. Not sure which to pay more attention to, William sat in the darkness in which he'd grudgingly become comfortable, back straight, hands resting on his thighs. He sat like this often, surely looking the fool. Perhaps if he appeared to be ready for anything, he would be. Unlikely. These days he wasn't ready for anything other than less milk in his tea.

Thank God for Olivia, though her desire to stand by him only reinforced his cowardice, a trait he had a hard time identifying with. His entire military career had been defined by bravery. He'd even been recognized for great courage during a training mission for recruits in '39, when a misfire sent an old barn up into flames, the three men inside shouting for their lives. William hadn't been afraid that day; he'd done what needed to be done, and those three lives had been saved.

Last spring, before North Africa, he'd been sent to protect mines in Norway from the Nazis. He considered himself a steadfast soldier despite the horrors he witnessed. Horrors like the wait time between an oncoming fighter plane and the mortars they released. Horrors like seeing fathers, sons, husbands, and brothers with limbs blown from their bodies, found hours later in sticky bogs. Some convulsed violently as they faced their mortality; others groaned and called for their loved ones. Uniforms were cleaned and sent home as mementos. How many more dead men's belongings would be sent to the grieving before it was all over?

As soon as war had been declared, he'd wanted to fight. He did his bit and did it well. His father had understood, and it bolstered William to have someone to share it with. But things were different now. The thought of going back to fight riddled him with fear. He'd become a slave to this new emotion. Deep down, he knew what had changed him and when. He knew what plagued his sleep and caused this confounded blindness.

And he wished to God it would all go away.

# CHAPTER 15

THE CRIES WEREN'T HUMAN. Shrill and persistent, they carried on like a defenseless skulk of fox cubs cornered by a predator. Though it wasn't surprising that the estate had been invaded by the thieving species, this was the first time Olivia had heard evidence of their existence. Were there four? Ten? She sought another pillow, anything to preserve the quiet.

Then the sound changed. The squeals lost their high pitch and transformed into something more intelligible: words.

"Take your bloody hands off her!"

She opened her eyes. All was quiet. Then, "She's nothing to do with this. It's me you want. Let her go!"

Light from the corridor ushered her back to reality: This was William as she'd never heard him before.

She left her dressing gown behind and raced to his room. Flat on his stomach he lay, blue pajama top bunched around his torso and his legs akimbo. His blankets lay in a bundle on the floor, and poor Jasper stood next to the bed as though he'd been kicked off. It was a sight similar to the first nightmare she'd ever roused him from, yet somehow different. Four months ago, he'd been frightened and weak; now, his eyes were open and he looked ready to kill.

For her own safety, she decelerated her approach and called, "William!"

A leaden foot struck her hip, and only swift reflexes kept her from sending his wardrobe toppling. Her elbows and palms stung as she smacked into the floor. Sweet Jasper licked her hand as though he knew how she felt. She drew the dog close as his master continued to thrash.

Once again, she approached the bed. "William, wake up!"

He lunged forward, cementing himself to her forearm. She surrendered to his pull and stumbled onto the bed, her face inches from his angry, wet mouth.

"So help me God, I will tear you limb from limb—"

She slapped him hard. "Damn it, William, wake up!"

His body deflated like a punctured balloon. He rubbed his cheek, his jaw shifting left to right as if he'd been walloped in a street fight.

"You're all right," she said. Still caught in his weakening grasp, she stayed where she was, teetering on her knees.

"Olivia?" His bobbing free arm found her shoulder and with the swiftness of a brushfire, he drew her into his arms and buried his face in her hair. "Olivia, oh, my dear Olivia."

She smoothed the damp fabric covering his mutilated back. "What were you dreaming?"

His breathing accelerated.

"You've got to get it out, or you'll return to the damned thing throughout the day tomorrow. You know this."

He spoke into the safety of her hair. "He had you. He was hurting you."

"Who had me? Wirth?"

He drew back. Memories deadened his face as though he were hypnotized. "I couldn't do anything to stop it. And I tried. He was doing it to punish me, and I couldn't do anything but beg him to stop, and—"

"What were they doing, William?"

He shook his head, pursing his lips.

"What were they doing?"

"They were taking turns."

"Tell me."

"You were bound, tied up. In the worst way, they were hurting you and they wouldn't stop. They were enjoying it, and you were screaming—crying my name—and I could do nothing."

The hand round her forearm tightened, close to marking her skin, but that wasn't what troubled her. What troubled her was the question she had to ask next.

"When you were prisoner, were you hurt this way? Did this happen to *you*, William?"

He dropped his head as sobs racked his body. She pulled him close, steering him back toward the sanctuary of her shoulder. Heavy breaths gave way to a fresh stream of tears that saturated her gown.

His response delivered a heavy blow to her gut. In her wildest dreams, she'd never imagined his experience had included suffering of this nature.

"I wasn't the only one," he said. "There were others who suffered. Some lost their lives; no one was safe. We were constantly reminded of that."

"I can't even imagine."

"Then you're lucky. It's all I've been doing these past six months."

She reached for the linens.

His grip tightened around her wrist. "Don't go. Please don't leave me."

"I wouldn't dream of it." She freely kissed the top of his head, holding him as she would a child.

Floorboards outside the bedroom creaked. Jasper trotted over to Mrs. Pollard, who stood in the doorway, her mouth agape.

"Everything is fine, Mrs. Pollard," Olivia said in steely tones. "In fact, would you mind handing me the bedclothes?"

William stayed fixed where he was as Olivia leant forward to take the wadded bunch. Mrs. Pollard's astonishment deepened to a frown, her disapproval clearly overshadowing her curiosity.

"You may switch the light off as you exit the room, as well," Olivia continued. "Thank you, Mrs. Pollard."

With great effort, Olivia spread the blankets over both of them, creating as little disruption as possible to the man grieving in her arms. She hadn't meant to sound so dictatorial, but the older woman's expression troubled her. This would not go unforgotten. It didn't matter. William wanted her there; more importantly, he needed her there.

Mrs. Pollard's judgment be damned.

Olivia woke to a whimper and a squeeze at her waist. William nudged her, seeking comfort against her rib cage. She slid further down to accommodate the head using her as a pillow. He snuggled in contentedly before suddenly stilling.

William sat up and hastily removed the arm he'd had wrapped around her for hours.

"Good morning," she said.

She kept her voice light despite her exhaustion. Stinging nettles coursed up and down her left arm and throughout her hand. She opened and closed her fist until the numbness subsided; after a few shakes, she could feel her hand again. The kink in her neck wouldn't be so forgiving. It was early, just after seven. A sliver of light entered the room between the blackout and windows.

The silhouette of William's Adam's apple bobbed up and down as he swallowed. "You're still here. I—I didn't expect that."

"Of course. How did you sleep?"

"Better than expected, considering. And you?"

She yawned. "Fine." She touched his forearm, her manner cheerful. "You must be famished. I know I am. I'll tell Mrs. Pollard we're ready for breakfast."

The relief that eased his brow emboldened her train of thought.

"We've the whole day ahead of us, William, a day to make new memories to replace those old ones. What shall we do?"

# CHAPTER 16

THE ROAR of crashing waves grew louder, telling William they'd emerged from the path. He'd finally consented to take Olivia to his beloved cove, where familiar scents, cool and salty, rushed his nose and provoked dozens of memories.

"It's beautiful." Delight flooded her voice.

"Even with barbed wire?"

"The wire is out beyond the surf. The beach is clear of it." She took his hand and tugged. "Come, let's go down to the water."

He pulled back.

"What's the matter?"

"Nothing," he said, eager to lose himself in his thoughts. "I mean it. Nothing is wrong. You go on ahead. Make your way in that direction, and I'll come meet you."

He pointed, he was sure, to the shelf of slate bordering the inlet's west side.

He couldn't remember the last time he'd been here. His mother had first brought him when he was very young. Though protective, she wasn't overly so, and she'd allowed him to climb and explore as any boy would. Natural consequences answered poor choices, but nothing too dire. Scrapes and bruises were the standard trimmings of the knee-length trousers and suspenders of his boyhood.

As he grew older, he came here alone; the cove became his refuge. In secret forts, an empty cave at low tide, or the hollow of dead bramble, he created battle plans after spying on make-believe enemies. His imagination was never void of storylines in which he saved the world (or his cove) from ruin. Twice, after his mother died, he'd brought mates here to play. Their envy of his own wild place boasting rocks, caves, and tumbling water reminded him how lucky he was to have it.

When he was older still, he came here to read over long holidays from school and in between assignments with the army. The cove was his alone; his father had never cared for it, and after those few visitors in childhood, he never shared it with others again.

Until now.

Olivia, the woman whose bare feet he imagined racing through the surf just yards away, had become his salvation. For weeks, an adoration he'd never felt for a woman before grew within him like a mighty oak, deep-rooted and unwavering. He desired her as well: her voice, her touch, and her smell were daily requirements. He'd intended to tell her so on Christmas Eve until the pain in his skull had reduced him to a blithering idiot.

Girlish giggles carried by a restorative breeze reached him where he stood, one hand shoved inside his greatcoat, the other gripping his white cane. Full of life, her laughter brought to mind her innocent kisses—the ones he'd received after giving her the moonstone and again under the mistletoe. Her inexperience was surprising. Professionally, she was unfazed by his caustic nature and horrendous mood swings. She could take a tense situation like the one last night and tame it to her will. Yet when it came to flirtation, her naïveté charged him to take control, beginning with the study of her face.

According to his fingers, it was heart-shaped, her nose small, and her lips—her lips were full and smooth like the petals of a burgeoning tulip. Though she'd never admit it, he knew she was beautiful. How could a woman who smiled so much be unattractive? And he could always tell when she smiled because her voice changed: The edges of her words softened and poured from her mouth like honey.

He had to kiss her again—but his way this time. The way her body melted against his told him she'd never experienced such a kiss. The way she sighed when they parted told him she wouldn't mind another.

"William?" A shadow crossed his face as her delicious scent encircled him.

He thought quickly. "I was wondering if you were enjoying yourself."

"From now on, I think you'll have a hard time keeping me away from here."

He pictured her twirling in the sand.

"It's hard to believe this is so close to the house," she continued. "The cliffs, the roaring ocean. I love how different it is from the quiet grounds."

He did too.

"Come with me?"

He let her tow him toward the water—briefly.

"Don't worry, I won't let you get wet," she said.

"I trust you." He let go of her hand and reached up, hoping to brush the silk of her hair or caress the side of her face. Nothing was there.

"A sand dollar!" she exclaimed, her voice feet away. "Oh, it's broken."

He lowered his arm and shoved his hand back into his pocket, disappointed and feeling a fool. "They're difficult to find whole down here, but sometimes you do."

"Can we climb the rocks? You climbed them as a boy, no doubt."

She took his hand, fueling his desire to pull her near. Instead, he followed her toward the uneven slate steps. He'd climbed them dozens of times, and under her careful direction, doing so blindly wasn't much different. His balance would've been stronger free of her hand, but he didn't want to let it go.

High above the roiling ocean, facing it head-on, they sat on the cool, hard surface of stone. William pictured the slopes that rose to the west. This time of year, the blackthorn dotting the windblown cliffs would resemble crippled old men, hunched and shaking in the wind. Though they were dark and skeletal, Cornwall's early spring would soon dress them in white flowers tough enough to withstand the next season's warmer gales.

A breeze kicked up, and flecks of seawater sprinkled them. Olivia shivered. Still holding her hand, he squeezed it, savoring the shared moment. Peace passed through their palms. Her touch did that to him, as it had in his bedroom less than twenty-four hours ago when she watched him cry, curse, and thrash about.

Before she asked the inevitable.

But even after learning the truth and seeing shame pummel him like a stone at the bottom of a waterfall, she remained his steadfast ally. Even when he was inconsolable, she gave no inclination that she thought him weak. His heartbeat quickened as he recalled lying beside her, his head nestled into her side whilst she protected him from his demons. His arms had clasped her tiny waist for hours, longing for her soft flesh and scorning her flannel gown. He'd imagined her in his arms and his bed more than once—but in fits of passion, not the throes of some bloody nightmare.

There was no avoiding it. He was in love with Olivia, and had been for some time.

"What are you smiling at?"

"What?" He turned his head to hide his surprise, and maybe his guilt, but his grin remained.

"Are you making fun of me? Do you think me silly for asking

127

you to climb ridiculous heights, and you're wishing we never ventured down here?"

"Not at all."

"What is it, then?"

He couldn't lie to her. He raised an eyebrow. "I was thinking about Christmas Eve."

"That was a horrible night."

Oh, no. "Horrible?"

"Your headaches. You were miserable, and I was a nervous wreck."

"Oh," he said, relieved that they were talking about two different things. "I meant earlier in the evening. The dinner and dancing. The mistletoe."

"Ah," she said, her voice turning dreamy. "That wasn't horrible at all. That was wonderful."

"I hope you didn't think me presumptuous for surprising you with the mistletoe."

"No, William." His heart warmed at hearing his name wrought into her smile. "But I wasn't sure if your plan that night was something you really wanted or some euphoria brought on by your pills."

"They served a purpose, I suppose. Without them, I wouldn't have had the courage to ask Mrs. Pollard to help me hang mistletoe. I certainly wouldn't have excused the staff for an entire week." He paused, hoping he wasn't revealing too much. "And though I wanted badly for you to have it, I don't think I'd have had the nerve to give you my mother's necklace. Do you ever wear it?"

She lifted his hand and left it resting on the pendant at her throat. "Every day. I cherish it."

His thumb smoothed over the large stone before traveling further afield. Clinging to her warm skin, his hand slid along her jawline to the side of her neck. "What if there were no mistletoe, no fire, and no holiday? Just a windy cove, an extremely hard surface, and what I think is a sunny day. Would you let me you kiss then?"

She responded by giving in to his gentle pull. He pictured her eyes closed in surrender. When their lips met, she stilled, as though awaiting his next move. Her reserve, as usual, left him wanting more. At her shoulder, he pulled her closer still.

She shivered.

"Chilly?" he asked, his forehead touching hers.

"A little."

"Should we go?"

"No!" she said, disrupting their closeness. "I'm not ready to go yet. Are you?"

"I'm rather enjoying myself. Here."

He stood and removed his greatcoat, draped its bulky mass around her, and returned to her side. She arranged part of the coat over his shoulders, too.

"We can share," she said, snuggling beneath its silky lining and his arm, now encircling her lower back.

Wind stirred her lavender scent, beckoning him to lean over and kiss her again. Perhaps he would lay her onto the rocks, his arms a cradle against sharp edges, his body a blockade from the incessant wind. If he could have seen what was behind them, he might have tried it, but he didn't want to make an unromantic fool out of himself.

He sought to veer away from the thought, but she did it for him. "Has the estate always belonged to your family?"

"Yes."

"Why do you look like that? Like you're hiding something?"

"My family's history is rather sordid. Some of it, anyway. And it's a rather long story."

"Tell me."

He was happy to—anything to keep her this close a little longer.

~

Long shadows stretched east, darkening Keldor's exterior. The wind had died, and a cool mist hovered over the lawn between the house and the cove's trailhead. Immune to the chill brought on by winter's early nightfall, Olivia strolled beside the "real" William as revealed by the magic of Steren Cove. Her William.

She wasn't sure how long he held her close, sheltering her from whipping wind and divulging intimate stories of his ancestors. He started with the treacherous Morgans who'd migrated from Wales and utilized the cove for surreptitious deeds that eventually financed the building of Keldor (*Keldor means "secret earth" in Cornish*, William had explained). Then there were the philanthropic Morgans of recent years and the remarkable story of how they'd entered his mother's life and forever changed it when she was still a girl. But after the story of Uncle George and his tragic end on the *Titanic*, William let escape a series of yawns. Her own yawns completed the volley, and neither one could deny the kip they both needed.

Out of the bramble and across the meadow, William gripped her hip as though he feared she might slip away. She rested her head on his shoulder, beaming when his playful pecks peppered the top of it. She'd never been so happy. The realization that she didn't have to fight or hide her feelings made her want to swing his arm and skip alongside him.

She longed to write her cousin. Should she disclose everything, including his advances on Christmas Eve, which she'd so conveniently left out of her last letter? Should she tell Katie how even though she was nervous about kissing him (because she wasn't sure she was very good at it), she couldn't wait to do it again? No, whatever she told Katie, she would do so in person. Words on paper could do nothing to express the joy warming her cheeks and broadening her smile.

They missed tea. Olivia hung up William's greatcoat as Jasper greeted them with a wagging tail in the foyer. Apparently he held no grudge for being excluded from the long walk and licked William's hand ferociously in greeting.

Mrs. Pollard waved off their absence, claiming it wasn't a bother at all. But she didn't turn to leave. Head cocked, she raised an eyebrow at them. Something had changed, and she knew it.

"Nice walk, then?" she asked.

Olivia hoped her certain flush would be attributed to the chilly air.

"Absolutely, Polly." William reached in Olivia's direction, and she gave him her hand. "I should've taken Olivia there long ago."

He brought her hand to his mouth and kissed it, stretching her guilty smile even further. She kept her eyes on the happy Labrador.

"We won't be late for supper, Polly, we promise," William said, oblivious to Mrs. Pollard's inquisitive face before Olivia steered them both toward the stairs.

~

"Do you need anything before I leave you to rest?" Olivia asked just inside William's bedroom.

He wore the same mysterious expression he'd worn at the cove. He was up to something, and it wouldn't be long before she was privy to it.

"I do."

Willingly, she followed his pull on her wrist. His left arm wrapped her waist and her hip met his. His right hand went to her face and found her mouth with his fingers before hurriedly covering it with his own, voraciously sapping every ounce of strength that kept her standing. If it hadn't been for the support of his arm and the wall behind her, she'd have sunk to the floor.

Unlike their brief embrace at Steren Cove, this kiss left no question of William's resolve. In an effort to match his fervor, she

131

rose on her tiptoes, her arms clinging more tightly, her palms flattening against his back. Her fingers curled as heat sprang from every place he touched her, sizzling through her body.

He pulled away. "Your hair. It's up."

Her hair had grown long since moving to Cornwall, but fashioning it into the latest twists and curls had always been beyond her. Assuming William didn't care one way or another (especially as he couldn't see it), it was easier to pile it on top of her head.

Out of breath, she whispered, "Should I take it down?"

"Let me."

Both hands patted her head, searching for hairpins. She ignored the tugging of delicate strands that would've rushed her to tears, had this been her mother's undertaking. Freed from the metal clips, her hair fell in thick hanks to her shoulders. He grabbed them in his fist, burying his nose in their layers until his mouth came to her neck. She'd never been kissed here before, an intrusion that left her bereft when he came away.

"I believe I've fallen in love with you, Nurse Talbot," he whispered.

She smiled against his face.

"Does that make you smile?"

"Yes."

"Good," he said, using his fingers to examine her eyelids, the tip of her nose, and each cheek. "Then you aren't opposed to more of these?"

He planted his lips gently between her eyebrows.

"No."

"Whenever I feel like it? They may come without warning from here on out."

Searching his face the way he had hers, she traced the arcs of his dark eyebrows, spellbound by the slate-blue orbs. Despite their ardor, the discoloration beneath them reminded her of his exhaustion.

"Whenever you wish. But William"—she tore herself away

from him as one would from a fire on a bitterly cold night—"you should lie down awhile."

An eyebrow ticked up as though reading more into her suggestion. But all he said was, "I suppose you're right, Nurse Talbot. Shall we resume this later, then?"

Unable to withdraw completely, she kissed his nose and mouth. "Of course. I find activity of this sort highly beneficial to your overall health."

# CHAPTER 17

It was late, but Olivia didn't sleep. Standing at the window, she peeked behind the blackout. Wind shook Keldor's windowpanes and blew branches wildly, reminding her of William searching the space around him before he learned how to use his white cane. How she wished it were William who'd got her out of bed and not the storm. Since the last horrific nightmare including her, his nights had been relatively quiet—a good thing, and she was back to honoring his request to allow him to get through the minor nightmares without her.

Still, she missed him. Was he sleeping? Was his top lip curled slightly toward his nose, his hair a black riot against his pillowcase? After so much time spent together during the day, emptiness crept over her when they were apart, like an oyster missing its pearl. True, she'd been with him every waking moment since October, but their days were different now.

In the mornings, they arrived at breakfast hand in hand. He insisted she sit close, not to help him eat but so he could keep a hand on her knee or smooth the length of her arm. Afternoons sent them down to Steren Cove, rain or shine, talking the whole way. Already somewhat familiar with her family dynamics,

William probed further. He inquired into the close relationships she had with her father and grandmother and the tenuous one she had with her mother. As an only child, he was curious about growing up with siblings; he learned straightaway that just because she was the only daughter didn't mean she'd been granted any favors. Open and honest, Olivia spoke as she would to her cousin Katie or as she would write in her personal journal. Not once did he interrupt. Even when she sounded petulant and spoilt, he never exacted judgment. Instead, he smiled and whisked her hand to his lips.

After their chilly walks, they retired to the library for hot tea and a book. She loved reading to him. Under a shared blanket on the library sofa, he lost himself in the stories, his face a canvas of reaction: laughter, worry, shock, sadness. Occasionally he touched her face as if making sure she was still there. Apparently, her legs draped over his lap and her voice in his ear weren't enough to tell him so.

Mrs. Pollard's presence had become rather intimidating. The housekeeper announced herself before entering a room, no doubt unsure of what she'd find there. In almost every instance, the besotted pair were clasping hands or leaning into one another in flirtatious laughter. Olivia avoided her glance at all costs, but William carried on as if caressing her shoulder or attaching his hand to her hip were customary behaviors between nurse and patient.

Yet forever the gentleman, he went no further. When they parted each night, he was careful not to pull her too close, and he shied away from exploring unfamiliar terrain. Olivia didn't tempt him, but her willpower was dwindling. The more comfortable they became in each other's arms, the harder it became to control herself.

Like this morning. After removing William's blackout curtains, she turned to find his face troubled. She instantly attended to the mismatched buttons on his shirt (she was beginning to think he dressed this way on purpose) and listened as he told of his restless night. Then out of nowhere and rapid as gunfire, he asked if she missed the city. If Dr. Butler said he no longer required a nurse, would she go back to London? Could she picture herself residing in Cornwall?

Despite the speed of their delivery, every word came across loud and clear.

"I love Cornwall! I don't want to go back to London." She bulldozed the man backward onto his bed. Her hands lost themselves in his hair, and her hungry lips adhered to his mouth. With her leg wrapping his hip, she rolled them until he lay on top of her.

He allowed his hands to wander under her skirt until, with remarkable restraint, he sat up.

"That's settled, then." He tidied his hair with one hand and found her arm with the other. "Exactly the answer I'd hoped for. Shall we go down to breakfast?"

These waves of desire were confounding. Olivia left the window and returned to bed, greeted by the mattress's squeaks as she collapsed onto the pillows. Dr. Butler's most recent report was holding off William's superiors, but how long would William remain blind? Too caught up in seeking his affections, she'd done nothing to fulfill her promise to help him get better.

The wind died. A scuffle, then a thud came from outside her room. She sprang upright. A heavy sigh outside her room told her she wasn't the only one awake.

She flicked her lamp to life and crept to the doorjamb. William sat against the papered wall, his shoulders hunched within his striped pajama top. His chin rested on drawn-up knees, and his right hand disappeared into his dark mane.

"William?"

His face rose; waves of misery lined the top of it.

"Have you had a nightmare?" she asked, crouching at his side.

"Not a nightmare. It's you."

"Me?"

"I'm across the damned corridor, awake and restless because all I want is to be with you. The nightmares are bad enough—but this, night after night, I'm finding quite difficult."

His words replicated her own thoughts. "I see. If that's the case, why are you sitting out here in the corridor?"

"I didn't want to wake you."

"So you thought you'd loiter out here like a gloomy teenager?"

Her playfulness finally resurrected his smile.

"Well, tonight's your lucky night, Major. I was already awake and thinking of you too. Come on." She stood, still holding his hand. "We'll stay up and talk. I've something to discuss with you anyway."

He stayed close until she deposited him on her bed, a short distance from the mussed bedclothes from which she'd emerged. After lifting a quilt from the wooden rack in the corner, she returned to find him sitting as stiffly as he had during his crippling paranoia. Feet on the floor, he faced the door she closed and fiddled with the bottom of his nightshirt.

As comfortably as she would sit next to her best girlfriend, she faced him, one leg stretched to the floor, the other kinked at a sharp angle, her knee touching his hip. She draped the quilt over both their laps.

"Are you all right?" she asked, unable to hide her amusement.

"Hmm?" He swiveled his head in her direction. "Yes. But is this appropriate? That I'm here, in your bedroom?"

"Of course," she whispered, taking his hand.

"I don't want to make you uncomfortable."

"You're not. This isn't the first time we've been together in the middle of the night."

If she kissed him, would he stop worrying? Since she'd become more confident in her abilities, it was an area she was eager to further explore. A war was on, they were in love, and they were alone. Nothing should keep them from advancing their relationship, should it?

Before her giddiness got the best of her, she pushed visions of passion from her mind. "I'm going turn off the light and tell you my plan."

She took his face in her hands. Afraid his lips would be too much of an enticement, she avoided them altogether and kissed his forehead and nose. Instantly, a drunken smile arose on his face.

She returned bearing pillows and coaxed the newly relaxed major down across the foot of the bed, undoubtedly more suitable than lying beneath the headboard. Eye to eye and nose to nose, they lay in darkness.

"We talked some time ago about you sharing your memories in hopes of ridding them forever. Do you remember?"

"Yes."

She propped herself up on one elbow. "I think it's time you start. We'll find a notebook to serve as your journal. We can sit together if you like, or you can be alone, but I want you to write from the start of your deployment to Africa, or even before. You could read it to Dr. Butler, or not. You could burn it, if you choose. But you've got to get the memories out."

"A journal?"

"Mm-hmm."

"Olivia, I don't need a journal." He smoothed his hand over her hair.

It took all her patience not to push it away. She'd been so happy when he told her he loved her. She loved him too, more than she ever loved anyone—but that wasn't going to repair his eyesight or lessen his night terrors. Hands bunched into fists, she curled her trimmed fingernails into her palms and remained silent, fighting the roar creeping up her throat.

"Olivia." Panic entered his voice and his body became as rigid as hers. He sat up. "I don't need a bloody journal."

"But I don't see why you won't try—"

"I don't need to write it down. Can't I tell you? A journal would take double the time. I don't know why—"

"You'd tell me?"

"I'll write the bloody mess out if you think I should, but I thought you said that I could tell someone. The only person I would tell is you."

"Oh, darling," she said, thrilled to use the endearment no longer relegated to her thoughts. She wrapped her arms around him, and her muffled voice spilt into his neck. "I thought we'd taken ten steps backward."

"Not backward, my love. Only forward from here on, I promise." He pulled away, tracing her lower lip with his thumb the way he always did before he kissed her. "It won't be pretty, and it won't be easy for me. I have many reservations about bringing you into my dark world."

She wasn't afraid. "It's time you were no longer there alone. And no matter how frightening it is, I'll be here, in the present, ready to bring us back to Keldor."

Replacing his thumb with his mouth, William kissed her. Locked in his arms, she fell with him back onto the pillows.

William hadn't planned on remaining in Olivia's bedroom all night, but when he insisted on leaving, she was adamant he stay, claiming he wouldn't sleep otherwise. She was right, of course. But had this been years ago and Olivia some woman he'd met at party, sleep would've been the furthest thing from his mind. He was in love with her, a feeling as foreign as fear, yet one he was rather enjoying. So after traversing her curves outside the barrier of her modest nightdress (and delighting in the way her body yielded in response), he planted several reserved kisses on her neck and face and allowed himself to succumb to sweet sleep.

He woke well after nine the next morning. Today, without question, was the day he would begin to recount his dark tale.

Olivia showered him with kiss after kiss, her voice jubilant. "You're sure? Are you sure you're sure?"

He was sure.

The clouds and rain outside would serve as an appropriate backdrop to the task ahead. He asked Mrs. Pollard to keep the rest of the staff away unless called for. She understood what the day would entail and was happy to help "her William" any way she could.

Just before their self-imposed lockdown, Mrs. Pollard charged Olivia with some mundane task in the kitchen and then asked him for a private word.

"Your friend Jasper has let me in on your secret," she said.

"Secret?" He accepted the teacup pushed into his hand.

He had expected this conversation. More than once Mrs. Pollard had entered the library, sitting room, foyer, or kitchen to find his hands shackled to Olivia, her mouth glued to his. The interruptions made Olivia uncomfortable, so he tried quelling her fears by delivering more kisses and laughter—but he refused to hide his feelings for her. Since she mentioned Jasper, Polly must have seen them in bed together; that was twice now. She must know he had the utmost respect for Olivia. They shared a sleeping space, yes, but he would do nothing to offend her honor. He wasn't that man anymore.

Regardless, he was in for an earful. Nanny, stand-in mother, and confidant, Mrs. Pollard was ever full of advice on how he should live his life, especially since his mother had died. She played the role of both parents, and he never doubted her love for him, even when it involved a lecture.

"If this is about Nurse Talbot," he said, "I say, it's hardly a secret."

"William, I've known for some time of your feelings for that girl. Ever since you asked me to find your mother's pendant, I knew something was brewing inside of you other than thanking her for her help." Her palm, covering his free hand, was warm and smooth, her tone motherly. He'd heard it often growing up and depending on the situation, it either soothed or aggravated him. Now it did neither.

"Go on."

"I'm concerned. Nurse Talbot is a sweet girl, like. She's sincere, selfless, and more than competent in her role as your nurse. But, love, she's no Jenna."

This wasn't about impropriety, then? He bit his tongue and let her continue.

"You were in love with Jenna once, and the things you found attractive in her, you won't find in your nurse."

"I'm uncertain what attracted me to Jenna besides convenience. But since I've found my true love, I can tell you honestly that I was never in love with Jenna."

"But Nurse Talbot, though a sweet and smart girl, is not of the same breeding as Miss Jenna. The two of you be cut from the same cloth. She too is from an old and prosperous Cornish family. Nurse Talbot's a city girl, a nurse. I may sound behind the times, but if you haven't done so already, I believe it's important for you to decide which type of woman and lifestyle you wish to capture. Jenna is elegant and sophisticated, like, yet Nurse Talbot is—well, she's common."

What the devil was she talking about? His mother's life before coming to Keldor was proof that background and breeding had never been a concern of the family's.

"Now, William, I have high regard for the nurse, and she's a pretty girl. She won't disappoint you there. But I want you to be certain, before any more hearts be broken."

He was certain—so certain, in fact, that he laughed. He laughed at her concern for him: overprotective at times, but he'd become used to it over the years. He laughed because as much as she thought she knew him, she knew nothing at all.

"This is nothing to laugh at," she said, her firm tone stilling him. "Whether she's told you or not, that girl in the kitchen is madly in love with you. I don't know what you said to her that day at Steren Cove, but she's not been the same since."

He came to attention as if his colonel had entered the room. "The day at the cove? What—how do you mean?"

"When the two of you returned, it was all over her face."

"What was? Tell me."

"Love. She's smitten. She's had an eye for you for some time, but since that day, something's changed. Her eyes follow wherever you go. For time on end, she gazes upon you with the same adoration a flower has for the sun. When she talks about you, she blushes like a schoolgirl—"

He couldn't help himself. "She does?"

"Yes, and—"

"Have you ever seen Jenna look like that?"

She exhaled. "Not since she was a girl—a young girl—chasing you around, eavesdropping on you and Peder."

He crossed his arms, smug.

She patted his knee. "Well, then, as long as you be truly happy, then I approve. Like I said, no more broken hearts." She stood and kissed the top of his head. "I'll send the girl in with your breakfast directly. Good luck today, my handsome."

## CHAPTER 18

"Before the war, I was stationed in Egypt, ordered to safeguard the comings and goings around the Suez."

William stood before the hearth, shoulders squared and confidence waning. He'd begun his tale and already he wanted to stop. He raised his head toward where the portrait of his father hung. The arched eyebrow and critical gaze felt particularly oppressive this morning.

"I lived there long enough to familiarize myself with the culture and the right people. With war looming, I came home to ready troops for combat. Last April, my company and I fortified mines in Norway and sought to keep the Nazis from gaining access to them. Norway was my first taste of carnage. Planes, bombs, bodies, blood, tears, regret. Regret?" He shook his head. "Never. Courage? Certainly. All those brave men, so ready to fight. Men who joined the army *before* word of war. Men like myself, hoping to fulfill their life's purpose: to fight for and protect their country. My God, I watched so many of them die."

He should've died that day as well. The bravery and skill his father had claimed kept him alive had nothing to do with it. Only luck could have delivered him from the attack unscathed.

Luck that, a month later, had run out.

"But it didn't last. Intelligence wanted me back, wanted the connections I'd made in Cairo restored. I went back not as a major but as a spy. I was to be the eyes and ears of the British, to live the life of a regular English bloke, to blend in—and with any luck, to be in the right place at the right time. I tell you, there was nothing right about it."

He made his way to the sideboard and poured a tumbler of whiskey. Sure-footed, he strode to the sofa, stopping once his shins flattened against it. Olivia guided him to the spot beside her, where he downed the liquid. It warmed his core and spurred him to continue.

"I reconnected easily with old friends and acquaintances who shared information on the Italians and their plans to declare war with Britain and France. The predicted consequences for the area were dire. Britain compensated my friends well for their troubles. Some, naturally, wondered why I had returned. There was a war on. Why wasn't I fighting in it?"

He laughed. "You'll appreciate this little detail. I had a cover: I'd been redeployed due to a battlefield accident affecting my eyesight. Ironic, isn't it? Rather than sending me back into the fight, they'd sent me to Cairo to improve communication technologies between Egypt and Britain, as a communications specialist. Which of course I wasn't."

He deposited his glass on the table by the couch. He should've brought the entire bottle.

"The first weeks were quiet. There was little to report, save intelligence regarding Italy's encroachment on Egypt—inevitable, just a matter of when. Come late May—it seems ages ago—I was to have dinner with my friend Ahmad. Though aware of my pending engagement to Jenna, he badly wanted his sister Alia and me to meet. I trusted him and enjoyed his company, so I went."

Ahmad. Young but wise, witty yet kind, he'd been his closest mate in Cairo.

"When I arrived at his flat, he—he looked different. I knew something was wrong right away." Ahmad wore a smile even on bad days. The panic supplanting it that evening would haunt William forever. "He said, 'Morgan,' then disappeared. In his place stood two men I'd never seen before. My gut told me to get the hell out, so I did. Ahmad yelled after me to run. I'd made it less than ten yards before two men at the end of the passage grabbed me. I was unarmed. What a fool."

The tremors were starting. Even sitting with his arms crossed, he couldn't make them stop.

"They wrestled a cloth over my head and cuffed my wrists. Before long, I was outside and shoved into a motorcar. The voices around me were all German, and I understood every word. Between their congratulations on my successful capture, I learned I was being taken to a base camp for questioning. Ahmad was being transported in the car behind us.

"For a fleeting moment, I actually thought quite highly of myself. I'd no idea the small role I played had been significant enough for Nazis to abduct me. My incarceration would be brief. People, important army officials, knew where I needed to be and when. But after we'd driven for what seemed hours, I started to panic. If they took me too far away, perhaps I wouldn't be found after all."

He could sit no longer. Damp with nervous perspiration, he moved to the hearth and extended his fingers toward its heat.

"When we arrived, the canvas was torn from my head and I was thrown into darkness—my first encounter with blindness. I tried to explore my cell, but my arms were still bound. It was empty anyway: no chair, no table, no toilet. I wasn't hungry or thirsty, not yet, but my unease was growing by the moment. That was nothing compared to how I would feel in the weeks to come. During the days when I wanted to die."

He wanted to die now. The account would only grow darker, and its completion was unimaginable. Then he remembered:

Olivia. Her presence on the sofa was a magnetic force pulling him to safety. At once he loped to her side and sat, regretting he ever left it.

"Two guards came in. Nazis. They tossed me to the floor and kicked me in the ribs, then dragged me to a room with bright white walls. Wirth was there." He hated the name—saying it, thinking it. "He was cordial at first. He apologized for the inconvenience of bringing me so far from Cairo. I sat in the chair opposite his small desk, and he offered me a cigarette—tea, even —all with a smile. I refused. There's no joy in a cigarette with bound hands, and the bastard had no intention of freeing them.

"When I asked where I was, he ignored the question and demanded I tell him the Empire's plans for expansion from the Suez, Egypt, and beyond—a ridiculous order. We wanted to hold on to what was ours. Britain was on the defensive, for Christ's sake. In no time, he backed down. I knew it meant he already had the facts and wanted to see what I looked like telling the truth."

"What did he look like?" Olivia asked.

William whirled his head toward her voice, startled. "He was older." From afar, the man's fine wrinkles had hid themselves well within his pale skin. But up close, each line cut a deep crag, punctuating his villainy. "By twenty years, maybe. His hair was close to white, eyes a light blue, almost translucent. I said he smiled, but it was a devil's smile, a smile that revealed pleasure, not kindness. I recognized the malice as soon as I saw it. He was still smiling when I killed him."

He stood and strode toward the hearth, raking his hair back from his face. The dead man's grin came with him. He'd never be rid of it.

"Wirth shifted the focus to maps and offensive plans against Italy. When I explained I knew nothing about that either, he didn't believe me. As gently as I could, I suggested he had the wrong man. Surely these maps and plans existed, but I wasn't the person with such information. I was there to listen, to observe, and to report back. I wasn't on the planning end; I was on the reporting end, the eyes and ears."

His voice rose. "His questioning and ridiculous accusations began to get to me. Every time he felt I was being impertinent, he nodded to the lieutenant on my right. On cue, the man smacked the side of my head with his open palm. Hard. I'm convinced the hearing in that ear isn't what it used to be. Eventually, he mentioned Ahmad and mapmaker in the same sentence. I didn't know what the hell he was talking about. I'd been so wrapped up in my own struggle that I'd almost forgotten about my friend.

"Wirth said, 'He is a mapmaker, no?' I laughed in his face and earned another wallop." His voice lowered. "I was bloody stupid, letting rage get the better of me. The more that bastard clouted me, the angrier I became. And he wanted it—a perfect excuse to do what he did next."

William covered his face. He'd share no more. He couldn't. His father had been right: Pain was private—something to be buried, forgotten.

He needed to get out of here.

He paused at the library's door, doorknob in hand, waiting for Olivia to urge him back to the sofa and for his chance to tell her how ridiculous she was to think that reliving this torment would erase it.

But she didn't. Stealthy as a Cornish house sprite, she came to his side, her touch gentle.

He sighed. "Ahmad wasn't a mapmaker. He worked for his father, who owned an open-air market selling Egyptian wares to tourists. Their business had suffered because of the war, even that early." Ahmad had dreamed of leaving the trade, of leaving Egypt and exploring new places. "He would've loved to have been a mapmaker."

Olivia's hand rested reassuringly on his arm like a tiny anchor.

"Wirth nodded to his henchmen. They left and returned with

Ahmad. His head was still covered, and his legs wobbled. They removed the canvas. I saw dark circles that hadn't been there hours earlier. He was terrified.

"Wirth asked if I knew him. 'Of course,' I answered, as though he was an idiot." William squeezed his temples. "Wirth couldn't wait to tame my impudence. This time, he delivered the blow himself. It knocked me to the floor."

His voice cracked. "Ahmad knew he was at death's door. I'd never seen a person so frightened before, not even in Norway, when men saw their comrades massacred in front of them.

"Wirth put the pistol to Ahmad's head, the pistol he'd hit me with. 'You swear on the life of your friend that he is indeed no mapmaker?'

"I shouted 'Yes!'

"Wirth shot him. He shot him anyway. In the head, no more questions. He went down, and I realized I wasn't far behind."

He leaned into Olivia's open arms, exhausted. She led him back to the sofa and asked if he'd like to be alone. He nodded and fell back onto the cushions, where her warmth still lingered. He nuzzled into it and the blanket she draped over him. After a light kiss on his forehead, she left him alone with his memories and his father's disappointment, cast from above the fireplace.

After supper, they retired to the library. Olivia leant against the armrest of the sofa, her legs draped across William's lap, and picked up reading *Jamaica Inn* where they left off the night before.

This proved difficult. Instead of listening to the story, William searched out wisps of her hair, tugging them gently or weaving them between his fingers. His hands, obsessed with the contours of her face, prevented her from seeing the words in the book. There wasn't much point in continuing.

"Never mind, then."

She dropped the novel to the floor as William drew her face even closer. His kisses grew fervent, seasoned with sadness and shame. She matched their ardor, imparting forgiveness and understanding. Bent on soothing him, she spread kisses down his neck. The button at his collar took a moment to release and as she did so, an eager hand arrived at her breast. She nudged forward, and like a flame set to dry leaves, William's passion flared. Before she could blink, he had her horizontal on the sofa where, hours ago, he'd fallen apart. His mouth caressed her jaw and neck as he tugged the top of her dress. Her bare shoulder melted under the warmth of his rapid breath.

Then he sat up.

Remorse tainted his handsome face in the flickering firelight. Though his legs still straddled her eager body below, he had reined in his hands and mouth. She had a mind to ask him what the hell he was doing. Desperate, she peeled away more of her dress and unhooked the back of her unimaginative brassiere. He moved to lift himself off her, but she seized his hand and placed it on her bare breast.

The maneuver worked. A groan in the form of her name crawled from his throat, and he brought his mouth to her ear.

"We're not doing this here," he whispered before delivering a rough kiss and latching his teeth to her earlobe. "I want you in my bed."

Loose garments in hand, Olivia barely got them both up the stairs safely. Laughter and the clatter of their missteps echoed throughout the silent house. Lips bound, they stumbled into William's bedroom, dimly lit by the corridor light. He kicked the door closed behind them.

At the edge of his bed, William slowed their frenzied tempo by raising her hands to his mouth. One by one, he kissed her fingers before finishing the job she'd begun in the library. In under a minute, her dress was in a bundle at her feet. Her stockings and knickers followed.

She'd never been naked with a man before, yet the embarrassment she once worried would keep her clothed remained at bay. Arousal thickened her breath, and she shivered.

"Are you cold?" His mouth headed south to her cupped left breast.

"No. It's just, I've never done this before."

He lifted his head to hers. "We don't have to—"

There was no backing out. Not letting him finish, she kissed his mouth and pressed her bare form into his fully clothed one. He hiked her leg around his hip and tumbled them onto his bed.

He searched her with his hands, as his eyes would have, if he'd had use of them. His mouth explored her too, whilst at the same time, he removed his clothes. She rose to help, but he wouldn't have it. With a gentle push, he whispered for her to lie still. Back at her side, his tongue tickled skin and attended to her breasts as if they'd been sprinkled with confectioner's sugar.

Meanwhile, adept fingers coaxed her legs apart before carrying out a sophisticated dance at their slippery apex. Her eyes fluttered in surrender. He flattened his lips onto her thigh, and they too joined the endeavor, delivering a mad ecstasy Olivia could hardly work out. Scarcely able to catch her breath, her mouth received his again whilst he commandeered her hips.

A quick jerk joined their bodies for the first time. It hurt. But then his movements became measured and massaged her core in pleasurable, pulsating waves. Like tall grasses on a breezy day, the two moved as one. At the peak of his passion, William cried her name before showering her face with kisses and declarations of love.

In silence, their pulses moderated and all Olivia could do was smile. Swaddled in her lover's arms, she'd finally grown up. She'd heard mixed reviews about losing one's virginity; some said their romantic expectations had been dashed and referred to sex as something one suffered through.

She hardly suffered.

"Had you an exotic mistress, in Egypt perhaps, who taught you how to seduce women?"

"I seduced you, is it?" William said, twisting hanks of her hair that fell down her back.

He was right. She'd have done anything to be where she was, naked in his arms. She giggled into his neck.

"I wonder if Dr. Butler knows he'd sent such a siren to care for me?" he murmured.

"A siren?"

"I tried very hard to ward off your temptations, Nurse Talbot, but you had me in your snare." He yawned and pulled her so that her head rested on his chest. "There was nothing for it but to surrender."

She trusted he was teasing, clearly happy with her advances. Surely he didn't think her promiscuous. Her mother had warned how little respect men bore for women who let lust replace their virtue, women who disregarded consequences and sought only to fulfill their carnal needs. Men never married girls who were "easy," as she'd called them. Yes, Olivia's needs had reached a level she could no longer ignore—but she wasn't "easy." Was she?

She needed to see his eyes, then she'd know for sure and would rest easier. She moved to switch on the light, but below her, William's breathing had changed. He was already asleep.

His steady heartbeat in her ear did little to soothe her. She let herself get carried away, and her greedy want of him had ruined the high regard he once had for her. From now on, conversation would be stilted, and if he still wanted to hold her hand, the intent behind it would be a mystery.

Under the weight of shame and her mother's reproach, she closed her eyes. Perhaps she wasn't so grown up after all.

# CHAPTER 19

THEY ARRIVED LATE for breakfast in the sitting room the next morning, but not as late as the day before. Though Mrs. Pollard made no comment, her displeasure was evident. Her stern eyes magnified the imagined judgments of Olivia's parents, Dr. Butler, and even William himself. The only words Mrs. Pollard uttered had to do with the erratic weather forecast and Jasper's need for a walk. William guiltily suggested they take him on a late-morning outing.

Happy to escape the housekeeper's unfurling chill, Olivia hastened to the foyer to help William into his boots and greatcoat. The weather Mrs. Pollard spoke of hadn't arrived yet, but it was best to be prepared. Foul weather never trickled into Cornwall; it gushed.

They crunched across the gravel around the garage, behind Jasper's swaying tail. Nose down and course set, he led them well past the slumbering vegetable patch and glasshouse to a run-down shed barely visible amidst an entanglement of broom and gorse.

And just in time. The sun dimmed and chilly winds blew clouds into a churning squall above their heads. Rain fell.

Olivia pulled William under the shed's eaves while Jasper, uninterested in going back indoors, plopped down in the long grass and rolled on his back. Peeling paint the color of a young fern floated to the ground as she creaked the door open. The shed was airless and still. She squeezed William's hand and reminded him to step carefully on the uneven floorboards. Cobwebs connected red curtains to the windows they flanked. Through them, thick vines blocked the sky and the garden beyond. Above, raindrops pounded the roof as if cast from giant slingshots.

"This place makes me sad," she said, her breath fogging the partitioned panes.

He wrinkled his nose. "Does it? What's it like, besides dreadfully stuffy? I can't say I've ever been in here."

Dangerous items like axes, mauls, and even a chain saw lined one of the rough-hewn walls. Any free space was littered with shovels of all sizes, garden hoes, and rakes. In one corner, clay pots stood in squat stacks. Clumps of decaying root balls littered the top of a splintered potting bench.

Olivia described all of it whilst searching the low ceiling for spiders. Despite the shed's neglect and the dust that clung to it like sand to wet feet, the structure held a certain appeal. She pictured their refuge as a child would, the four walls a sanctuary —a playhouse even, where a little girl might have tea and read Beatrix Potter books to her stuffed animals or cat.

"A thorough cleaning and some paint, and it'd make a charming retreat."

"You're welcome to it. Perhaps when the weather improves." He seemed distracted. In fact, he'd been quiet since they woke when he kissed her forehead sweetly and was out of bed as though escaping any reminder of their night together.

"Is something bothering you?"

"A lot on my mind, I suppose."

She couldn't bear to see his regret so she kept her eyes on the warped panes of the window.

"What happened last night, Olivia, what we did—I don't want you to think I consider it lightly, because I don't."

This was it. They made love and he was through with her. Any decency he thought she had disappeared as soon she removed her brassiere in the library.

But he was wrong. She had morals. He was her first and, she hoped, her last. "Will—"

"Olivia, I want you to marry me."

The rain stopped; amplified gusts battered the shed from all directions.

She must've misheard him.

"I should've asked weeks ago. I love you. I want you to be my wife—to always be with me. Forever." His words picked up speed. "I know I'm damaged goods, not an ideal package of a husband. You don't have to answer me today. But I wanted to ask, informally, at least. This must seem like it's coming from nowhere, standing in this shack. Not at all romantic."

As his proposal petered into blithering nonsense, words like *wife* and *forever* cleaved to Olivia like sticky burrs. Her worries had been for naught. William respected her character. He loved her as she loved him.

She rose on her toes and brought her lips to his.

Relief sent his eyebrows skyward, and he enfolded her in both arms. "Is that a yes?" His breath bled onto her cheek where he rested his mouth.

"Of course it's a yes."

"Thank heavens." He pulled away, his face dreadfully serious. "Can we keep the news to ourselves? For a short time? Would you mind terribly?"

She couldn't think of a thing she wanted more than to be Mrs. William Morgan. Shouting it to the world would be icing on the cake. Then again, she'd been away from her family and friends for months. They—her mother—would ask a slew of uncomfortable questions. The last thing she wanted was her mother minimizing her newfound happiness.

"I don't mind."

"I have things to do before asking you properly. I realize we're in the middle of a war, but there are a few traditions I'd like to uphold, you under—"

The room flashed just before the eruption overhead. The thunderclap bellowed with the fury of a hundred air strikes.

Arms out, William hurtled Olivia to the floor. His forearms broke their fall, and his body protected her like a cage from whatever might come at them from above.

Nothing came.

His voice was an unsure whisper. "That was thunder?"

"That was thunder."

She was dismayed by the ferocity with which he shook. Dirt and dead leaves stuck to her hands as she propped herself up. Eager to change the subject, she kissed his chin.

"Bloody hell," he said, his face cut with angry lines. "I told you, I'm damaged. Broken."

He moved to stand, but her prolonged kisses held him fast.

"Not broken," she whispered. "A little bent, love, but not broken. Nothing we can't iron out with time."

She let one elbow collapse and drew him closer. Her mouth consumed his whilst she wrenched a leg free and coiled it around his calf.

Once he could breathe properly, he said, "How clever you are, Nurse Talbot. Is diversion something they teach in nursing school?"

"It is," she said with a giggle, "and as your nurse, I suggest we leave this cold shack and withstand the jaunt through the storm so you can rest. And once we're back in your room, Major, I'll need to help you out of your wet clothes. I'd hate for you to catch cold."

~

"Ahmad's execution was only the beginning," William said. They lay on his bed, a warm fire at their feet and a setting of tea at the bedside. The weight of Olivia's head on his chest eased him into continuing his tale. "Wirth recognized early that the best way to torture me was to hurt or threaten innocent people in my life. Days after Ahmad's death, they moved me to a cell with a wooden bunk, a metal table, and a chair. I even had a window—a tiny square, really, too high to see out of. At least it gave me light.

"They questioned me again about maps and connections, accusations I continued to deny. When the guards returned me to my new cell, there was a handful of photographs on the table. The first was of my friend Omar's wife, Bahiti."

He fought to remember Bahiti as she was when he'd first met her. Warm and welcoming, she'd made William feel a part of their family.

He tightened his arm around Olivia's hip. "They'd gagged her and tied her wrists together. The next photograph showed Omar beside her in the fetal position, gagged as well. He looked dead. The horror in Bahiti's eyes killed me."

Olivia sat up, freeing his hold on her.

"I tore the pictures into pieces, shouting every German expletive I knew." He'd never forget the rage of that day. Or the fear. "Two grinning lieutenants secured my wrists and brought me back to Wirth. I demanded he tell me where my friends were. He assured me they were close. Smug bastard. He admitted they'd been brought solely to get to me. He knew they were innocent."

Olivia seemed a million miles away, so he sat up as well, determined to keep her close.

"I was frantic. I repeated the same things I'd been saying since my arrival, that he had the wrong man, that I had no information for him. He was pleased by my familiar babble, which set him up for his next move."

He paused. His memory of what happened next could not be relayed in great detail. He didn't want Olivia having nightmares too.

"They brought Bahiti in first, Omar right after. They threw him to the floor, and she was—she was raped." In front of him, in front of her husband, she was flattened against a wall and violated by a handful of men. Wirth had watched, his eyes not on the assault but on William. "She called my name. Over and over, she begged me to help. I fought to free myself until my wrists bled and the brutes knocked me to the floor. I screamed for them both. I pleaded to Wirth to let them go because I had nothing, absolutely nothing to tell him.

"All he did was smile."

William brought his hand to his face. It was wet when he took it away.

"Her calls will never leave me. In my nightmares, she accuses me of killing her and Omar, and I did. She floats above my bed at night, repeatedly asking why I did nothing to help them. All I can do is say how bloody sorry I am."

Olivia thrust a handkerchief into his hand. He wiped his face.

"I should've given the Nazis what they wanted." Even if the nightmares ended and his senseless fears ceased to exist, the guilt at causing their deaths would plague him forever. "If I'd told them what they wanted to hear sooner, maybe my friends would still be alive."

Olivia bent forward. "How could you have given them what they wanted if they had the wrong man?"

He toppled back onto his pillow. "I can't talk about this any more today. I'm sorry."

She didn't understand. She would never understand. He was a fool to think anyone, even his beloved Olivia, ever could.

157

# CHAPTER 20

"HOW'S OUR MAN, NURSE TALBOT?" Dr. Butler asked, seating himself in the stout wooden chair next to William's desk in the library. It was the two of them—a quick debrief, he explained, before examining the major. The doctor had phoned a full day before his arrival, creating a wakeful night for Olivia. She'd have to answer each of his questions carefully, so as to not let leak that she'd fallen madly in love with their patient.

"Better, sir. As you're aware, the major's paranoia has vanished and his depression is far less prevalent."

She kept herself from tugging at the neck of her stiff uniform. The fire James laid moments earlier was roaring, a normally welcome comfort that felt stifling this morning.

"All good to hear," he said. "And how are the nightmares?"

"Infrequent, for over a month." In fact, the last serious nightmare had been about her. She swallowed, realizing that after that horrific night, everything between them had changed. Now they were a couple, an inseparable pair, unofficially engaged and exceedingly in love.

"Interesting. What's changed?"

"Changed?"

"Yes, what are you giving him before bed that's helping him sleep? Have you got a hold of more of your grandmother's tea?" He snickered.

"I—no." Her mouth went dry. In all her imagined conversations with Dr. Butler, she hadn't once considered that he might ask how William's nightmares had subsided or why.

"Then you're positive they're 'infrequent,' as you say? Has the major told you this? You've explained how he made a terrible uproar, enough to wake the house at times. Do you think perhaps he's become quieter in his restlessness? How do you know for certain he's not having the nightmares?"

She tried not to smirk as she pictured herself in William's arms, there to comfort him at the slightest whimper, but she marshaled her composure. "I've spoken with him, sir. He's sleeping more soundly, and I believe it's because he's talking about his experiences."

There. That sounded quite reasonable. She sat taller, relieved.

"I beg your pardon?"

"He's been telling me about his time as prisoner in North Africa."

"And why on earth would he do that, Nurse Talbot?"

"Well, because I—I suggested it." She raised her eyes bravely and kept them there. "I thought if he discussed his ordeals during his waking hours, perhaps his sleeping hours wouldn't be so full of them. Whenever I was down as a child, my mother always said I'd feel better if I aired out my misery, in writing or by talking. I suggested both methods to the major, and he was willing to try."

He closed his eyes and sighed as if she were a simpleton. Lines she'd never seen before dug a chasm between his brows.

"My dear Nurse Talbot." He began gently, but irritation quickly whittled away his decorum. "These aren't the whimsical and insignificant troubles of a schoolgirl with a broken heart or a lost puppy." He slapped the top of his clipboard, almost sending it to the floor. "Giving these experiences the light of day could have dangerous consequences. It's too soon for this, far too soon. He's still grieving the death of his father." He folded his hands but appeared too agitated for such a calm gesture, so he jerked at his tie and adjusted himself in his chair instead. "And if discussing these recollections *is* helping him sleep, which I seriously doubt, he shouldn't be talking to *you* about them. He requires a trained physician, an expert in psychoneurosis."

Olivia bit her lip, her eyes never wavering.

"Well, I suppose this may be a good time for you to take your leave," he concluded, "before more harm is done. Your father said you wished to leave Keldor by the end of March if possible, and we're close to meeting that mark, are we not?"

Her rage was replaced by a wave of nausea. "You wish for me to leave Keldor, sir?" She'd forgotten all about the deal she'd made with her father, back when the thought of living at some remote country estate seemed more confining than a nunnery.

"You were interested in a children's hospital, correct? Perhaps caring for children is more your forte, hmm?" He winked as though he'd never been cross with her.

"Sir, I—"

"Not to worry. I'll still give you the glowing recommendation I promised. How does Edinburgh sound? You have relations up there somewhere, don't you? Should be a tad safer than London —in the eyes of your parents, that is. Not that anywhere is safe these days." He pushed up his glasses and jotted some notes. "And I'm happy to keep this little muck-up between the two of us. We needn't tell your father unless you wish to. Is that agreeable, Nurse Talbot?"

He didn't wait for an answer but continued to yammer away, completely unaware of how close she was to falling out of her chair.

"I appreciate your dedication to the major, but you must remember your place. You are a nurse, not a doctor. Your job is to nurture, to offer conversation and keep the patient's mind off their distress. Your words should be nothing but sunny and supportive." He leant toward her and patted her knee. "I realize you've been without proper guidance over the past few weeks, but decisions as large as this are not for you to make, not ever. As your career moves forward, let this be a lesson to you. Are we clear?"

He peered over the glasses resting on the bridge of his nose.

"Yes, Doctor," she said, lowering her woeful head.

"Good girl. Now then, would you collect the major?"

Olivia made haste for the sitting room. Heated strides brought her to William's side, where her white skirt, stiff as a thick paper napkin, brushed his knees.

"What's the matter?" he asked.

She could have wept at how well he knew her. Keeping her voice low, she explained: "Dr. Butler says I've done a terrible thing suggesting that you talk about North Africa. I wouldn't have mentioned it, except he asked why you were sleeping better. I thought it wiser to say you were sharing your trauma with me than your bed—"

A noise somewhere between a whimper and a giggle burst from her mouth. Her head was spinning, and she leant into him. He swiftly wrapped his arm around her waist, giving her the comfort she needed and the impetus to continue.

"He says you're not ready to talk, and if you were, you certainly shouldn't speak to me, because I've no idea what I'm doing. And because I'm a complete failure and he's worried I'll do more damage, he's sending me to Edinburgh."

"Edinburgh?" he said with a laugh.

She nodded miserably. "To work at the children's hospital there, an opportunity I'd have died for when I entered nursing. Dr. Butler promised me a shining reference to work anywhere I

liked if I stayed here at least six months, which I haven't. Not yet."
Another small sob escaped her. "This is a dismissal. I've failed.
I've failed you. I've failed Dr. Butler. I've failed my parents;
they're going to be crushed."

She'd ranted enough. What would William think after seeing
this side of her, the petulant one her mother despised and whose
ugly head still reared up from time to time?

William cradled her face. "No matter what Dr. Butler says,
you haven't failed me. You could never fail me. He's merely
offering you Edinburgh assuming that's what *you* want. Dr.
Butler may have arranged this job for you, but you don't work for
him. You work for me." He found the top of her head with his lips
and kissed it. "Let's go meet the doctor. And don't fret, Nurse
Talbot. I'll sort it out."

Dr. Butler and William came out of the library shoulder to
shoulder like old mates.

"Well, Nurse Talbot, it seems I owe you an apology," the
doctor proclaimed.

He nodded toward William, and they both laughed.

Olivia sprang from her chair in the receiving room, eyeing
William, whose lighthearted grin did nothing to cure her
puzzlement.

"Your patient appears to be in superb shape, aside from his
blindness, of course. I must say I wasn't expecting such progress
in his physical *or* mental condition. Well done, Nurse Talbot, well
done indeed."

The doctor's jovial smile faded as he turned toward his
patient. "Now, William, you said your depression is still present.
Like you, I can't say if it will ever abate completely, but the next
obvious phase would be the return of your vision. Nurse
Talbot"—he nodded toward her—"continue as you are with the

major, despite my earlier remarks. I'm back in Cornwall for good this time. Therefore, I'm available should you need me for anything—if sleeping habits change, if the depression increases, or heaven forbid, if the paranoia returns."

Dr. Butler patted William's shoulder before finding his hand and shaking it. He shook Olivia's hand as well and then took his leave.

"What just happened?" Olivia asked once they were alone.

She walked into William's outstretched arm and allowed herself to become enfolded in it. As soon as he had both around her, he pinned her against the closest wall, his breath hot near her ear. "I told the doctor of my plan to ask you to be my wife. He promised to keep it a secret."

They hadn't spoken of the proposal for days. "And he took the news well?"

"Very well. A little shocked at first, but he quickly warmed to the idea. Edinburgh's no longer a concern. I'm afraid the children there will have to contend with some other nurse." His left hand caressed her face whilst his right arm molded round her waist, smoothing the starched fabric of her nurse's attire. He frowned. "What have you got on?"

"My uniform," she grumbled. "I'm going upstairs to take it off."

"Excellent. I'll help."

# CHAPTER 21

"I STILL WONDER IF I'd lied from the beginning, would my friends have lived?"

It had been one week since Dr. Butler's visit. William had continued to share his North Africa memories, although the "sessions," as Olivia referred to them, were becoming mere snippets of memories, out of order and incomplete. His tale was nearing its end, drawing closer to the elements that filled him with dread.

Tonight, though, he talked nonstop and she let him. Normally, talk of his time as prisoner so close to bedtime was against her rules, for fear the dark memories might prevent him from getting any sleep. Maybe she wanted him to get the inevitable over with. He nestled his head safely in her lap as they sipped brandy in between his accounts. The wireless had been switched off and replaced with the crackle of wood in the hearth.

"I started telling him stories—extensions, really, of the ideas Wirth had planted in my head. It was easy. Most of his questions required yes-or-no answers, and even weak as I was, I knew which would satisfy him. I figured if I stopped being a defiant ass, he'd eventually let me go.

"As the weeks passed, the more elaborate my stories became. I

164

started believing them myself, something I didn't realize until after I'd returned home. I told him I'd lived in London with my wife and three children. In January, I'd signed on as a spy for General Wavell, feeding him information leaked by the Italians about plans to declare war on Britain and France, including the location of their initial attacks. I named places I was familiar with, claiming they had something to do with the information Britain sought. By then, Italy had declared war. Battles raged in the desert. I heard fighting from my cell—the long-reaching booms, the ones that rattle your gut."

He closed his eyes. "The tales poured out of me. The flat I grew up in and lads from school materialized like actual memories. I told him how my family went to Brighton for my tenth birthday—a lie. I recalled the first time I kissed a girl, fumbling like an idiot by the playground swings in our neighborhood— another lie. Sometimes I wonder if Wirth poisoned the little food that was given to me or dosed my drinking water."

Like a writer creates characters, settings, and events, he'd invented a life with recollections he still remembered so clearly: his childhood flat, the neighborhood playground—even the girl. She was tall, blond, and as inexperienced as he was. As a man, he'd served under Wavell, a valuable asset that the enemy would've loved to get their hands on. Wirth's smug smile had confirmed this. Hands behind his back, he paced the room as he listened to William's stories, eager to finally report that he'd captured the right man.

William sat up. "My God, Olivia. Why didn't I think of this before?"

"What? What didn't you think of?"

"I became who he wanted me to be!" he whispered.

"That seems obvious, doesn't it?"

"Perhaps, now that I'm saying all this aloud. But it didn't occur to me then. Being this made-up person was heaven compared to the nightmare of being William Morgan—and

Wirth wanted to believe it as much as I did! It justified the murder of my friends. It kept him from failing his superiors or looking a fool to his minions. And that's why he was so upset when … when …"

"When what?"

"When he was forced to believe the truth."

Olivia placed the brandy in his hand.

He drained what was left in the snifter. The end was coming, and there wasn't enough brandy in all of England to get him through it. Not tonight.

"I can't. Not tonight."

"And I don't want you to." She kissed his forehead. "So what will it be: the wireless? Or shall we finish *Jamaica Inn?*"

Olivia groped lazily across the comfortable span of William's bed for his broad shoulders and warm body. The empty mass of damp linens woke her with a start. Powerful retching echoed from the bathroom, followed by moans of pain. She threw on her dressing gown and dashed toward the noise.

With one flick, light illuminated the kneeling, naked form in front of the toilet.

"William," she said, landing at his side.

He heaved once more before settling onto his folded legs. She seized the towel draping the tub and patted his damp face.

"What is it? Tell me. Flu? Something you ate?"

"Worse."

"I was afraid of that."

"I'm sorry, I didn't mean to wake you."

"You're shaking. Let me get—"

"No," William found her arm. "Don't leave me, please."

The harsh overhead light bounced off the green and yellow tiles, coating his bare body in peaked hues. Dark hollows beneath his cheekbones had changed her William back into Wirth's prisoner, his eyes into black wells of terror.

She smoothed the shadows sagging below them before kissing his forehead. "In a few minutes, you'll be freezing. I won't leave you for long, I promise."

In defeat, he leant back on the white wainscoting.

She returned a mere ten seconds later with his dressing gown and a face flannel. She ran the cloth under cool water from the tub and pressed it firmly upon his neck, shoulders, and chest. She lay the dressing gown over his bare legs.

"Tell me what you've dreamt."

He pinched the skin between his closed eyes. "I'm sure you can imagine."

"All right then, don't tell me about the dream. Tell me what happened as you lived it."

The pain on his face tormented her, but she knew what needed to be done.

He knew too. "Very well." Eyes closed, he rested his head back on the wall. "Some weeks before I finally escaped, two guards blindfolded me and brought me to a room I'd never been to. It was cold and smelled clean, almost clinical. Later, I did see it: a laboratory with white walls and stainless steel counters and tables."

His voice cracked. "Someone gagged me and ripped off my shirt. Chest first, I was thrown on top of a table and tied to it. Wirth was there, ranting about liars and how they deserved to be punished. He bragged about ways he'd punished his own men for lying and said as his prisoner, I could expect far worse. Then his hands were on me, stretching the skin on my back so far in places I almost cried out. I tried speaking. He laughed at my muffled drivel, so I stopped. Sulfur filled the air, and because of the chill, I felt the heat instantly. He was about to perform an experiment, he said, to see the difference between cutting skin with a cool blade versus cutting with heated metal."

He sniffed. "I'm sorry, is there no liquor up here?"

She returned as quickly as possible with the bottle of whisky from the library. She filled glasses for each of them.

"Thank you." He threw his head back, draining the glass. His eyes watered. "He said he loved art, like the führer, and complained that not enough people appreciated it. On my back, he would make a masterpiece to rival all others and as a favor, he'd photograph it so I could see it. Would you say my back looks like art?" His lips became a quivering, derisive curve.

Over the months, her eyes had memorized every mark on his back, from the time when they'd still gushed red to their sealed disfigurement. Her hands knew them, too, tracing each hardened line as lovingly as she kissed his mouth. But imagining their formation made her queasy. She lifted her glass and swallowed everything in it.

"Before every cut, he announced which blade he'd use, hot or cold. I didn't bother to reply, not a grunt or a groan. Apparently my shaking and convulsing satisfied him. He liked the reactions my body gave and told me he was glad for once not to hear my voice." He unsteadily poured more amber fluid into his empty glass. "For days, he did this to my back and legs, creating new wounds most times. Other times, he'd reopen old ones. More than once, he extinguished lit cigarettes on my back. After many tries, he determined they expired quicker with more pressure."

Olivia wiped her wet face, careful not to exhale the sorrow choking the back of her throat. He mustn't hear her grief. For his sake, she must be brave.

"That day in the glasshouse, months ago, when you helped me find those old cigarettes—do you remember? The goddamned smoke was revolting. I thought I would be sick. I fought it as hard as I could. I didn't want you to know how ill it made me. How did I do?"

So much had changed since then that it was hard to

remember the details. "You were a decent actor on some days. Other days, I saw right through you."

She took her glass and refilled it, not caring if they both got drunk tonight. It was two thirty in the morning, and though her brain remained sharp as a tack, her body tingled in that warm way a glass of whisky delivered. Beneath the unflattering light next to the toilet, she held the hand of the man she loved. The floor on which they sat felt as merciful as a giant block of ice.

There was nowhere else she'd rather be.

"Five days before I killed the bastard, I was back in the lab for what I thought would be another cutting session. This time, they undressed me completely. Instead of being tied to a table, my arms and legs were spread and trussed to a wall, my face smashed against it. Wirth and I were alone, or that's what he said." William emptied the remaining whisky down his throat. "It doesn't bloody well matter, anyway."

The words flew faster and faster. "He'd become bored with cuts and burns, but I could tell he wasn't ready to kill me yet, though I knew it would be soon. He beat me again, with what I couldn't tell you. When he was tired of that, he prodded me with something else, maybe a poker from a fireplace. Then, before I knew it, he—"

For weeks, she'd listened without response, a silent pillar of strength until disgust sent her scurrying to her room, where she found release by screaming into her pillow. She'd fall still then, silently weeping for every terrified hour he'd spent in that horrid place. And though each session had been a stepping-stone to this darkest moment, its truth was impossibly heavy. She was reaching for another drink when William's labored breath reminded her to quit thinking of herself.

"He tore me apart in the worst way imaginable." William's words poured out of his mouth like hot tar. "There's no more to tell you except that my soul died that day. Oh, Christ—"

He pitched over the porcelain bowl, spilling her whisky and

almost knocking over the decanter. Abysmal groans rose from deep within his belly.

She rested one hand on his scarred back. The other caressed his neck with the damp flannel as her own tears joined the brown liquid on the floor.

A heady vapor of rose and verbena settled around the pair in the tub. Replenished by clean teeth and a warm bath, William finally stopped shaking. He drew strength from Olivia, who sat between his legs, encircled in his arms. The tiled room echoed with the occasional slosh of water and sporadic sob.

"Talk to me," she whispered, turning her cheek to his opened mouth.

From what he could tell, she'd neither judged him nor indicated she thought him weak. She was nothing like his father. He drew a long shuddering breath. He could continue.

"It happened more than once," he whispered against her cheek. "Each time, I became less of a man, less of a human. In my cell, I picked at any lesion I could reach, hoping for infection and death."

With his cheek resting on her shoulder, he locked his arms more tightly around her. "He knew he'd tortured the fight out of me. I was compliant; by then, I deserved the abuse. Bound hands and blindfold were no longer necessary. When I was brought to the lab, I stripped without objection. No doubt he considered me a willing submissive."

William's heart rate spiked, and he sat taller. "But that last day, when he chained my right ankle, something awoke in me. Maybe it was the flash of the silver pommel at his waist. I'd never seen him without his dagger, and it'd caught my eye more than once. Seeing it this time resurrected enough of me to recall my training in close-quarters combat. Killing this man should've come to me as naturally as saluting a superior officer." He could count the number of men he'd killed directly on both hands. Taking a life had never given him pleasure—until that day. "My rage had been smothered by self-loathing, but at that moment it consumed me, and I welcomed it like an old friend.

"When he reached for my second ankle, I stomped his hand with my foot. I found enough strength to unsheathe his dagger, and before he grasped what was happening, I cut his throat." Wirth's confusion had turned to anger in seconds, but it was already too late. "In my state, he should've been able to over-power me, but he had no reason to expect it. He had no idea what he was dealing with. Perhaps if he'd done his research in the first place, he might've known."

He ran a hand through his wet hair, raining drops onto his eyelashes. "The building was a maze of dark passageways and locked doors, but when I left it appeared to be empty. I heard nothing except my own hammering feet. I assume the place had been evacuated—and Wirth, in his disgrace and madness, had stayed behind.

"I made it outside and ran far from the camp, away from the sounds of battle. I remember sand, bloody sand, everywhere. After that, I don't remember anything else except waking on the hospital ship, where all I saw was black."

He'd shared his name, rank, and that he'd been a Nazi pris-oner. Nothing else. "In Plymouth, army superiors threw ques-tions at me, but I wouldn't talk. Anyone with the impudence to keep badgering me bore the brunt of my bitterness, no matter who they were. They summoned kind Dr. Butler from Cornwall, and he made sure I was sent home, declaring my mental state 'extremely delicate.' The man's known me my entire life. What a shock he must have had when first he saw me. He drove me to Keldor himself." William's voice dropped. "And on the way, he told me my father was dead."

It was the only thing he remembered from the drive—that

and the endless fear that the doctor would ask questions. No more questions.

"I was almost relieved at the news. I could never tell him what had happened to me. He would've considered me a coward for allowing Wirth to abuse me in such a way. He would never have forgiven me for such weakness."

"Do you still believe that?" she asked. "After what you've told me of how you were tortured and brainwashed? And what of your brave escape?"

"I can't say. That will take time to sort out."

"Do you forgive you?"

"Sorry?" he barked, though he didn't mean to.

"What about you? Have you forgiven yourself for what happened?"

Her question overwhelmed him. "I don't know, Olivia. I don't know."

# CHAPTER 22

WILLIAM EMERGED from the coastal path with Mrs. Pollard at his side. Rain had moved in, and both were in need of a cup of tea. She'd been a sport getting him outside whilst Olivia trained WVS recruits at Dr. Butler's surgery. Jasper jaunted ten strides ahead, Mrs. Pollard said, looking back occasionally to check if they were still coming.

Olivia's upcoming journey to Plymouth topped the afternoon's conversation. Olivia's mum would be there to move her recently widowed great Aunt Hilda to London. Her cousin Katie, newly posted as a Wren in Plymouth, would be there too. William shared Olivia's enthusiasm at getting to see family again after so many months.

Apparently Polly was happy about it, too. "What do you think Dr. and Mrs. Talbot would say if they knew their daughter slept in her employer's bed night after night? I know you intend to marry the girl and you be waiting on your mother's ring so you can propose 'properly,' but God doesn't care a tithing about a ring. He does care about people living in sin, like, as do I. Nurse Talbot's parents do as well, I'm sure."

William swept his white cane and kept walking. This wasn't

the first time God had been disappointed with him, and it wouldn't be the last. In the end, all would be made right. As soon as the ring arrived, he would phone Dr. Talbot for his blessing, and then he'd ask Olivia to be his wife the way he'd intended: at Steren Cove, on one knee and as close to sunset as he could manage. He hoped Mrs. Pollard hadn't complained to Olivia as well. Knowing Olivia, Polly's disapproving expression alone would be enough to make her uncomfortable.

So engrossed was he in his private thoughts that he never noticed the quiet whir in the distance, mingling naturally with the shuffling of branches and the calls of local birds, until it drew close, buzzing toward them like an angry hornet. He didn't need sight to know its source: a German Luftwaffe warplane, careening toward them so fast that the ground trembled.

In his mind's eye, his men scattered below the shadows of sharp cliffs and into the cold sea, unable to find cover. Their shouts rang in his ears; their haunted faces, open-mouthed and pale, bobbed in the water. The warplane whizzed closer. What came next would be much louder than the rumble of thunder.

He broke free of his reverie. He had to get them out of here.

Propellers whined, and bullets struck the ground with dogged force. If he could get them back under the trees, they might survive. They couldn't be far from the tree line. He grabbed Mrs. Pollard and dragged her toward the shrouded footpath. Her indecipherable questions added to his dark chaos. He ignored them.

"We've got to run, Polly. Toward the trees, now!"

He dropped the white cane; he moved faster without it. Hitting a tree head-on would be nothing compared to suffering a strike from above. Bullets tore into the turf around them. Clumps of grass and dirt pelted his exposed skin, stinging it.

"William!" Polly shrieked.

He'd lost his hold on her. She clutched at his side in a flurry as she went down. He fell beside her, but only for a moment.

Above the plane's dwindling drone and Jasper's frantic barks, her voice rang loud and clear. "The bugger's leaving, William. Please—I can't run anymore."

"He'll be back—and yes, you can. Now get up, Polly. That's an order!"

He stood and tugged, almost too forcefully. He teetered. The buzzing grew louder. As predicted, their adversary was making a turn back for another go.

"We're going to die out here!"

"No, we aren't."

William regained his balance and led them, he hoped, toward the trees. Bullets hissed, tracing their every step. He pictured his meadow pocked with divots like a battlefield awaiting to embrace two more bodies. He coughed and struggled to open his eyes, which were coated with soil and burning badly.

His pace slowed amidst the tangle of brush catching at his ankles. With his free hand, he patted the air for tree trunks. Finding one, he reached for more, tugging Polly the entire time. Once they were deep enough in the bramble, he dropped, pulling her flat beside him.

"Get on your belly and as far under the brush as you can."

She let out a muffled scream and lurched forward.

"Lie still!"

"But Jasper! He's frightened. He doesn't know what to do. I think he's run away!"

"That means he's alive."

The pair lay flat and silent through a third onslaught. William's grip on Mrs. Pollard's wrist was fierce, as were the thorns snagging their clothing and skin.

Finally, the menacing sound faded south.

He loosened his grip. "Are you all right, Polly?"

"I—I think so."

Every muscle pulsed with adrenaline, and he fought the urge to stand and run it out. His eyes, mostly cleared of dirt, blinked open to a blurry stone fortress looming over the shredded green-

and-brown vista. The round figure of Mrs. Pollard, her hair in fuzzy disarray, materialized before him.

"Mr. William, what is it?" she asked, kneeling beside him. "Are you hurt? Were you hit?" She smoothed his hair back from his face.

"No, Polly." His eyes met hers. "I can see."

~

Captain Dinham had already phoned by the time the bedraggled pair returned. James, highly agitated, hurried William to the receiving room, where Annie stood by the waiting telephone. James had been stoking the fire in the sitting room when the gunfire had drawn him to the window. He couldn't spot the plane, yet the scrim-covered panes had rattled as though they'd shatter. He'd grabbed Annie, and together they'd run to the wine cellar.

James's shaky voice rose as he asked after their well-being. Were they hurt? Would the villain return? Mrs. Pollard, patting his shoulder with her cleaner hand, led James and Annie away so William could deal with the captain.

With no time to appreciate his fuzzy yet regained vision, William listened to the captain's update. The south coast of Cornwall was in an uproar. Falmouth had been machine-gunned yet again, and numerous witnesses had seen a single plane separate from the group and head northeast, skirting the southern coast. The plane had taken shots at Portloe and Gorran Haven before reaching Mevagissey.

William thanked Dinham for the call and rang off. He and Polly had survived. What-ifs were unnecessary.

His heart pounded, but not out of fear. Ignoring the waves of blurriness and the translucent, asymmetrical shapes swimming everywhere he looked, he let exhilaration at seeing the well-known objects of his family home crowd out his unease. Like a familial embrace, the wing-backed chairs and stout hearth calmed him. He lifted his hands, still callused and etched with deep, telling lines. Through caked mud and smears of red, he recognized his boyhood scars. The last time he'd seen them, they'd been covered in blood.

After finding Jasper near the shed, spooked but safe, William retired to his bedroom, thinking only of Olivia's arrival home. This would be her celebration, too. The prospect of seeing her— every inch of her—for the first time was so thrilling that he turned down luncheon.

Outside his bedroom window, the rain fell in sheets. Impatience shifted him up and down on his toes. When the hell would she get here?

"William! Mrs. Pollard?"

Finally.

Urgent footfalls came up the stairs. Her cool arms embraced him from behind; her face dampened his linen shirt. "Darling, are you all right?"

Unable to wait any longer, he turned and folded her in his arms. "I'm fine. We're all fine, even Jasper."

She pressed her face into his neck. "Oh, thank God."

She tried lifting her wet head, but he held it still, smothering it in kisses. Her disorderly halo of glorious golden strands did rather match that of spent grass. But it glinted, too, like a wheat field in autumn.

He laughed.

"What?" she asked, trying futilely to raise her head.

"I was right about your hair. It *is* golden. In fact, I'd say you're more of a blonde than a brunette."

She forced her head up. Her deep-set brown eyes searched his —and for the first time, he searched back. A surge of desire tethered him to her as he appraised the widening almonds and sharpening circles of black and brown at their center. Cherubic cheeks, remnants of a healthy childhood that had yet to be completely shed, reddened above full lips.

How incredibly lovely she was.

Her hand went to her mouth, as though he'd crowned her May Queen.

"It came back," he whispered. "The plane, its noise, its proximity—I couldn't let the bastard take us, and I didn't."

"Oh, William! That's wonderful, darling!"

Her arms went round his neck. Then she abruptly dropped back from her tiptoes, her clutch gone slack.

"What is it?"

"I—I look like a drowned rat!" Her muffled words morphed into a hysterical giggle. "And, and you've never seen me before."

She buried her face in his neck.

"Olivia, let me see you."

"No."

"My love, I've glimpsed your pretty face for less than thirty seconds. Please."

"No."

Gently, he pushed her back and coaxed her face upward. Her eyelashes clung together like the ends of a wet paintbrush, and the dimples on either side of her mouth magnified her nervous smile. He smoothed his thumb along the line of her jaw and over her pink lips, the same way he had before he could see them.

"My love, you are beautiful."

He kissed her.

But instead of melting in his arms like she normally did, she remained rigid.

"Olivia, what is it?"

"A part of me always wondered if you'd be disappointed when you first saw me, and I've just ridden a bicycle over four miles in a rainstorm and I'm feel rather … ugly."

William threw his head back and laughed, hard. Before she could list more flaws, he scooped up her wet form and strode to the door. A swift kick slammed it shut before he deposited her emphatically on the bed.

"You are a stunning example of perfection, Olivia Talbot."

"Willi—"

He hushed her complaint with a kiss. His hands went to the buttons at her throat. Despite her protests, he would unwrap this package that he could finally see, and he would take his time doing it. Her uniform, saturated to pliancy, came away easily. After releasing the top three buttons, he pushed back the scratchy fabric to reveal her light pink brassiere, practical yet feminine. Modestly tucked away, her breasts took away his breath, and suddenly he was no longer intent on lingering.

"You'll pop the buttons off my uniform," she whispered, arching her back.

"Would that be a problem?"

"Not if you can sew them back on by Monday."

"I have my sight," he said in between devouring her supple skin. "I can do anything."

He sat up and tore open her uniform down to her navel. Her graceful curves, symmetrical and flawless, sent a ripple of urgency through his core. He pulled her uniform down over her hips.

"What the devil are these?" he asked, fingering the cream-colored lace hugging her waist.

"My knickers," she replied, red-faced.

"I'd no idea nurses wore such racy undergarments."

Each hipbone received a kiss before his lips moved to the hollow of her abdomen.

She inhaled sharply as his tongue traced a ring around her belly button, then propped herself up on her elbows. "Tell me what happened, in the meadow. The ground is shredded. Were you hurt?"

He lifted his head and raised an eyebrow. "Am I making you uncomfortable?"

"No." Her guilt was plain as the lovely swell of her lips. "I want to know what happened. Was Jasper with you?"

He crawled forward on his elbows and brought his face close to hers. "He was. And he was scared, but he'll recover, as will Mrs. Pollard. I'll happily relay all the details to you—later. But right now, will you allow me to indulge myself? Would you not agree that after all this time, I deserve it?" He tenderly removed a band of wet hair from her forehead. "Unless you really want me to stop. Then I will."

"I'm not used to you seeing me—"

What had happened to his seductress, the woman who taunted him with her body until he was at her mercy? She'd taken advantage of him, and by God, he wanted to tease her about it.

But not now.

"You're studying me." Her eyes sparkled like imperial topaz. "And despite the dark day, it's awfully bright in here—"

Yet again, he silenced her with his lips whilst he continued the job of removing her blasted uniform. Once she lay bare, he savored her the way a thirsty man drinks a pint of lager: in gulps. His hands already knew the curves of her hips, the topography of her breasts, and the angle of her jaw. His eyes were learning the shades of her skin, the light hairs on her arms, and the small asymmetrical birthmark above her left hip.

He prized her legs apart, finally releasing her inner temptress. She pitched her head back. Did she always look this sensual when he made love to her? This aroused him more than anything his imagination had ever marshaled. Christ, he'd missed out on so much.

He undid his trousers. He hoped she was prepared to help him make up for it.

# CHAPTER 23

"MR. WILLIAM?" Mrs. Pollard asked, pushing the library doors open an hour after Olivia had left for Plymouth. "A parcel has arrived for you."

William sat at his large desk diligently pecking away at his father's typewriter. The fact that his sight had returned had done nothing to improve his typing.

He stood. "It's about time! Bring it here, will you, Polly?"

He grabbed a pair of scissors and jabbed at its taped seams. Tucked inside the package was a cylindrical leather box fastened by a dull brass hook. He opened it to reveal a diamond ring nestled in blue velvet.

"What do you think?"

"As beautiful as ever," she said, taking it from him. "Just stunning."

She held the ring up to the window before placing it into his open palm. He smiled, recalling the kind face and gentle hands he associated with it.

"Do you think she'll like it?"

She chortled. "She'd be happy with a rubber ring."

He traced a fingertip around the ridges of platinum safe-

181

guarding a circle of small, twinkling stones. At their center, a larger diamond sparkled in the light, celebrating its escape from decades of darkness in the family vault.

He smoothed over the bigger stone with his thumb. "Will it fit her?"

"Your mother had small fingers, as does your future wife. Looks like a perfect fit."

"Excellent. I can call Olivia's father and ask for his daughter's hand." He looked up at Mrs. Pollard frankly. "I understand it's taken some time to get to this point, Polly, and we haven't been necessarily above board when it comes to our behavior. But we'll be married soon, and you'll sleep more soundly because of it. I hope."

She smoothed her apron. "Well, thank heavens for that."

"Dr. Talbot here."

"Dr. Talbot, hello. This is William Morgan. Your daughter, Olivia, is my nurse."

"Yes—Major Morgan, isn't it? Is everything all right? I thought Olivia was in Plymouth with her mother."

Despite his confusion, the man at the other end of the line sounded reasonable. This might be less torturous than William had feared.

"Yes, sir, she is indeed in Plymouth." He'd never experienced this brand of nervousness. His dry mouth was already thirsty for another cup of tea. He couldn't pause too long. "She left this morning, and all is well. I'm calling you, sir, to ask for Olivia's hand in marriage."

The line fell silent. William imagined all sorts of rejoinders: *To Olivia? But she's my little girl, my only daughter—my only child, for heaven's sake. Who are you that I should give my daughter?* William's life suddenly depended upon convincing a complete stranger that he wasn't a rake set on defiling the man's pride and joy.

"Sir?"

"Major, I'm afraid I don't understand." He drew the last word out, as if William might be playing a practical joke he didn't want to fall for.

"No, sir, I imagine you wouldn't, and I apologize. I hold your daughter in the highest regard. In fact, I wouldn't be here today if it weren't for her, sir. Despite this dark war, Olivia has illuminated my world—and for a man who can't see, that's saying a lot." He forced an uncertain chuckle at the bit he'd worked out weeks ago. "She's brought joy into my life, Dr. Talbot, an emotion I'd considered lost forever, and I love her for it. I wish to spend the rest of my life with her—with your blessing, of course."

As a soldier, he'd avoided mortar shells and bombs. As a spy, he'd escaped torture and death. He could overcome this, couldn't he?

"Well, this is rather sudden, isn't it? I mean, *marriage?*"

"Sir—"

"Major, please, take no offense, but have you any idea of how she'll respond to this proposal? I haven't spent time with her recently, as you're well aware, but had you known her a year ago, you'd realize the last thing on her mind was a relationship of any sort, let alone marriage. She's always been career-minded, dedicated to purposes far beyond her own."

William gripped the telephone cord and leaned forward. "And that's why I love her, sir. She's committed herself to my well-being since she's been here, and I intend to spend the rest of my days doing the same for her. I'm certain she'll say yes. We're in love, Dr. Talbot, and we've discussed spending our lives together. Nothing official, of course. I wanted to ask you first."

Hope sprang up within him, and thoughts of Olivia swarmed his mind: how she'd lain by his side that morning, nude and fetching, her lips so close to his, begging for another kiss. Christ, the man on the other end of the line would kill him if he knew.

"Well, it wouldn't be like Olivia to broadcast your shared affections, and I suppose you've had a decent amount of time to get to know one another."

"Yes, sir," William replied, imagining Olivia's smooth skin quivering beneath his fingertips. He swallowed, powerless against the guilt enveloping him like fog creeping over Bodmin Moor. "I assure you, my priority is your daughter's happiness. I love her, Dr. Talbot, more than I've loved anyone in my entire life."

As though digesting William's outpouring, the doctor took his time before replying. "Well then, Major, I by all means give you my blessing. What a nice surprise, truly."

"Thank you, sir. I plan on asking her as soon as she returns from Plymouth, so if you wouldn't mind not—"

"Rest assured I'll not share our conversation with Mrs. Talbot whilst she's away. I trust that close to the time she returns home, you'll have proposed properly and she can share the news with her mother on the telephone or what have you."

"Thank you, Doctor."

"Good man. Now, I'm due back for a night shift. I look forward to meeting you, Major, and to that phone call from Livvy regarding the happy news. Congratulations."

Not thirty seconds after Dr. Talbot rang off, Olivia phoned. Overjoyed at hearing her voice, he smiled despite her complaints that the line had been busy. She accepted his lie that Mrs. Pollard had been speaking with her sister and proceeded to describe her trip so far. Leaning back in his chair, he rotated her ring in his fingers and focused on her anecdotes about her aging aunt and overprotective mother.

"Mother's brought clothes for me to take back to Keldor, as well as some books. I'll see Katie Thursday, but until then, I'm helping Mother pack up Aunt Hilda. The old bird hasn't changed.

She's still as chatty as ever. She'll drive my poor aunt and uncle crazy in London."

She paused to yawn.

"Is she overworking you? You sound exhausted."

"I suppose I am. I've been on my feet since I arrived. I'd sit, if I could find a free space." She laughed.

He enjoyed her rambling and wished she were here telling her stories in person. He pictured her leaning against the wall of an old woman's stuffy house, surrounded by half-filled boxes. Her blond hair would be parted on the side, hanging straight save for the subtle curls surrounding her face. Her orange scarf, the one that brought out the small flowers in her blue skirt, would still be wrapped around her neck, offsetting her white blouse.

"And how are things there?" she asked. "Are you still following the plan?"

"What plan?"

She lowered her voice. "Your blindness. Please tell me Mrs. Pollard is still the only one who knows."

"Ah, yes, of course," he said uncomfortably.

The truth was that the day William's eyesight returned, his desire to fight had, too. Fear had buried his courage for far too long. The intruder had awakened William's true self—a soldier who'd see rights wronged until the day he died. He'd soon seek to return to active duty, though he had yet to determine how to tell Olivia.

"Be careful, will you? Don't do anything rash whilst I'm away. Have you your journal handy, in case of nightmares?"

"Yes, and Jasper's promised to keep your side of the bed warm whilst you're away."

"You're lucky my mother isn't on the line to hear that."

"In that case, I'd say *you're* the lucky one."

"You have a point there. Oh! Thank you, Mother. Mother's handed me a nightcap."

Mrs. Talbot's voice hummed through the line. "Tell the major how grateful we are for his letting you escape for a few days."

"Tell your mother she's welcome, though I'm not too keen on sleeping without you these next four nights."

"He says you're welcome, Mother, and it wasn't a problem." He could almost see the wicked smile lacing every word. "All right," she whispered. "I'll ring off. Sleep tight and think of me. I love you."

A taxi brought Katie to Aunt Hilda's at seven o'clock. From there, the girls walked to The Mast and Anchor to catch up and enjoy a half-pint. The pub was crowded for a Thursday night, and they were lucky to get a table away from the noisy revelers celebrating the coming weekend early. Like all the buildings in Aunt Hilda's neighborhood, the pub had been there for over a century, its antiquity marked by framed maritime maps, heavy anchors, and an old fishing net coated in years of dust. Olivia checked her glass for floating trespassers, then sipped her bitter hoping it would calm the upset stomach that had nagged her the past three days.

Across the table, her bubbly companion settled in. "My goodness, Livvy, all I've done is talk, talk, talk!" Katie removed her navy cap with a laugh. Opposite her dark widow's peak, her bun gave her an authoritative air that was broken whenever she opened her mouth. "You've told me nothing of what's happening with you."

Katie had hardly changed since Henry's funeral, and for that, Olivia was grateful. She'd depended upon her cousin's innate optimism more times than she could count. And though Katie could listen as well as she could talk, she wasn't quite finished on her end. So as Katie continued nattering about her desire to meet

Mr. Right and her miserable failure as a wireless telegraphist, Olivia let her.

"And so now I'm an office clerk. It's an area I'm rather clever in, really. I've always had a knack for filing." Katie's expression turned coy. "But even tucked away in that little office, I suppose I have a better opportunity of meeting that special someone than you do, since you and the major are only *friends*. How is Major Morgan? Not still paranoid, I hope? Did you have a terrible time getting a few days' leave? I know your parents are glad you're away from London, so that's something. I just hope you aren't bored to tears out there in no man's land."

Olivia's eyes blurred over the froth of her ale. She took a big gulp. "No, I can't say I'm bored. Not bored at all."

Katie's eyes widened. "Wait a minute, what's this? What's happened? He's taken a shine to you, hasn't he? And you to him. I knew it!"

Through a smile that rivaled the Cheshire cat's, Olivia shared the recent details of her life. Happy scenes from the past four months fit squarely like patterns on a quilt: the kiss underneath the mistletoe, William's declaration of love, even the loss of her virginity. This was the first time she'd spoken to anyone about the man she loved, and steeped in the compliments and congratulations of her rapt audience, she beamed like Ginger Rogers must have after her Academy Award triumph for *Kitty Foyle*.

"Why Livvy, you're absolutely radiant!" Katie exclaimed. "I've never seen you like this. I'm so happy for you. Wait—does your mother know?"

"No one knows."

"Why so secretive?"

"I'm not ready to tell my parents yet. I'm sure they'd find it all too sudden, especially Mother. Daddy would go with whatever made me happy. But it's been fun having this be our secret, the two of us, away from the war and the world. William's healing has been my priority, which not surprisingly has brought us even closer."

The miracle of his returned vision shimmered inside her, and she fought another secret smile by raising her half-pint. "We'll tell people eventually."

"All right, then. So what does your dictator-turned-Romeo look like?"

She described William as she pictured him: his tall frame capped with dark, unruly hair and slate-blue eyes that sparkled like sapphires when he laughed. She spoke little of the trauma he'd endured and more of the passion and strength he embodied. At their small table, he had a presence, which helped her miss him a little less. She smoothed her blouse over the moonstone around her neck. She'd kept it tucked beneath her neckline so far; she didn't need her mother asking questions.

"Hang on," Katie said skeptically. "Aren't you the least bit concerned that your William has no idea what you look like? What if you're not his type, if and when his sight returns?"

"He knows the color of my hair and eyes, and his hands have a marvelous way of identifying features." She grinned impishly. "But I won't deny the consideration."

"Don't get me wrong. You'll forever be the cousin I envy, with your light hair and dimpled cheeks. He'd be a fool not to think you're the bee's knees. But honestly, when I put myself in your shoes—well, I'd be worried. I mean, what happens if you find he prefers brunettes?"

"I'm not worried." William had his sight, and none of this was an issue any longer, but she couldn't tell Katie that.

Instead, she grinned, recalling a certain rainy afternoon six short days ago.

"Wait—what's that cheeky look for? What else aren't you telling me?"

It was close to nine when the girls parted.

After a warm hug, Katie laughed and cupped Olivia's face in her hand. "To think you were so bloody miserable last autumn, and now look at you. You can thank the war, I suppose. Strange how things happen, isn't it?"

Though positive, the observation left Olivia with a sense of emptiness. If only she and William could've fallen in love without the shadow of war, when an enjoyable evening out wouldn't bring with it the worry that tomorrow might be worse than today. She lifted her head as she rounded the pub's corner into darkness. Patience was what she needed, and faith—patience for the war's end, and faith they would outlive it. By then, their lives would be normal. Their children would run circles round their grandparents, and the biggest obstacles they'd face would be whether to send the children to boarding school or allow them to attend locally. William would likely want them to be sent away, as he'd been, but perhaps she could convince him otherwise.

She halted, her heart a thumping racket. The periodic nausea that'd plagued her since she disembarked in Plymouth—perhaps it wasn't motion sickness. And her chronic sleepiness as of late. No, she couldn't be pregnant. They'd been careful—hadn't they?

Visions of William holding their little one set butterflies flapping in her belly. She resumed her course at a faster pace. They'd be together the day after tomorrow. She couldn't wait.

A giggle burst from her throat just as the first siren sounded.

She hadn't forgotten the inconvenience of being caught in an air raid, especially in a strange place. She'd survived many, and though her brother had died in one, they didn't frighten her like they used to, but she needed shelter, and fast. The meager light produced by her pocket torch made it impossible to see where the scurrying feet she heard were headed.

"Hello?" she called. "Can you help me?"

Another piercing alarm drowned her voice. She was still ten minutes from Aunt Hilda's; it wasn't likely she could make it there unscathed. Perhaps she should return to the pub; she'd only gone a few blocks.

The ground beneath her feet vibrated. The planes were coming. She couldn't stay here; a sudden explosion ten doors down told her as much. Was this how Henry had felt the day he died, trapped in uncertainty and short of time?

The pub would have to do. Fixed on the luminous paint lining the pavement, Olivia ran. As she reached the intersection, she could scarcely make out the silhouette of the pub's signpost yards ahead. Close to victory, she darted across the broad street, clinging to the stout wall on the other side to hide from the demons above. She clutched her ears to protect them from their high-pitched whine.

A hard blast rocked the area. The next heaved her across the deserted street. She landed face down, her body seesawing against the high curb.

Scenes of her life flickered through her mind like film clips:

John tattling on her for sticking her tongue out at Mother.

Tea in Grandmother's garden, just the two of them.

Her interview at St. Mary Abbot's.

Henry's funeral.

William.

In the shadow of a burning market and a decimated pub she lay still, unconscious. Alone.

# CHAPTER 24

"Mr. William! Mr. William!"

The shouts shot William upright.

"What is it?" he asked, struggling to wake.

A breathless Mrs. Pollard hugged her dressing gown tightly across her large bosom. A thin cotton cap crowned her head, and a long gray braid draped her shoulder. "It's Plymouth. The city's been bombed, like. My sister phoned from Saltash saying they heard blasts for close to four hours."

Jasper jumped down from the bed as William pushed past Mrs. Pollard to his wardrobe.

"What are you doing?"

"I'm going to Plymouth," he replied, pulling up his woolen uniform trousers.

"You can't go to Plymouth. It's one in the morning. The ferries won't be running at this hour. You'll have to drive all the way to Gunnislake, and light regulations won't let you drive safely. You'll be stopped and charged a fine."

"I'll use the slit masks and go slowly. No one else will be on the road at this hour."

"And we're almost out of petrol, William." She only called him

191

"William" when she expected to get her way, and yet here she came toward him, hands out to help with his necktie.

"My father kept spare liters. Not even James knows about them."

"And your sight. Blind men don't drive. What if you're found out? What about James, when he wakes and sees you and your father's car missing?"

She tugged at his tie. Her breath was warm and smelled mildly of port. He was six again, being scolded by his loving nanny for being awake and playing with army men when he ought to have been sleeping.

"It's a sacrifice I'm willing to make."

He slipped his arms into his satin-lined olive tunic. His reflection in the mirror showed a tired man who'd aged considerably. He placed a peaked cap on his head and straightened the visor, noting the shadow it cast about his eyes. The lines of his face had become deep ravines compared to the last time he'd worn this uniform. Though fuller than they'd been in October, his cheeks resembled those of an emaciated street urchin. How Olivia found him attractive, he hardly knew.

"William!" Mrs. Pollard stepped further between him and the mirror, irritated at being ignored.

He hardly noticed. He cinched his leather belt over one more hole than he liked.

"This is a bad idea. The city is a burning war zone. Dorothy said she'd never seen flames so high."

"That's exactly why I need to go. How do I look? The uniform might help get questions answered. The more official I look, the better."

She stepped back, recognizing defeat. "I'm sure she's safe, hunkered down in a shelter waiting for the phones to turn back on so she can call you. She's used to this sort of thing, coming from London. Do you even know where you be going? There aren't signposts on the roads anymore. Home Guard's taken them all down."

"I know Plymouth. Her aunt lives on Greenbank Avenue. I'll start there."

She'd never been so hot. Olivia blinked her stinging eyes open and hoisted herself up. Pain stretched down her right side and sliced into her stomach as if she'd been filleted from breast to belly button.

As excruciating as it was, the agony was a passing considera-tion compared to the horror surrounding her. Smoke from the charred remains of town houses and businesses thickened the air. Flames sneered overhead. Massive beams, once powerful enough to support walls, lay scattered like Tinkertoys. Sirens blared between the buzzing of low-flying aircraft.

Another blast. A wall of fire toppled, smothering her with dirty heat. Olivia high-stepped between window frames and chimneys, looking for any place to take shelter. She gathered her might and cried for help. Her calls, though shrill in her own ears, couldn't cut through the sirens. The pain in her side was unbearable. She pressed her hands onto it, as if important parts might fall out if she didn't.

She finally sat on a portion of ground that wasn't burning, stooped like a beggar woman, her silhouette flickering in the glow of hell. She could escape this. She needed to find the pub. But was the pub still there? Had Katie got off all right? What was hurting so badly inside her?

Was she moving?

The ground grew farther away. Someone gripped her arms until she was turned and tossed over someone's shoulder. She screamed as her rib cage slammed against it. After an eternity of flopping like a rag doll, she was set down.

An explosion rattled the earth as soon as her feet met it. A stout woman in a nurse's uniform steadied her flailing arms. "You'll be all right. You're safe now, miss."

"She's bleeding all over the place," a deeper voice said. An old man with gray hair and wrinkles lining his grimy face shook his head with worry. "I think she's been hit."

She stood in what looked like an above-ground bunker, where mothers and grandmothers tended to children and each other, shushing fears and calming nerves. Scrapes marked their dirty faces and peeked through their tattered clothing, but no one appeared to have been struck by anything other than shards of glass or metal. If she weren't so ill, she'd help. And if the air weren't so stifling ... Was there no window?

"She hasn't been hit," said the nurse gravely, as if this were bad news. "And I can't help her here. She needs a hospital straightaway."

Vertigo swept across her vision. She might faint. She latched onto the nurse and prayed she wouldn't vomit; the pressure would shatter her rib cage. The grime in her eyes stung, producing tears that blurred her surroundings. Why were her legs and feet wet?

The nurse must have read her thoughts. Olivia followed the woman's uneasy gaze to the splotches of red that covered her skirt and shoes.

Her grip on the nurse's forearm slackened and like a drunkard, she tumbled to the ground.

# CHAPTER 25

"Blast!"

William slammed his fists into the steering wheel. There were at least two miles to go, but the car hadn't moved in twenty minutes. A line of emergency vehicles snaked in front of him, their lights just bright enough to keep them from running into one another. He was glad to see aid pouring in from neighboring towns, but wished he wasn't caught in their traffic. In the opposite lane, cars sped by, no doubt filled with families anxious to leave the burning city. Ahead, the horizon glowed.

Polly was right. Olivia and her mother dealt with this sort of thing regularly in London. But he couldn't help worrying. Not knowing her situation drove him mad. Plymouth wasn't used to this kind of attack, and even if Olivia was safe, her family would somehow be affected.

And once he arrived, then what? He'd never manage to drive or park the motorcar in town. At this rate, he'd never get there. To his right lay a pasture bordered by a short wall of stone. He dodged the oncoming traffic, crossed the road, and parked his father's Daimler along the shoulder.

The decision was whether to stay on the road or cut across

the field. He wasn't the only one on foot. Silhouetted against the bonfire of destruction behind them, throngs of people filled the meadow: elderly men and women, mothers with their children and pets. In an exhausted daze they moved to safety, away from their shattered homes, businesses, and lives. William searched their faces. Could one of them be Olivia or her mother or aunt? If Olivia was amongst this crowd, he would eventually find her. But if not ...

A new urgency set him jogging over the uneven ground.

At the edge of the city, the streets looked unfamiliar. He asked passersby how to get to Greenbank Avenue, but their directions proved difficult to follow. Landmarks had been blown apart or burnt to the ground. He followed a path of disappearing bread-crumbs down lanes no longer bordered by tall buildings, bright awnings, or painted doors. Narrow passageways had become main thoroughfares, whilst wider streets lay cluttered with rubble.

Finally he found Greenbank, where the first neighbor he encountered directed him to Hilda Thornton's house. Still stand-ing, thank God. He rapped upon the door, and his heart leapt at the sound of footsteps within. A young woman in a Wren uniform greeted him, her starched white blouse a sharp contrast to her open navy jacket and the dark hair pulled back from her pale face.

Nervously, he removed his hat. "Is Olivia here?"

"No, she's not." She raised a torch in her left hand. "Do I know you?"

As he explained, her confusion melted in the reflected light. "Ah, you're Olivia's William! I'm Katie, her cousin. But how on earth did you get here?" She looked behind him for a possible companion. "Olivia told me—"

"Ah, yes, my vision—it returned a short time ago. The doctors said it might, and—do you know where she is?"

"Sorry, yes. She was injured in the raid, just after it started, we think. She was brought to City Hospital. By whom, we haven't the foggiest. My aunt's on her way there with a change of clothes. We're told she'll be all right, but she's rather banged up and was still unconscious when her mum first got to her."

"City Hospital. Do you know the fastest route in this mess?"

She began giving directions, then stopped herself. "Never mind. I'll take you." She withdrew briefly into the house before emerging again with her hat and greatcoat. "Come. It's about a mile."

Torch in hand, she locked the door behind them and led him down the hazy, littered streets. Greenbank Avenue writhed with activity. By the light of burning debris, people hefted buckets of water or flagged fire engines that weaved round the wreckage. Everywhere someone called for a missing loved one or pet. Those who weren't crying were valiantly escorting others to the nearest First Aid Post or helping dig through the impenetrable rubble.

Each new sad situation lent extra weight to his. "You say she was hurt right after the attack? But she'll be all right? Did Olivia's mum say anything else? Where was she? Why was she alone?"

"We'd been together at a pub down the way. We'd just parted. I'm not certain of her injuries; Aunt Jeanie said they'd stitched up her face, and something about bruised ribs. We didn't talk long."

He quickened his pace. "How much further?"

"A few more blocks. Am I going too slowly for you?"

They marched down the middle of a dark street until footsteps scampered toward them.

"Help me!" A young girl in a dirty dressing gown entered their torchlight. She tugged William's arm. "This way, please!" The child's desperation stirred memories of a Norwegian girl he'd met in Narvik nearly one year ago.

At that time the Nazi's claim to the city had been inevitable. Civilians hid in their homes whilst British soldiers dodged enemy fire from above; their attempts to protect them, futile.

William was delivering new orders for Private Curtis, and after an hour of searching, still couldn't find him. Then, stealing down an alley, he did. At the feet of a girl he lay, shot in the neck by a sniper.

"He was helping me," the girl whispered in perfect English. "My brother's run off. I can't find him." Eyes averted from the soldier toppled at her ankles, she hovered her hands above his body as if attempting to move it. There'd been no time to mourn the loss of his comrade. William rushed at the girl, pushing her away from the sniper's line of fire. He'd helped her look for her brother before leaving her in the arms of her sobbing mother who was stricken with dread over what had likely happened to her son.

Katie had taken the child's hand. The pain on her face told him she'd never seen such despair.

Olivia was safe at City Hospital and being cared for by doctors. Her mother was with her. Here, another life could be saved. He crouched down. "What can we do?"

"It's mummy. She's stuck. She left the shelter to get the kitty and then it hit, and she got stuck."

By the light of Katie's torch, the two followed the child to a nearby house. They stepped over shards of glass and entered what used to be a kitchen. A table lay on its side and pantry contents were scattered beside the remnants of a brick wall.

"Out here. I'm out here," a tired voice called from the dark.

William grabbed the torch. Its light found a dusty hand at the base of the doorjamb. Beyond that, a heap of bricks covered the woman like a blanket, short of her head. Her eyes were open and her panic was evident despite her immobility. These breaths she took would be her last.

"Katie, take the child away from here."

"Away? But where?"

"Anywhere but here!" he barked.

The girls melted into the darkness and William got to work. Each brick he removed was tossed, making a new pile feet away.

"What's your name?" he asked.

"Angela."

"Tell me where we can take your daughter, Angela."

"Her grandparents, my husband's family. They live two streets over." The woman's speech was labored, yet she continued. "I went to get the cat. For Millie. She was crying for the bloody animal and then I heard it—"

"Quiet, now." If they were careful, she still might make it. "No need to agitate yourself."

Finally, he could see her clothing—a few more armfuls should do it.

He hefted another load then stopped. The dim light was playing tricks on him. He picked up the torch. The woman's legs were impossibly twisted. She'd never walk again, but at least she was still alive.

"Is that feeling better?" he asked.

The woman did not answer.

"Ma'am?" He placed a light hand on her shoulder, careful not to move her. "Angela."

"Mummy! Mummy!" Millie had returned pulling the hand of an older woman who stopped abruptly at the sight before her. She held the girl's shoulders. "Stay here, pet."

Katie emerged from behind them. "These are Millie's grandparents. We've flagged an ambulance."

The family's grief was too much to bear. William stood and drew Katie away by the arm. "It's too late for that, I'm afraid."

Her eyes glistened. She nodded silently, as though she too knew their rescue mission had been doomed from the start.

A man with tired eyes and thinning hair approached with his hand out. "Thank you for your help, ah—?"

"Morgan. Major William Morgan." William shook the man's hand. "I'm sorry I couldn't save her."

"Taylor's the name, and you did what you could. We'll not forget it."

Millie hid her face in her grandmother's greatcoat. "There, there," the woman said, rocking the child as two men appeared and hefted Angela's broken body onto a stretcher.

Mr. Taylor joined his wife. Hand-in-hand they walked the girl away, promising they'd come back once the sun rose to look for her kitty.

Pandemonium reigned outside City Hospital. An incendiary had hit the maternity wing, and a skeleton crew of firefighters struggled to extinguish it. Fresh flames and flashing red lights bathed the flocks of weary victims. Wounded men, women, and children were rushed through the main entrance, either in the arms of others or carried on planks of plywood or damaged doors. Those well enough to leave did so in varied states of rehabilitation. Somber figures carried the dead of all sizes.

Inside, the waiting rooms and corridors were littered with war victims, some on beds, some in wheelchairs, some on the floor. William and Katie followed the stream of traffic to a large ward. At least fifty beds had been packed into the room, and the smell of disinfectant had been overcome by blood and charred flesh. Blackout curtains hung floor to ceiling, and the flickering emergency lighting—hurricane lamps and dripping candles— made the job of discerning faces incredibly difficult. The motionless bundles on each bed could have been corpses or they could have been living, recovering patients. In this wretched light, it was hard to tell.

Katie pointed. "There she is, back on the left. The woman in the blue greatcoat next to her, that's Aunt Jeanette, Olivia's mum."

"Thank you," he said, tearing his eyes from the busy ward. "And thank you for your help back there." He placed a hand on her shoulder. "Are you returning to your aunt? Have you your torch?"

She laughed, erasing an hour's worth of stress from her face. So he'd become overprotective of her. It seemed appropriate even after their short acquaintance.

"Tell Livvy I'll write. It was nice meeting you."

Once Katie left, William made his way to Olivia's metal-framed bed. The bedside lantern illuminated the form of Mrs. Talbot, bent in silent prayer over her unconscious daughter. She was as oblivious to his presence as she was to the loud voices and bustle throughout the room.

"My love," he whispered at his first glimpse of Olivia's face.

Even with her injuries, she radiated beauty like a field of red poppies under stormy gray skies. A stitched gash on her forehead lay far too close to her right eye. He longed to kiss it.

He sank to the edge of the bed.

Mrs. Talbot's head popped up. "May I help you?"

"Forgive me—Mrs. Talbot?" He stood at once and pressed his cap to his chest. "I'm William. William Morgan."

He wasn't sure if he should say more. Dr. Talbot had recognized his name, and he hoped Mrs. Talbot would follow suit.

"Major Morgan?" She took his outstretched hand warily.

"Yes, ma'am. I came as soon as I heard of the attack. I was afraid Olivia might've been hurt in this madness." He cupped a hand centimeters from her wound whilst forcing Angela's misshapen body from his mind. The water in his eyes distorted his sight of the milky stone pendant above the collar of her hospital gown.

He looked up. "Can you tell me what happened? Will she be all right?"

"I don't understand. Two days ago, Olivia told me it would take time before your sight recovered. How on earth—"

"My sight returned days before she came to Plymouth." His nerves rocketed even higher than when he'd spoken to Dr.

Talbot. "I asked Olivia to keep the news under wraps until I was sure it had returned for good." His voice quavered at the lie, ashamed that he'd ever entertained the notion of keeping his returned vision a secret.

"It appears she's kept a lot from me recently," she murmured.

He ignored the remark. He just wanted Olivia to wake and to be well. Without regard for propriety, he sat and fished through the nappy blanket for her hands. Her soft skin calmed him despite their minor cuts and dirt-filled creases.

"How long has she been here? Your niece mentioned damaged ribs. Is that all she's suffering from, aside from these cuts here?" He touched her forehead. "Any internal bleeding? Have you spoken with her or—"

"She was pregnant, Major," Mrs. Talbot snapped. "Your doing, I presume?"

A tingle crept up his neck, and a high-pitched ring muted the room's clamor. He stared at Olivia. Had she known? For how long? Was she waiting to tell him?

Mrs. Talbot awaited an answer, but he couldn't give it. Shock and sadness dampened his cheeks.

"That's a yes, then." She was relentless. "And because of her miscarriage, Major, she lost a lot of blood. When she wakes, she'll remain incredibly weak. Her ribs are bruised, her body covered with contusions. No, I haven't spoken with her. She's been unconscious since she arrived."

William gaped at her, grasping for meaning.

"I realize it's been months since she's lived in such conditions, but"—the pitch of Mrs. Talbot's voice dropped as she covered her face—"she should've *known* to find shelter when the sirens sounded. My girl is smarter than that!"

He reached across Olivia. "Mrs. Talbot—"

The woman raised her head and pulled away. Though ringed in red, her eyes held their water. "Tell me, Major, were you planning on marrying my daughter? Or, since you have your eyesight, you're not sure she's up to snuff?"

"I—"

"What were you thinking, taking advantage of an innocent girl in this way? You're at least ten years her senior!"

"I love her, Mrs. Talbot. That's why I'm here. She knows I want to marry her, but I've been waiting for this." He stood and fished his mother's ring from his pocket. "I wanted to propose properly so—"

"There is nothing proper about getting an unmarried girl pregnant."

He slowly curled his fingers around the ring and sank back onto the bed. What a fool he'd been.

Isolated by Keldor's serenity, he'd forgotten how the rest of Britain was struggling to survive. Cities were collapsing, people were dying. How ridiculous of him to stay fixed on tradition, waiting for a flaming ring. He should've called Dr. Talbot weeks ago. Mrs. Talbot was right setting her fury on him. If this were his daughter, he'd have been even more explosive.

Mrs. Talbot rose, as though preparing for another battle. One at a time, she smoothed her hands down her sleeves and the front of her blue greatcoat. "Well, she's not yours to worry over anymore, Major. Once she's awake and able to walk out of here, I'm taking her back to London with me. She's lost her baby, so that's no longer an issue—and you, with your miraculously returned eyesight, won't need her services in Cornwall any longer."

"Mrs. Talbot, I understand your frustration, and I'm sorry you feel I've taken advantage of your daughter. But—"

"Did you even know she was pregnant?"

He cringed as her bullet hit its target. In past relationships, he'd been careful to take the necessary precautions to prevent pregnancy, but all that had changed with Olivia and the day she agreed to marry him. He'd become lax in his diligence, and both looked forward to whatever might come of it.

"No. But we welcomed the possibility." He drew up to dispense some shots of his own. "The ring came the day she left. I phoned Dr. Talbot straightaway and asked for Olivia's hand. Though surprised, he gave it."

As hoped, his words left her stunned.

"Since arriving at Keldor," he continued, "your daughter has done nothing but commit herself to my recovery. She has forced me to reckon with my demons and continues to teach me how much I have to live for—her companionship, for one. We belong together, and we *will* marry." Despite the clout in his tone, he gave a timid smile to the woman he hoped to one day befriend. "I love her, Mrs. Talbot, and I would be honored if we had your blessing as well."

He caught her pained expression before she covered a fresh batch of tears, sitting abruptly in her chair. "She's never even hinted at a change in your relationship. We were close! Why didn't she tell me about you and this love affair? I wouldn't have expected details, but I thought daughters were supposed to share happy news with their mothers. How could I not have known?"

Though a part of him wished to comfort her, he stayed put, distracted by the twitching feet under the worn blanket.

Olivia stretched. Her lips drew back in discomfort, and she muttered, "William?"

He must be the one to relay the news. Frantic, he reached toward Olivia's mother. "Please, Mrs. Talbot, let me tell her about the baby, will you?"

Her face softened in consent. "Very well. She's said your name more than a few times since I've been here. Maybe this time, she'll wake up."

## CHAPTER 26

THERE WAS NOWHERE TO RUN. Someone's drawing room lay in her path, and the sofa had caught fire. A frightened dog with pointed ears and a fluffy tail darted past, whining incessantly.

Unbearable heat wrapped her body like a sarcophagus. Olivia kicked in protest. "The fire ..."

"They're out, love. You're safe."

A well-known hand caressed her face. She leant into its perfect mold, enjoying the coolness.

"You're being well cared for, and soon you'll be home."

The familiar voice forced her eyes open. "William?"

Smartly dressed in a well-decorated army uniform sat the man she loved, as she'd never seen him before. Combed to perfection, the threads of his obsidian hair glinted in the light of a large and busy room.

Relief softened his face. "I'm here."

In an instant, her arms were around his neck.

"Oh!" she cried. The pain on her right side was unbearable. She relaxed her hold and gingerly surveyed the damage.

William's hand closed over hers, spanning the length of her rib cage. "Careful. You're hurt."

In the nest of his arms, she was safe. The fires wouldn't chase her again despite the scorched air that draped her like a dirty coat.

"Here, lie back," he said.

She nuzzled into his neck until he guided her down toward the meager pillow. "How did you find me? How long have I been here?"

"A few hours, I think." He kissed her hands before turning toward the person at her right.

"Mother—" She extended an arm but remained on the pillow as William directed.

Her mother looked as bad as Olivia felt. Dark semicircles bobbed like tiny boats beneath her bloodshot eyes. Black flecks of ash peppered her yellow hair and the shoulders of her blue greatcoat, on which she'd done the buttons all wrong.

A trillion questions swamped Olivia's mind, but what rose to the top was the need to defend her lie about William, clearly no longer blind.

"This is Major Morgan" was all she could muster.

"Yes, dear." Her mother's lips narrowed, spreading out rather than up, and lines of disappointment streaked her forehead. "We've met."

"Oh." Olivia tried sorting that out and couldn't. She was glad she'd missed it.

"How do you feel, dear?" her mother asked.

She swallowed and scanned the room, where important people bustled about with clipboards and stethoscopes. "I'm thirsty." Her heart had yet to calm, and each new question sent it hammering. "How did I get here? Did you bring me? The siren sounded, but I'd no idea where to go. There was an explosion. A nurse found me, and"—she swallowed again, unsure if she'd dreamt the next part—"I saw blood. Loads of it."

Her mother's distress deepened, so she turned to William. "What happened to me?"

He glanced at her mother expectantly.

"I'm going to fetch the nurse and get you some water." Her mother patted Olivia's hand before nodding toward William and leaving the bedside.

Like a lost child, Olivia faced William directly.

"I'm not sure what happened exactly," he said, "except that you came awfully close to being killed. By the looks of it, the explosions knocked you unconscious and possibly covered you in rubble, causing these bruises and scrapes." He stroked her forehead and cheek. "Strangers brought you in. Very kind strangers."

"But the blood? It was all over my shoes." The intensity of her own voice frightened her.

His eyes were mournful, but they never left hers. "You had a miscarriage. Were you aware you'd started a baby?"

For one sweet moment, before hell rained from above. "I had an idea. More of a hope, really." A tear slid down her cheek, the image of William snuggling their bald bundle no longer an imminent reality.

He secured a stray lock behind her left ear. "In the future, we'll have many children if that's what you want. I envision a little Olivia, hands on her hips, telling her parents a thing or two. For now, we'll enjoy each other's company, the two of us, a little longer."

He was right, of course, but still, the grief hurt worse than her ribcage. "Does my mother know?"

He nodded tersely. "She's the one who told me."

"I sensed she was unhappy with me. She has a hard time hiding her disappointment—and with me, she's always disappointed."

"You're all she has left. She wants what's best for you. She certainly wasn't happy with me when I arrived, but I think we've come to an understanding. For a moment, she was planning to take you back to London."

She inhaled sharply, painfully. "What?"

"Calm, yourself. You're coming back to Keldor. *I* get to be caregiver, and you've got to do what I say."

"Oh, no." She rolled her eyes.

Ignoring her cheek, he dug into his trousers pocket. "But first, Olivia Talbot." He opened his fist. "Will you marry me?"

In William's palm lay the prettiest ring Olivia had ever seen. Elevated above a platinum filigree, small glittering diamonds encircled a glowing solitaire like happy spectators cheering the leading lady.

Finally.

"It's beautiful."

"Is that a yes?"

"Yes, of course it is. I told you already!" The question's absurdity, the timing, and the backdrop set her to laughing until pain transformed her gaiety into a muted yet earnest nod.

He slipped the ring onto her finger. "Do you like it?"

The diamonds dazzled her eyes, even in the dim room. "I love it, but … Was this your mother's? Are you—"

Before she could finish, he seized her face. His lips made up for what explorations he couldn't make to her broken body with his hands, and her desire outwrestled her pain.

Nose to nose, he took a breath to say, "I'm sure. And I'm sorry for making you wait. I hope you never doubted my commitment."

"Never. Every time we made love, every time you kissed me, every time you held me, I knew. An implicit bond. I could feel it here." She flattened her palm to her chest.

"I wasn't the only one, then. How pagan of us." He kissed the top of her head. "I was a fool to wait for the ring. It finally arrived the day you left. I phoned your father and—"

"My father?"

"Of course. I wanted to do this properly, remember?" He backed away and brought her hand to his lips. "This is far from the proposal I'd planned, but that doesn't matter anymore. Let's get you home."

Home. To Keldor—their home, miles away from destruction and death, where she would heal in comfort and safety. Where she could mourn the loss of her baby, and thank the heavens she herself hadn't been added to the war's collection of casualties.

Then, as though disentangling from the thronging darkness, her mother's grim face emerged. Every muscle in Olivia's weak body stiffened. William sensed the change and followed her gaze. Here she was: an adult officially engaged to be married. But none of it mattered—Mother served as judge, jury, and executioner, as masterful as the war itself when it came to ruining everything.

The main routes to the hospital and surrounding neighborhoods were the first to be cleared of rubble. After planting a swift kiss on her cheek (and her mother's), William set out on foot in search of a lift to his abandoned motorcar. Mother and daughter stayed behind on a bench in what used to be the ornamental courtyard opposite the hospital's entrance. Beneath the sun's paltry light, victims continued to arrive, fewer on foot but more by way of ambulance, lorry, or motorcar.

With the hospital well over capacity, the staff had been happy to see Olivia stand and walk out of the building with help. Free of her threadbare hospital gown, she wore her own dress under a greatcoat of Aunt Hilda's and a clean pair of shoes. Her mother had patted a cool cloth over her face and pulled her unwashed, oily hair into a bun, leaving her somewhat refreshed. She'd been released long before she should have, her mother opined, but Olivia didn't care; she just wanted to go home.

But until that happened, she had to suffer through her mother's uninformed opinions over her unseemly behavior with "the major," as she kept calling him.

"Funny," Mother finally said with a sniff that meant her next sentence would be miles from humorous. "Sending you to Cornwall was supposed to keep you *out* of harm's way. Had quite the opposite outcome, did it not?"

"Mother, I was never in harm's way."

"Pregnant by your employer, a man years older than you, spells nothing but ruin, Olivia. Tell me"—Mrs. Talbot turned to face her—"did the major ever use his age or position to threaten or intimidate you? I know he was rather disagreeable in the beginning. Katie told me all about it."

With no time to dwell on her cousin's loose lips, Olivia snapped, "William has been nothing but a gentleman, Mother, even early on."

"That kiss in there hardly looked gentlemanly." Mrs. Talbot nodded toward the hospital.

William's kisses rarely were. That's what she liked about them. Olivia crossed her arms carefully against her tender midsection and suppressed a smile.

"If the major is truly the man you've chosen for yourself, then so be it," her mother said. "Lord knows my opinion, whether it matched yours or not, would go unheard."

For once, Olivia agreed.

"So rather than give you motherly advice, I will relay the following instead, as a seasoned midwife: If you want more children, you must permit yourself time to heal before succumbing to the major's wants and needs—or those of your own."

Again, Olivia hid her smile.

"And when the time comes—after you're wedded, of course—pregnancy can be prevented. Were your father and I wrong to believe you were more conscientious than this? Honestly, Olivia, sometimes I think you're *trying* to disappoint me."

Her mirth faded. Mother would never have spoken to John or Henry in this manner, no matter what their age or circumstances.

But she hadn't the energy to argue. Shades of her sixteen-year-old self simmered in silence.

"And as much as I'm eager for grandchildren," her mother continued, "I can't understand why anyone would want to bring a child into the world as it is. I'm certain you agree, especially after what you've undergone."

Was it selfish to disagree? More than anything—especially after what she'd experienced—she wanted a child. William's child. The war wouldn't last forever. Her mother knew nothing of the safety and tranquility of Keldor, the place where they would raise their children, war or no war. It was too long before she'd be there, lying comfortably in William's gentle arms, at home where his presence alone would take her pain away.

"Will you be all right?" William asked her as they drove away from the Exeter train station, where they'd left her mother and Aunt Hilda.

"Yes," Olivia said with a sniffle. "Thank you for being so sweet to Mother. She's certainly taken with you. Well done."

His campaign to win over Jeanette Talbot hadn't taken long. It'd begun with his sincere condolences over the loss of her two sons. From there, he'd made sure Aunt Hilda's home would remain secured during her indefinite absence.

"The major's invited your father and me to Keldor, Livvy," her mother had said on their way to Exeter, as though the king himself had invited them.

"That'd be a wonderful treat," Olivia said honestly, shifting her grateful eyes to William.

In the car park, goodbyes hadn't taken long.

"She's a terrible patient, Major," her mother said, kneeling at Olivia's open car door. "She won't complain about pain and will try convincing you that she feels better than she does. And good luck getting her to do what she's supposed to." She took Olivia's chin in her hand. "Perhaps that's why you've chosen nursing as a profession? It's easier for you to manage everyone else."

Olivia couldn't disagree, even though she'd gladly listen to William. Listening to her mother, however, was another story.

"I'm happy for you, dear," her mother finished. "I have a notion you're in good hands. Get well, now." She turned to William, who stood beside the open car door with their bags. "I look forward to when we'll get to know each other better, Major. In the meantime, take good care of my daughter. She's all I've got left."

Olivia wiped away a tear. Outside the car window, the streets grew more congested, the buildings closer together. She'd never been to Exeter, but William knew his way around. The war had touched this place, but it hadn't leveled it. It was comforting to see structures still intact and people going about their lives as usual. Children attended school, adults went to work, the post was delivered, and restaurants and pubs served luncheon.

"Where are you going? I said I was hungry, but I can wait to eat. I want to get home."

"We're getting married." He glanced in the rearview mirror, then back at the road ahead. "Right now. Is that all right?"

Her surprised smile expanded as her new ring winked in the dappled sunlight.

"I told your mum we'd be married as soon as you were well enough, but I'm not sure I can wait. Can you?"

"No."

"Will she be disappointed if we do this so soon after her send-off? The register office in Plymouth is no longer in existence, thanks to the Germans, or else we'd be husband and wife by now."

As overbearing as her mother was, she'd always loved a party, and she'd have been brilliant at helping to plan their wedding. However, Olivia was fairly certain she'd be equally happy to celebrate that her daughter was no longer living like a tart.

"In light of recent events, I imagine she just wants us married."

"I've a mind to agree with you."

# CHAPTER 27

"Wait here."

William's day-old stubble scratched her cheek when he pecked it. He left her on a bench next to a noticeboard cluttered with employment announcements and alerts for missing pets. His long strides carried him across the spacious chamber to a window marked INFORMATION. There were fewer people here than she'd expected, and everyone spoke in hushed voices, aware that the marble floors and tall ceilings amplified the quietest sounds.

William returned with a clipboard and pen in hand. "We should be married in twenty minutes." He filled out his portion of paperwork before passing it to her and tugging at her ring. "Let me have this, and I'll return it to your finger during the ceremony." The ring had been hers for only a few hours and already her left hand looked naked without it.

In less than fifteen minutes, a woman with short gray hair and wire-rimmed glasses appeared in an open door at the far side of the lobby.

"Major Morgan?" she called, her voice echoing across the distance.

"Yes." William rose, bringing Olivia with him.

"How do you do, Major?" She glanced over the clipboard and smiled keenly before turning her attention to Olivia.

The woman's face seemed kind enough, but Olivia wilted under her gaze. The cut above her eye throbbed, as did her ribs. An ugly wretch—and on this, her wedding day.

"You'll be after this couple," the woman said, motioning toward a young pair holding hands in front of a man whose bald head shone like a cue ball. A long black robe covered his equally round body.

The young bride grinned from ear to ear beneath a peach bow turban decorated with white silk flowers. Though humble, her dress matched the turban perfectly, as did its white buttons and the carnation corsage on her chest. The groom wore an RAF uniform dreadfully similar to the one John had been buried in. At their sides stood an older man and a young woman who could have been the bride's twin sister.

The bespectacled woman gestured to the man in the robe, seizing Olivia's attention once more. "Once you're called, take this to the superintendent registrar. After your ceremony, he'll sign this and—where are your witnesses?"

"Witnesses?" William asked.

"You're supposed to bring your own witnesses."

"I'm sorry. We'd no idea."

"Well," her eyes raked over Olivia once more, "since we're a little slow today, I suppose Cherry and I can do it." She nodded toward the secretary in the corner of the long green room, shaking her head as though they should be eternally grateful.

They were.

"Thank you!" William gripped the woman's arm.

"Of course. You're to both sign here after the ceremony." She pointed to two giant *X*'s next to two empty lines. "Once the document is signed by all parties, return it to the front window. We'll prepare a copy for filing, you'll be given the original, and then you'll be married. Congratulations."

Olivia could have sworn the woman's teeth squeaked when she smiled, but maybe it was someone's shoes on the marble floor.

"Thank you." William took the clipboard as the woman headed away across a stretch of sunlit olive carpet that muffled her footsteps.

He pulled Olivia close as they moved further into the room.

"I know I'm not supposed to kiss the bride yet," he murmured, "but I'm thinking of breaking the rules." His lips brushed her ear. "You're beautiful. You know that, don't you?"

She almost believed him. Was she doing the right thing, marrying so excellent a liar? She pressed her face self-consciously against his scratchy wool tunic. The musky pine scent of William's bedroom filled her nose, for one satisfying moment transporting her there.

"Morgan, is it?" the Superintendent Registrar called.

William passed off the clipboard, and they stepped forward and faced one another before the officiant.

Arms outstretched, Olivia locked hands with William. On either side stood their witnesses, as promised, Cherry the secretary and Eloise, the woman in glasses.

The cue ball of a man went through his routine regarding the legality of their union.

"Excellent, we're ready for vows, then," he said. "If no other couples are queued behind you?"

He glanced at Eloise.

She shook her head. "They're it."

He beamed at them. "In addition to the standard, then, you'll have time for vows of your own, if you'd like."

She'd had nothing prepared; neither did William, surely. "That's all right. I don't think—"

"Brilliant!" William cut her off.

In his eager eyes, there was only blue.

Shoulders straightened, he repeated after the officiant, "I call upon those present to witness ... that I, William Jack Morgan ... take thee, Olivia Jean Talbot ... to be my lawfully wedded wife."

He continued on his own. "As your husband, I promise to celebrate my love for you by making your happiness and the happiness of our future children my top priority. I shall remain devoted to fulfilling your needs"—his left eyebrow twitched surreptitiously—"and securing our bond as companions in sickness, health, heartache, death, and beyond. I give you this ring, Olivia"—he produced the treasure and slid it back on her finger —"as a symbol of my undying affection and loyalty to you."

She'd heard these words before in the dark, whispered in her ear as they lay alongside one another and his fingers traced lines of ecstasy over her body. Heat spread from her cheeks to her neck.

And it was her turn.

She took a dry swallow as the superintendent registrar cued her lines.

"I call upon those present to witness ... that I, Olivia Jean Talbot ... take thee, William Jack Morgan ... to be my lawful husband." Still swimming in the blue depths of his eyes, she calmed. "As your wife, I promise to remain your closest friend and confidant. I will put my love for you above all else and will continue to strive to replace your sorrows with joy and your anger with laughter for all eternity."

"In the presence of these two witnesses, William and Olivia have given their consent and made their marriage vows to one another. By the power vested in me, I pronounce them man and wife. William, you may kiss your bride."

As if he'd been waiting to hear those words his entire life, William took her face in his hands and brought her mouth to his. His kiss was gentle, and the sweetest thing she'd ever tasted.

"I love you, Mrs. Morgan. If you weren't hurt, that kiss would've been much more scandalous."

Mrs. Morgan: a new name for a new beginning, and one she was eager to shout to the world. She nuzzled inside the arms of her husband and smiled. The day's date, their wedding anniversary forever: 21 March, 1941, marked another new beginning. It was the first day of spring.

# CHAPTER 28

ON A CORNER outside the register office, Olivia sat clutching their marriage certificate. She was exhausted. William was too. Hand up, she blocked the bright sun and spotted him across the street at a small outdoor market. The air had warmed since morning, asserting the changing season. Partially opened buds dotted tree branches lining the street. Pink and purple hyacinth as vibrant as Easter eggs peppered the gray concrete with color.

Olivia closed her eyes and let her tension melt under the sun until she sensed William's presence. There he stood like a gallant knight presenting her with riches. His hair, a straight shelf of black across his forehead, emphasized his crooked smile.

"For my wife." He knelt, thrusting a bouquet of daffodils her way. "I promise to make today up to you. One day, you'll have a proper wedding."

She buried her nose in lemon yellow, allowing the tangy scent to linger. "But we have had a proper wedding. Even if all our friends and family had joined us, the only person I'm interested in celebrating with is you."

"And celebrate we will, every day for the rest of our lives." He dusted yellow powder from her nose. "How my parents would've loved you."

"You've thought of them a lot today?"

"Even more so since you've come into my life. You and my mother are kindred spirits. Like you, she was selfless and compassionate. And my father—why, he'd dote upon you and claim I wasn't doting upon you enough. I daresay they'd be proud of me marrying such a brilliant woman."

"They'd be proud of you regardless."

"I've phoned Mrs. Pollard and told her what's happened. She's overjoyed at our marriage, as you can imagine."

She laughed, though it hurt. "Yes, I can."

The poor woman had tolerated their indiscretions for months. Once they were home, she would apologize and beg Mrs. Pollard's forgiveness. They needed each other now—especially since William's returned eyesight was still a secret. The two of them would have to ensure that the circle of those who knew the truth remained small. And though a few of the insiders included members of her family, they knew nothing of the army's demand that William return to war as soon as he was well.

And he wasn't well. His trauma as prisoner remained deep-rooted. This jaunt to Plymouth had surely agitated earlier war memories: the bombed-out buildings, the decimated houses, the fires, the bodies …

"The weather isn't as fine in Cornwall as here," he said. "A spring squall has commandeered the southwest and is moving east. We're likely to hit rain on the way home."

A chill crawled up her arms as though the tempest had already arrived. A shadow pinched their sun.

She glanced up.

"Major Morgan?" asked a deep voice. "Is that you?"

Olivia's squint landed on a man in a uniform similar to her husband's. A sense of foreboding replaced her chill with a shiver.

"By Jove, it is you! I haven't seen you since Norway!" He stood straighter and saluted.

William rose, his stunned expression changing into more civil acknowledgment. "Lieutenant Blackwood." His arm rose to his forehead just as swiftly.

"Last I heard, you were recovering from bad business in North Africa, miraculously found on a beach in the Mediterranean, blind and a mess—but look at you! Not at all as I expected, though I don't think I would've recognized you without your uniform."

Whatever William muttered, Olivia couldn't make out, but the lieutenant came across loud and clear: the unseen damage from abuse, torture, starvation, and rape were inconsequential, especially if one wore a uniform.

"Are you off, then? Where are they sending you this time?" Lieutenant Blackwood's eyes finally connected with hers before moving between her, the flowers, and the register office. "Wait! Have you just been married?"

"Yes, this is my bride—my wife. Olivia."

She wanted to enjoy those words, but instead she drifted, removed from the shell of her broken body to the space above. From there, she observed William square his shoulders, his stature confident, commanding, and seemingly natural. She watched her own hands tighten, entwined in a death grip around the stems of her drooping daffodils. Their secret had been blown apart—another fatality of this merciless war.

"Brilliant!" Lieutenant Blackwood made a move toward her, his arm outstretched.

Back on the bench, her posture refused to soften and she fashioned her war-torn face to suggest the interloper depart sooner rather than later.

The man's eyes shifted uncertainly before turning back to William. "I'm off in a few days—south this time. I've had a short leave, but sadly no sweetheart to call on." He ventured a glance at

Olivia once more. "I'll tell the others I've seen you and that you're in better shape than we'd feared. You've been in contact with the colonel, I'm sure."

William nodded but kept silent.

"Well, I'll let you alone with your new bride, Major. I'm glad to know you're doing so well, sir."

A final salute sent Lieutenant Blackwood on his way—on his way to tell the army that Major William Morgan was ready to return to a war he was mentally unfit to serve in.

William knelt at her side, but she couldn't look at him. Her back withered and her face crumpled into her hands. The daffodils, once cheery and robust, lay beside her worn shoes in a strangled heap.

Rain hammered every car slogging along the A30, and William welcomed it. Perhaps the moisture would dissipate the charred odor that seemed permanently trapped inside his nostrils. The stench was making him nearly as ill as Olivia, who'd vomited twice since leaving Exeter. Despite the low visibility on the motorway, the drumming shower comforted him. The cool temperature meant he was home. Home—where he couldn't wait to shelter his wife from Plymouth's fetid inferno.

Forced to decelerate behind a slow-moving lorry, he glanced at her. Her eyes were closed; wavering creases above them spoke of lingering pain. The brake lights stole his attention, but amidst the blinking red ahead, her drawn face emerged, followed by Angela's, the stranger he'd watched die. Plymouth's night of terror at the enemy's hand was a cruel reminder of what he'd been avoiding these past six months: Whilst he wallowed in self-pity, the Nazis had grown bolder and more powerful.

He pressed the accelerator. Over the next few days, he and Olivia would celebrate their long-awaited union, but after that, he had a duty to uphold. Keldor's assumed safety was fleeting, as proven only one week ago in his own back garden. He wouldn't be fulfilling his wedding vows if he continued to sit back and allow his God-given talents go to waste.

Blackwood had been fated to recognize him today. How else might his new wife be persuaded to accept his resolve to reenter the war?

Gravel crunched under halting tires as he parked outside Keldor's gate. Olivia opened her eyes.

William faced his bride. "Listen, I can't say what the future holds, but please, let me worry about it. Today is supposed to be a happy day, and I won't let anything ruin that. All I want is to carry you over the threshold as my wife and get you upstairs, soaking in a hot bath." He pulled a few stray hairs from her face. "I can't believe how lucky I am to have you."

A tear rolled down her cheek. He wiped it away.

"Can we focus on the present, then? Will you try not to worry and let me care for you the way you cared for me?"

As expected, she succumbed to his wheedling. Olivia's lips turned upward.

"I will."

# CHAPTER 29

MORE THAN ANYTHING, Olivia wanted to please her new husband. This meant shutting out their recent encounter with Lieutenant Blackwood and its implications for William's future. Instead, she would relish in their new status as married.

The homecoming helped. Mrs. Pollard had whipped the staff into a frenzy of preparations to welcome the newlyweds. When William (mindful of Olivia's injuries) carried her over the threshold of Keldor's grand entryway, Mrs. Pollard, James, and Annie greeted them with cheers. All three were sharply dressed in the black-and-white livery of yesteryear. A cork popped. Champagne frothed and dripped onto the tiled floor. Annie handed them squeaky-clean crystal flutes, likely unearthed from the depths of storage along with the champagne.

James grinned as he poured, not at all bothered by the effervescent stickiness running down his hand. How changed the man looked when he genuinely smiled. Keldor was her official home now, and this small party of residents welcomed her with open arms.

She remained bundled in William's arms as they followed Mrs. Pollard upstairs to William's bedroom—*their* bedroom. She rushed ahead to the door and opened it with a flourish, as though revealing an expensive piece of artwork to the crowned heads of Europe. The gray rain pelting the windows couldn't diminish the explosion of pale pink tulips and flowering magnolia branches inside. Soft flames swayed within pillar candles scattered about their honeymoon suite. Oil lamps added to the glow, making the day outside look darker than it was. A crackling fire roared.

Already Mrs. Pollard had drawn a bubbly bath. Once the others had gone, Olivia sank gratefully past the rising steam unfurling like mist off curling wave crests. She drew a deep breath of satisfaction as William lathered her back and dribbled warm water over her shoulders. Her empty stomach had assisted the champagne in melting away the upheaval of the last twenty-four hours, and the embracing heat soothed her. Even the loss of her baby—the inkling that had become a reality all too late—would heal with time.

"Would you have hoped for a boy or a girl?" she asked, one hand tracing patterns in the bubbles.

"I would be happy with either."

"You must have a preference."

He sat back on his heels. "I don't. Do you?"

She poked a few bubbles, making them pop. "I want a boy first and then a girl. I loved having an older brother. John loved to tease me, yes, but he was also the first to cheer me, especially after rows with Mother." Her memories wandered, and she let them. "He said I took her too seriously, said I was too sensitive. How different it is for boys."

"That's it, then? Two children?" His fingers spread across her shoulders, rubbing her aching muscles.

"Not necessarily, but it's a start. So what would you have hoped for?"

"You mean, what *do* I hope for." He leant forward and pecked the top of her head. "I hope for healthy babies and a healthy mummy. You'll be pregnant again soon, if I have anything to do with it. Now let's get more food in you."

Mrs. Pollard and Annie had delivered their meal in grand fashion: a large platter crowded with the finest china, polished silver, and sparkling crystal. Olivia ate fresh fishcakes, nestled into the covers and propped up by pillows, whilst William enjoyed his plate and toasted his new bride from a chair beside the bed.

Finally, James came in to stoke the fire and replenish their wood supply for the evening. Dinner had been cleared and the blackout put in place. Candles glimmered. Olivia had never seen the bedroom look so romantic. Everyone had devoted such tremendous attention to detail, treating them like royalty on this special day.

More than anything, she wanted William to make love to her —but she knew he wouldn't. She wasn't the only one who'd received an earful from her mother about abstinence and future children. Something told her that her new husband would be overprotective and inflexible about her recovery.

She had to beg him to remove her nightdress. "Please, can we lie next to each other as if we *had* made love?"

With the pursed lips of a know-it-all, he relented and carefully removed the nightdress he'd put on her an hour earlier. He kissed the hollow of her stomach.

"You're perfect," he whispered, evidently satisfied with the removal of her clothing.

She blushed and squirmed as he examined her dimples and blemishes under the wavering light.

"This was your idea, remember?"

"Yes, but—"

His kiss silenced her, a kiss that began at her mouth but didn't end there. Down her neck it traveled, visiting each shoulder via her collarbone. It then made its way to her torso before cutting a trail across her belly button. There, it turned into kisses up and down each hip. Olivia gasped with pleasure as the kisses made their way inside her thighs, where—

She recoiled in pain.

William sat up.

She held her breath against the discomfort. She didn't want him to stop. She could live with the pain for a little longer. Maybe.

"What?" she asked innocently.

"I'm sorry," he said. "I'll stop."

"Don't, please."

It was no use. His eyes told her that until she healed fully, anything below her neck was for viewing only. He gathered the blankets and brought them up to her chin, stoked the fire and extinguished the candles, and took his place beside her. As gently as he could, he wrapped himself around her bruised body.

"How are you feeling, besides frustrated?" He placed a gentle kiss on her forehead.

"Better—because of you. And because right here is where we both belong."

Endless rain fell outside. Nose in her pillow, Olivia inhaled a scent she was growing tired of: sleep. Since she'd come home, every day had been spent in this bed as William, endorsed by Dr. Butler during an exam a week ago, had ordered. She didn't mind so much when William was acting as her pillow, but once he determined that she didn't rest when he was there with her, she spent naptimes alone. Without him, lying around was no fun.

All this resting did nothing to hurry her healing. After seven days, she felt little improved. At least she could walk, but only if she took her time to avoid becoming winded, which meant she wasn't out of bed often. It hurt to even breathe, and laughing was out of the question.

Crying hurt most of all, but that didn't stop her from doing it anyway. Images of torched buildings under an exploding sky, some from memory and some of invention, occupied the space in her head that wasn't distressed over William's impending return to the front. She'd avoided the latter topic, hoping that if they didn't talk about, it wouldn't happen. As a result, ten-minute spells of melancholy littered her days. These she cleverly hid. They might've lasted longer if they weren't so bloody painful.

The bedside clock read 3:04 p.m. It seemed as though six hours had passed since William had brought her lunch. Through their partially opened door, his deep voice broke the silence of the sleepy afternoon. Butterflies raged through her abdomen as frantically as they had the day after their first kiss. Was he on his way up to commend her on a long nap? Maybe not, for there were other voices too—all men. One belonged to Dr. Butler, but two others she didn't recognize.

She swung her feet to the floor and lifted her dressing gown from the foot of the bed, holding her breath at the pain of stretching so far. After a whispered curse, she put it on and padded to the door.

At the bottom of the stairs stood a tall man with graying hair wearing a uniform similar to William's, with more decoration. His eyes were kind, and he was smiling at William like a proud father. This was Colonel Adams, she was sure of it. Next to the colonel stood a dour, spectacled figure with a puffed chest and a self-satisfied smirk.

She hadn't expected this so soon. To keep her shaky legs from buckling, she sank onto the top stair. From this perch, Dr. Butler also came into view. Her stomach tightened. Last week, she had barraged him with questions about William's mental state: Could he endure combat? Would he come back a different man— someone she didn't know, someone who would lose interest in life and possibly try to end it? She'd seen that before, she warned. Dr. Butler had seen it too, he said, but even if he deemed William mentally unfit for battle, it would do little to change the minds of the powers that be. As long as William could participate in some capacity, then he'd be utilized. He was an officer, after all, not some reckless youth who'd rashly signed up but now suffered beyond recovery.

"The expansion in Durham is almost complete," the colonel was saying. "You'll hear from us sooner rather than later."

"You mustn't get too comfortable in the interim," the other man said with a cheeky smile. "Time's ticking. The war won't wait."

The colonel placed his hand on William's shoulder as though giving him an accolade, not a death sentence. "Glad to have you back, Major."

Unwanted warmth wrapped Olivia's rib cage, and the faint smell of smoke stung her nose. The image of her mother sobbing at John's funeral and then at Henry's months later chilled her limbs. The vision of another funeral entered her mind: an empty casket, a symbol of William's unrecognizable corpse.

An involuntary whimper escaped her lips.

"Olivia," William called before turning back to the visitors. "Excuse me, sirs. My wife, she's not been well."

Dr. Butler gripped his arm. "I'll see to her."

"Thank you, but no. I'll go. Would you be so kind as to show the colonel and captain out? Colonel, Captain, thank you for traveling to Cornwall. Until I hear from you."

William saluted and turned on his heels, taking the stairs two steps at a time.

Olivia leant into him as he led her back to their bedroom, her eyes lingering on the powerful men below. Her objections would mean little to them. She felt as fettered as surely her mother had the day John came home saying he'd signed on with the RAF. Of course she'd been proud of him. But hours after his funeral, Olivia overheard Mother say that once she'd seen her son in uniform, she knew the day she'd bury him wouldn't be far behind.

At least William would listen to her, if they wouldn't.

"This is what you want?" she asked, her arms clenched at her side, even as he helped her sit on the bed. Each of her rapid breaths delivered small punches to her rib cage.

"Olivia," he said, sounding frighteningly like her mother, "I can no longer watch this war happen. Too much is at stake. I won't shirk my responsibilities."

"But when I found the letter from the colonel, you knew then you were unfit to—"

"At the time, I *was* unfit. Things have changed. I've changed. Plymouth reminded me first hand of what our country is suffering. I must do this."

Her grandmother once said that war made men think they were stronger than they were. She'd lost two sons in the first war as well, a husband too.

"But aren't you afraid you'll be captured again? Or killed?"

He shook his head as though she was too thick to understand. Perhaps she didn't want to understand.

"I'm more frightened of what's happening to Plymouth, to Coventry, to London, and the rest of Europe. The blighter that shot at Polly and me? And Falmouth? How many more hits before it's completely obliterated? None of us are safe, not even in Cornwall. This isn't the world we want to bring our children into, is it?"

She let him rant as she stared at the oil painting behind him. Twisted with knots of gold, the frame bordered an image of Steren Cove. Sun gleamed off the whitecaps and gulls flew above the surf. The artist had captured the scene long before metal posts and barbed wire contaminated its splendor, an oasis of beauty tarnished by the need to defend it from barbarians.

" ... know I wasn't raised to stand by and wait for trouble to sort itself out. I realize I can't end the war on my own, but with my skill and knowledge, I can surely make a dent." He was pacing. "Britain has a history of strength. Everything we hold dear must be safeguarded. If we care at all about our way of life, then we cannot lie down in defeat and allow ourselves to be bullied by a madman and a murderer!"

Rage sat on the edge of his voice as though everything he was saying had been bottled up for some time. He apologized for the outburst, but he needn't have: Loss was abundant and horror widespread. Her ordeal in Plymouth was a reprimand for forgetting. And there was no end in sight. To act as though she suffered worse than anyone else was incredibly selfish.

Perhaps William was well enough to fight and her protests merely stemmed from wanting to keep him out of harm's way. It wasn't wrong, but considering the strength of the other side and their talent for destroying lives, it wasn't right, either. More had to be done.

"I agree," she said.

"You do?" His smile came quickly.

Falling in love had distracted her from her own drive to do her bit. There was no way she could remain cocooned in safety whilst men, including the one she loved, were risking their lives.

"It won't do to cower at Keldor, away from the war, not for either of us."

"What do you mean, 'for either of us'?" He crossed his arms, his expression not quite as triumphant as it had been seconds ago.

"I told my parents I wanted to work with children, but that was my dream before the war started. I once had a notion to nurse abroad. I've got talents too. The Red Cross is—"

He raised a hand as if she'd lost her mind. "Your parents won't allow it, nor will I."

Was he serious? "You won't *allow* it? So I've two mothers now?"

She stood in preparation to huff out of the room, finished

with the quarrel until she had more ammunition, but William trapped her in ready arms. She struggled to escape until her weakness stayed her and he dissolved in laughter.

She wasn't laughing.

"I'm all right," she said through gritted teeth. "Let me go."

In one gentle swoop, William placed her back in bed, the last place she wanted to be. "Have you always been so difficult, Olivia Jean?"

His amused eyes tormented her, but this wasn't a joke. She had phone calls to make and bags to pack. Where she was going, she didn't know. If she were feeling stronger, he'd have witnessed a tantrum he couldn't have imagined.

Temporarily derailed, she flopped back onto the pillows and reluctantly accepted the kiss planted on her forehead and nose.

"Relax, love," he said. "We'll speak more on this later. I've some things to discuss with Dr. Butler. Before I do, I'll send Polly up with tea."

Whether her parents liked it or not, her notion to leave wouldn't surprise them. And it shouldn't surprise William. She was a nurse, after all, and her country needed her as much as it needed him. As he himself said: Lying down in defeat is not an option. We must do what we can to protect our way of life. *We* meant everyone—including her.

# CHAPTER 30

SORENESS STILL PESTERED her right side, but Olivia would waste no more days in bed. William would be gone soon. And once she received a clean health report from Dr. Butler, she would follow suit—a topic they had yet to agree upon. For days, over meals, lying in bed, and now, as they walked the coast path on her first day out of the house, the dispute went round and round like a dog chasing its tail.

"Do you think I can't take care of myself? That I'd foolishly put myself in harm's way?" she asked. She wasn't a child, though he was certainly treating her like one.

"The fact that you're asking this incredibly asinine question tells me you know absolutely nothing about what's really happening out there," he said. "Actually living and working in a war zone has nothing to do with worrying over whether or not you'd use your head."

He may have had a point. When she pictured herself helping injured soldiers—in a tent, perhaps, or on the deck of a crowded and chaotic ship—her visions were nothing like the way she imagined him dodging bullets or recoiling as bombs rained from above. John, Henry, and countless others had lost their lives thanks to this war, but she had made a narrow escape; William had, too. Only luck would spare them both a second time.

She erased the unsteadiness from her voice with a swallow. "It doesn't matter, anyway. You'll be off soon; I'll be on my own. I can do as I wish. You'll not stop me then."

She scrunched her face and looked out over the choppy sea. The desire to risk her life for Britain quickened her heart, yet the acrid fires of Plymouth that still coated the back of her throat soured her stomach. For a moment they stood there, Olivia struggling to hold the ground she was on the precipice of losing, and William in desperate need of recouping his.

But then his expression changed, as if whatever wild card he'd been saving was about to be played. "You're my wife, Mrs. Morgan, which also makes you mistress of Keldor." Practically smiling, he took a step closer. "You have responsibilities here and to the community. Polly, James, and Annie can't expand the garden on their own, and as he's told us more than once, Dr. Butler could use your help at his surgery. Will you do this for me, love? Will you stay here and care for the home we'll one day share with our family? Will you let this be your contribution to the war effort?"

No one had told her how similar married life would be to living with her parents. The perks of love were brilliant, of course, but this submission? This forced confinement? Would she ever be trusted enough to make her own decisions?

"You may not regard your tasks here as very important, but think of the peace of mind you'll give me knowing that Keldor is in your competent hands."

He wouldn't worry about Keldor if she left. He'd worry about her, and he mustn't. In order to live, he needed to stay alert. He needed to win, and he needed to come home.

Translating her loss for words as the acquiescence she wasn't ready to give, he put his arm around her and suggested they head back for lunch.

"Mr. William," Mrs. Pollard said, rushing across the garden and waving a bit of paper. She thrust a telegram into William's hand.

It was exactly what everyone thought it would be. The telephone call to confirm his pickup would come within twenty-four hours.

He was leaving.

Already.

Her eyes were dry when they met his, but inside she was mourning the time they'd wasted quarreling. They would waste no more. Seemingly thinking the same, William said he'd pack later and suggested they enjoy their luncheon at Steren Cove.

"I'll gather items in the kitchen," she said, matching his urgency. "You grab a blanket."

Ambling along the overgrown path to Steren Cove, William carried the picnic basket and a tartan. Olivia followed closely behind. The trail narrowed, and errant branches, alive with green, stretched across the footpath as if barring their entry to paradise.

Despite her raging curiosity about where he was being sent, she was trying to respect his transition back into soldiering life by not asking too many questions. Military confidentiality often kept wives in the dark, but she had a mind to pry a little more.

"You said training would last through summer. Then what?"

"We'll be off come autumn. Could be earlier, depending on circumstances."

"So soon," she muttered, apprehension slowing her steps.

Growing up, Olivia had seen her mother's fears determine with whom the Talbot children could associate, where they could go, and when they were needed home. With one eye on the back of her beloved and the other on the trail ahead, she understood her mother's fretting. Full of questions and opinions, she was acting just like her—yet another thing to worry about.

A strong breeze assailed Steren Cove, but the air was warm. Olivia's toes welcomed the sand's dry warmth before wriggling beneath the surface to enjoy a cool, damp massage. Not far from where she stood, William wrestled mighty gusts as he laid out their rug. The sight of it whipping above his head before clinging to him like a starfish to a rock made her laugh.

"I'm glad you find this amusing," he grumbled through a smile that melted her core.

Since Plymouth, Olivia had craved William the way she'd once craved chocolate and ice cream. But food cravings were short-lived. She hadn't laid eyes on a chocolate bar in over a year, making it easier to forget what one tasted like. But William had flaunted himself before her for weeks, sometimes sharply dressed, other times undressed. Beside her in bed every night, his hands caught in her hair and his warm breath on her neck sent her into a tizzy. His careful kisses were granules of sugar dotting her lips without the cake and frosting to follow.

And soon he would depart, out of her life for an indefinite amount of time. Would her hunger for him subside? Would she forget what it felt like to kiss him, to lie with him—something they still had yet to do as husband and wife?

He had yet to flatten the disobedient blanket when she fell upon the man who would likely be gone by this time tomorrow. Without hesitation, his unruly kisses crushed her playful lips, but she didn't complain.

He moved her beneath him onto the blanket. "It's only been three weeks. You're sure?"

She nodded, though she wasn't sure, not at all. She also wasn't sure if, after tomorrow, she'd ever see him again. Shoving that thought from her mind, she lifted her chin, inviting the fierce assault along her jawline and down her neck.

"I've missed you," he whispered once his body joined hers.

She'd missed him too. Defying minor discomforts along her rib cage, she sought his eyes. Steadfast, they summoned her life force the way mystics conjured spirits. Using hers as a portal, they elicited the inner workings of her heart. Her nature, the good and the bad, rose out of her like steam off a cup of tea. He drank them all in: her compassion and generosity, her penchant for justice, her stubbornness, and her need to win arguments.

He had seen even her frailty, and yet his eyes promised that no matter what he saw, he would love her still.

"How afraid are you?" Olivia asked him.

She'd worry no matter what he said, so he went with the truth. "I'm mildly afraid."

It was three o'clock in the morning, and he was due to leave at eight. They'd fallen into bed after a late supper, but not for sleep. Now that they'd finally consummated their marriage, they couldn't stop. Outside, the wind whipped angry raindrops against the blackened windows, having long ago erased the sun and warm breezes from the day.

The atmosphere had changed indoors, too. The inevitable telephone call had finally come: a car would arrive for him first thing the next morning.

"Tell me what you're afraid of."

Olivia lay within the circle of his left arm. Besotted as always by her scent, he contemplated how to capture it and take it with him. She'd encouraged him to sleep, but he'd refused; he would sleep plenty on the train north. Tonight, he only wanted to enjoy her company.

"I'm afraid this war will last much longer than we first thought. And I'm afraid of how dreadfully I'll miss you. But most of all," he lowered his voice, "I'm afraid that if something happens to me, something will happen to you."

"What do you mean?" she asked sharply, sitting up.

"I don't know how to explain this without sounding like I've got an enormous ego and that you're not a brilliant, strong woman." He traced his fingers up and down the locked bare arm supporting her.

"Just say it."

His eyes shifted to the wall of black behind her. Flashes of hand-to-hand combat and months of imprisonment swept the canvas of his mind. "I'm not afraid of fighting. And I'm not afraid of being captured, because it wouldn't be like before." Saying the words aloud helped convince him; he hoped they helped her, too. "Knowing I have you to come home to once it's all over, I could survive it. And dying—I'm not afraid of dying. My whole life, I've never been afraid of that."

He too sat up, unsure of what compelled him to continue. Perhaps it was the deep disappointment that resurfaced whenever he thought of his father. Or maybe he was looking in the mirror: The bond with his wife was impenetrable and their love so intense that he wasn't sure how he'd behave had their roles been reversed. Was it Olivia's changeable behavior over the past weeks—the bouts of tears, the fear and instability that incited the words he was loath to utter?

"But I'm afraid of how you might react, should that happen."

She said nothing, but the way her eyes avoided his told him she knew exactly what he was talking about.

"Promise me you'll always look after yourself no matter what you think is happening to me. Don't—don't be like my father." This was the first time he'd spoken of his father's death himself. He wished he didn't have to and was careful to spare her the unpleasant particulars.

"Your father?"

"He killed himself, Olivia, in the library. Not long before I was found in North Africa."

Dr. Butler had been the one to tell him about the suicide, but he'd refused to elaborate. Mrs. Pollard's telling added details she didn't want to share, like how she found him dangling beside his desk one night when bringing his supper. How once he'd learned William was missing, he'd refused to believe it and assumed his son was dead, just like his mother. Polly had piled excuse upon excuse as to why he'd done it, and none William could accept. His father had been incredibly selfish, and the more he thought upon it, the more it hurt.

"And you think—"

His hand went up. "Please. Keep your faith in me. If you don't hear from me after a time, once I'm abroad, don't assume the worst and consider me gone—because I may not be. I couldn't bear it if you gave up on me, too."

That quieted her. She ducked her head as though to hide, validating the misgivings he'd rather have kept to himself.

"Promise me that." Impulse forced his hand to her chin, and he lifted it with a firm jerk. "Promise me you won't be like him. I beg you."

Obediently she met his gaze, blinking back tears as if she'd been slapped. "I promise."

He released her, appalled at the white marks his fingers left on her jawline.

In the candlelight, her wet eyes twinkled as her smile overtook the moment. "You won't have to worry. I'll be here, cheering for you, awaiting your return, and warming this bed. I'll not give up on you. I promise."

Lieutenant Hugh Jenkins arrived at Keldor sharply at 8:00 a.m.

"Good morning, sir." Jenkins saluted his superior the moment the front door opened on the torrential rain outside.

After William's returned salute, Jenkins began dutifully loading his bags.

William folded Olivia in his arms and kissed her once more. The short moments before the lieutenant's arrival had been spent in each other's arms. William had covered her face with kisses and offered encouraging smiles. She accepted both whilst futilely forcing images of her immediate future from her mind: whether enjoying a book in the library or strolling to Steren Cove in the height of summer, she would be alone. She would go to bed alone; she would wake alone. Her one piece of William—his child and possibly her chance to ever conceive another—was lost in Plymouth. Should something happen to him, her distant future would be just as solitary.

"I love you," he said. His eyes reminded her of the ocean he would cross in the months to come. "Remember what we talked about. Don't give up on me."

The heat of his hand and the pressure of his lips remained after he walked out the door.

Frustrated at her inability to stop time, she followed him halfway down the stone steps. Water cascaded down the waxy material of his long greatcoat and beaded along the brim of his cap.

At the motorcar's open door, he looked up. "What are you doing?"

She squinted against the downpour. Rain pelted the top of her head and soaked through her dressing gown and everything underneath. Water raced down the bridge of her nose, dripped over her lips, and trickled into her open mouth.

"Olivia," he shouted over the cacophony of falling water.

Lieutenant Jenkins leant forward to get a closer look at the major's potentially mad wife.

"Olivia, what is it?"

"Don't die."

"What?"

John had died, shot from the air. Whether he died from the plane's explosion, the impact of its crash into the Channel, or simply drowned, it didn't matter. Henry too had died, found dead under a pile of bricks. Was it a slow suffocation that killed him? Or was he crushed instantly? How would William die?

Gripping the balustrade tightly, she took one step down, then another. "Don't die. Please, William. Don't—"

He lowered his head into the car. "Lieutenant, one minute."

"Certainly, sir."

William slammed the door and sprinted up the handful of steps to her. Forcefully, but with care, he backed her against the balustrade and pressed his forehead into hers.

"I won't," he said roughly before cradling her cheek in his hand. Immersed in the unsympathetic rain, he kissed her again. "I love you, my sweet Olivia. I'll return. You have my word."

# CHAPTER 31

It took Mrs. Pollard three hours to coax Olivia from her damp bed and into a hot bath after William left. Reprimands that sounded strikingly similar to her mother's did nothing to budge her from her sad reverie. She was being childish—she didn't need a reminder—but the clever Mrs. Pollard didn't give up. Arms crossed, she approached the bed like a formidable headmistress.

"Where's your strength, then? Your courage?" she asked.

"What are you talking about?"

"The strength you came here with. You lost half your family, then came here to care for a devil who wanted nothing to do with you. You weren't crying in those days. So where'd you put it, then, your pluck? What've you done with it?"

No wonder William had turned out so well under her watch.

"Mr. William is to ring tomorrow, is he not? Do you want him to be proud of the woman he married, the woman he fell in love with, knowing she's all right so he can focus on staying alive and winning this bloody war?"

Olivia wiped her wet nose and cheeks. Head low, she trudged to the bathroom and slammed the door.

The next evening on the phone, before William had even uttered her name, she apologized for her dramatic send-off. She promised that all was well, and each passing day proved this was true.

Spearheading Keldor's extended victory garden allowed no time for heartache. With her knees in the dirt and the sun on her shoulders, Olivia channeled the green thumb of William's mother and prayed her spirit wasn't devastated to see Keldor's sprawling lawns plowed and sowed with root crops. Harvests came in waves assisting local families, schools, and hospitals. Keldor benefited as well, but no one gained more than Olivia. The sway she held over her garden gave her immeasurable comfort and a sense of purpose she hadn't expected. Ripened produce and dead weeds enriched her long days. Thanks from gratified recipients ended them happily.

And yet stormy summer nights were unbearably lonely, and she often went sleepless. Cooler temperatures reminded her that summer would end, as would William's training. By then he'd be off fighting, and she'd be stuck at Keldor, suffering through shorter and colder days without him. She needed another occupation, far from here. Yes, William wished her to stay, but she'd never actually said she would. Joining the Red Cross meant she could work in Britain, an option William might swallow, but if she joined the army she could be stationed abroad—perhaps even someplace close to him. Though images of Plymouth still haunted her, she could manage the front. Helping others would expel her fears.

Come September, she'd make inquiries.

But then August arrived.

Whilst William relayed how his men were finalizing their training, Olivia curled at his desk in the library, cleaning dirt from underneath her fingernails and savoring the warmth of his voice across the miles.

"What will you do this autumn after the final harvest?" he

asked. "Will you see Dr. Butler for a job? Didn't I say Keldor would keep you well occupied this summer?"

"I've been to see him, but not for a job." She tried keeping the smile out of her voice but couldn't. She wasn't sure how she managed the first five minutes of the conversation, as bursting as she was with the news.

"What is it? Is someone ill?"

"Just a touch of nausea. It's usually gone by midday."

"Nausea? It's you? What did he say it was, something you're eating?"

"I'm going to have a baby."

"Do you mean it?" he shouted. "My love, that's wonderful news! So, what is the protocol? You're cutting back in the garden, I hope? How careful do you need to be? If you must hire help, do."

She could hear the voices on the other end of the line more clearly. It sounded as if the others in the room had guessed what had happened and were congratulating him.

"Dr. Butler says physical work is healthy, as is being out of doors. I promise, I'm taking excellent care of my—" A whimper hijacked her voice.

"Love—"

"I'm fine," she finally managed. "I promise. Truly, all I do is cry and vomit. I wish you were here to hold back my hair." She feigned a weak laugh.

The line grew quiet, exposing the sadness they both fought to deny.

"I hope you don't mind," she continued, "but I told my parents. Mother validated my hopes and urged me to see Dr. Butler."

"Of course I don't mind."

"They're delighted. I knew as soon as she learned she'd be a grandmother, war or no war, she'd be thrilled. I've asked her to deliver the baby. He or she will be here in January."

"January?"

"Can you be here?" she asked biting at her jagged and rather stubborn thumbnail.

"I'll put in a request right away."

The line fell quiet again. Was William questioning whether or not he'd make a good parent? The baby wouldn't arrive for months. Did he doubt he'd even live that long? Her hand went to her flat stomach, a place it'd visited quite often lately. She would remain positive for all three of them—another promise she'd keep here on the home front.

⁓

POST OFFICE

TELEGRAM

25 SEP 41

COMING HOME ON SHORT LEAVE STOP SEE YOU IN 12 HOURS STOP LOVE WILLIAM

The telegram had arrived at noon, and sleep got the best of her after midnight. Snug with a book under a blanket in the library, Olivia listened for an approaching motorcar on gravel. None came. By dim light and a toasty fire, she reread the same page over and over, her mind too busy anticipating William's arrival to focus on anything else. Why was he coming home? How long would he stay? Did this mean he'd get to come home often?

At one o'clock she awoke with a start, freezing. Intent on checking the fire, she sat up, but the broad silhouette of someone bending over her blocked her view.

William's fingers swept back the curls flattened to her face, and though she couldn't make out his features the way she'd like, her heart sped.

"Finally!" she cried.

"Hello, my love."

His careworn smile and creased brow surprised her. She was about to say so until her mouth was assailed by a burning kiss, stirring places in her body that had lain dormant for too long.

She quelled her passion to draw back and get a better look at him. Though her fingers could barely span the developed bulk of his arms, his normally squared shoulders followed the corners of his mouth in a downward slope. She hadn't seen him this forlorn since January.

"What's the matter?"

"Nothing. I've just missed you. My God, Olivia, how I've missed you." He enfolded her in his arms and lifted her, cradling her as he had on their wedding day.

She locked her arms about his neck, unsure of the quaver in his voice. "I've missed you too."

# CHAPTER 32

THEIR BEDROOM WAS A WELCOME SIGHT—THE rich wood tones of ancient furniture, the red bedspread, and the black dog sleeping on it were comforting mainstays to William's weary eyes. Head up at hearing his master's voice, Jasper fell into a fever of panting. The happy reunion of licks and ear scratches was short-lived, however, as William relegated the Labrador to the floor.

Eyes fixed on his wife, he couldn't remove his confining uniform quickly enough. He threw his belt, tunic, and tie to the floor and fought with the small buttons of his shirt. Olivia watched him struggle with the seductive smile of a courtesan curled against a wall of pillows. Her golden locks had grown a great deal and fell down her bare arms in hunks. Her new curves called to him from beneath a white nightdress that clung to her as if wet, starting with the tiny ball of her abdomen.

His hand smoothed over her hard, swollen stomach before he leant down and kissed its summit. "My God, Olivia, you're more stunning than ever. This is all right?"

He slipped the straps of her nightdress off her shoulders.

"Absolutely. As soon as I knew you were coming home, I rang Dr. Butler and asked."

"You didn't."

"I did. I hadn't the nerve to ask my mother. Anyway, he said intercourse wouldn't hurt the baby and we should carry on as usual. Although if we couldn't, I can't say what I'd do. Now that I'm no longer sick, I, well, I'm not sure how to explain it."

"Try," he said, eyeing the supple skin inside her splayed thighs, a vision he'd dreamt of for months.

"Well, it seems I've entered a new stage of my pregnancy. Instead of feeling sick, all I feel is this mad desire for you."

"And this is a new sensation?" he asked, taking his time revisiting neglected territory.

She tilted her head back, uttering something or other about switching off the light, and he closed his mouth over hers. With no time to remove his trousers completely, he kicked off his shoes and found his way between her opened legs.

Time slowed, as did his impetus. Dizzy with her heady lavender scent, he cherished this intimacy that he shared with no one else. Collarbone, eyelids, and earlobes, his lips sought the smallest plots of her skin. In return, her caresses dismissed the anxiety and loneliness that had come to define him.

Neither spoke, not one word, until they were well spent—tired, but not sleepy.

"When your telegram came this morning, my heart stopped," she said, breaking the silence. "I thought something terrible had happened."

"I was worried you might. I thought of surprising you, but then I changed my mind. I apologize for not phoning. It all came about so quickly."

She wrapped her leg around his hip, giddy. "How long do you get to stay?"

"A week." His eyes drifted, unable to mirror her excitement. "That should be enough time, they think."

"Enough time for what?"

He rolled away from her onto his back. "Olivia, I've—I've

done something dreadful." He pinched his nose with his free hand and squeezed his eyes shut.

"What do you mean? What's happened?"

Yellow hairs tickled his neck and shoulders.

"My nightmares have returned—the violent ones, the terrors. Ever since we started simulating hand-to-hand combat. Not that they ever truly went away. I haven't mentioned them because I didn't want you to worry." He smiled ruefully, hoping for forgiveness. The soft hand on his cheek deemed it granted. "But lately they've been worse, more like they used to be. Neighboring officers have had to wake me in the middle of the night due to the screaming and, hmm, the crying. Two days ago during overnight wilderness training, I role-played the enemy. One of my privates stole up behind me."

The exercise was to be swift, precise—a dramatization, not real. And still.

"I knew he was coming, but as soon as he laid his hands on me, I—I snapped." He closed his eyes to block the vision of a man crumpled on the ground with two broken knees and a head speckled with contusions. "I almost broke his neck. He may not recover."

He couldn't read her expression. Was she judging him as he judged himself? Did she think he'd become unhinged, that he might snap again and hurt her too? That would never happen. Her presence was his therapy. He'd spilt the truth and was already absorbing the calm she exuded.

"What's next? For you, I mean." Her voice was hardening, every syllable more brittle by the second. "You're not dismissed, then?"

"We ship out as soon as I return."

She sat up. "Will you be ready?"

His laughter lacked mirth. "Yes. In fact, I've had a psychiatric evaluation—two, actually. Much to the delight of my superiors, the doctors say I'm more than ready. If I can do to the enemy what I did to Private Schroeder—well, that's exactly what they want."

She slammed her fist onto her bent knee. "Damn it, William! Their solution is for you to come home for a week before they ship you out to war? This is supposed to cure you?"

"There is no cure. I'm to stay out of current trainings in case I hurt someone else, someone on our side. In war, though, I'm an asset. If I use my rage and fury on the enemy, I win. We win."

Thumbnail between her teeth, she said nothing.

The colonel had joked, calling him a killing machine. It wasn't funny. "I almost killed him with my bare hands. I was pulled away before I could draw my knife, that's what they told me. I remember nothing except a sense of drowning once I realized what I'd done. Once I saw his misshapen body being lifted away."

After delivering a kiss of forgiveness, his angel of mercy crossed her arms. "I don't think you should go."

"Olivia."

"You have a war injury. You do this—you go on this assignment—and you'll come home in a poorer state than ever imagined. I don't care if you *are* an 'asset.' "

He was mute with disappointment. He hoped the subject would be over so he could make love to her again and savor the world he'd missed these past four months—the world he'd miss overseas whilst dodging gunfire or dying at enemy hands.

He raked his fingers forward through his hair. "As well as you know me, Olivia, you'll never understand this. You'll never know what this feels like. Not that I have a choice, but I will go. And I will fight."

She cast her eyes down and gave a reluctant nod. He read the tiny gesture as a positive and drew her on top of him. Settled in his embrace, she rolled with him as he switched off the bedside lamp. The room became pitch-black, the curtains doing their job of blocking the full moon sliding toward the quiet horizon.

≈

"Oh, Mr. William, I'm so glad to see you."

Mrs. Pollard opened her arms and hugged the breath out of him. He wiped a tear from her eye when they parted and kissed each cheek.

"And you're to be a father," she said, turning back to the counter to pour him a cup of tea and regain her composure. "I couldn't be happier for you and Mistress Olivia."

"Thank you, Polly. We're counting on you to act as the little one's grandmother when he or she arrives. You understand that?"

She lowered her head bashfully—an unusual expression for her. She pushed a cup of tea in his direction. "It would be my honor. Now get Jasper outside before he has an accident!"

The early autumn air was brisk but considerably warmer than that of Durham this time of year. William embraced the balminess from the stone terrace overlooking the back garden. Straight ahead in the victory garden, new vegetable beds joined their smaller, older counterparts. The closest housed potato plants bunched beside one another like old chums, their leaves hinting at treasures beneath the soil ready to be unearthed.

He finished his tea and set the teacup carefully near the door, admiring the floral pattern of his grandmother's china. What would his tea come in next week or in a month? A tin cup? Would he have tea at all?

He left the terrace in search of Jasper, who'd gone to relieve himself somewhere behind the trees west of the vegetable patch. On his way, he clung to sunny spots for warmth. If only this were his final homecoming—the one when the war was over and he was home to stay. But that was months away. Christ, who was he kidding? Based on military intelligence, it was more likely to be years.

Having sensed his approach, Jasper trotted out of the trees, tail wagging and happy to have his master's undivided attention.

William delivered a few ear scratches that lead to multiple belly scratches. Jasper snorted as he rubbed his nose fervently in the dewy lawn.

He wished Olivia understood his need to fight. Her side of the argument was valid: She loved him and wanted him out of danger. In her eyes, he'd already served his country, leaving him with unseen scars worse than most. He remained constantly on the defense, wary of strangers, and ready to defuse any threatening situation with intuitive violence.

But there was so much she didn't know. Things in Europe had gone from hot to boiling. Hitler's surprise attack on the Soviet Union had been his largest yet. Axis powers were gaining steam, and Britain needed aggressive and surprise attacks of her own. The closer William was to news from the Continent, the more enraged he became. What he'd suffered as a POW was a mere fragment of the führer's larger plan for his enemies. This was evident from the horror stories delivered by those who'd seen what the Nazis were capable of on a much grander scale than a private compound in North Africa.

The Nazis must be defeated. If William's damaged temperament benefited his country, then he would use it. Olivia had no inkling of what he was capable of as a soldier, a fighter. He had nightmares, yes; he was disturbed, highly. But he was also determined to win. His thirst for victory had never been so strong. If he could lead his men into a battle that might weaken the Nazis even slightly, surely this would offset the damage inflicted upon him over a year ago.

So far, he'd kept this scenario to himself, afraid Olivia would disagree. The last thing he wanted during their precious time together was row. He loved her like no one ever in his life, and it was because of her that he'd regained the will to recover. But this part of his healing had nothing to do with her. Only he could mend what had been broken inside him. And mend it he would, to become the best husband and father he could be. She needed to trust his will and remain optimistic that he would survive to emerge from war a stronger man.

"More tea?"

Mrs. Pollard held a teapot aloft at the side door.

"Yes, thank you, Polly."

She poured milk followed by the steaming tawny elixir into the teacup he'd left by the balustrade, then left him alone with his dog and his thoughts.

In the wee hours, Olivia woke to the broad wall of William's back, her left arm draped over his bare hip. If she got up to use the toilet, he'd wake as soon as she left the bed. Perhaps he'd like to wake up a different way. Deep need for her absentee husband still thundered, and she wasn't about to let his time at home go to waste. She liked being in charge and having her way with him, as she had earlier that night. She trusted he liked it, too. Under the disorderly bedclothes, she sought her prize before seizing it.

She was thrown onto her back faster than she could move or speak.

"Are you ready to die?" seethed a menacing shadow with William's voice. He held her arms high above her head as he hovered above her.

She twisted impotently in his grasp. He could hurt the baby; he could kill them both. He completely overpowered her. But even so, she understood what he did not: He was still asleep and at the mercy of a nightmare he thought he was living.

As though reminding her of his presence, he grunted a string of profanities and thrust his weight into her wrists so roughly she expected to hear a *crack*. Sharp knees pressed her thighs into the mattress. Her voice was her only defense, and panicked as she was, she struggled to speak loudly enough to penetrate his stupor.

"William!" Breath hard to catch, panting. "William, it's Olivia. O-*livia!* Wake up, darling. Wake *up!*"

Ignoring her completely, he stretched his free hand toward his right ankle as though searching for something. It returned as a balled fist, inches from her face and ready to strike. Silhouetted by the fireplace's dying embers, his head tilted back and forth, up and down like a boxer loosening up before a fight.

"William! Wake up, damn it. You're hurting me!" She shoved against him with every syllable.

The ominous profile stilled.

"What?" he whispered, looking back and forth between his fist and his victim. "What the bloody hell?"

In a flash, he freed her wrists. Once his knees left her soft thighs, he slinked away, a looming shadow absorbed in the room's darkness.

Olivia clambered to the bedside lamp and switched it on. His face displayed not an ounce of the fury it held seconds ago. Dilated pupils as black as the center of a blood-red poppy crowded out the blue as he stared back at her. She'd never seen William look at her like this, as though he wished the person in front of him were anyone but her.

He gathered his garments and left the room.

She brought her knees in close to her quaking body. Rapid breaths filled her chest and she rubbed her wrists, willing the return of circulation to her cold, trembling hands.

William sat at the foot of their unmade bed, waiting. When Olivia emerged from the bathroom, her tired eyes showed no sign of surprise at his presence. That was good.

Wet and combed back from her face, her hair looked darker than normal. Her dainty feet approached with quiet footfalls, and her light blue dressing gown swished at her ankles. He had no idea what she would say; only what he deserved. He wanted to reach out and take her wrists—gently, this time—but rose to his feet instead, humiliated, awaiting punishment.

"How badly did I hurt you?"

She held up her arms. Purple splotches covered her wrists.

"Christ." Not meeting her eyes, he turned toward the wardrobe. "That decides it, then."

"Decides what?"

"I'm off. I'll get a room in the village or St. Austell. It's not safe for you and the baby if I stay. You were right." He heaved his leather bag onto the bed and began to rummage through it, trying to determine what else he might need over the next week.

Olivia's hand smashed down onto the top of the bag.

"You can't leave!" She took his hand and placed it on the small mound of her belly. "I'm fine. *We're* fine. Your leaving will solve nothing."

"Coming home was a bad idea. You were right, Olivia. Going back to war has made me far worse than before. I'm lethal. My mind will remain fixed on the enemy until this fight is over." With hands on her shoulders, he moved her aside and returned to his bag. "But I still want to see you. We'll have dinner tomorrow, someplace public."

"No!" She hurled the bag to the floor.

He squeezed the bridge of his nose.

"What happened was an accident," she said. "A mistake. You didn't know what you were doing. I should've known better than to—"

"Goddamn it, it's nothing to do with you!" The rage he possessed after realizing what he'd done returned. He stepped back, tempering his voice. "This is my problem, and you know it."

"Fine," she said, crossing her arms. "Go."

She dropped onto the bed, but the hard line of her mouth crumpled.

He knelt in front of her. "My worst fears were realized

tonight: My demons took over and I frightened you. I hurt you. I can't risk that happening again, especially with the baby coming." He rotated her bruised wrists, their softness reflecting her innocence in all this. Overcome with shame, he buried his face in her lap, where her dressing gown absorbed his tireless laments. "I'm so sorry."

"What were you dreaming? Can you tell me?" In one fluid movement, she slid to the floor beside him. The bedside lamp shined on her bare legs. Her calves were muscular but supple, her knees smooth. Her pink varnished toes reminded him of sugared almonds.

He forced himself to focus. "Wirth. It's always Wirth. I can't get the bloody bastard out of my head. Ridiculous to think I can fix this."

"Fix your night terrors?"

"Fix all of it. If I use my talents to aid my country, then the nightmares will go away. I'll be myself, like before—before this darkness clouded every thought, waking and dreaming."

"Revenge won't help, and—"

"This isn't about revenge. It's about facing my fears, and I'm ready. I've been ready. But, well, what if it doesn't work?"

"Your nightmares aren't going away. They're a part of you and always will be. You need to learn to live with them in a way—"

"In a way that doesn't harm the people I love."

She frowned. "Including yourself."

He snickered. "I'm afraid I make a better soldier than husband. Fatherhood will likely be just as disappointing."

"My grandmother says it's often our attitudes that fulfill our destinies."

"And what the devil does that mean?"

"It means that if you really believe those words—and I don't think you do—they will come true."

He raised his hands before her. "I've killed with these hands. These hands that I touch you with are the same hands that have taken numerous lives. And to imagine they'll soon hold our infant child—that doesn't bother you in the slightest?"

"I married a soldier. And though I prayed it wouldn't happen, I knew you'd likely return to war." Her eyes locked on his. "But we're in this together. We always have been. Don't separate me from your suffering. Let me help you work through it, please?"

Her kind brown eyes expected consent.

His remorseful nod gave it.

"Good."

She stood. A swift pull untied her dressing gown. The fabric fell from her shoulders as gracefully as a petal tumbling from a flower.

"I'm going back to bed. I expect you'll join me."

Her ample breasts and the protrusion of her little tummy advised him that only a fool would linger on the floor by himself.

# CHAPTER 33

5 OCTOBER, 1941
   Mrs. William Morgan
   Keldor
   Mevagissey
   My love,
   When I think back to where I was last week, my heart aches. After this letter, I've no idea when you'll hear from me, but have faith, Olivia, that I am alive and well. Remember, I won't be alone: A band of well-trained, intelligent, and level-headed men accompany me. We look after each other. As soon as I'm able, I'll send another letter. For now, keep sending yours to Durham. Eventually they'll find their way to me.
   Private Schroeder is recovering well. He's still in the care of doctors and vigilant nurses (thank God for nurses), but he's conscious and should be released soon. I'm happy to report he holds no grudge against me and promised that with a little more training, it is I who would've landed in hospital, not him.
   How is our little one treating you? Are you sleeping better or are her movements still keeping you awake at night? I hope your premonition that she (yes, I'm still convinced we've got a little girl in there) might be a restless sleeper is false, for then you'd have two of us on your hands.

*But not to worry, I can care for the angel during the night whilst you get your beauty sleep. In fact, HQ confirmed I've been given leave for early January. I've put in a special request to stretch my visit at least two weeks past the birth of our little girl. I can't wait to meet her.*

*As much as I regret the events that led me back home recently, I am likewise grateful for the opportunity. Time with you heals my soul in inexplicable ways. To hold you in my arms delivered the boost I needed to stay focused on getting back to you as quickly as possible. Remember, if you don't receive a letter from me in the coming weeks, find comfort knowing I am fighting for you and our family. I'm fighting for our country and our world. May it one day be inundated with peace.*

*I love you forever, Olivia.*

*Yours,*

*William*

~

*28 November, 1941*

*Major William Morgan*

*Brancepeth*

*Durham*

*Dear William,*

*I hope my letters are finding you well, wherever you are. Though I haven't heard from you in some time, I expect you've been writing and your letters are sitting in a mailbag somewhere on the Continent awaiting safe passage to England. Don't worry, I shall keep writing and apprising you of the goings-on here.*

*Pretty Jenna and her brother Peder came to Keldor today. Peder said how grateful he'd been to receive your letters over the summer and how his last visit had him worried that you'd written off a very old friend-ship. It was an interesting call, actually. Both knew you were away from home, yet Peder was keen to introduce himself properly to the wife of his oldest friend during his short leave, whereas Jenna looked as though she longed to be elsewhere. Neither knew of our expected addition, and whilst Peder embraced me with congratulations and sincere best wishes, Jenna struggled to produce a smile. Has she always worn her feelings so blatantly on her sleeve? The smirk on her face whilst examining my big belly would've been discernable to a blind person.*

*We managed tea, though, as well as two civil women in love with the same man could. For almost an hour, Peder kept me entertained with stories of your rambunctious boyhood whilst Jenna spent much of it chatting with Mrs. Pollard, who adores her. Apparently clerical work for the ATS wasn't a lofty enough assignment, and she's training as a nurse in London. She enjoys it and coyly asked if you were still in need of one. You never told me she had a sense of humor. And she is beautiful. Are you sure you made the right choice? I hope you don't mind that I gave her your address. You've been friends for many years. Even your jealous wife shouldn't stand in the way of that.*

*Between tending winter crops (nothing too arduous, I promise) and dodging raindrops, I've been nesting, getting ready for baby. Mrs. Pollard, Annie, and I have used what resources we have to make clothes and even new curtains to hang in your former nursery. We've unearthed some of your old toys, as well as your bassinet. I've spent hours of rainy afternoons knitting a baby blanket in your mother's rocking chair overlooking her favorite garden. How calm I feel in that room, absorbing the lives that once inhabited it.*

*Christmas is a month away, and I can't help but to reflect on the magic of last year's holiday under the mistletoe. I look forward to the ones we'll celebrate together in the years to come.*

*Stay safe, William. I love you.*

*Yours,*

*Olivia*

~

"Mrs. Morgan!" Annie called up the stairs.

It was morning, before breakfast. Jasper had been following Olivia around the bedroom, waiting for her to take him out. The doorbell rang and now, hearing her name, the toll was for her. In no mood for company, she threw on her dressing gown (much too small) and stood at the top of the stairs.

"Who is it?" she whispered loud enough for to hear.

"A delivery for you. A telegram."

She hadn't heard from William since early October. A message could only mean he'd returned safely to England. A rush of joy spurred her down the stairs as fast as her swollen body would allow, with Jasper wagging and trotting behind her. She snatched the envelope from the waiting telegram boy, whose dubious face gave her pause. It didn't look like other telegrams sent by William. She tore it open.

It wasn't from William. It was from Colonel Adams.


URGENT TELEGRAM

15 DEC 41

I REGRET TO INFORM YOU THAT YOUR HUSBAND MAJOR WILLIAM MORGAN WAS POSTED AS MISSING ON 9 DECEMBER 1941 STOP A DETAILED LETTER WILL FOLLOW STOP

COLONEL ADAMS

151ST INFANTRY BRIGADE

SIXTH BATTALION, DLI


Olivia backed away from the open door as it pitched to and fro. The tall oriental vase in the corner teetered, threatening to crash into a million pieces. At her feet, tiny tiles swirled in colorful symmetry like images through a kaleidoscope. She lowered herself onto the bottom stair with help from the handrail and put her head between her knees, fighting the rising bile in her throat. Thwarted by her ever-growing stomach, she was forced her to lie on her side, her left cheek kissing the step's dusty hardwood.

"No," she panted, "no, no, no."

A gritty puddle spread the length of her flattened face, pooling near her mouth. He was to be home soon.

"Good news?" came a lilting voice from somewhere. "Mrs. Morgan?"

His leave was just weeks away.

"Is it the baby? Are you in pain? Tell me, what is it?"

The hand on her forehead was warm and soft, smaller than William's.

"Mrs. Pollard!" Annie's voice sounded above her. "Come quickly!"

Missing?

"Mistress Olivia! What's happened? Has she fallen? Is she hurt?"

"It can't be," Olivia moaned. "It can't be."

The baby was moving, clearly uncomfortable, as was she. Slow to emerge from her fog, she sat up and wiped the wet off her cheek and the bridge of her nose. But the tears kept coming. Through their blurry lens, Mrs. Pollard excused the anxious telegram boy and closed the front door.

Annie, her eyes quivering with sympathy, took Olivia's hand. "Missing doesn't mean dead. My cousin was thought missing at first, but they found him in a prison camp. He'll be home after the war." Gently, she uncurled Olivia's fist and smoothed her palm with her own.

Olivia rediscovered her voice. "John was declared 'missing' before they found him dead," she said in a lethal tone. "'Missing' means William's body is shredded so badly there's nothing recognizable left."

She blinked through an imagined scene where rivulets of blood meandered through the streets of what once was a village where the remains of homes, business, and soldiers lay lifeless in the pink light of dawn.

She looked directly into the eyes of both women, one after

another. "Until they find his identity discs—his cold meat ticket. That's what my brother's friends called them. That's what 'missing' means."

"Let's get her upstairs," said Mrs. Pollard.

Close to lunchtime the next day, a letter arrived from Colonel Adams. Jeanette Talbot arrived as well. Annie led Olivia's mother into her bedroom, where she'd been since the previous morning.

"Has she eaten?" Mrs. Talbot asked, sitting on the bed.

"Soup last night, nothing yet today."

"Olivia, look at me."

She refused. Who'd called her mother?

"It's time you returned to the land of the living. The colonel's letter has arrived, and Mrs. Pollard is on her way up with luncheon."

Laced with venom, her mother's voice evoked memories of the row that almost sent Olivia off to live with her grandmother a handful of years ago. So she'd missed her curfew by a few hours; contacting the police was hardly necessary. She was safe. She'd just lost track of time.

"Your grandmother sent this tea." Her mother shook a small tin she retrieved from a paper bag. "It's made of oat straw and nettle leaf, meant to calm—and safe during pregnancy, but I daresay it most likely tastes like something that's crawled from the sewer." She set the tin down and folded her hands around the crumpled bag. "She almost came with me. I had to convince her to stay home, seeing as I'll be here for a while."

Olivia's head jerked. "A while? What's a while?"

"At least until the baby is born. And some time after that, I suspect." Still wearing the navy hat she'd traveled in, her mother tilted her head as though her daughter should have guessed this.

Olivia lay back on the pillows. "I'm fine, really. I don't need you here."

"You don't need me here? Because you can look after yourself and this baby on your own? Because you're eating regularly, getting fresh air, and keeping energy up for yourself and your unborn child? Is that it?" The pitch of her mother's voice pierced Olivia's eardrums like shards of glass. "Listen, I know you're heartbroken—all of us are sad with the news you received yesterday—but you've got someone else to think about. Whatever you deprive yourself of and for whatever cause means you're also depriving your child. William's child. Are you listening to me?"

The little one inside her kicked—hard. It seemed the women in her family (if indeed she was carrying a girl) were coming at her from all sides. Her mother was right. Damn it, she was always right—well, almost always.

Olivia seized her mother's hand and brought it to the side of her great belly.

Her mother smiled as though she'd single-handedly won the war. "There. It seems someone agrees with me!"

Olivia's eyes met her mother's; it was like looking in a mirror. "I'm listening, Mother. Will you read me the letter?"

Her mother opened the note.

" 'My dear Mrs. Morgan,' " she read. " 'It is with the deepest regret that I write you this letter. As of December 9, 1941, your husband, Major William Morgan was posted as missing.

" 'Let me be clear that a missing report does not mean death. Since his body has not been found, the major has likely been separated from his company and remains in hiding or has been taken prisoner. Official notification of a prisoner taken by the enemy may take days or even weeks to reach us. If we receive word of his whereabouts, we will contact you at once.

" 'International law states that any person taken as prisoner has rights to food and humane treatment. If the major is held as prisoner and exhibits good behavior, his captors will grant him permission to contact you directly. If you hear from the major before we do, please forward the notification to us and we will return it as soon as we are able.

" 'My thoughts are with you, Mrs. Morgan, as well as my deepest sympathies and regards, Colonel Adams, 151st Infantry Brigade, Sixth Battalion, DLI.'

"A lovely letter," her mother added. "Very thoughtful."

Olivia sat back. "International law means nothing to the Nazis." She spat the last word. "Why do you think William needed a nurse to begin with? If he's recaptured, it will kill him."

"I believe you're underestimating how strong William is. He's strong because of you, and he remains strong because of you. And the son or daughter he's longing to meet."

Right again. William was strong, the strongest person she knew. She nodded through renewed sobs.

"He's got to survive, dear. People are depending on him, and I believe he'll do everything in his power to live through this. Have faith."

She closed her eyes, remembering a similar conversation she'd had with William the night before he left for Durham, when she thought she was saying goodbye forever. But he'd returned. They were having a baby. He'd asked her to have faith that he was still alive even if his letters stopped coming. He'd asked her to stay strong for him, and she'd promised she would.

When Olivia opened her eyes, her mother captured a strand of her hair and tucked it behind her ear—proudly mindful, Olivia was certain, that mother knew best.

Emily Charlotte Morgan was born on the fourth of January, 1942. The shivering bundle, with her torrent of dark hair, was wrapped loosely in a thin yellow blanket and delivered into the arms of her mother by those of her grandmother. Cries of angst poured from the baby at her abrupt removal from her quiet, snug environment into one of noise and infinite openness. Three generations of Talbot women shared an embrace amidst tears and smiles.

"You were like this when you were born," her mother said, "loud and intent on letting us all know you'd arrived."

Olivia marveled at the tiny life in her arms. She took hold of her daughter's crinkled fingers and laid them over her own, making comparisons. Emily's pinkies curved at the middle knuckle the same way her own did, and the beds of her thumbnails lay wide like William's. Olivia counted every finger more than once before pressing each tiny cushion to her lips.

She was in love. And still so bloody sad.

William was alive, she didn't doubt that anymore. But where was he? Did he suffer? She hoped he wasn't worrying about her or the baby. She'd had enough worry these past weeks for the entire family. Compounding her worry was frustration. Her inability to prepare the vegetable plots the way she wanted caused immeasurable guilt as the staff bore the burden of turning soil and pulling winter weeds. In fact, due to her "condition," as everyone had called it, they wouldn't let her do much other than serve tea and knit, which did nothing to take her mind off images of William starving, cold, hurt, or scared.

Her mother was still here, a fact that wasn't all bad. She'd proved helpful in preparing for the arrival of the new life at Keldor, thinking of all the things that kept slipping Olivia's mind, like clothing for a growing baby or registering for green ration books as a nursing mother, in addition to registering a book for her child (something she hadn't even thought of). Now she had first choice to milk, fruit, vegetables, and a double supply of eggs. When summer came, she'd give the eggs and her veg ration away, since Keldor's chickens provided plenty for its inhabitants, and the patch would be in full swing then.

The daughter William knew they would have had arrived, and

everything about her reminded Olivia of him. With each passing day, Emily's blue eyes grew wider and darker, like storm clouds reflected on the ocean. They warmed Olivia's heart at just the right moments. So young and helpless, the little girl had powers beyond anyone's imagination: power to comfort her grieving mother by channeling her father and bestowing her mother with great responsibility.

Despite his absence, William's spirit and love for her and the daughter he had yet to meet would keep her going. She would wait for him as long as he needed.

# CHAPTER 34

By May, the vegetable patch was keeping all of Keldor's residents busy, including Olivia's mother, who'd chosen to extend her visit through spring. Determined to help as much as possible, Olivia pitched in between feedings and changings. Last summer had affirmed Charlotte Morgan's creed: Nothing was more relaxing than spending time with plants and the creatures that appreciated them as much as she did. Under warm sunshine, busy honeybees called upon pink and purple sweet peas, and ladybugs crawled around dutifully, full, Olivia hoped, of the nasty aphids threatening to infest her roses. Birds provided background music as they hopped from branch to branch. Even Jasper, who was no help at all in the garden, proved to be a marvelous guard dog and companion to the sleeping baby in her pram. Silent breezes stirred the dappled light, peaceful enough that baby and dog remained undisturbed despite the surrounding activity.

It was on such an agreeable afternoon that Captain Dinham arrived. Olivia hadn't seen him since his congratulatory visit with Mrs. Dinham shortly after Emily's birth. Today he came alone. Annie ran around back to announce him and then went inside to start tea. Something about the captain's solemn expression made Olivia wonder if she might need a whisky instead.

Arms outstretched, Captain Dinham carried a brown box as though it led the way.

She met him on unstable legs. She clapped her garden gloves together before clenching them at her side.

"Captain Dinham," she said finally.

"Mrs. Morgan, I hope you don't think me interfering, but imagining you learning this news by post seemed particularly cruel."

The lines of his face were etched with sympathy, sending Olivia to her knees. Her mother came from behind, cradling her as she crumpled to the ground.

The captain knelt. "These were the major's identity discs, Mrs. Morgan."

In her hands, their warmth startled her. The markings on the green and red discs were indecipherable in the bright sun, but once shaded, the word MORGAN took her breath away. The last time she'd seen these discs, they'd been hanging around William's neck.

"Knowing my relationship with the family, Colonel Adams contacted me personally with the news," Captain Dinham was saying. "Apparently, an offensive on the Mediterranean coast northwest of Cairo went terribly awry. German patrols attacked in large numbers. Those who weren't killed in the ambush were taken prisoner, though a handful were not. Once the area was reclaimed several weeks later, these discs were found next to the burnt remains of eight men. It's believed the major was amongst the dead. I'm terribly sorry, Mrs. Morgan."

Her mother took a dramatic breath.

Jaw tight, Olivia remained quiet. She kept her eyes in steady line with the captain's as William's suffering clouded her vision: Eight brave men, each one bound to the next, awaiting the flames that would end their lives. Their screams rose under the enemy's satisfied gaze. Was William conscious when the fire consumed him?

The birds still chirped, and the breeze continued to blow. Time stood still until finally, her daughter's wail whipped Olivia's head back to the scene she'd forgotten she was a part of. She stared at the pram blanketed lovingly by the shade of an enormous Cornish oak. Beside it sat the regal form of William's ever-faithful Labrador, sniffing the air, sensing a change.

Olivia stood and squeezed her mother's arm before running to her daughter. For the infant, it was mealtime.

Keldor's stunned inhabitants stirred in a daze. Mrs. Pollard, informed of the tragedy secondhand, stared quietly out a window in the sitting room. Her posture, stiff like armor, kept all who passed well away.

Olivia found her mother in the kitchen and told her she'd be out for a time. Mrs. Talbot begged Olivia to stay; clouds had gathered and threatened a downpour. Olivia won the argument by not engaging in it. She deposited her daughter into the arms of her grandmother and dashed out the kitchen door and down the stone steps.

As quickly as her legs would take her, she ran across the expansive garden and through bramble and vines obscuring the path to Steren Cove. The cove was their place, the place where William told stories of his family and the area's history, where they had picnics and made love.

She smiled at the recollections. And then she cried.

"Damn it!" she shouted into the gathering winds.

She teetered, and the sand drew her down. Her bare knees made contact first, stoking her rage. The wind taunted her, whipping her hair about her wet face until it stuck there. She groped for anything within reach, closing her fingers around a smooth stone. She hurled it with all her might, frightening a sandpiper looking for food, and she didn't care. She let loose with angry shouts about how she had known this would happen and the unfairness of this cruel war.

Finally, exhausted, she listed to the left, and her torso met the soft sand with a thud. Head on one arm, her mouth hung open inches from the damp, clinging granules. She rooted into the sand as if it were a pillow.

Out at sea, the turquoise waves darkened to gray; their billowing whitecaps matched the temper of the ceaseless wind. In rhythmic time, they crashed feet from hers, their violence lulling her muddled mind.

William was gone.

She was a widow.

Forever.

All she'd lived for since moving to Cornwall had been torn from her. As often as she'd told herself that this day would come, nothing had prepared her for its arrival. Even if Churchill announced peace tomorrow, with Hitler dead and all the rest, she'd still be without her true love—the one who even during wartime had brought her a happiness she didn't know could exist.

She sat up and pulled William's discs from the pocket of her cotton dress. This time she studied them without shying away from the markings. The indented letters and numbers formed a pattern her fingertips would get used to smoothing. She slipped the rope around her neck, where they landed companionably next to her moonstone. Emily would have two more trinkets to reach for when Olivia held her.

Emily. The child may have lost her father, but she still had a mother—a mother with two roles to fill.

In an instant, she was up and running.

"I'm coming, sweet Emily!" she said as she panted up the path. "I'll be there for you. I promise, I'll always be there for you."

~

The house had quieted after Keldor's residents retired for the evening. Even little Emily slept heavily beside her parents' bed in what was once William's bassinet.

Under soft lamplight, Olivia opened the wooden box left by Captain Dinham. A red paper poppy greeted her. Its wrinkled tissue petals and crooked wire stem suggested a child had made it —his or her contribution to the war effort, perhaps. Aware of its artificial nature, she still brought it to her nose before wrapping the wire stem around her finger. Beneath the flower lay stacks of her letters to William, nestled in their envelopes. Next to the letters was a writing tablet of lined yellow pages affixed to firm cardboard backing. The pages were covered in William's writing, the first dated 11 April, 1941, just over a year ago.

*My love,*

*I've boarded the train and although I told you I'd sleep, I cannot. You are on my mind and since I have the time, I shall write.*

*Is it redundant to say I miss you? Hours ago, you were in my arms. Our noses touched and your eyes looked into mine with such fire. I'll not forget that look or the kisses that followed. They sustain me, as does the taste of your lips and your neck. The scent of your hair is still strong despite the drenching you withstood following me to my motorcar.*

*I say, Olivia, you scared the bloody hell out of me when I left. I hope I never see you so distraught ever, ever again. Nothing in your life should cause you such torment. Try imagining our lives after the war. I envisage our future at Keldor like a summer Sunday afternoon, the hours stretching as we relax in the lazy sun. I'll weave you a crown of flowers and watch you laugh as our noisy children chase Jasper through the tall grass. Our lives will change once our children arrive. You'll be diligent keeping up with their busy feet and growing bodies, but I'll be there to help. My father barely partook in my upbringing, even after mother died. But I've told you before, I intend to be there from their first cry to their first steps, their first lost tooth, and beyond. I cannot wait.*

*Will you keep your nursing career after we have children? The masses of returning wounded will no doubt enjoy having such an attractive woman caring for them. I promise to rein in my jealousy, and I pledge to support you in whatever you decide.*

*Meanwhile, I'd like to separate from military life. You might find this shocking, as in the same breath I must tell you how committed I am to my new position and service to my country. And it's true, I am. But when war is over, I'd like to try something different, like designing and constructing furniture. Did I tell you my grandfather liked to build things? He had a talent for it. He even built that monster of a desk in the library. My father had a go at craftsmanship (I believe he built a bookshelf for my mother), but it frustrated him. I tried my hand earlier in life and quite enjoyed it. Perhaps I could build you a vanity or a bassinet for our firstborn so he or she isn't subject to sleeping in the rickety one I once used. Ultimately I'd like a specialty shop in the village where I could sell custom-made furniture, tables, and things. Does that sound silly? I hope not.*

*Ah, I'm tired. Maybe catching a few winks isn't such a bad idea.*

*I love you, Olivia.*

She inhaled deeply before turning back to the first page. Wet with tears, the petals of the paper poppy had separated and clung to her fingers, parts of which were stained red. With blurred vision, she reread the entire passage, focusing on William's desired career change. The idea of her husband's head bowed over a creation of his own design, his meticulous fingers smoothing grooves in the masterpiece he carved himself sent a shock of longing through her. It distracted her from the discomfiture of not already knowing he wished to build furniture, a fact that wasn't silly at all. It was terribly romantic.

Would she have continued with nursing? Yes, but not until the children were old enough to be without their mother during the day. Babies grew and changed quickly as it was, and she'd not miss a moment of it.

Two lines skipped on the yellow tablet before the next entry, which carried the same date as the first. Olivia's wet hands returned the tablet to its original state before she tucked it under the pillow behind her. No more would be read tonight. The following entries would give her something to look forward to—perhaps one per day. The tablet was thick.

Hands back in the box, she removed William's uniform. She frowned at its stiffness. Cleaned and pressed, it held no trace of him. Her hand smoothed over its stitches, embroidery, and buttons as she recalled how handsome he looked in it, especially when they married.

Beneath the uniform, a portion of her orange scarf he'd taken with him when he left blanketed the bottom of the box like a layer of gold coins. She discarded the poppy and wrapped the remnant around her stained hand, futilely wondering what had happened to the rest of it. She pushed the box to the foot of the bed. Envelopes and letters dotted the expanse to her left, and some had fallen on the floor. The poppy lay forgotten like a pulled weed. William's uniform remained folded and rigid beside her.

After another peek at Emily, Olivia switched off the light and nestled under the bed linens. She brought the silk scarf to her nose. Was it her imagination, or could she catch a trace of William within it? It had lost her scent, he had once complained, only to capture his own. Thank God.

At once he was there in spirit, thinking of her as she did him. She squeezed her eyes shut. She missed her husband, her greatest friend, the man who would never become a craftsman.

# CHAPTER 35

GRIEF CLUNG to Keldor's residents like clouds on a craggy moor. The only person Olivia would talk to was Emily, and she managed all her chores, inside and out, with the baby on her hip. Mrs. Pollard kept to the kitchen, making meals and delivering them without a word. Annie tidied house in her usual silence but with less spring in her step, and James simply resigned. He'd been at Keldor since the colonel was a boy, and the death of his son was more than the elderly man could bear.

Only Olivia's mother, who extended her stay through summer, could penetrate the fog, especially as harvest time approached. She coordinated extra community help, much to Olivia's silent relief, and made sure the bounty had been distributed appropriately. But by early autumn, she had returned to London. Olivia missed her, to a certain degree, but enjoyed the independence that came with her absence. Now she could try her hand at mothering without her own mother chattering in her ear, filling her with doubt. "Not to interfere, dear," and "are you certain …" were two phrases Olivia could happily live without.

Midmornings became mummy and daughter time. Walks with Emily, who lay in her pram mesmerized by the changeable skies, helped Olivia begin most days with optimism. As they walked, she talked about William, how they met, and the history of this home they shared. Emily would grab her foot and chew it idly. When their eyes locked, the smile that lit the baby's face sent Olivia's heart into successive somersaults.

After their walks, Olivia would take tea and read the latest condolence letters and cards that were still trickling in, many from people she'd never met. They littered William's desk for months, each reiterating how much her husband had been loved. Peder Werren's touching sentiments had made her cry: "There was a time when William and I were as close as brothers; I'd do anything for him. This I extend to the woman he chose to spend his life with. If you need anything at all, Olivia, you shall have it." Peder's current assignment had taken him far from England but as soon he returned, he'd give his sympathies in person. Even Jenna had sent flowers and a nice note stating that she'd be round to see Olivia and meet new baby Morgan as soon as she could.

Surviving members of William's company had written as well. These letters were Olivia's favorites. Over and over, they exalted her husband as a valiant leader who'd instilled allegiance in his men. How dismayed they were by his demise. They mourned as Olivia mourned, and to her surprise, their blatant sorrow comforted her.

Setting aside correspondence, Olivia gave Emily her second breakfast. Eyes closed, the suckling infant breathed steadily through her nose; her hair, lightening by the day, lay feathered across her forehead. War beset the world—homes and cities destroyed, people displaced and starving—yet everything this new life needed was right here.

The wooden chair creaked with the shift of Olivia's weight. Her eyes surveyed the walls of books, rich-toned oil paintings, and expensive trinkets that had once belonged to Colonel Morgan. He'd been nothing but a lowly ghost before she got to know William. Now he was a member of her family. She wasn't sure how he'd taken his life or where Mrs. Pollard had found his body. Had he hanged himself? Or was it the revolver? How long had he planned the suicide? Had he planned it at all? Perhaps he awoke one morning and decided to make it his last.

A sour taste crept up her throat. How wrong the colonel had been, assuming the worst. How weak. Waiting without answers was never easy, but surely someone in his position had connections. If only he'd done some digging, he'd have learned the details of his son's disappearance and that he was actually alive.

Olivia shuffled through the letters, searching for the stack from William's company. Amidst sentiments of how they would've died for William, given the opportunity, many had asked if, after the war, they might visit the wife of the man they so admired. What if she made their acquaintance now? Surely, the last people to have seen William alive would know if he'd had any chance of survival. If their stories held even a glimmer of hope, and surely they would, perhaps through her own connections she could be stationed as an army nurse close to where William allegedly lost his life. Once there, she could learn for herself what really happened that day on the north coast of Egypt.

"Gah!" shrieked the bubbly infant.

A cleansing breath propelled Olivia back to the life in her arms. She touched her nose to Emily's and smiled as a line of bubbles ran down the baby's chin. Pudgy fingers tapped Olivia's cheeks. She caught the baby's wayward hand and smothered it in kisses.

She'd obliged when William had begged her not to work abroad, but that was long ago. Nothing could stop her from leaving now. Once this little one was weaned, they'd go to London. Hitler had sent his might elsewhere, so the city wasn't nearly as dangerous as it had been, and her parents would love to have Emily whilst Olivia did her bit for her country and her family.

Intent on making a few telephone calls, she rose to find Annie.

But Annie found her first.

"Mrs. Morgan?" A light knock accompanied her voice as she opened the library door. "There's someone here to see you."

"Oh? Who is it?"

"Introduced himself as a doctor. Needs to have a word with you. May I show him in?"

"No, thank you, I'll come out. Would you take Emily?"

In the foyer stood a man Olivia had not met before. With a lazy smile and eyes that didn't meet hers, yet rather roved his surroundings, he held out his hand. "Nurse Morgan. How do you do?"

The title took Olivia by surprise; she hadn't been addressed as "nurse" since she married.

"My name is Dr. Davies. I'm the director of the auxiliary hospital at Hartford House in St. Austell."

"How can I help you?"

"I'll come right to the point. Our patient numbers at Hartford are rather high, and I've known for many weeks of your estate—Keldor, is it?" He leant forward as if doing so might reveal to him the rest of the house.

"Yes."

"From what I hear, the size of your home and its location would provide the perfect annex for Hartford—a convalescent annex, if you will." His smile grew to an unnerving width. "We'd like you to house ten to fifteen soldiers during their recuperation, men with physiotherapy needs—exercise, massage, and occupational therapies."

Though the doctor kept talking, a ringing in Olivia's ears drowned his voice until Mrs. Pollard whisked into the receiving room bearing tea.

Remembering her role, she offered the man a seat. "Shall we, Doctor?"

She poured his tea as he continued.

"They'd require general care by sensible nurses equipped with a worthy bedside manner. Dr. Butler tells me you are more than qualified, and your colleagues from St. Mary Abbot's say the same. The Red Cross is prepared to send you two nurses, and Hartford will send two orderlies. The Joint War Organization will provide someone to prepare meals for your patients and small staff."

She stopped pouring. "My small staff?"

"Yes. You'd serve as head nurse, naturally."

"Doctor, I've got a baby. I can't work."

"How disappointing. We've already postponed this entreaty by two months at Dr. Butler's request. He assured us that if we afforded you time to adjust to motherhood and to mourn the loss of your husband—for which I was sorry to hear," he added, his voice lacking the sincerity his words claimed to convey, "you'd be more than happy to take on the job. To avoid the alternative, that is."

"The alternative?"

"Why, yes. You and the other residents here would have until the weekend to vacate the premises. We'd like to get the annex operational right away, you understand."

"I understand," she said, lying through her teeth.

That was as much assent as he needed. "I'll be by tomorrow for a proper tour with members from the JWO. What time would work best?"

They settled on midmorning.

Olivia ushered the doctor out as graciously and as quickly as she could. Head down, she bit the insides of her cheeks until she gasped for the breath she'd been holding since she closed the door. She'd never find William now. The home she'd come to love—the place where she longed for him to return—had become her prison.

# CHAPTER 36

THREE MEN ARRIVED with Dr. Davies the following day just after Emily had gone down for her morning kip. Each was friendlier than the doctor and far more personable. Still dazed by the ultimatum that would apparently clip her wings for good, Olivia led them through her home. After hours of griping and many cups of weak tea the night before, she and Mrs. Pollard had devised the plan she delivered: "Both the drawing room and the ballroom will be opened and available for beds. I'd like to split the men up and put half in each. Upstairs is off limits to patients and staff. It is to remain private, for family only—the library, too."

The men responded more positively than she'd expected and reassured her of their support. First, they sent beds, physiotherapy equipment, and games and sports gear. Two nurses would arrive next, young and inexperienced but quick learners, they promised, especially under the guidance of such a "seasoned" nurse.

"All we ask is that you do what you're already good at, Nurse Morgan. Help those in need, and ensure your nurses do the same. See that patients receive regular exercise and decent meals, with kind words in between—anything to distract them from their mental and physical discomforts."

By Friday, both large rooms had been cleaned, dust cloths removed, and furniture pushed to the side or stored elsewhere in time for the delivery of fifteen standard hospital beds. Seven were placed in the drawing room and eight in the ballroom. The Central Hospital Supply Service brought pajamas, bed linens, towels, and bandages.

Food arrived too, along with two women with whom Mrs. Pollard was to share her kitchen. Clare and Maggie were sisters, one year apart but practically identical. Born and raised in Cornwall, they were familiar with the likes of Mrs. Pollard and had no qualms about being commanded by the territorial and sometimes formidable woman.

Fresh from a London nursing school, Cora and Danni arrived two days later. Green indeed, their only nurse–patient contact had happened as volunteers at a hospital where they'd looked after children and the elderly. They rushed into Keldor as though it was the Paramount on a Friday night, buzzing as city girls do about the latest film, *Much Too Shy*, and already mourning their absence at the National Gallery for lunchtime concerts. Olivia tried not to judge them too harshly; at least they seemed excited about their new assignment—a contrast from when she'd first arrived in the country. Pretty, sweet, and rather giggly, they'd make the men's hearts swoon and no doubt "distract them from their mental and physical discomforts" without much effort.

Nurses and kitchen staff were billeted in rooms once occupied by Keldor's larger wait staff. James's room, empty since his retirement, belonged to Clare and Maggie. Annie moved upstairs to be closer to Emily, leaving her vacated room to Cora. Danni also had her own room, since the two nurses would work and sleep at different hours. Two rooms remained available for orderlies, should they appear, or perhaps another nurse.

The day the patients arrived was exhausting. The idea of

organizing them according to their needs didn't work as Olivia had hoped. They all arrived at once, forcing her to fill empty beds willy-nilly. She only saw Emily to feed her. The rest of the time she was on her feet, scurrying to and fro, eager to get the men comfortable and her nurses on a working schedule. Hartford House took back their promise of sending orderlies, so Annie stepped in to run errands and serve as a messenger between Olivia and Mrs. Pollard, a task easily performed with Emily in tow.

Five days in, and Olivia no longer spent all her time cleaning up someone else's mess, giving friendly suggestions, or tackling a task herself to ensure it was done correctly. She carried Emily back and forth between the drawing room and the ballroom, known as Wards D and B, with a serene smile. Her ship was running smoothly. The part she loved best and missed most about nursing could begin: getting to know her patients.

The men ranged between the ages of eighteen and thirty-five. Five of them required stationary leg exercises, as they were confined to wheelchairs and it was uncertain if they'd walk again. The lucky ones received attention to both legs, whilst others focused on strengthening a remaining leg. Four soldiers had lost hands or arms and were learning to cope, both emotionally and physically. Another four were relearning how to use their limbs after severe burns or breaks. The final two had lost their sight. Reluctantly, they practiced seeing the world without the use of their eyes.

Billy came from the latter group. It wasn't just his name and blindness that reminded Olivia of William, but his disposition as well. He was ornery and bitter, two traits she looked forward to eradicating.

"Why don't we go outside for our walk today, Billy?" she asked, coming to Danni's rescue one sunny morning six days after his arrival.

Having received a vulgar response to the same question,

Danni flew out of the room in tears.

Seething with resentment at his condition, Billy parted his lips in a sneer that exposed gritted, horse-like teeth. "Nurse Morgan, how many times do I have to say it? I don't want to bloody go outside. I don't want to go anywhere. Why can't I be left alone?"

Olivia crossed her arms. "Doctor's orders, Billy. We can send you back to Hartford if you'd like, but you won't have myself or the nice girls to look after you, and I assure you the cooking won't be nearly as good as it is here at Keldor."

"Humph."

"Please, Private."

Olivia insisted that nurses and staff alternate between addressing the men by their military titles and Christian names. Military titles indicated respect and helped the men retain their dignity after fighting so hard for their country. Hearing their given names helped them recall who they were outside of war, before they became pawns in a conflict that continued to crush the lives of so many.

Once clothed against the chill, Olivia and her charge inched down the front steps. "I'll help guide you today, but I expect that soon you'll be able to navigate by yourself with the help of your white cane—if you ever consent to using it, that is."

"I feel ridiculous carrying it. I look like a fool, tapping a damned stick in front of me all the time."

"How do you know what you look like? I daresay you look more the fool walking into tables and walls. It's time you swallow your pride, William, and—"

Billy laughed, drowning out her gasp of dismay. "How old are you, Nurse Morgan?"

"I've just turned twenty-three."

"Then you're too young to call me 'William.' I know you're trying to sound like my superior, but you aren't. That name is reserved for me mum and our vicar, and maybe the doctor."

"I'm sorry," she mumbled, unnecessarily looking away to conceal her hot cheeks.

"No need to be sorry." He gave her a crooked grin that would've likely been accompanied by a wink had his eyes not been bandaged. It wasn't the first time she'd glimpsed his good nature.

Reading this as a good sign, she thrust the white cane into his right hand. His sporadic tapping joined their footsteps as they crunched across the gravel toward the quieter footpath.

"I wanted to travel," Billy said after many steps. "Visit South America, climb the Andes. Now I'm stuck—stuck in rainy England, which isn't the worst thing, except I can't bloody see it."

"You'll be happy again. You will."

"Happy?" he said with a bitter laugh. "Happiness doesn't matter. It's having dreams. Having dreams and having them realized, having something to live for. That's what matters."

"And when you're healed and this war is over, you'll have dreams again. They'll be different dreams, but you'll find your purpose, your something or someone to live for." She tightened her hand around his arm and added with more enthusiasm than she thought she was capable of. "I promise you."

"'Someone,' you say?" He offered another grin, a pleasant change from the snarl his mouth produced when he yelled.

She grinned in return. "It could happen. But not if you're still walking into walls and furniture. Keep tapping."

Each night, in case of emergencies downstairs, Olivia slept with her bedroom door open, as did Annie. Most nights, the annex remained quiet. The soldiers took strong pills to help them sleep; it wasn't what Olivia would have prescribed, but it proved good insurance against fifteen men crying out with nightmares at all hours of the night. But sometimes the pills weren't enough.

A bloodcurdling shout yanked Olivia from a deep sleep.

"Benny! Run! Run, you fool!" Groans and cries followed.

She grabbed her dressing gown and flew down the stairs as if the house were on fire. Annie bustled behind her. By the time they reached D Ward, a light in the corner was already on and the cries had changed to sobs. Danni sat with Billy, holding his hand and smoothing the bandage along the side of his face.

"Mum? Is it you?" Billy asked between heaving breaths. His hands patted the face, neck, and shoulders of the woman beside him.

"No, Private. It's Danni. Nurse Johnson."

The news produced a fresh flood of tears. Stricken by his pain, Danni cried too.

Olivia soothed other patients awakened by the outburst as the reality of Billy's condition descended upon the new nurse. His anger wouldn't run Danni off again, for she now understood the cruelty these men continued to endure.

"In a few more weeks, Private," Danni said, "the doctor will remove your bandages, and then you can go home. Home to your mum."

The image of Billy's shadowed, terrified face followed Olivia back to her room afterward. She tossed and turned. The lines of fear around his open mouth and sallow cheeks sent chills through her, despite the warmth of her bed.

William's night terrors had been like Billy's. If William had truly survived war a second time, a belief she still firmly held, he'd be even worse off this time. The only comfort in the possibility of his demise is that he'd no longer scream out in the night. Death would bring William the gift of peace, unlike the young soldier downstairs who'd never see anything again but his own images of carnage and ruin.

She buried half her face in William's pillow, where she inhaled only lavender. Was it selfish to wish him alive, when if he'd left this earth, he would truly be free?

# CHAPTER 37

BY CHRISTMASTIME, Olivia still remained loyal to optimism. Bolstered by the laughter of her daughter and driven by duty, those who knew her well—Annie, Mrs. Pollard, and her parents, who'd come for the holidays—wondered if she'd finally cleared her massive hurdle of grief.

For the most part, she had. Instead of wallowing in worry, she was keeping her promise to William by indulging in the giggles of their growing child and the joy they brought to patients and staff alike. Her parents were especially affected by little Emily's enchantments. She was constantly in the arms of one of them, each party entertained by the other. Dr. Talbot gushed with pride at the baby's dazzling smiles, and like everyone else who met the little charmer, he was thoroughly besotted.

This was Emily's first Christmas, and her eyes grew large at the change of scenery: the extra candles, the three spindly trees (one per ward and one in the sitting room), and the wrapped gifts (she particularly liked the shiny ribbon). Despite the shortage of frivolous holiday items like freshly glittered ornaments and tinsel garlands, everyone on Olivia's small staff delighted in adorning the house with locally picked sprigs of holly and evergreen boughs. Gift wrap from previous Christmases had been reused, and Mrs. Pollard cooked with vegetables such as carrots and beets to add as much color to Keldor's holiday menu as exotic fruits had in Christmases past. Yes, there was a war on, but God help this family if they couldn't make the only Talbot grand-child's first Christmas (and that of Keldor's patients) an extra-special one.

Most hands remained on deck over the holidays, including Mrs. Pollard's. Though Olivia offered to bring in a temporary cook for a week, the housekeeper had no wish to leave Keldor for Christmas. Annie journeyed to her parents' home at Olivia's insistence, but Mrs. Pollard shared in earnest her desire to spend the holidays with the Morgan girls. William, the son she'd never had, was gone, but Olivia had become as close to her as a daughter. And Emily—Emily was the apple of her eye. She knew she'd be sharing the sweet babe with her real grandpar-ents, but would Olivia mind if she stayed at Keldor this year? With a tear in her eye and a heart full of gratitude, Olivia hugged the older woman, overjoyed to have her at Christmas. She questioned how she would have survived the holiday without her.

After singing Emily a few Christmas carols at bedtime, Olivia sauntered downstairs, stopping by each ward. It was Christmas Eve, and as expected, Cora, Danni, Clare, and Maggie kept the atmosphere festive with games and songs.

Olivia joined her parents and Mrs. Pollard in the sitting room. Though her heart was set on enjoying Christmas present, she couldn't help but think of Christmases yet to come: after the war when William would be home, alive, well, and a fixture in the holiday hubbub. Accompanying her father in a whisky, he'd observe the dynamics of her family, making casual comments about the sometimes volatile interactions Olivia had with her mother.

"Is it always like this?" William would ask.

ERICA NYDEN

"Yes, I'm afraid so," her father would reply before taking a drink, "but you get used to it."

These sanguine thoughts had Olivia practically floating into the room, ready for a nightcap and an opportunity to relax next to the cozy fire. Her mother's stern brow stopped her short. Mrs. Pollard stood, excused herself, and shuffled out.

Her parents had arrived two days earlier and so far, their company had been enjoyable. She hadn't seen her father in years, and despite recent tragedies, she'd never seen him so happy. Grandparenthood suited him. Even her mother had been pleasant. She hadn't uttered one critical comment on Olivia's parenting or her management of the annex. She'd laughed and smiled and cooed, as grandmothers should. What could possibly be wrong?

"What's the matter?" Olivia asked.

"We need to talk," her mother replied.

She swallowed hard and settled in the cushioned chair closest to the hearth, hugging the rose-patterned pillow on her lap.

"Your father and I are worried about you."

Already not appreciating the direction of this conversation yet needing to hear more, Olivia awaited the onslaught.

"Earlier today, I was alarmed to overhear you talking to Emily as though her father is alive. I've asked Mrs. Pollard about the matter, and in so many words, she's confirmed my fears."

Olivia looked down at a fingernail she feigned obsession over and picked at it. She was a grown woman with no one to answer to. She would not deny her beliefs. "It's true."

"Why would you do that? I realize Emily is still a baby, but you cannot fill her head with falsehoods. Because one day, sooner than you think, she'll understand what you're saying, and by then it'll be too late. When her father fails to return home, she'll think you've lied to her."

"But I'm not lying."

Her parents exchanged glances. "Do you know something we don't?"

"I suppose I do," she replied, her tone challenging.

"What is it, Livvy? Has Colonel Adams contacted you?" For the first time in the conversation her father spoke, his voice hopeful.

"No." She raised her head and looked squarely at her attackers. "It's a feeling I have. I can't explain it."

"A feeling? A *feeling* that William is alive is what's driving this? I can't believe it." Her mother shook her head, readying for another foray. "When I heard your brother had been shot down, I struggled to accept it, but did I go around believing he survived because I had a *feeling* he had?"

Olivia strangled the pillow. "Of course you didn't! Why would you? They found Johnny's body on a beach. You viewed it. It may have been unrecognizable to most, but you knew it was your son. That was all the proof you needed. But me, I have no proof. All I have are these!" She tugged at the identity discs around her neck. "Someone out there knows exactly what happened to my husband, and until I'm told the story of William's death by someone who witnessed it—whether it's our men or the Nazi who killed him—I'll keep believing he's alive."

The room fell quiet save for the crackling fire and the Glenn Miller Orchestra's festive horns over the wireless. Olivia released the pillow, smoothing its creases. How could someone live through the hell William had just to die two years later? Or survive just to live in another POW camp, back under the thumb of Nazis? Surely he was living out a different scenario—in hiding, perhaps, injured yet clever enough to escape the roundup of prisoners. Perhaps he'd traveled on foot for many days and a nomadic caravan had discovered him unconscious and at death's door. Camouflaged as one of them, he'd been nursed back to health. He couldn't send word of his whereabouts, but as soon as the Allies won the war, he'd be on the next boat home.

"We're worried, dear," her mother said, splintering Olivia's daydream. "The captain told you William was dead. The man knows what occurs at the battlefront; he'd have told you if there was chance of William's survival. You're living in a fantasy, Olivia, a world of make-believe that you're passing on to your daughter. It's unhealthy. It's time you let William go."

Couldn't they understand that she'd never let William go?

"I'm not living in a fantasy, nor would I ever lie to Emily. I made a promise to William that I wouldn't give up on him the way his father had."

They both knew about the colonel and had been saddened to hear it. But their doubtful faces—especially Mother's, with her flair for blending uncertainty with disapproval—told her that this line of defense changed nothing. They still thought she was mad.

She didn't care. Their concern had given her the chance to state her convictions aloud for the first time. Lingering doubts were banished for good, and oddly, like when the sun shines on a bitterly cold day, she felt less sad. She stood and hastened to the sideboard, in need of that nightcap. Lifting the crystal decanter, she poured more liquor into her glass than she normally would, but that was all right. She'd find some way to celebrate the holiday, even if she did so alone.

"I'm Emily's mother," she said, her confidence at its zenith though her back was to them, "and I'll speak to her about her father as I wish. For him, we shall carry on, positive and hopeful. You needn't agree, but you'll not contradict me in front of her."

Finally, she turned and looked at her parents over the lip of her tilted snifter. Their doubt had changed to bafflement— mouths were open, yet nothing came out.

"Don't look so forlorn," she said almost smiling before taking another sip. The brandy was sweet and warming. "It's Christmas —we're to enjoy our time together, war or no war."

Their silence was too much. She cranked up the wireless then lifted the decanter. "Who'd care for another drink?"

Despite the Christmas Eve quarrel, the overall holiday was a pleasant one. On Christmas Day, Emily's delight at ripping paper and shoving it into her mouth kept everyone laughing and distracted from the row of the night before. On the following days, the family lived amicably, hoping to emulate the peace they wished to see in the world. Her parents must've understood that no matter how outrageous they considered her position, she'd not waver. Rehashing it would only waste the little time they had left together.

"A smashing success," Dr. Talbot remarked as he and Mrs. Talbot readied to board their train. In his arms, he bounced Emily with a rhythm that matched his mood, jovial and light-hearted. "Not only the rearing of this adorable little gem, but your contribution to the war effort as well. You ought to be proud of yourself, my dear."

"Thank you, Daddy," Olivia replied. Not meeting his eyes, she toyed with Emily's shoe instead. Praise from her father was hard to accept, especially so close to his departure.

"I'm proud of you too, Olivia."

"Thank you, Mother."

"I'm serious. What you're doing, helping these men and training these nurses. The patients' eyes light up when you enter the room. They know you have their best interests at heart, whether it's something they want to hear or not."

Her mother gently tugged one of Emily's honey-colored curls. "And remember, dear, whilst you're working hard to help so many, you also need to put your daughter's best interests in the forefront of your mind. I'm not asking you to stop loving

William. I'm asking you to think of your daughter. It's time you make *her* your priority. William would agree."

The woman was still an expert at twisting a compliment to serve her purpose. Olivia determinedly widened her smile.

Dr. Talbot laughed, as always, steering the topic away from conflict. "All right, then, one more big kiss for your granddad."

Obliging as usual, Emily planted a wet one on his cheek before he transferred her back to her mother and assisted his wife onto the train.

She was sorry to see them go, especially for Emily's sake. The holidays were over, and it was back to war as usual. Routines would resume, decisions would be made, and she'd be in charge, answering to no one but herself. Olivia smiled and gave Emily a squeeze as she walked to the car park, her head a little higher and her steps lighter.

# CHAPTER 38

WEEKS AFTER EMILY'S first birthday, she used her chubby legs to walk for the first time. Granted, she fell onto the grass almost at once but was keen to try again, encouraged by her mother, Annie, and several patients passing through the early spring garden.

"Aaaagh!" her tiny mouth screeched as she stood and had another go.

Five more successful steps brought her to Olivia, who lifted her to the sky.

"Marvelous!" cheered Private Kinney who limped by with Cora on his arm. "You've an athlete there, sure enough, Nurse Morgan."

Emily brought delight to Keldor's ailing residents no matter how gloomy their disposition. Her jolly nature increased as she grew and proved contagious, especially when she imitated Jasper's barks or the moos of cows. The names she gave people received laughs as well. "Polleeeee," in a high screech not unlike that of a monkey, was reserved for Mrs. Pollard. Annie was known as "Nanny." "Mamamamama" was a common word, repeated in a singsong pattern. Sometimes "Dadadada" rang out during their daily perusal of photographs of William, which got Olivia laughing and crying at the same time.

By Emily's second birthday, the beds had been emptied and refilled at least seventy times since the annex's opening. But in recent months, vacant beds remained vacant, a fact that hadn't escaped the fastidious Dr. Davies. In May 1944, he deemed the annex overstaffed and insisted one of Olivia's nurses be transferred straightaway. He didn't allow her to choose—she wasn't sure how she could have—and slated Danni for Southampton on June first. Danni admitted that a part of her was excited for the move, since Billy lived close by in Portsmouth with his mother. The two had been corresponding since he left Keldor over a year ago, but still, she didn't want to abandon the annex. Therefore, Olivia had fought to keep her with all the fire she'd become known for, arguing that patient numbers were sure to increase.

Her point was proven, to no avail, days after Danni's departure.

"You're listening to the BBC Home Service. This morning at dawn, the Allied troops began a surprise attack on Hitler's European stronghold …"

Mrs. Pollard smiled at Olivia over the kitchen's wireless. "This is the turn we've needed, Mistress Olivia. Peace be on its way. You can hear it in his voice, can't you?"

She had a hard time adopting Mrs. Pollard's enthusiasm. Yes, the consequences of the Allied actions of 6 June, 1944, would be monumental—and as the lead nurse of a convalescent home, Olivia's mind was fixed on the immediate future.

In a matter of days, they acquired fifteen more beds to accommodate twenty-six new patients. Many of the injured British, American, Canadian, and Free French Forces soldiers who'd survived the Normandy beaches went to Plymouth and Portsmouth hospitals for medical attention. Those who didn't die at the hospital yet weren't well enough to go home were referred to convalescent homes throughout England, including Hartford House and Keldor.

"Will they send more help, then?" her mother asked during their weekly telephone call.

Petrol for private use had become a thing of the past, and the ban on nonemergency travel not specific to the war effort made it difficult for Emily's grandparents to get to Keldor. After fragmented and often confusing conversations with the two-year-old, they updated one another by telephone instead. Olivia pictured their cheeks almost touching above the telephone mouthpiece, her mother attempting to wrest it from her father.

"No more help, no, and I've no idea what I'll do with only one nurse," Olivia said. "It was difficult before with fifteen patients and two nurses, and I worked as much as they did. But thirty patients with just Cora and me? I know how hospitals operate, but this isn't a hospital, and these men aren't confined to their beds. They need exercise and one-on-one assistance. The two of us won't be able to care for them, not properly."

"Knowing you, I'm sure you'll make it work, Livvy," Dr. Talbot said.

Unconvinced, Olivia twisted the telephone cord round her finger.

"What would you think about adding me to your staff?" her mother asked. "I promise I won't try to take over—it's your ship, you're the captain. I would follow all orders obligingly."

She couldn't be serious. Olivia dropped the cord and tapped the desk with her fingernail. It took zero imagination to picture her mother wielding her experience for the "betterment of the annex" whilst sacrificing all the systems Olivia had put in place. She'd be supplanted as head nurse of the annex in no time.

"What about your patients in London?" Dr. Talbot asked.

Yes, what about her patients? And what about Daddy, for that matter? He'd be terribly lonely without her again.

"Oh, I've got plenty of capable girls who can deliver babies in my stead," her mother said, "and Virginia is brilliant at telling them what to do and when to do it. What do you say, Livvy? I could help with patients and with Emily. Yes, you've got Annie, but having the babe's gran around might be nice for her too."

She did need the help, and her mother's years of medical practice and tough love were the antidote the injured soldiers needed. For Emily to have her gran at Keldor would be a blessing. And maybe, just maybe, her mother would stay true to her word and let Olivia rule the roost.

"Dad, how would you feel about it? If Mother came to Keldor for a spell?"

"My dear," he said in the soothing tone she'd drawn comfort from her entire life, "if it will help you in your efforts, I'm all for it."

"All right then, Mother. You start as soon as you can get here."

By the twentieth of June, soldiers of nearly every rank filled Keldor's infirmary beds. To accommodate the growing population, two beds were added to B Ward and three to D Ward. Permanent residents no longer used the sitting room. Aptly named the S Ward, it held beds for ten patients, forcing the staff to use the dining room for meetings and meals.

The library remained Olivia and Emily's domain. Whilst Olivia buried her head in paperwork, Emily sat at her own small desk producing masses of impressionistic art with wax crayons and watercolors. A collection of these masterpieces went into a leather-bound album on a shelf, whereas the outstanding works were hung on the library doors. Most were pictures of her family: Mummy, Daddy, herself, and Jasper. Polly had a portrait on the door as well. Today, Emily worked on one of her daddy, using a photograph Olivia had given her of him in his uniform as a model.

It was toward this secluded refuge that her mother's voice quickly approached. "Olivia!"

"Yes, Mother," she lowered her papers before looking up.

"The men are all settled in S Ward, and—"

"Good."

"One of them says he knows you. Says he was a close friend of William's, a Lieutenant Werren? It must be in your papers there. Do you recognize the name?"

Olivia sprinted to the other end of the house.

S Ward was quiet. Two men tapped tentatively on crutches around the room, whilst six lay in their beds reading or trying to sleep. One had joined Cora outside for a turn in his wheelchair, and the very last sat in his own wheelchair by the window looking out onto Charlotte's Garden.

"Peder?" Olivia asked, her breath in short supply.

"Olivia!"

Peder's smile, though genuine, contrasted with his condition. A sling held his left arm in place, and his shoulder bulged with a hefty bandage. The side of his head was covered in gauzy wrap and an enormous bruise blackened the side of his face, reddening the whites of his eyes.

"How I wish William were here to see this: me, recuperating in his home and under his wife's care, no less," Peder said. "My parents told me Keldor had become a convalescent home. I'm grateful. I'd much rather be here in the home of my best mate than at Hartford House. The Pearns were never great friends of our family's, anyway, not the way the Morgans were."

He winked as though Olivia knew what he was talking about.

Her eyes flitted to the blanket over his lap, cascading down to the one foot that peeked out from under it.

She knelt beside him and took his hand. "Have you lost your leg then, Peder?"

"It got away from me at Sword Beach." He sniffed. "But I'm alive, wouldn't you know?"

"Yes, you are" was all she could say. She was so happy to see him, but considering the circumstances, she had no idea how to relay this.

"You received my letter, I take it?" he asked. "About William? I'm terribly sorry I couldn't tell you in person. Not until now, that is. This war … I'd no idea it would take so much."

He looked down at his lap, and his merry disposition threatened to crumble.

"You'll be in good hands here, Lieutenant."

"Ah, no titles, please. We're family. Call me Peder, understand? This 'lieutenant' business died with my leg." He chuckled. "I still can't believe I was ever promoted. I suppose William would've been proud. Jenna says you've had a baby girl. Has she been round to meet her yet?"

"Not yet." She was certain Jenna's offer to visit had been made out of politeness.

"Not surprising. She's been in the Middle East, hopping from one military hospital to another. Leaves aren't as plentiful when you're posted that far away. She's met an American."

"An American?"

"Mm. Tell me about your little one. Dear God, I pray she's taken after you." His grin was infectious.

"Olivia," her mother called. "Hartford House is on the telephone."

"Thank you, Mother."

"This is your mother?" Peder said as her mother approached. "I should've guessed. You two could be sisters."

A deep breath helped Olivia rein in the overwhelming nature of the last five minutes. After a brief introduction she needn't have made, she smiled. "I haven't read over your paperwork yet, Peder, but I'll tell you what we tell all the patients here." She stood and glanced at her mother for corroboration. "The more you cooperate and work hard during your physiotherapy, the quicker we can get you home."

"Home," he repeated. "Looks as though Mother will have to make room for me in the dower house. This certainly won't get me up to my old flat." He lifted his remaining foot and faked a laugh that Olivia disregarded.

"I have work to return to." She placed her hand on her mother's arm. "Nurse Talbot will help you if I'm not available. I'll return later with Emily and perhaps get you outdoors for a walk before tea. Tomorrow we'll start physiotherapy specific to that shoulder injury, and we'll exercise your leg. Shall I send for Mrs. Pollard? She'll be delighted to see you."

His smile was dazzling. "Please! A squeeze from Polly is exaclty what I need. Thank you, Olivia. And it was nice meeting you, Nurse Talbot."

With thirty patients and three wards, Olivia did her best to divide the duties fairly amongst the three caregivers. Each nurse managed a handful of patients from each ward, depending on the patient's needs. Olivia carried the lightest caseload with six patients, which allowed her time to process ongoing paperwork, manage the staff, and communicate patient progress to the doctors at Hartford. Cora and Nurse Talbot split the other twenty-four patients between them.

Peder Werren was the sixth patient on Olivia's caseload, and by three o'clock on his first day at Keldor, she had him outside. To her delight, the sun was shining, though lingering moisture left the air pungent with life. The fine pea gravel wasn't the easiest thing to push a wheelchair over, but once they made it to the garden's tamped dirt paths, the going was a little easier.

"Have you seen your parents yet?" she asked.

"Not yet. We've spoken on the telephone. Mum was a wreck. They're happy I'm alive and thrilled that I've been sent here."

"They're welcome to visit. The annex can seem a bit claustrophobic, especially on wet days, but we'll find a place where you can enjoy a proper visit."

"Thank you. I might wait a week or two. I'm not sure I want Mum to see my face like this—or Father either, for that matter. His health is little improved since the war started. It's as though this new war has resurrected days of old, bringing back all his horrid memories. The Werrens aren't resilient fighters like the Morgans, you know."

If he wasn't so serious, she might've laughed at the comment. No one, especially the Morgans, was strong enough to avoid war's ruinous aftermath. But since Peder had lost his leg, it's no wonder he felt down. Best not to keep the event bottled up, no matter how painful. "Do you mind my asking exactly what happened, Peder, on Sword Beach?"

"Not at all," he said, sounding matter-of-fact. "We arrived early to clear the beach for invasion. We disarmed and removed mines, all whilst under constant fire, mind you. The Germans knew we were there." He was quiet for a moment, as though his memories had yet to catch up with his words. "I can't say how many mines I'd successfully deactivated before that morning. I know how they work, and the pressure's never bothered me. I focus on the task—it's not so different from solving an intricate puzzle—and let it carry me."

She stopped walking and came around to face him. He'd raised a hand to his face, covering his mouth. "But no matter how much training you have, I'm not sure it can truly prepare you for death."

He looked away. She took the hint, and after touching his hand, resumed their walk. They rounded the wych elm. Birdsong filled their stalled conversation.

"So many were depending on me to be perfect—actual *lives* were depending on me, and I failed. Nerves took over, and I let them. I still can't believe I'm alive. A mine that size should've killed me. It did kill three others. Hopkinson didn't die on the spot like Mitchell and Ellis. He waited until we were in hospital long enough to hear he lost his legs, an arm, and both eyes. Considering the news, he died hours later."

As if programmed, the wind stirred. Peder shuddered. Gently, she removed the rug from his lap and placed it around his shoulders.

In the process, he clasped her arm, his red eyes flooded with worry. "Do you think me weak?"

She knelt. "I do not."

"Would William, do you think?" His grip tightened. "Would he think me a coward for breaking as I did? For being afraid to die?"

"Not at all—don't let the perception of your old friend fool you," she said, recalling William's own terror and how he was never truly rid of it. "There's no shame in being afraid to die."

That night Olivia sat at the foot of her bed, bent over William's journal, unnerved by the anguish that would possess his oldest friend for years to come, if not forever.

She found the haunting excerpt easily.

*30 September, 1941*

    *Olivia, what I'm about to write will not make you happy, but I must write it and pray you never read it. If you do, I hope you'll forgive me. I'm afraid. For the second time in my life, fear is shaking me to the core. If I die, I leave you to raise our child alone. You'll become a widow at twenty-two, and we haven't even been married a year.*

    *For obvious reasons, I can't back out. I wouldn't anyway. I'm committed to our operation and to the men in my company. But I'm terrified, Olivia. Fully awake, I have the same mind I had as prisoner— full of dread, hopelessness, and loss. For so long, my dreams were the only place where I'd suffered such misgiving.*

*If I don't come home, will you stay at Keldor? The estate will not collapse into bankruptcy. My father was shrewd with money, as I've discussed with you before. You know to contact Mr. Bather in Truro if you or Polly are in need of anything.*

*Please tell Polly how much she's meant to me all these years. Tell her how sorry I am if I've ever hurt her or taken my pranks too far and for being beastly to her when I returned from North Africa. Thank her for me, will you? Thank her for stepping in and caring for me when my mother could not.*

*I love you more than life itself, Olivia Jean Morgan. Forgive me for the pall of doubt descending over me this morning. I actually prayed to God that I would be home to you by January, so I could be there for the birth of our first child and to support you in any way I can. I promise I'm trying to be positive. This can't be goodbye.*

Her fingers traced her husband's hasty scrawl. She'd been wrong to argue with him when he'd been so set on returning to war. He said she didn't understand, and at the time, she hadn't. The mind of a soldier was complicated and none were the same—a fact she'd been learning these many months from the men in her care. Most fought for love of country and a loyalty to the soldiers with whom they served, as William had. But he had other reasons, too. His return to service was supposed to end the terror he withstood in North Africa. Talking to her about it had helped, but it wasn't enough. He needed to once again risk captivity and torture to prove to himself that he wasn't a coward.

He'd once told her he wasn't afraid to die and never had been. Was the fear he'd written of in his journal a first for him, then—a new brand of courage, perhaps? For a fighting man to admit his fear of death took unimaginable courage. Surely, wherever he was, he knew that now. And for Peder, as with all things, time would help him to realize the same.

# CHAPTER 39

PEDER DESERVED MORE than the bare support they scraped together for the patients at Keldor. Surely his relationship with William called upon Olivia to go above and beyond for him. Though he was billeted in S Ward, she contemplated giving up the library so he could have a room of his own.

"Don't be ridiculous," her mother had said. "Lieutenant Werren's proximity to the other men gives him the camaraderie he needs, and you need the space and privacy to get your work done. I realize he was William's friend, but I believe he'd be the first to say that whilst he's here, he wishes for no special treatment."

But whether he wished for it or not, it was difficult to avoid. Whilst Clare delivered supper to the rest of S Ward on Peder's first night, the chef herself delivered his meal, as if he were the king of England. The other patients, many who had been there for days already but had yet to lay eyes on the woman who provided such tasty meals morning, noon, and night, clapped and whistled. Those who could stand did, causing Mrs. Pollard to shoo them off and shake her head as if they were full of nonsense.

"They've every right to cheer for you, Mrs. Pollard," Peder said, encouraging the ruckus around him.

"Agreed," Olivia said coming up behind her with Emily in her arms. "Your cooking, you realize, reminds them of their mother's. All they want is to thank you."

"Nonsense. I cook for Mr. Peder and for all the boys like I would my William. When you all get home," she announced to room, "you make sure to thank your own mums, not me. I'm just doing my duty."

She delivered Peder a kiss and sailed from the room, a dozen cheers in her wake.

"So this is Emily?" Peder asked.

"We're soon to have our supper, but first I wanted you two to meet. Emily, this is Mr. Werren."

He laughed. "No, no, Emily, don't listen to your mother. My name is Peder, and that's what you shall call me. How do you do?"

He stuck his hand out, but the toddler crashed into her mother's neck, utterly embarrassed.

"If she's not the spitting image of Charlotte!" he said, glancing at the woman's portrait above the hearth. "But with your hair."

"Her hair has lightened since she was born. For months, it was dark like William's." Olivia buried her nose in the golden strands.

"I'm afraid I haven't spent time around children since I was one myself," he said, his face open and kind. "But I wonder, Miss Emily, if you'd like to meet Morveren."

Out of his pocket, he pulled a small mermaid made of silver. "She's my good luck charm. Tell me, Emily, do you believe in mermaids?"

The child's round eyes grew rounder. She took the mermaid.

"Mm," he said. "I thought you might. You're welcome to play with her, but she mustn't go into your mouth. She's terribly small, and we wouldn't want her getting lost in there."

"Perhaps you should only play with her when we visit Peder. She's a very special mermaid."

"Yes, she takes care of me when I'm far from home or in need of help."

Emily, clearly enraptured by the silver trinket, would likely have exploded if it were taken away from her so quickly. Peder sensed this.

"Would the two of you join me here for supper?" he asked. "Or does that violate annex protocol?"

Olivia scanned the room. Three men lay in bed with meal trays on their laps. Others shared small tables. Peder's meal sat on one such table, which he had to himself.

Olivia chewed her lip for a moment. "Why don't we join your new friend, Peder, for supper? And then you can play with Morveren a little longer."

The giggles the little girl emitted gave Olivia her answer.

"May I leave her here? I'll only be a moment."

"Of course." Peder drew Emily onto his lap.

Stalling at the room's exit, Olivia watched as he gestured grandly with his hands. Emily's eyes followed their every movement. When she wasn't overawed by whatever he was telling her (though how much Emily really understood was debatable), she was smiling. And for the first time since his arrival, without the veil of civility, Peder did the same.

"Nurse Morgan," Cora summoned from the corridor.

Olivia ignored the call, simply delighting in the scene across the room. She too was smiling as a piece of her wounded heart edged back into place.

Peder hadn't been joking when he said that he hoped Emily took after Olivia. He wasn't sure he could handle looking at the spitting image of his best friend in the face of this child. But as her tiny fingers smoothed over the charm that had saved his life in Normandy, things were different. William and Charlotte's wide cheekbones and pointed nose sparked memories this child had no part of. Her innocence and curiosity distracted him from his woes and selfish deliberations.

"What do you think of her?" he asked, pointing to the charm she clutched in one sticky hand.

Emily stared, her blue eyes shielded by the longest eyelashes.

"She's magical, you know. She tells fishermen when it's safe to go to sea. And she protects those of us who wish to stay on land."

His nursemaid had given him Morveren before he'd left for Blundell's, claiming it would bring protection and happiness whilst living away from home. It worked: he'd enjoyed school, passed his exams, and moved through life fairly contentedly. He even met pretty girls, thanks to William, of course, who'd laughed at his superstitious obsession with the trinket.

William wasn't laughing now.

Peder bounced Emily gently with his good leg, more optimistic than he had been in months. He hoped the feeling would hold. "I'm here today because of Morveren—not just alive, but here, at Keldor, meeting you and getting to know your mum. Making new friends."

Emily's attention went back to the charm. She petted the deep grooves of the mermaid's hair and the scalloped scales of her fin.

"Have you had a nice visit, then?" Olivia returned with two plates, which she laid on the table. She brought up a chair beside them, then took Emily and sat.

Peder laughed. "Your daughter's quite talkative."

Olivia wrinkled her nose fetchingly. "I know you're joking, but I'm afraid she rather can be. Though most of what she says is gibberish, she does go on and on. The future implications frighten me."

"I'm afraid, Miss Emily, that Morveren must take her rest." He held out his hand, curious as to whether or not his request might trigger a tantrum.

306

She looked up at her mum, who raised an eyebrow but said nothing. Sticking her bottom lip out, Emily plopped the mermaid back into Peder's hand.

"Good girl." He closed his fingers tightly around the charm and slipped her back into his trousers pocket, eager for the next bit of luck she might send his way. "I wonder what delicious meal Mrs. Pollard has prepared for our supper this evening."

~

"Okay, okay. That's enough. I can't lift it any further." Peder gritted his teeth against the pain grinding his shoulder.

"All right, we'll stop." Olivia rolled the unused gauze into a tight coil, her eyes steady on him. "But over the next few weeks, with hard work and a willingness to suffer a little pain, you *will* lift it."

Already, Peder hated physiotherapy. "Because losing a leg isn't enough pain."

"On the contrary," she replied, helping him with his T-shirt. "It's enough to last a lifetime. But sadly, if you want to use that arm the way you used to you, you'll have to endure a bit more. Remember, you're one of the lucky ones."

"Am I?"

She sank onto the bed across from his wheelchair. "You are. And you know it."

He said nothing. If he were truly lucky, he'd have someone to go home to other than his aging nervous mother and infirm father. But when it came to women, despite his good luck charm, Peder was far from lucky. William had always said he lacked confidence—this from the man who could charm the skirts off girls with a simple hello. So whilst his best friend luxuriated in the caresses of whichever beautiful woman he chose to spend the night with, Peder ruminated alone, reflecting on words he wished he'd said or hadn't said until he finally fell asleep. At least now he'd no longer sulk within William's shadow.

"You know, I never thought William would marry," he said.

Olivia lifted her head as if she'd been pinched. "Excuse me?"

He glanced about. Where was little Emily? Surely she could dispel the negativity he was so good at summoning at the most unwelcome times. No wonder he couldn't find a wife.

"Y-you mentioned luck," he stammered. "William was lucky to have you, if even for a short time."

"You never thought he'd marry? Not even your sister?"

He wrinkled his face. "Especially not Jenna. A doomed relationship from the start. I've no idea what he was thinking when he first asked her, not when he could've had anyone."

"Anyone?" Her eyes twinkled, and she raised her brows.

Did she think he was joking? He ought to steer the conversation away from William's many conquests, though she might've appreciated knowing that none had held his attention more than a fortnight.

"When he finally wrote telling me he'd married, I didn't believe it," he said. "He apologized for being a rotten friend and for not staying in touch as he once did, and then the rest of the letter was about you. That's when I realized he was telling the truth and wondered: Who is this nurse? How did she ensnare my friend, the terminal bachelor? Was she dosing his tea?"

He laughed, but Olivia looked uneasy.

"It seems we knew two different men, the one before North Africa and the one after," she said.

"Perhaps. You know, he'd been incredibly tight-lipped about that whole ordeal, including his father's death. Did he ever talk to you about it?"

"Yes," she said.

Had she bristled?

He smiled. "Of course. I therefore repeat: William was a lucky man."

~

It had rained for five days. Cornwall could be a wet place, and the low gray clouds stretching for miles mirrored Peder's mood. His parents were visiting for a second time, and though Olivia's library provided privacy, their visits brought a pang of guilt for the other men who wouldn't see their families for weeks or months yet. His mother's fawning brought on still more guilt; her affections weren't always reciprocated.

"I've brought you something," she sang, pulling two enormous books from her bag. "They're scrapbooks I made when you and Jenna were children. I thought you'd like to see them and maybe share them with Nurse Morgan?"

"Whatever for?" he asked.

Mr. Werren stepped forward. "William is in here too, as well as photographs of his parents. I'd meant to pass on the ones of Charlotte to William years ago, but …"

"It seems your father couldn't still his infatuation for Charlotte Morgan enough to part with them," Mrs. Werren snickered, reminding Peder that the long-running joke was anything but.

Once his parents stopped their petty bickering, they indulged in walking Peder down memory lane. His mother had done a brilliant job of recording the short history of his immediate family, and the more he scanned the carefully preserved photographs, locks of hair, postcards, and dated newspaper clippings, the more he appreciated this. It turned out to be a lovely afternoon.

"Your mother said you had something to show me," Olivia said after showing his parents out.

"I do." He held out the smaller of the two books. "Here."

She sat down beside him and rested it on her lap, turning the pages slowly and respectfully until Peder could no longer stifle his excitement and flipped half a dozen at once.

"Do you recognize that face?" he asked, pointing to a young

boy with unruly dark hair in short knickers, whose head rested against the skirt of the woman beside him on the beach.

Olivia's hand flew to her mouth. "William! And Charlotte Morgan?"

"Mm." Peder nodded, turning a handful of pages. "Here's another taken at Tredon, our estate, in the south garden."

Two women, both with coal-black hair, stood together whilst clasping the hands of their young sons. "Through thick and thin" was written in his mother's flowery handwriting.

"Mother said this was taken shortly after Mrs. Morgan had lost a baby," he said. "A miscarriage."

Olivia studied the photograph's every detail, her finger tracing the length of Charlotte's faded face. "So they were friends, your mum and Mrs. Morgan?"

"Not at first, I don't think. I'm told my father had hoped to marry Mrs. Morgan until he learned she had eyes for someone else—always had and always would."

"What a beauty. And how sad she looks—for good reason, I know. What do you remember of her?"

He flipped back a few pages to three photographs taken outside a school. Both families were showcased, and the year 1915 was etched under them.

He tapped the glowing face of William's mother. "Here. Do you see her smile? I remember this day well. William and I had finished our first year at Blundell's. My mum, Jenna, Mrs. Morgan, and the colonel, who had a few days' leave, came to retrieve us. Summer holidays at last."

"She had both her boys with her, if only for a short while."

He nodded. "This is how I remember her: radiant, warm, and forever beautiful." Fixed on Olivia's mournful yet pretty face, and curiously unable to stop speaking, he continued. "It's no wonder William married you, for you're very much like her."

She reddened and closed the book. "Thank you, Peder, for sharing these."

He'd embarrassed her; he hadn't meant to.

She stood. "I'll phone your mum to thank her as well. Might I show these to Emily before they go back to Tredon?"

"Of course. They're for you both to enjoy. I'll leave you to your library. Thank you again for its use."

# CHAPTER 40

By August, Keldor's patient numbers remained at thirty, prompting the Red Cross to send another nurse as soon as they could. Nurse Talbot would return to London, much to Dr. Talbot's delight, in a matter of weeks. In the meantime, Olivia worked more than ever. She spent less time alone and less time alone with Emily. On top of her regular duties, she played games, listened to the wireless, and even ate meals with the soldiers— well, with one soldier, anyway.

Her mother, of course, was the one to bring this to her attention.

"It seems Lieutenant Werren has taken a shine to you, or is it you to him?" she asked one morning as Olivia fluttered past in search of jam.

She stopped, and looked sharply at her mother. "Sorry?"

"Oh don't get defensive, Livvy. It's marvelous! And look how he is with Emily. She adores him."

Both women turned to the pair by the window. Emily was tilting her head, chatting away to Peder, whilst he nodded with interest as though he understood everything she said.

"Mother." Olivia pinched the back of her mother's arm and steered her toward the door. "Are you mad? We're friends."

"I'm not trying to ruffle your feathers, dear, but we're all aware of what's been happening between the two of you. And no one's condemning it, least of all me. It's as though you've hit your stride since he's been here. Running this annex isn't easy, and yet with a man like Peder here to uplift you, you seem born to it."

"It's because of Peder that I'm doing my job well?"

"All I'm saying is that it's healthy for you to have a man in your life again. I don't think you've realized how much you've needed it."

What she needed was her mother to go back to London. Certainly Peder had uplifted her; he was her friend, after all, as he was William's.

"Was your mother getting after you for something or other?" Peder asked when she returned.

"Oh, no." She set the jam on the table and fiddled with the napkin on her lap, keen to lay it just right before making eye contact.

"Then what's the matter?"

"Nothing's the matter." She looked up. "But tell me, is it true you're not interested in a prosthetic leg?"

"That's true, but why are you bringing it up now? Is that what you two were discussing?"

"No, nothing like that." She slopped a dollop of jam on Emily's biscuit, hoping the new topic would stick.

"Peeeeder, biscuit?" Emily asked.

Her tiny, plump fingers gripped too tightly, causing chunks of biscuit to escape between them. Olivia cocked an eyebrow at the jam stain growing on her sleeve.

"Why thank you, Miss Emily," Peder said. "I'd love a biscuit."

"I read the report sent from Dr. Banister earlier this morning," Olivia continued. "Why don't you want the prosthesis?"

Peder caught the larger remnants as Emily handed over the

crumbly treat. When his smile faded, his expression was unlike any Olivia had seen before. He rested his arms on the table, his hands fisted.

"Because they don't work well. My uncle has one. They're painful and cumbersome. I've got a wheelchair. I may as well use it. Now would you mind pouring the tea and perhaps changing the subject?"

Olivia poured the tea. Despite his resistance, this was a matter she could tackle.

"Fine, then," she said serenely. "Starting today, expect a more rigorous round of physiotherapy involving your good leg. If you think you're going to let it grow weak because all you do is sit in that chair hour after hour, then you don't know your nurse very well."

Peder hadn't seen Olivia for a few hours, but still he waited, expecting she'd take him outside. They'd walked the halls the last two days because it had been raining so hard, but today his view of Charlotte's Garden looked less wet.

Weather aside, he feared she might not come at all. This morning during physiotherapy, she'd been aloof and distant. After days of bringing Emily to "help" during his sessions, when he'd indulged the little girl's high-pitched giggles and curiosity that often got her in trouble, today Olivia had come alone, leaving her daughter and her good humor behind. True, he'd snapped at her during breakfast, but he hadn't meant to. He'd grown sensitive about his leg—or rather, his lack of one.

Since his arrival, he'd kept his ailments to himself. She'd think him weak if he complained, and anyway, he'd rather listen to Olivia. Her voice soothed him. It also removed his earlier doubts as to how William of all people could have fallen in love with a woman before he'd even seen what she looked like. What delight he must have felt at seeing her kind eyes, her sparkling smile, and her perfect little shape for the first time. Peder suffered through dozens of tales about William in order to stay near her; she was a constant reminder of his friend's appeal.

But William was no longer here.

Peder had long resented picking up where William had left off —both men shared similar tastes in women: shapely legs, modest breasts, tiny waists—but this would be different. Olivia needed a husband, and Emily needed a father. The child's soft curls and playful spirit sent his heart spinning like a top, especially when she ran into S Ward shouting "PEEEDERRR! BREFFAST!" with William's drooling black Labrador at her heels.

But if this was truly to be his future and not another fantasy, then he had work to do. Any lingering displeasure after the morning's disagreement must be remedied. Perhaps abandoning his brave façade would bring her back around. She was his nurse, after all.

"Ready for your walk, Peder?" Olivia asked, briskly entering the room.

"Not today." He shifted in his chair, his face contorted in pain.

She stopped cold. "This doesn't sound like you. You love our walks, even in the rain. What's the matter?"

Replacing his usual smile with a grimace, Peder exposed a truth he'd long kept secret. "My stump. It burns constantly. And regardless of what you think, I don't plan on relegating myself to a wheelchair for the rest of my life. I'm happy to use crutches."

"But why not the prosthetic? You wouldn't need crutches or a chair—"

"Because if resting in a chair is this painful, I can't imagine cramming my stump into an artificial device." He buried his face in his hands.

"Peder." Her breath was sweet and tickled his ear as she bent over him. Traces of lavender delivered instant solace, as did her nearness.

He hadn't planned on breaking down, but if it kept her this close …

Head down, he mumbled more regrets. "I shouldn't have survived the beach. This war should've taken me, too."

She stood and wheeled him toward the door. He lifted his head when they entered her library, where a small blaze dispelled the day's dampness.

"What's this nonsense about not surviving? When you came here, you said yourself how glad you were to be alive." She squeezed his wrist, her warm fingers kneading away his sorrow. The other touched his chin, coaxing his watery eyes to meet hers. "Is the discomfort making you say this? You need to tell me when you're in pain so we can work through it. That's why you're here. This isn't a holiday, you know."

"I don't need special treatment," Peder said, though the idea pleased him immensely. "Our time together shouldn't be marred by my aches and pains. It's not how I want to live the rest of my life. By suffering through it now, maybe I won't have to. I can be strong."

"Of course you can. No one's ever doubted that. Only I'm not so sure you're going about it the right way."

She walked to the desk as if driven by an invisible force. "I'll phone Dr. Banister this afternoon. You require something stronger than what he's prescribed for pain. I wish you would've told me as soon as you felt discomfort, not to mention the itching and burning." After scratching notes on a clipboard, she bit at the end of her pencil and looked up. "Are you at all opposed to homeopathic remedies for phantom pain?"

Trusting it wasn't too early to claim victory, he let the tension drain from his shoulders.

"I have the utmost faith in whatever you think best," he said. And he meant it.

~

That evening and every night afterward, Olivia spent a good hour at his bedside, issuing massages and dispensing encouragement. Her thumb, as good at burrowing as a badger, sought the knots in Peder's back and leveled them like a German buzz bomb. Sweet and reassuring, her voice relaxed him, as did her words.

"Your future awaits you, Peder. The world is close to peace, and you contributed toward that effort. Though your body may at times feel old, you're still young. So much life awaits you."

She tended to his stump, too, which wasn't nearly as enjoyable, with a rose geranium oil concoction of her grandmother's. He chose not to scoff at the home remedy, afraid his doubt would propel their tenuous truce back into unsettled waters. Surprisingly, the oil wasn't at all disagreeable. It helped calm the phantom sensations where his leg used to be.

Tonight, she rubbed in a circular motion up and down his spine. Peder worked hard to keep the word "arousing" out of his internal accounting of this nightly ritual. Thank God three of the other men in the room were blind and the other four were too immersed in their heated games of poker to notice that he was on the precipice of losing his composure. It took everything he had not to moan at her touch or reach up to pull the pins out of her hair and watch it cascade around her shoulders before he took her in his arms.

He appraised her delicate brow and curved mouth as she wiped oil off her palms with a towel. Her lips were luscious in the pale light, and he wished he had the nerve to bring her face to his. She pulled a fresh T-shirt over his head, bringing his eyes parallel with the buttons of her uniform. Her breasts were small, round. He pictured encasing one in his hand or his mouth—

"I don't think I've seen you look so content, Peder," she said. "I told you the oils would work."

"Mm," he said, wanting to keep her close a little longer. "But I leave next week. You don't make house calls, do you?"

"I'll come by to see you at every opportunity. If beds weren't so badly needed here, I'd petition for another month, at least. You'll be in good hands with your mum, though. She's excited to have you home." She gathered her bag and flannels and switched off his small lamp. "Good night."

"Good night, Olivia."

He lay back, mesmerized by the sway of her hips as she left the room.

Footsteps pounded down the corridor. In her dream they were her own, running not down the corridors of Keldor but of St. Mary Abbot's Hospital. Every door opened to empty rooms. Her patients had disappeared.

"Nurse Morgan, wake up." Cora's voice hovered inches above her, and someone was shaking her. "Nurse Morgan, you're needed in S Ward. It's Lieutenant Werren."

She sat up, her heart pumping at a mad rate. The light in her bedroom had been turned on, and Cora stood over her in her dressing gown.

"I'm sorry to wake you, but the lieutenant is calling you by name, insisting he see you."

"I'll be right there."

She grabbed her dressing gown and raced down the stairs barefoot.

"Tell me you're all right!" Peder shouted as soon as she entered the dimly lit room.

"Of course I'm all right! What is it you've dreamt? Will you tell me?"

He leant toward her, his hands and arms shaking.

"I can't," he blubbered.

She took his hands. "Peder, tell me so I can assure you that none of what you've dreamt is real. Then tomorrow we'll have breakfast together like we always do."

He snatched the handkerchief from his bedside table and blew his nose heartily.

"The mine was supposed to be dead," he finally said. "I'd disarmed it, and the city block was secure. I'd promised you and everyone else there that they'd be safe whilst we awaited its removal. Then as soon as I turned to find the captain, it, it exploded. You and Emily—"

He threw himself forward into her arms, shaking as all her patients did when sorting fiction from reality. He whispered into her neck. "Please, stay with me awhile."

"I'll stay as long as you like." Unlike William, Peder wasn't a born soldier. He wasn't cut out for war. Despite his brave face, his sensitive side hungered for a tenderness she was happy to provide.

"I thought I'd killed you both," he whispered.

"Shh now." His arms, though trembling, were sturdy and comfortable around her. It'd been a long time since she'd been held so.

Once his whimpering subsided and his breathing stabilized, she lowered him onto his pillow, cradling his neck and shoulders as she did when tucking Emily into bed. She would've given him a sedative, but his dreamy face didn't call for it.

She combed his hair away from his forehead with her fingers. "Will you be all right?"

"I will. I'm sorry to have got you out of bed."

"I'm here for you. I always will be. Good night, Peder."

"Good night, Olivia."

# CHAPTER 41

"It won't be the same here without you, Lieutenant," Nurse Talbot said, helping Peder into his trousers.

He nodded in agreement. This was his final day at Keldor, one he no longer dreaded.

"I know a couple of girls who are going to miss you." Olivia's mother was a pretty woman. She winked and smiled.

"And I them," he replied, "but not for too long, I hope. The war has to end some time, and when it does, I plan on seeing much more of the Morgan girls."

Olivia had accepted his advances last night after that horrifying nightmare. In the meager privacy of S Ward, she'd clutched him tightly, as though she'd wanted them to stay that close forever. And when his lips grazed the skin under her ear, she hadn't backed away; she hadn't chided him.

"Olivia will like that. You're good for her, Peder."

The footsteps of a rambunctious toddler padded into the sitting room, and every soldier within earshot perked up at the arrival of the little madam.

"GOOMORRING!" Emily shouted.

Her voice revived the scenes from Peder's gruesome night-

320

mare. He quickly bridled the tears that threatened to accompany them before responding, "Good morning, Miss Emily," along with the other patients.

"Good morning, little dove." Her grandmother kissed the top of her blond head and helped her to the table.

"Thank you, Mum," Olivia said, approaching. "After breakfast, I'll be in the library sorting Peder and Captain Riley's paperwork. We've three new patients coming tomorrow. Will you check with Cora and make sure B Ward is ready to receive them?"

"Of course, dear. Enjoy your breakfast."

Olivia settled into her seat. "How are you this morning?"

"Much better, especially after seeing this little gem." He tickled under Emily's fleshy arm. She giggled furiously.

"Now, now, not at the table." Olivia winked at him over her teacup.

His heart might burst.

"I thought we'd go on our walk earlier today," she said, "well before your parents arrive."

Perfect. Soon he'd execute the best part of his plan, and then he'd be the happiest of men.

He grinned. "I'm looking forward to it."

"I'm happy to see you smiling, Peder," Olivia said, pushing him as usual toward the wych elm.

The sun hadn't stayed out as long as he'd hoped, but the tree's canopy would prove ample cover if it rained.

"You were right. Today is a new day." He tilted his head back, hoping to catch a glimpse of the smile in her voice. "It's so difficult believing all is well after waking from such horror."

"Realization comes quicker the more nightmares you have. That's what William used to say."

William. Always William.

ERICA NYDEN

But Peder was determined: Olivia would be his, and Emily too. A litter of Werrens would follow: boys and girls, towheads and gingers, inheriting his name and his wife's winsome features.

All he needed was to ask.

Parts of the path were bumpy, but Olivia had a way of keeping his ride smooth. As they neared the tree, Peder turned his head as far as it would go, wishing he could see her better. "What are your plans when the war is over? Will you stay at Keldor, do you think?"

She laughed. "Of course I'll stay here. Where else would I go?"

"Oh, I don't know. I suppose maybe you and Emily could come and live with me at Tredon."

The chair stopped.

Perspiration dotted his temples. He couldn't even see her properly, but if he didn't ask now, he never would.

"Olivia, I wondered if you'd marry me."

The chair moved again. In jarring silence, she pushed him toward a nearby garden bench and sat opposite him. Her face, a stunning portrait of pity and dismissal, told him all he didn't want to know.

"I realize I'm no match for the man that was William, but I promise you, Olivia, I can care for you and Emily just as well. Please"—he leant toward her, wanting to take her hand but afraid to—"won't you be my wife?"

Rejection from women always looked the same: a friendly smile capped with shining eyes. Olivia enhanced the expression by placing a hand over her heart. The other stretched toward him as if to keep his words from going any further.

"Thank you, Peder. Your proposal is very kind, but I cannot marry you. I'm sorry."

A hint of lavender reached his nose, propelling him back to last night's intimate embrace. "Even after last night?"

"Last night?"

"Yes!" He shook the wheels of his chair. "Last night, when you

322

held me like a lover, when you let me kiss you. Trust me, Olivia, I wouldn't ask if I didn't think you wanted this too."

Her brow wrinkled. "I was comforting you, as I do all my patients."

"With kisses?"

Her voice and color rose. "What kisses?"

"The ones below your ear, on your neck."

His tears had wet her skin before his lips took over, showering it like the softest rain. He could still taste the saltiness.

"Peder." Her face, so sweet, so sincere, was sickening him more by the second. "If you had kissed me, I would've asked you to stop. We're friends, and I'd like to remain so."

But she wasn't speaking to him as a friend. She was speaking as though he were a lame fool. How idiotic of him to think that he, a cripple, could capture such a beautiful creature.

He looked down to where his leg used to be. "Because I'm only part of a man, is that it? You're concerned I can't satisfy you?"

Wherever William was, he was laughing at him.

"Peder!" Her eyes gleamed as if she were laughing, too.

Incensed, he gripped the arms of his wheelchair as if he might rise out of it. "Your former husband was lucky to have had you when he did, but don't think for a moment your marriage would've lasted beyond this war. William was a fickle bloke, and beautiful wife or no, as soon as another attractive woman crossed his path, he'd be on her like a deerhound on a doe."

His words had nothing to do with desperation, he told himself. She deserved to know the harsh realities wetting her chocolaty eyes. "He was always on the prowl for the next female to warm his bed. A handful of wedding vows could do nothing to change William Morgan's true nature. Why do you think he broke off his engagement to my sister? Marriage meant chains to a man like William."

Her face softened as though he was finally getting through to her. "Why are you telling me this?"

"Because I love you! And I am steadfast in that love, more than William could ever have been. I'll not hurt you, Olivia, not ever."

"You're hurting me now, Peder!" She stood, ripped the nurse's cap from her head, and fumed back toward the tree where she paced, each step hunching her shoulders as though she'd been struck in the stomach.

She believed him, then—all of it, even the bits he wasn't so sure of. And she was crying, hard.

He had done this.

~

Olivia was finding it difficult to catch her breath, but walking helped, as did the mizzle, though she wished it would rain.

"I'm sorry," Peder mumbled from his chair.

She pretended she couldn't hear him. Back and forth and around the tree, she walked.

"Why, Olivia?" he shouted. He rolled toward her. "Why don't you care for me as I do you? If it's not my broken body that appalls you so, then what is it?"

She turned and faced him. "You're my husband's best mate, Peder!"

"You mean your *former* husband."

Finished with this conversation and intent on taking him back inside, she strode back to take control of the chair.

He grabbed her wrist, stopping her. "Hold on a tick. You think he's still alive, don't you?"

He gazed at her. His eyes widened; he may've even smiled.

She glared back, unwavering. "I do."

He let go of her and laughed, his callous chortles slicing through the belief that'd kept her afloat for years. Suddenly

desperate to state her case, she spoke between his scoffs, sharing
her theory of how William had been helped by local residents
and was hiding somewhere in the desert, alive. But no matter
how loudly she said them, the words lost their sway when they
slammed into Peder's derision.

"You're out of your mind." He shook his head, still smiling.
"North Africa is a desolate wasteland dotted with land mines.
The Bedouin were pushed out long ago. There's no one to help,
and there's nowhere to hide."

"William's a skilled fighter, trained to live in the harshest
conditions. He's outsmarted Nazis before. He can do it again."

"And he's human, which means he can die like the rest of us—
by bullet, bomb, grenade, and fire, amongst many other means."

She covered her face. Peder had been to the front more than
once; he knew of what he spoke.

"You're right." She knelt beside him and stared at her shoes
and the muddy ground soiling them. "Dear God. You're right."

His hand gently smoothed her hair. "The war has taken everything we hold dear. But if you'll let me, I'll make you happy."

Yes, the war had taken her brothers. Her father-in-law.
William. It'd almost taken her beautiful home, where so many
life-changing moments had unfolded, from William's cries to
Emily's. And yet without the war, she'd never have come to
Keldor; she'd never have met William or had his child. And
though she sometimes agonized over life without him, she
wouldn't trade her mourning for never having had the experience of lying in his arms or kissing his lips.

Peder said he could make her happy, but she was already
happy. She had an adoring little girl who lifted her spirits daily.
She had her job. Caring for soldiers healed her wounds as much
as it healed theirs.

She stood. Ignoring her stuffy nose and puffy eyes, she lifted
her chin. "I care for you, Peder, even after your disastrous
attempt to make me doubt my husband's fidelity. But my heart

belongs to William." She paused, hardly able to utter the words that followed. "It will always be his—even if he doesn't return to me."

"So you'll remain alone, then? For the rest of your life?"

She grasped the handles of the wheelchair and pushed Peder back to the house in silence.

~

In Olivia's arms, Emily waved goodbye as Mr. and Mrs. Werren drove their son away from Keldor. Olivia did the same, as did her mother beside them.

She should've discharged Peder weeks ago. Instead she'd kept him here, hoping he'd fill the void William had left. But she hadn't needed a man in her life, as her mother had suggested; she needed a friend. The one she'd found was a living almanac of William's life, keeping him alive in ways that even Polly couldn't.

Though some of Peder's tales had stabbed her heart like a dagger, part of what he'd said was true: William's past was far from unsullied. He'd hinted at that more than once. Her husband was eleven years her senior, but however he'd lived before they met had only brought him, by some stroke of good fortune, to her, the love of his life—a position she'd hold for all eternity.

She kissed Emily's chubby cheek. "We'll visit Uncle Peder soon. Once he's settled, you, Polly, and I will call on him."

"Yes, Mummy." Emily dropped her head onto her mother's shoulder.

"He'll miss you both," her mother said.

Olivia stared ahead as the car crept from sight. "He asked me to marry him, you know," she added, unsure of what compelled her to do so.

"I gather you declined? Poor man." Her mother turned to her, eyebrows raised. "But Peder isn't the only man out there. There are plenty of others who—"

"Mother."

Mrs. Talbot closed her mouth.

"I'll put Emily down for her kip, then I'm taking a bath," Olivia said. "Will you tell Cora?"

"Of course. Will you be all right, dear?"

"Yes, Mother." She patted her mother's cheek, a gesture of which she was typically the recipient.

After two readings of *Miss Moppet*, Emily's current favorite, Olivia went to her bedroom, lit a fire, and started a bath. As the tub filled, she flopped onto the bed with William's journal. His final entry, read dozens of times, uplifted her more than ever before. She smiled wanly, confident that she could soldier on without him.

*30 September, 1941*

*Soon I'll depart, leaving this journal behind. I've released my soul amongst these pages. If anything tragic happens, read them and find comfort knowing my body may be elsewhere, but home is with you and home is where I will return. Even if you leave Keldor, I will find you. If you remarry I would not object (though the notion of you with another man delivers bile up my throat). But honestly, love, my utmost desire is for you to be happy.*

*I can't say what my existence will be like after death (no pearly gates for me), but I will keep an eye on you, making sure you're treated well and are content. I'll flutter as leaves in the wind or rest as mist on your skin from spray off the sea. I'll be the brightest flame in the library hearth or the pesky weed that keeps popping up in your garden. You'll find me, my love. I shall return to you.*

# CHAPTER 42

"Mummy! Mummy!" Though a small child of three years, Emily's voice rang through the garden like cathedral bells.

By mid-May 1945, Germany had surrendered to the Allies. Recovering soldiers continued to pour into Keldor, and Olivia still had summer crops to plant. The annex was running more smoothly than ever. Since last autumn, she'd gained three additional nurses, leaving her solely in charge of administration. She still had plenty of contact with patients (the best part of nursing), but now she engaged without the strain of a schedule. She also had more time in the garden and more time with Emily, who sometimes was and sometimes wasn't the best helper.

Hands on her hips, she followed her daughter's call. She spotted her ankles deep in an empty vegetable patch slated for a second round of broccoli and cauliflower seedlings. Between the child's fingers, a fat earthworm wriggled lazily.

Olivia kicked her shoes off onto the grass and joined her in the dirt. "Well, isn't he an attractive fellow?"

Emily's belly laugh caused the worm to drop, just in time, into Olivia's open palm. This sent Emily into another fit of giggles, and Olivia couldn't help but join her.

The day was fine. After weeks of rain, the sun shone and spring flowers perfumed the still air. Keldor's rather unkempt landscape suffered in comparison to the massive victory garden, but the convalescents strolling the grounds didn't seem to mind. The weather had brought almost everyone outside, and Olivia marveled at how the sun's healing rays influenced even her most downtrodden patients. They all wore smiles today.

"Where should we put your new friend? Shall he stay in this bed, or shall we deliver him across the way to the potatoes?"

But Emily had lost interest in her discovery. Her chubby legs churned as her feet pounded through the grass toward the house.

"Where are you going? You haven't said what you'd like to do with your new friend!" If Polly had arrived with luncheon, the toddler's voracious appetite took precedent. Olivia carefully dropped the worm onto the welcoming earth and stood. She too was ready for lunch. "Sorry, Mr. Worm."

But Emily hadn't run toward Polly. A man in a dark suit was kneeling under the apple tree that shaded the back entrance, smiling at her daughter as though he knew her. Lieutenant Cleary, perhaps, though patients didn't normally arrive looking so smart. And he wasn't due until tomorrow, anyway.

Stepping out of the garden bed, she shook her head at her overly friendly child and followed. "Emily? Who—"

Her eyes met his. She halted with a jolt as though she'd struck an invisible wall.

"William?"

Stability left her legs. She reached out, but there was nothing to hold on to. And then there was. William was there, grasping her arms and saying her name.

"But ... I, I don't—"

"It's me. I'm here. I'm home."

With each syllable, he jerked her gently closer until their foreheads met. His lips caressed her nose and cheeks. She recognized these kisses, tender and earnest. And like William's, they left her wanting. Thirsty for more, she closed her eyes and leaned into them, selfishly aware that if this were a dream, she'd drown in as many as the figment was willing to impart. Blindly, she studied his shoulders and arms. They too felt familiar—this man even smelled like William.

But what if it wasn't truly him?

Risking all, she opened her eyes.

He was still there, staring at her, his face marked with worry. She traced her fingers over his cheekbones and across his lips. All was where she remembered it, and couldn't have been more handsome.

"William. It *is* you! But I—I—"

"I'm here, I'm home, and I'll never leave you again. I swear it, Olivia. I swear it."

"This—this is real," she said, trusting that the more she stated it, the truer it would be. But the fact, no matter how wonderful, baffled her. "But how? Over and over, I was told—"

"—that I'd been killed? The Nazis believed it, my superiors believed it too. It was the lie that kept me alive. I'm just so sor—"

Needing more of him and unwilling to wait, she pressed her mouth to his. He returned the kiss, pulling her close yet letting his hands wander in ways that indicated he hadn't forgotten her body and was eager to revisit every part of it.

Dizzy with desire, she staggered. William held her fast, and their eyes met. The connection evoked years of fear, worry, and bottomless sadness.

She gripped the lapels of his tunic. "But what happened? Where the hell were you?"

He closed his eyes. "I've been living as someone else, under strict orders to keep my true identity dead. Even to you." He opened them, and it was as if he had to force himself to look at her. "If you've found someone else … If—"

He was here—he was hers, and she was his. Always. She

brought their wet faces together. This kiss, less violent than the first, carried a tenderness she hoped would soothe his worries.

He sniffed and kissed the top of her head. "I'll tell you more of what I'm allowed to later. But first, I want to meet our little girl." He crouched down to where Emily stood staring at him. "Hello, Emily. I'm your daddy."

Miss Genial had grown shy. Uncertainty brought her dirt-stained finger dangerously close to her mouth.

She let him take her small hand and shake it. "*My* daddy?"

"*Your* daddy. How do you do?"

Once her smile emerged, it was all over. Her shyness evaporated as though it had never been there in the first place.

"*My* mummy and daddy!" Then she said it again and again, hopping in place, her hands in tight little balls until she dissolved in uncontrollable laughter.

Olivia knelt beside William and enfolded Emily in their first familial embrace. Her questions disintegrated; doubts and fears disappeared. For the first time in a long time, she let everything go and let the joy of the moment carry her.

# CHAPTER 43

WARM BREEZES SHIFTED the dappled sunlight above William and Olivia. With his back propped against a sturdy oak tree near the gardens, he twirled her wedding ring idly on her finger before bringing her hand to his mouth and kissing it. All was calm now, but Keldor had been in quite an uproar since his arrival. It had begun in the garden with Jasper, who had sprinted toward them after Emily had joined Olivia on his lap, knocking all three Morgans over with his aged white face and wagging tail.

"I knew!" Polly had exclaimed through her sobs when they entered the house. "I always knew you'd come home to us, Mr. William, you naughty, naughty boy."

Thankfully, her arms were full of linens and not china when she first saw him, for everything in her grasp had plummeted to the floor. Hand to her heart, she gasped for air as though she'd been thrown into the Channel. Olivia had had to calm poor Emily, who began to cry until Mrs. Pollard, also in tears, drew the toddler into her embrace.

Polly had served vegetable pasties and tea outdoors for luncheon that afternoon, but both William and Olivia were still too elated to eat. After a few bites, he pushed his plate aside to bask in the sights and sounds of home. At his side, his wife's slender legs stretched parallel to his, and across the garden, their energetic daughter bounded like a playful fawn. Olivia had challenged her to pick as many dandelions as she could find, and by her careening laughter, she was delighted with her assignment. Up and down, her blond head bobbed like a seabird on the ocean whilst her fleshy legs carried her through grass taller than her knees. Close behind loped Jasper. Emily gripped a fistful of wilted weeds in front of the dog as though employing his help. Annie had put her into a clean dress free of grass stains, and now she rolled on the earth with glee, creating more.

"That should keep her busy for a time," Olivia said.

She pulled her legs up underneath herself, and a splash of green fell away to reveal her enticing bare knees. Aware that Emily was well occupied and safe in Jasper's charge, William closed a hand over the one closest him and slid it down her shin.

She jumped.

"What is it?"

A smile lit her face. Her hand topped his, encouraging it to proceed with quick pats.

"What's the matter?" he asked.

"Noth—nothing, darling."

He frowned playfully, waiting for the truth. For more than three years, he'd been ignorant of life at Keldor except that his wife had given birth to a healthy baby girl in January of '42. It was only after he returned to England that he learned of Keldor's transformation into a convalescent home. Funny thing—he knew the name of every patient, including that of his childhood mate, Peder Werren, and how long they'd been there. Six nurses had come and gone since the annex's inception; he knew their names as well. But knowledge of Olivia's heart was still a mystery. She still wore his ring, but had her love for him faded? If she felt uncomfortable being intimate with him, the sooner he knew, the better.

It appeared the composure Olivia had displayed over the past two hours was a façade. She crawled into William's lap and snaked her arms around his middle, her face crushed against his neck.

"I still can't believe it, that you're really here." Her words were terribly muffled. "That you're not the ghost in my dreams, always off by morning." When her wet red face emerged from the folds of his shirt, her eyes drooped and her lips pouted, full and supple. Her hair was long, and she wore it in a single plait that lay on her shoulder. She was lovely. "I thought I'd live the rest of my life with this gaping hole."

"I'm so sorry to have put you through all this."

"You keep saying you're sorry, but you've nothing to be sorry for. Whatever happened, whatever you had to do, it brought you home to me. You're here and that's all that matters." A spurt of laughter sent tears spilling down her cheeks. "These are happy tears, you realize."

But guilt and deceit went hand in hand. While his unresponsive body had been found before the Nazis could dance around his burning corpse, his rescue had led to the utmost secrecy regarding his whereabouts, along with three and half years of lies. Even Colonel Adams had believed he was dead until four days ago. William's special operations executive director spent hours trying to convince the colonel that his talents had been better served as a secret agent than as a light infantry officer. William sensed that the deception had bothered the colonel more than anything.

So far, his wife had been more forgiving. Beyond grateful, William's eyes began brimming as well, but she wouldn't allow it. She cushioned the back of his head with her hands, protecting it from the jostle her lips caused when they tethered to his.

Tears forgotten, he unfolded her legs and drew them around his waist. Between his gasps and quiet moans, he drowned in lavender. His desire for her ignited, and he pushed her back on the quilt. After giving her lips their due, his mouth journeyed down her throat before Olivia wrenched his head, demanding his mouth again.

He was vaguely aware of his foot upending his half-eaten pasty and tossing over his tea. It didn't matter—nothing mattered but the woman beneath him and the life they would finally have together. He forgot about the little girl in the grass and the aging dog beside her; the wandering convalescents and their caregivers vanished.

"I can't tell you how much I've missed you," he murmured between nibbling her earlobe and grazing her face and neck with the tip of his nose, "and I will continue to say it, even when you tell me to stop. I—"

"*Jasper, no!*" A shrill as high as a peacock's sliced across the garden. "*That's my Daddy's food!*"

William sat up, hair tousled and eyes boggled, searching for the origin of the chaos. Olivia rose more tolerantly. At their feet lay a rapidly diminishing pile of root vegetables and pastry, as Jasper lapped frantically at the gravy.

Emily stomped toward the aging dog, fit to be tied.

Mrs. Pollard appeared and whisked the little girl from her feet. "All right, that's enough, young miss. You've yelled enough at poor Jasper."

"POLLY, NO!" Emily wailed, her arms thrashing as lustily as her legs. "He is a *bad* dog!"

"Jasper is not a bad dog—and he's your daddy's favorite doggie. I'm sure your daddy didn't mind sharing his lunch."

Annie had joined them, arms out, explaining that it was someone's naptime.

Emily twisted toward them. "Mummy? Will Daddy—"

Olivia kissed the little girl's face, which was still fixed on Jasper and the man petting him. "Yes, dove, Daddy will still come read to you. Let Annie get you undressed, and he'll be up soon." She wiped the blond strands from the child's forehead. "We've

talked about how you're to speak to Jasper. He's a good boy and
he's getting older, so we need to be even kinder to him. Yelling
does no good at all. Do you want your daddy to think you've got
a wicked temper?"

Emily's eyes grew round. "No."

"Brilliant. Be a good girl and do as Annie says. Daddy will join
you shortly."

Through the open door of Emily's bedroom, Olivia beheld a sight
she once feared she might never see: her husband lying beside
their daughter in blissful slumber. His left arm cradled the
sleeping girl, her cherubic face resting in the bunched material of
his shirt. The book they'd read had fallen to the floor next to
William's shoes, which were lined neatly beside the bed.

William had come home, and he would stay home with her
for good. Forever. Her greatest wish had come true, and yet his
actual return seemed unreal. But happiness overran her disbelief,
fierce and clamorous, buzzing inside her as she continued to
review the irrefutable facts: Her daughter had a father. She
wasn't a widow. She and William would grow old together. Like a
complicated jigsaw, the pieces of her splintered heart came
together, each insight filling her with eagerness for the years to
come. Answers to *Where the hell have you been?* and *Could you not
have sent one clue that you were alive? Just one?* didn't matter. He
was home.

She'd already phoned her parents to share the news. At first
they were speechless, but once it sank in, their interruptions ran
up against her limited information until she finally yelled "I don't
know!"

"—yet," she'd added sheepishly. "I wanted you both to know
he's alive, he's home and"—the rest turned into a tight-throated,
high-pitched whisper—"we're so, so happy."

One person she hadn't phoned was Peder. It'd been eight months since his stay at Keldor. In that time Olivia had strived to return their friendship to its original ease by visiting when she could and pretending he'd never alluded to William's likely infidelity should he return from war. The charade worked—maybe too well. In April Peder proposed again. It was the last time she'd been to Tredon, and she was no longer accepting his telephone calls. His disregard for her word—that "no" meant no—wounded her deeply. William, if apprised of the situation, would be furious. But she'd not interfere with their old friendship. She'd keep the last year's events involving Peder to herself, for surely William's reappearance alone would knock the madness, if not the breath, out of his oldest mate.

She glided into Emily's room and laid a hand on William's broad shoulder. Still a light sleeper, he stirred at once. New lines he'd accumulated reappeared, and his eyes searched until they found her amused face. He kissed the top of Emily's head, then looked dubiously at his imprisoned arm.

"Will she wake?"

She shook her head. "She may be a little grumpy when she wakes up to find you've gone, but she'll get over it."

"Should I stay?"

"Absolutely not," she whispered, holding out both hands. "Come with me. It's my turn."

# CHAPTER 44

"I THINK she was as tired as me," William said as Olivia eased Emily's door closed. "She fell asleep not two pages into the story. I watched her sleep until I surrendered myself. I was worried it would take her more time to warm to me, but it's like we've been friends all along."

"Are you joking? Of course she warmed to you. I've spoken of you every day since she was born."

The smallest movements Olivia made captivated his attention, from the careful manner in which she closed the door to the way her eyebrows rose at its soft *click*. She'd replaced her garden dress with a satin dressing gown—and heaven help him, nothing else.

"Come." She took his hand and led him down the corridor.

She got to their bed first and untied her dressing gown. The subtle curves of her breasts and hips were more luscious than he remembered. Overwhelmed, he stood drinking her in whilst she unbuttoned his shirt.

The assault of her soft breasts on his chest sent his eyes to the back of his head. She guided him down onto a mass of pillows, where her delicate hands overran his neglected body. She delivered tiny, concentrated circles to his shoulders and chest, focusing solely on his pleasure.

His urgency waned and he rolled onto his back, steeped in Olivia's healing caresses. His dream of survival had come true; years of tension and uncertainty rolled off like a distant nightmare. The laughter of his adorable, accepting daughter and the loyalty of his beautiful, clever wife were just the beginning.

He hadn't been there for Emily's first words or steps, but he'd be there on her first day of school. He'd walk her down the aisle when the time came, too. And there'd be more children—many more, if Olivia was willing. The chatter of their family would fill the rooms and corridors of Keldor with vitality and joy. They'd teach their children to embrace every day, even the bad ones, for he'd learned that sometimes a string of bad days could lead to a life happier than one could ever imagine.

He might even attend church again. He smiled, picturing their brood filling an entire pew. And he'd pursue his woodworking. The first thing he'd build was a vanity for Olivia, in time for her birthday—but he'd keep it a surprise, although he wasn't sure how, since he had no intention of leaving her side even for a few hours. And every night he'd make love to her—during the children's naptime, too, like today. A perfect routine, allowing them their well-deserved time alone.

The kisses had stopped. He cracked open an eye to see Olivia climbing on top of him. She bent forward and smothered him with her hair, giggling as she effortlessly joined her body to his.

He was paralyzed.

Unperturbed by his stillness, she placed a crown of kisses across his forehead. "Relax."

"Whatever you say," he murmured, nuzzling the breasts that lingered above his mouth.

Olivia let him indulge for a short time before rising. She moved above him, naked and goddess-like in her determination to please him—until he remembered how he'd envisaged this reunion: not like this.

He seized her waist and rolled her back onto the mattress. "What—"

Nestled between her legs more properly than in the garden, he devoured her with his eyes.

"I'm making love to my wife the way I've always imagined I would these last three years," he responded with a forceful thrust.

This silenced her words, but not the moans of pleasure filling the space between them. Fully entranced, she opened her arms in surrender. Pleased with his coup, he hovered above her, waiting for her eyes to open. And then they were locked with his, shimmering with delight.

"We've outlived the war's worst days, Olivia, the three of us a proper family. I'm—" Unexpectedly, his eyes welled. "I'm so happy."

He pressed his forehead to hers. He wanted to ravish her with passion and romance, not with the sentimental reflections of an aging veteran grateful for the woman in his arms.

With a coy curl of her lips and a gentle squeeze at his hips, Olivia reminded him they were still joined.

He hadn't forgotten.

A long kiss, enlivened by his wife's coquettish submission, reestablished his reign. In one hand, he gathered her honeyed locks whilst subjecting her to his heightened need. Husband and wife occupied the familiar soul of the other, crowding fear with love, sorrow with joy, and war with celebration until his cries matched hers.

On their sides, she twined her arms and legs around him as they became servants to exhaustion and bliss.

"Never again will I leave you," he said, lazily tickling her back.

"I know."

"Were you told I was missing first?"

She nodded against him. "A telegram came on the fifteenth of

December. A letter from Colonel Adams followed—a nice letter, reassuring me that 'missing' didn't mean 'dead.' "

"How long before they told you I'd been killed?"

"Not until May. I knew you were still alive, though, because—"

"The scarf? Surely that gave you an inkling."

"The scarf?"

He sat up. "Your orange scarf. I took half of it with me to North Africa. I asked a nurse to send it to you when I was recovering in Tunis. Did you never receive it?"

She frowned. "I only received the bit that came in a box with your effects. I'd wondered why it'd been torn."

He rolled onto his back, annoyed. Nurse Baldwin, his primary caregiver in the desert, had held firm to the directive that he have zero contact with anyone outside the agency—even his pregnant wife. For weeks, he'd protested the cruelty of the deception until she finally yielded. She agreed to send only the well-loved remnant of Olivia's scarf. No note, no return address.

He hoped the post had failed and not the nurse.

"What were you recovering from?" she asked.

"A bullet wound. To my leg, here." He pulled the linens down, revealing an ugly scar on the outside of his left thigh.

She tried examining it as though he were one of her patients, but he shuffled her hands away and readjusted the bed covers.

"There was a skirmish a few miles from my former prison camp, if you can believe it. We'd been ambushed and were brutally outnumbered. I don't remember anything after I went down. Many were killed and even more taken prisoner. Those assumed dead were—"

"Burnt."

"Yes," he said, surprised she'd been given such details.

Hot air, dust, shouting, machine-gun fire—it had been so long ago, but he'd never stop reliving the chaos. He still wasn't sure if his memories of Wirth and the prison nearby had jostled his nerves and caused him to fight like an inexperienced cadet that day. Carelessly received or not, the injury had saved his life.

He stirred. "I awoke two days later, hundreds of miles away. Those at my bedside assured me I'd been rescued by a reliable organization, people who'd never leave me for dead and who'd utilize my talents in ways the army never could. They knew all about me: my prior undercover work for the SIS in Cairo, my escape in '40, even you and the imminent arrival of our child."

He'd never lived through a more infuriating day, when strangers had informed him that he would live—but until the war ended, it would be as someone else. Officially, Major William Jack Morgan had died on 9 December, 1941, along with seven other men at the enemy's hands.

"But why? Why couldn't I know? I wouldn't have done anything to muck up their plans—"

He held up his hand and shook his head. "No one could know. Not the colonel, not my men, not even you."

The disorder of war had easily concealed the five identities he'd inhabited, some good, some evil. Concealed, too, were his exploits. He'd been to every corner of occupied Europe, sometimes living in luxury amongst shameless Nazi bureaucrats and other times crawling on snowy forest floors, unsure of when his next meal would come. He came close to death twice and was saved by the enemy once—unknowingly, of course—the aftermath of which put a price on his head higher than that of any other agent.

Telling Olivia none of this felt as grave a sin as hiding a mistress from her.

He took her briskly into his arms. "My reward is being here now with you. I was promised I'd be sent home for good once the Nazis surrendered, and here I am. I have dozens of reports still to write, but I'm finished with the war. I'm done living a lie and doing as others bid me. I'm retiring completely from the military.

From here on, I plan to live a quiet life with you. The only ruckus afoot shall be issued from our ridiculously happy children."

He kissed her forehead and nose, hoping to reach her mouth before her questions resumed.

"But—"

He relented. "But what?"

She lay still. "Nothing. I know you can't say. I understand."

This was a first. Was she not going to ask for details of his whereabouts? Or criticize the way his life had been manipulated in a way that could've done irreparable damage to their marriage? Would she not even hound him for information regarding his psyche and his ability to cope with previous traumas whilst creating new ones?

"Not a day went by that I didn't think about you. Though I lived as someone else for all that time, in my mind, I was still your husband. Thoughts of you were like a distant holiday I knew I'd eventually enjoy, even though it was years away."

Her face softened as though all she needed was confirmation that he still loved her.

Of course he did.

# CHAPTER 45

THE HAMMERING of toddler feet approached rapidly down the corridor.

"Daddy?"

The high-pitched voice drew closer and closer to their bedroom. William countered Olivia's smirk with a grin.

She inched out of his robust embrace. "I look forward to resuming this later."

The door burst open, and a crown of golden tresses atop two big blue eyes peered upward, followed by giggling like Olivia had never heard from her daughter.

"She enjoys laughing, doesn't she?" William asked.

"That she does."

She helped Emily onto the bed. The child jumped and bounced until she tumbled against her daddy in fits of laughter as a result of his gentle tickling.

Olivia pulled on her dressing gown and held out her hand. "Shall we go see Polly about this afternoon's tea party, madam?"

She herself had not been invited to the father-daughter engagement. Her job was to help Mrs. Pollard prepare the meal and deliver it to the garden shed, now a proper playhouse—

cleaned, spruced up, and according to William, hardly recognizable. As her most reliable servant, William was to assist Emily in
gathering her favorite teddy bear and dollies. The occasion
would provide him with an opportunity to get to know his
daughter on his own while giving Olivia time to catch up on
neglected paperwork.

Once she was alone in the library, she sat staring at the files.

William's life over nearly four years would forever remain
hidden from her.

And it didn't matter.

He said he was leaving it all behind; why shouldn't she? Not
to say that his slumbering demons (if indeed they slept) wouldn't
rear their ugly heads from time to time. And maybe he'd carry on
like other veterans she'd become acquainted with, those with a
knack for arranging events in their lives as one might items in a
desk: fond recollections that remained nearby where they were
easily retrieved, regrets and torments hidden well away, buried
beneath mundane memories like a drive to the grocer's or
choosing which shoes to wear.

She closed her files. It'd only been thirty minutes, but already
she missed William's hands, his mouth, his body on hers. She
longed for his smile, his confident shoulders, and even the new
hitch in his gait, which only added to his appeal.

Laughter burst from her lips, sudden and sharp. What was she
was waiting for?

Outside, birds sang in the afternoon's warmth. Patients who
could were out and about, and she spotted Cora walking hand in
hand with her new beau, a lieutenant from North Wales. Spring
was well underway, the promise of summer and its bounty seen
in every new leaf, blooming flower, and amorous couple.

It had been a long winter for Britain. Each family had weath-
ered their own cold snaps and blizzards, and as with any storm,
the survivors were left at the mercy of its aftermath. Though he
seemed as robust as ever, trauma would live within her husband

forever. It was a part of him, as much as his dark hair and slate-blue eyes, his dashing smile, and his undying love for her. But together, and with gratitude, they would weather the squalls, for without their existence there would be no Olivia and William.

Olivia slowed her pace and admired the small outbuilding. Its exterior walls were white as clouds, its shutters sky blue. Through the warped windowpanes, red curtains blushed as brightly as masses of Flanders Fields poppies. Inside that little building were the most important people in her life. They were the perfect family, with a lifetime ahead in which to make up for the moments behind them. In love and sadness, they had come full circle back to joy.

Olivia knocked lightly and opened the door.

THE END